By TINNEAN

NOVELS
Bless Us With Content
Two Lips, Indifferent Red

SPY VS. SPOOK SERIES
Houseboat on the Nile
Not My Spook!
Forever

NOVELLAS
The Best
Call Me Church
Greeting Cards
No One Should Be Alone
To Love Through Space and Time

Published by DREAMSPINNER PRESS
http://www.dreamspinnerpress.com

TWO LIPS, INDIFFERENT *Red*

TINNEAN

Dreamspinner Press

Published by
Dreamspinner Press
5032 Capital Circle SW
Ste 2, PMB# 279
Tallahassee, FL 32305-7886
USA
http://www.dreamspinnerpress.com/

Two Lips, Indifferent Red

Cover Art by Reese Dante
http://www.reesedante.com

ISBN: 978-1-62380-402-2
Digital ISBN: 978-1-62380-403-9

Printed in the United States of America
First Edition
March 2013

As always, this is for Bob, who empties the dishwasher, folds the laundry, picks up takeout, runs the vacuum over the carpet, walks the pup when he visits, takes the car for an oil change, and makes the coffee so I have the time to write.

ACKNOWLEDGMENTS

Many people helped with this, and I give heartfelt thanks to: my sons—Bobby, for the information about tests taken online, and Joey, sports maven extraordinaire, for what I needed to know about football (and also for giving me a Zune for Christmas a few years ago.); Tracy Nagurski, for the questions and suggestions; Tim Mead, who, as a professor, gave me invaluable information about colleges; Tony, who's willing to brainstorm, and David, for his contribution regarding country rap; Trish, who listened patiently as I complained because the guys wouldn't cooperate; Tisha, who wanted the Richardsons to pay for what they did to Kipp; Silk, for the skinny about MTV (what can I tell you? It's been a lot of years since my kids watched it) and iTunes; and finally, to Gail Morse, for all her unceasing help over the years.

AUTHOR'S NOTE

The T-shirts Kipp wears can be found on the What On Earth website at http://www.whatonearthcatalog.com/whatonearth/Tees-Sweatshirts_3aa.html

And this is the song that inspired it all, Chuck Berry's "Brown-Eyed Handsome Man": http://www.youtube.com/watch?v=gOIe-At7DNw

CHAPTER 1

Charlestown, Pennsylvania
May, 2017

CHARLESTOWN, Pennsylvania, was beautiful in May. The trees that lined the streets of the small university town had leafed out earlier in the month. Flowers bloomed in a riot of color and scents in front of the stately homes that now served as dormitories for Charles T. Armand University.

Of course, I wasn't able to enjoy that balmy spring day. The semester had come to an end, and while I'd taken most of my finals, there were two left, and I intended to do as well on them as I'd done on the others. Scholarships funded my education at Armand U, and I needed to maintain my GPA.

I took a break when my bladder informed me in no uncertain terms that if I didn't pay a visit to the john *now*, things were going to get ugly.

And since I had already interrupted my studying, I decided to go down to the first floor, where there was a vending machine. I could use the sugar rush, and a bag of M&Ms would do the trick.

It would take a little while for the sugar to work its magic, so I went out onto the front porch and leaned against the railing.

The air was like warm silk against my face, and I closed my eyes, tipped back my head, and breathed in the lovely fragrance of the flowers I'd helped plant earlier in the spring.

Well, standing here doesn't get the studying done. "Time to get back to the books, Llewellyn."

I returned to my room, opened the door, and frowned.

"Hey, Kipp! I thought you'd fallen in!" My roommate, Andrew Scott, was sprawled casually on my bed. Of course he wasn't on his own bed—that was piled high with the clothes he was packing to go home.

I could have lived without him, but I hadn't been given much choice. I'd learned early on in life not to make waves, and so I generally wound up with the roommates no one else wanted: players, partiers, and general pains in the ass. The room would be mine alone during the summer semester, but hopefully, come the fall I'd have someone who didn't get *quite* as much on my last nerve.

"*Kippers*! You with me, boy?"

I paused for a minute before turning and closing the door behind me. I hated when people called me Kippers, but I hated being called "boy" even more. Hearing that always made me look around for my father.

"Yes?"

"Phone call for you!" He waggled my cell phone.

"And you felt the need to answer it?"

"Hey, we're genetically programmed to do that. Besides, that ring tone…."

"Oh?" My heart felt like it was doing somersaults. "Was it 'Brown-Eyed Handsome Man'?"

He shrugged. "I didn't recognize it, but it sounded like elevator music to me."

That didn't surprise me. If it wasn't something like "I Wanna Sex You Up" or "Bust a Move," he had no idea what it was.

I rarely got phone calls, so I assumed it was a prank he had set up. "Tell whoever it is that I'm not interested and hang up my phone."

"You sure? She sounds sexy as all hell!"

Now I was certain it was a prank. Sexy-as-all-hell women didn't call me. Not that I minded; I'd much rather have received a call from a guy, and one guy in particular. He was older, and so sexy, although that wouldn't have mattered—I'd have been content with someone who loved me, no matter what he looked like.

I'd learned better than to let a handsome face draw me in. I thought of Daniel, who'd not only made a fool of me in high school, but who'd broken my heart as well. We'd gone to grade school together until second grade. At that time, I was sent to a boarding school in upstate New York, where no one knew me as Marcus Llewellyn's son, and where I was happy. That lasted until I was fourteen, when, as abruptly as I'd been sent away, I'd been ordered to return home and informed that I would start Benjamin Martin High in the fall.

I ran into Daniel when it turned out we had homeroom together. And embarrassingly, I popped wood. *Every time I looked at him*, I wound up with an erection, and so I got into the habit of wearing my shirt untucked.

By our senior year, not only was Daniel a jock, he headed the debate team, played clarinet in the school orchestra, sang in senior chorus, always got the lead role in drama club, and was president of the student body. Added to that, he was so handsome there wasn't a girl in school who'd say no to him. Rumor had it that included some of the teachers as well.

CHAPTER 2

I'D SPENT the past four years—my entire high school career—wishing he would notice me but knowing he never would, not even to say hi; I wasn't anyone special... just a staffer on the magazine and the guy who designed sets for the school plays. It turned out I was good at the latter, and no one needed to know that I'd first gotten involved as a way to be in Daniel's vicinity.

But then, about four weeks before graduation, he did notice me, asked me out on a date, and I... I was dazzled, walking on air until the evening I was to see him. I didn't ask myself why a straight boy would be interested in me, but if I had, I'd simply have asked, why wouldn't he? Aside from being a nice person, I had the blond looks from my mother's side of the family; people didn't run screaming when they saw me.

I had my hair styled, bought a pair of jeans with a zip instead of a button fly and a shirt that unsnapped so he could open my jeans and shirt easily, and found a cologne the nice woman at the fragrance counter promised would melt my young lady. Of course I couldn't tell her it was to melt my young man.

Daniel had offered to pick me up at my house, but if Sir—my father had insisted I call him that from the time I'd learned to talk—if he realized I was dating a boy... well, I was certain he'd order me to never darken his doorway again. So to avoid the *Sturm und Drang* it would cause, I told Daniel I would meet him in front of the Main Street Soda Shoppe, a very popular throwback to the diners of the forties and fifties.

I hadn't been angling to get a meal out of the date as well, but Daniel took me inside and bought me a cheeseburger and fries, and we shared a chocolate milkshake.

He took me to the movies, up to the balcony, where he put his arm around my shoulders, and I was the one who melted. I spent the entire movie with my head on his shoulder, and from time to time he'd rub his cheek against my hair.

Oh God, I was so in love!

I was looking forward to the end of the movie, to a good-night kiss, but the best was yet to come!

After the movie, he murmured, "There's a lunar eclipse tonight."

There was?

"I know this wasn't part of our plans, but...." He smiled at me, his teeth a brilliant white. "Would you be interested in watching it with me?"

I'd be interested in watching grass grow if it was with him!

"Yes," I said, somehow managing to keep the anticipation out of my voice. I could have danced and done a fist pump, but I knew how to conceal my excitement. Even though I wasn't my father's favorite son, I still knew what was due to the family.

So I sat beside Daniel in the classic Jaguar his father had given him, my hands folded primly in my lap, while he made the drive to Lila's Hill. He'd lowered the top of his convertible, and the soft evening wind blew in my hair.

Martinsburg had been founded by my great-great-great-grandfather, who'd chosen to settle in Pennsylvania in the middle 1800s, and we'd lived there ever since. Legend had it that Great-Great-Grandfather Martin's youngest daughter was a little... wild, and she often went there with her beaux. I wasn't as wild as my great-aunt, not because I couldn't be, but simply because I'd never had the opportunity: no one had ever wanted to drive up there with me.

Until now.

No sooner had Daniel set the parking brake and turned off the headlights than I forgot my heritage, my upbringing, everything. I was out of my seat belt and all over him, licking his neck, nipping his earlobe, whispering passionate words into his ear. "I've dreamed of feeling you naked against me! Do you want to touch me? You smell so good! I want to taste you!"

He turned his head away. "I don't kiss guys." I'd meant I wanted
to go down on him—I'd jerked off in the shower to thoughts of us
sixty-nining each other—but before I could tell him that, he said,
"You're going too fast, Kipp. A guy likes to make the first move."

It was as if he'd doused me with a bucket of ice water. I didn't
even object that *I* was a guy. "I'm sorry." Had I ruined my chance with
him? Was that why he wasn't hard? "I... I guess you want to take me
home?" I started to slide off his lap, but he tightened his hands on my
hips.

"Not yet, sweet pea."

I hadn't ruined our evening! He'd even called me by a pet name!
Okay, I wasn't crazy about it, but... a pet name! I was happy. A little
confused, but so happy. He unsnapped my jeans and worked a hand
beneath the waistband. And then he sucked in a breath. Was he shocked
that I hadn't worn shorts?

His fingers were inches from my dick. "Please! Just a little more!
Please!" I panted, and I leaned forward to work the patch of skin
beneath his ear. He didn't want to kiss, but surely this....

"Don't mark me!"

I sagged into his arms. Was there nothing I could do right?

"C'mon!" he whispered impatiently. "Fucking act like you want
to be with me!"

Thoroughly confused now, I started to sit back on his thighs.

Abruptly, flashlights lit up the moonless night, there were raucous
yells and catcalls, and the car was surrounded by boys. Daniel yanked
his hand out of my pants and pushed me away, his action causing me to
catch my inner thigh on the gear shift in the center console. I bit back a
cry as I flailed and started to slide off the seat.

Somehow I managed to regain my balance, and I looked around,
for the first time in my life physically afraid. Martinsburg was a quaint
little city, not some movie setting where kids would have sex and then
get killed. I hadn't even had the opportunity to have sex!

"Daniel?" This had to be a nightmare.

"Knock it off, guys," he ordered, and I realized he knew them.
They must have been the boys he hung out with. He held out his hand
and waggled his fingers. "We had a bet."

"Yeah, and you won, Danny!" They started tossing bills—fives and tens—into the car. "Your reputation as stud of Martin High is solid! You can get in anyone's pants!"

It was a bet? I sat there, frozen, staring through the windshield, trying to shut out their coarse words, trying to conceal the way my jeans gapped.

"Now that my reputation has been substantiated, go on home!"

They didn't, not right away, just continued asking what base he'd gotten to, if my dick was as small as they were sure it must be, what it was like to kiss a guy.

I kept hoping Daniel would... defend me, perhaps? But when he did speak, it was just to say smugly, "A gentleman doesn't kiss and tell." He was suddenly a gentleman? "Now, I told you: go home!"

His friends finally left, but he continued to sit there, counting the money.

"Sweet! We made a cool two hundred bucks!"

"Why me, Daniel?" I zipped my jeans, fortunately not catching any pubic hair or flesh in the process. It took a minute to fasten the button because my hands were trembling so hard.

"The guys know I can get any girl in Martin High, so they bet me I couldn't get a boy."

"That still doesn't explain why you chose me."

"You're Marcus Llewellyn's son. The guys thought you should be taken down a peg. You've got a reputation for being stuck-up."

Stuck-up? Me? I gave a choke of bitter laughter. With a father who refused to have anything to do with me, and a brother who didn't have time to spare for a sibling eight years his junior? I was just incredibly shy.

"No hard feelings, Kipp."

"No feelings at all." I clenched my teeth, afraid he would hear how they were chattering. "Would you mind taking me home?" My thigh began to throb. Or maybe it had been throbbing all along and I was just now noticing it.

He turned on the ignition and drove away from Lila's Hill.

"Daniel." His name was like ash in my mouth, and I was afraid the cheeseburger I'd eaten earlier would come back up. "My father doesn't know."

"Know what? Oh, shit. I didn't even think—Look, don't worry about it. I'll make sure the guys keep quiet."

How did he intend to do that? A secret stayed a secret only as long as not more than one person knew it.

And this… it was such a juicy tidbit. But apparently he thought he had enough sway to have them refrain from passing on what had happened this evening.

I must have made a scoffing sound, because he looked at me, puzzled. "No, seriously. They're good guys."

What had happened this evening that would make me concur with that? "Watch the road, please."

He drove with one hand on the steering wheel, his other elbow nonchalantly cocked on the open window, and he whistled tunelessly through his teeth.

It seemed to take forever for him to reach the road where Llewellyn Manor was located.

"Please let me out here." We were still some distance from the house, but I couldn't bear remaining in the same car with him. I'd sneaked out through a side door no one ever used, and I'd have to hope Higgins, Sir's butler, hadn't bothered to check that it was locked.

He pulled over to the curb. "Here, take twenty dollars. That's the least I owe you."

So he could blacken my name even further, adding "whore" to it? "No, thank you." I got out and walked toward the house, staying in the shadows of the hedges that shielded Llewellyn Manor from the hoi and the polloi.

He idled along beside me, so I didn't even have the luxury of wiping the tears that streamed down my cheeks.

There was another way to get onto the grounds, and I slipped between the shrubs. They had leafed out, and although they scratched my face and tangled my hair, at least the scratches didn't break the skin. As for my clothes, it wouldn't have mattered if they were torn—I intended to throw them away as soon as I got them off my body.

For a second I thought maybe Daniel would get out of the car to make sure I was all right, but then I heard the engine rev, and he drove off.

I was alone in the night. The pain in my inner thigh was excruciating now, and I was biting back whimpers as I made my way to the side door, let myself in, and got to my room unseen.

My bedroom had its own en suite bath, so it was a relief that I didn't have to worry about crossing paths with Sir or someone else in the household. I went into it and peeled down my jeans. The bruise that was starting to form looked bad, but what made me almost vomit was how close I had come to castrating myself.

I'd need some ice. I stripped off my clothes, put on my bathrobe, and hobbled down to the kitchen to get it. Higgins caught me.

"I'm thirsty," I lied. I'd filled a carafe with ice cubes, and I had to add water to it.

Higgins merely nodded and returned to his room.

I went back upstairs, poured out the water, and made a compress with one of the washcloths. It was a toss-up as to which hurt more... the bruise, or the ice on my hot skin.

Even though I took a couple of ibuprofen, I didn't sleep well. I dreaded going to class the next day.

There was no escaping it, however. Of course Jackson, Sir's head chauffeur, wouldn't drive me to school; that was left to Pierce. As underchauffeur, it was his job to drive everyone else in the household.

"Are you all right, Master Kipp?"

"Yes." My thigh hurt too much for me to put my full weight on my leg, and so I'd limped to the Rolls Ghost used for Higgins, me, and Mrs. Wales, our cook. "My leg must have cramped during the night."

He opened the rear door and didn't say anything else.

I hoped slow paces would make my limping less noticeable, but I wasn't about to wager the manor on it. And, oh my God, was everyone going to think that Daniel had fucked me? I entered Martin High braced for taunting and derision.

But no one said anything or even looked at me cross-eyed. Mr. Madigan, who taught English and who was also the magazine advisor, didn't take me aside to inform me I was being talked about. He was one of the few teachers who didn't compare me to my brother Geoff. Even though Geoff had graduated from Martin High eight years before, he was still the big man on campus, still a legend. He'd had even more extracurricular activities than Daniel, and he'd been Prom King.

Mr. Madigan did say he was pleased to see I had my shirt tucked in for a change. Well, there really wasn't any need for me to wear it out anymore. I'd caught sight of Daniel in front of his locker, talking to one of the girls who constantly hovered around him. He'd glanced up and grinned as I'd walked by—the same grin as the day before—and my body hadn't reacted at all.

It was cold comfort.

The day passed, and nothing was said to me or about me at school.

But there was still the ordeal to be faced at home.

I generally ate alone in the small dining room unless Sir was having a dinner party where the presence of both his sons was required—a very infrequent occasion—but this evening I could hardly force myself to take a bite as I waited with dread to be called into Sir's study.

There was no summons.

As it turned out, my anxiety was for nothing; Sir never brought up my sexuality. Perhaps Daniel had convinced his posse to keep their mouths shut. Perhaps they didn't think I was worth outing. Or perhaps it was just that none of the Families—as the wealthiest residents of Martinsburg referred to themselves—dared to say a word to Sir. He wasn't a good man to cross. Whatever the reason, I was grateful.

But no matter how grateful I was, it didn't stop me from making a point of looking the other way whenever Daniel and I passed in the halls. I knew well enough what he thought of me, and I didn't need to see him staring right through me to prove it.

Fortunately there was only a month or so until graduation....

CHAPTER 3

"EARTH to Kipp!"

"Sorry." I sighed, unhappy to realize that even after three years, thoughts of Daniel could still disturb me. Although even now I would walk out of the room or turn off the television whenever *Terminator vs. Predator: Earth's Last Stand*, the movie he'd taken me to see, came on. "So what does she want?"

"Beats me. She says she's your father's personal assistant."

"You could have told me that to begin with!" God, he was such a dick!

"What? And spoil seeing you get all flustered that some deluded woman was willing to give you the time of day?"

We'd roomed together this entire school year, and never once had I looped a tie around the doorknob, indicating I was entertaining someone of the feminine persuasion and he should find other accommodations for the evening. How could Scott not have picked up that I was gay?

But I had other things to worry about, and I brushed thoughts of him out of my mind. The only time Sir had Ms. Clive contact me was to tell me it wouldn't be convenient for me to come home or when my allowance was going to be reduced again, and by now there really wasn't much left to it.

As for my tuition, that had become strictly my responsibility. Originally, it was going to be paid out of the trust fund my mother had set up for me before I was born, but when I'd declared my intent to pursue a degree in interior design, Granddad became so furious I thought he'd have a stroke. He refused to allow me access to that money. He refused to see me.

For the majority of my life, the one person I could depend on loving me was my grandfather. To have that love withdrawn hurt more than the indifference my father had always shown toward me.

I tried calling Granddad, but Beauchamp, his butler, told me he wasn't available to speak to me.

During my first month at the university, my roommate thought I was a "horny bastard" because of all the showers I took, but it was simply because that was the only place where I could cry without being heard and made fun of.

But I'd learned over the years that crying accomplished nothing, and so I stiffened my spine and determined to make the best grades I could, for myself, if not for Granddad.

Sir had never gotten along with my maternal grandfather, and I suspected that was why my father had paid for my freshman year, but I'd been stunned when he informed me he would not pay for my remaining three years at Charles T. Armand University. I wasn't eligible for a Pell Grant, since the family income was considerably over the maximum amount allowed, and I'd had to scramble to apply for every scholarship available. I was also working part time at Georg's. Hunter, the owner, had chosen a German lover's name for his interior design business.

He had started with a single store eighteen years earlier and had eventually taken over the entire strip mall. I did some rapid calculations. If Hunter could increase my hours, and if I took on students to tutor, I might have enough to cover next semester's expenses.

Well, standing here was only delaying the bad news. I took the phone from my roommate and pointed toward the door.

"Don't I get to listen?"

"In a word? No. Please leave."

"You're no fun!" he said petulantly. But he walked out.

"Good afternoon, Ms. Clive. I'm sorry for the delay. How are things in Martinsburg?"

"The city is as it's always been. Your father needs you to come home immediately." She never had been one for small talk.

"I'm in the middle of finals for the spring semester."

"That's immaterial. A ticket is waiting for you at the Greyhound depot."

A bus instead of the family jet? The last time I'd been... instructed to come home, Sir had sent the jet. Of course that had been seven years earlier, when I'd been at boarding school, but.... I shook my head and set that aside for the time being.

"I have two finals left. If I don't take these tests I'll get an incomplete and won't be able to—"

"I'm sorry, but Mr. Llewellyn expects you home immediately. At any rate, you won't be returning to college. As per your father's instructions, I've already spoken to the registrar."

"But—"

"Llewellyn, Inc. is on the verge of... an important merger."

Something was going on. I might not want to become part of Llewellyn, Inc., but I'd been around Sir enough to pick up on that slight hesitation. What was happening?

"Why does Sir want me? Geoff's home, isn't he?"

Geoff had gone to Harvard Business School, as Sir had wished, and was being groomed to take Sir's place one day.

Parents were supposed to love their children equally, but I'd known since forever that Geoff was the favored child.

"Geoffrey isn't... suitable. Mr. Llewellyn wants you."

I felt as if I'd taken a blow to the chest. After all these years, there was finally something I could do that my brother couldn't! Of course I had no idea what that might be, but....

"I'll be home as soon as I can."

I almost dropped the phone before I could end the call, and I stared at my hands. They were shaking. I curled my fingers into fists and drew in a breath.

All right. Sir wanted me. But I wasn't about to throw away the education I'd worked so hard for. I'd go to see my professors and ask about taking the finals now.

PROFESSOR MONTGOMERY permitted me to take his final right then, without batting an eye, but when I went to see Dr. Fordham afterward, he stared at me over his glasses and said, "The final is at three forty-five. You will be here to take it, or you will get a fail. And it will bring down your GPA."

"I'll be here." I didn't bother trying to argue with him. After midterms he'd said the same thing when one of his students asked to take it again, because he'd spent the night in the hospital with his ill mother and had blown that test.

There was no way I'd be able to take Fordham's final and still make the bus. It was too bad there wasn't another bus this evening, but *ce qui sera, sera*, as Granddad was fond of saying. What must be, will.

Fortunately, I was able to exchange my ticket for the next day. It was only a matter of twenty-four hours difference, and I was sure Sir could spare me that. I called Ms. Clive. She was out of the office, so I left a message.

"I'm sorry, I was able to reschedule one of the finals, but I have no choice about the second. I'll arrive in Martinsburg tomorrow by midafternoon, four o'clock at the latest, I promise. Please offer Sir my apologies and ask him to send Pierce at that time. Thanks very much. Good-bye."

I half expected a blistering call in response, but to my surprise, none came.

With some time to kill before Dr. Fordham's final, I decided to call my dream man.

CHAPTER 4

WE'D met about a year or so ago—all right, who was I kidding? It was seventeen months, three weeks, and five days. He was leaving Georg's and I was coming in for my shift. He nodded at me, and I nearly fell over my own feet. I stood staring after him, and when he glanced back, he'd grinned and winked.

And just like that, I was in love.

Oh, I knew it was hopeless—he must have been about twenty years my senior and was probably used to lovers who were soigné and debonair, and shit, he was most likely straight, so those lovers would be chic and svelte.

But he had brown eyes, the kind called honey eyes, skin the color of caramel, and thick, curly hair as dark as a moonless night.

What could I say? He brought out the poet in me.

And if he'd asked, I'd have sprawled on the nearest flat surface and let him have me.

Wait, what? That startled me. I'd kept my distance from anyone who looked like he might be even remotely interested in asking me out. After what Daniel had done to me, I just didn't trust my reaction to anyone.

Why was I drawn to this man?

Oh, of course. I chuckled sheepishly to myself. That walking wet dream would never look at me that way even if he was gay, and so it was perfectly safe for me to fantasize about him, about licking that skin and running my fingers through that hair. Would his skin taste as sweet as it looked? Would those curls wrap around my fingers, clinging to them? Would—

"Kipp!" My boss's voice shook me out of that pleasant reverie. "There's a delivery out back. Get hopping."

"Yes, Hunter."

Of course I thought about trying to find out who the man was, but how much luck would I have if he paid cash? And if he used credit cards, how would I know which was his? I simply had no way of discovering who he was....

All right, I knew that was bullshit. If I really wanted to discover who he was, I could track transactions. But he was out of my league, and it was foolish to set myself up for a fall.

But I could dream of him. And oh, momma, were my dreams good!

The man came back about six weeks later. Hunter had me filling clear glass vases with multi-colored glass stones and potpourri. Once I was done, I was supposed to place them around the shop, in various nooks and crannies, demonstrating my ability to create something that would pop.

The scent of the citrusy potpourri irritated my nasal passages, and I sneezed, and then sneezed four more times in a row.

"God bless you." The voice was like a warm brownie with two scoops of vanilla ice cream, drowned in hot fudge sauce—no nuts, though, thanks very much—and topped with a mountain of whipped cream. Without even seeing the voice's owner, I was in lust.

"Thank you." I looked up, pressing my index finger against that spot under my nose to prevent another sneeze, and it was him, the man of my dreams! The grin that spread across my face had to be the broadest, silliest thing he'd ever seen, but his eyes were kind, and he handed me a handkerchief.

In one corner was the initial H.

"Thank you," I said again. I tried to be cool about blowing my nose, but I had the feeling I was a complete failure at that. Well, at least I didn't sound like a Canadian goose. "I'll have this laundered and get it back to you as soon as I can."

"There's no rush."

I sighed. I'd thought that was the perfect excuse to see him again. "What does the H stand for?"

He tilted his head and grinned, and I went from "Whistle While You Work" to "Oh, Mamma, Buy Me That!" in two seconds.

"What do you think?"

"Harrison? Henri?" Lots of people were suckers for accents, so I gave that the French pronunciation. And then I gave him an innocent look from under my lashes. "Handsome?"

He burst out laughing, but a blush rose in his cheeks. His skin wasn't so dark that I couldn't see that, and I'd put it there! I'd never flirted with anyone before, and it was like heady wine.

"May I help you with anything, Mr. H?" Maybe it stood for his last name. This would be the safest way to address him, in the shop at any rate. If Hunter heard me coming on to one of his customers, I didn't think I'd have a job for very much longer.

"I think you should call me something else, Kipp." Wait, how had he learned my name? I'd never told him. Unless he'd asked Hunter?

Did I really care, one way or the other? I was going to find out his name!

"Sure. What did you have in mind?"

"Ham."

"Um…." All right. "Like that character in *Doc Savage*?"

"You're much too young to remember that!"

"I'm not that young!" I muttered under my breath. The last thing I wanted him to see me as was a kid. "I saw the movie once."

"Ah. Well, I never stole hams." That was how the character had gotten the nickname. Ham must have gotten bored with the subject, because he changed it. "Is Hunter in?"

"Oh. Yes, of course." He was here to see my boss, not me. I felt as if I was back at home, and I sighed.

"Kipp?"

"Yes, sir?"

He frowned at me. "I thought we'd agreed you'd call me Ham?"

"Yes, Ham?"

"Hunt called me. He ordered a bronze piece for me, and he said it had come in."

"He's in the back room. I'll go get him."

"Thank you, Kipp." He ran his fingers over my cheekbone.

Not only did he know my name, but he'd touched me!

I was almost dancing as I went to get my boss.

Hunter had the radio playing his favorite station, which aired songs of the fifties and sixties. Just then Chuck Berry was singing about a brown-eyed handsome man, and how apropos was that?

"Yes, Kipp?"

"We have a customer who's waiting to see you."

"Who is it?"

I wasn't going to tell my employer that a customer had told me to call him "Ham." Not only was it too familiar, but it was… just between the two of us. "I don't know. He said you'd ordered a bronze piece for him?"

"Ah. That would be—"

I held my breath. I was about to learn my dream man's real name!

Hunter paused in the doorway and beamed at me. He was a big man who looked like he should have been on the football field taking down offensive linemen rather than helping wealthy women change the décor of their living rooms, but he was also the sweetest-tempered person I'd ever met. And he was damned good at what he did. In fact, I wanted to be him when I grew up.

"Finish up those vases, all right?"

"Yes, Hunter."

He took Ham into his office and closed the door, and I sighed again and went back to work.

But that was meeting number two.

And so it went: he'd come into the shop, greet me, and tease me. It almost felt as if he was flirting with me, but I couldn't let myself even consider that someone as gorgeous as he would be interested in a sophomore at Armand U. Or a junior, as I was now.

Until the day last week when he'd found me in the stockroom. "Ham!" I could have kicked something. Why did he have to see me looking like this? Because I was cleaning the stockroom, I was wearing my oldest clothes, the ones even Goodwill wouldn't accept. My hair was in my eyes, cobwebs draped over one ear, and dust and sweat streaked my cheeks. I pushed the hair off my forehead and rubbed my shirtsleeve over a cheek.

"Kipp." The expression in his eyes… I'd never seen anything like it before, not directed toward me.

He came right up into my personal space and gripped my shoulders. I stared at him with my lips parted. He stood about six feet two, maybe an inch or so more, while I was five feet ten. I had no clue about what he intended when he pulled me up onto my toes. And then he kissed me.

His lips were soft, and they pressed against mine in kisses that were chaste and gentle. That was the last thing I wanted.

I struggled to get free, and the warm color of his skin seemed to leech out.

"I'm sorry—"

"Don't you dare be!" I wrapped my arms around his neck, moistened my lips, and fastened them to his. He made no effort to slip his tongue into my mouth until I touched the tip of my tongue to his lips, and then…. "Oh, yes!"

Of course I'd been kissed before—well, on the cheek—but this was the best kiss I'd ever had. I could stay here forever. I could—

"Kipp!" Hunter was calling me from the showroom, and Ham set me away from him. I could read his expression now; it was serious. I remembered Daniel's words: a guy liked to make the first move, and… oh, God, Ham was going to tell me I'd blown it, and not in the good way—

"He'll be right with you, Hunter!" he called, and then he lowered his voice. "I want to take you to dinner, Kipp. I'm booked the rest of this week with… business, but perhaps next week?"

"Yes!" We were going to dinner! An actual, honest-to-God date!

He smiled and caressed my cheek. "Let me have your cell phone."

"Shit." I bit my lip. I shouldn't have sworn in front of someone I wanted to impress. "Sorry. I must have left it in my dorm room."

"Okay." He took out his cell phone. "Give me your number." He programmed it into his phone, then took a notebook from the inner pocket of his suit jacket, tore off a sheet of paper, and wrote down his number. "Here." He handed it to me. It had an out-of-state area code and extra minutes on my prepaid plan cost the earth, but who cared? I rarely called anyone anyway. "I'll call you later in the week to firm things up."

"Sounds good. Thank you, Ham."

He tugged on the hair that curved over my ear. "Thank you. Now you'd better go see what Hunt wants, or he'll think I'm having my wicked way with you."

I went out into the showroom, grinning the whole way.

"Kipp, I—" Hunter frowned. "Are you okay?"

"Never better."

"Hmm. All right. Would you—" He looked me up and down. "Never mind. I was going to ask for your help with that new customer, but you look like you've spent the day in the coal mines."

"Give me a couple of minutes to get changed. I have the clothes I wore here."

He patted my shoulder. "Good man."

I blushed and hurried to the back room, once again almost dancing across the floor. And while yes, this was an important job Hunter was giving me, most of my pleasure was because I had a date with the nicest man I'd ever known. The fact that he was also the handsomest was just a bonus.

When I got back to the dorm after work, it was to find my roommate out, probably trying to get into the pants of the newest girl he was dating. I just hoped she knew the kind of guy she was dealing with.

I logged Ham's number into my phone and dialed it.

"Hello there, blue eyes."

"Hi, Ham." I could barely catch my breath. I loved that he knew it was me, that he had a pet name for me. "I just put your number in my phone and I wanted to be sure I had it right. I... I didn't interrupt anything, did I?"

"No. I'm here, all alone. I wish you were with me."

"Oh!" Oh, God! His voice was smooth as honey this time. I'd never heard anything like it, and the way it coiled around my dick.... I nearly came in my pants.

"Kipp?"

"I...."

"Next week can't come soon enough for me." Was this what he sounded like in bed?

"Me neither." I would have danced across the room, only that would have left me breathless—more breathless—so I hugged myself instead. "Where... uh... where will we go for dinner?"

"I thought I'd take you to the Gramercy Tavern."

"Isn't that in Manhattan?"

"Yes."

"We're having dinner in Manhattan?"

"Yes. We'll take my jet. And afterward I thought we'd go for a carriage ride around Central Park as well."

It was a good thing he was on the other end of the line. I didn't want him to see how my mouth was gaping. We were going to fly to New York to go to one of Zagat's top-rated restaurants, and then a carriage ride....

This was going to be the world's best first date!

It was probably too warm for a blanket to cover us, cover what our hands might be doing, but I could picture it. He'd unzip my fly and reach in—oh, I'd go commando!—and he'd stroke the pad of his thumb over my dick, gathering up precome. He'd take his hand out of my pants, press his thumb against my lips, and I'd—

I rubbed my palm over the bulge in my jeans and bit my lip to keep from moaning.

He must have misunderstood my silence, though. "Of course, if you'd prefer to go somewhere else...."

"No, no, that's fine!" I could feel the heat rise over my cheeks. "I... that's fine!" Thank God he couldn't read my thoughts!

"I'm glad to hear that. I think you'll enjoy the duck breast and confit."

What? Oh, food. "It sounds delicious." I'd enjoy gator nuggets and seaweed if I was having it with him.

"The flight to JFK will be about forty-five minutes, and I'll have a limo take us into the city, so suppose I pick you up about six thirty?"

"Yes." I'd learned my freshman year at Armand U that there were only a few occasions throughout the school year that required dress clothes. At that time, my allowance had been enough for little extravagances, and since a growth spurt had resulted in me outgrowing all the clothes I'd brought from home, I'd purchased a quality blazer and trousers, a couple of button-down shirts, a silk tie, and a pair of dress loafers. They were almost three years old now, and while I didn't doubt they'd meet the Gramercy Tavern's dress code, I wanted something new, something nicer.

I groaned. Oh, God, how girly was that?

"Are you all right, Kipp?"

"Yes." I tucked my phone between my shoulder and ear and pulled out the key for the drawer in my desk that locked. It wasn't that I didn't exactly trust my roommate but... I didn't.

I took out my checkbook and turned to the last entry in the transaction register. The balance was a little more than three hundred dollars, and I sighed. I had to strictly budget my funds, and I wouldn't have enough for a new suit even after my next paycheck was deposited into my checking account at the end of the week. But I could get my blazer and trousers dry-cleaned, and... maybe the shirt and tie as well? Yes, the whole thing shouldn't cost more than twenty dollars. I could swing that.

I was about to put the checkbook away and somehow I managed to drop my phone. "Shit!" I scooped it up. "Ham? Are you still there?"

"I'm here."

"I'm sorry. I dropped my phone. You were saying?"

"Kipp, is everything okay?"

"Certainly." I replaced my checkbook in the drawer, locked it, and put the key away. "Why wouldn't it be?"

"You sound a little... I don't know... distracted?"

"Ah. I'm sorry. I was...." How could I tell him I'd been fussing over what I would wear?

"I know I'm older than you. Am I too old? Would you rather not—"

"Oh, God, no! I want to go to dinner with you! It's just…. When you hear what I've been thinking about, you're going to change your mind about going out with me."

"I doubt that." His voice had taken on that honey quality again, and hearing it made me so hard…. "Tell me."

All right, I'd just have to bite the bullet. "I was wondering if I should buy a new suit."

"Really?" I could hear his amusement in that one word.

"You're laughing at me." Not that I really minded.

"No. I think it's very sweet."

"I just don't want you to be embarrassed to be seen with me." As a Llewellyn, I knew how important it was to make sure I was always dressed appropriately.

"As if that could ever happen."

"Now that's very sweet."

"I'm a cutthroat, Kipp. Any of my competitors will tell you that."

"But I'm not your competition, am I?"

"No. I hope you'll remember that. Excuse me a moment. Yes, Armitage?" He must have put his hand over his phone, because I couldn't distinguish his conversation with whoever this Armitage was, but after a few minutes, he said, "I'm sorry, Kipp. That was my personal assistant."

"You're busy. You should have told me. I'd better let you go."

"I wish you wouldn't."

That did it. Between his voice, fantasizing about what he'd do to me during that carriage ride, and the memory of his kisses, I gasped and climaxed.

"Are you all right, Kipp?"

"F-fine. I'll see you next week."

"Next week."

CHAPTER 5

ONLY here it was, next week, and I wouldn't be having dinner with him, I'd be going home. Scott was taking his last final and hadn't returned to our room yet, so I'd take advantage of his absence to call Ham. This wasn't a call I wanted my nosy roommate to eavesdrop on.

I still had my cell phone out, and I dialed the number.

And Ham knew it was me, even before I'd said a word!

"Hello, blue eyes." God, I did love when he called me that!

"Hi, Ham."

"Are we still on for tomorrow night?"

"I'm afraid not. I've been called home on family business."

"I hope it's nothing serious?"

"My father needs me." I couldn't help the pride in my voice.

"Your father? May I ask why?"

"Of course, but I can't tell you. I have no idea!" I hurried to assure him. And while Ms. Clive had said something regarding a merger, I knew enough to keep my mouth shut about it. "I... I'm really sorry I have to break our date. I was looking forward to it."

"As was I."

"May I have a rain check?"

"Of course, Kipp. *À bientôt.*"

Soon? Was that the best I could hope for? I guessed so. "*À bientôt,* Ham." I waited for him to disconnect the call.

"Kipp."

"Yes?"

"I *am* sorry you had to cancel, and I *will* see you soon."

"I won't be leaving until tomorrow morning. Could you meet me for dinner this evening? My treat," I wheedled. "T.G.I. Friday's has the best loaded potato skins."

He laughed. "As tempting as that sounds, I'm afraid not. I need to finish firming up a business deal. And regrettably, I'm not in town."

"Damn. I'd better let you go." Was this the way all our phone conversations were going to end?

"I'll talk to you soon. Dream of me tonight, blue eyes."

"Will you dream of me?"

"Don't doubt it. I've been losing sleep because of you."

"Are you trying to make me come in my jeans again?" Oh, my God, had I actually said that?

Fortunately, he didn't question me on it. He just chuckled and said, "Good-bye, Kipp."

"Bye, Ham." I hit "end" and….

Hunter! I had to call Hunter too, to let him know I wouldn't be coming in anymore!

CHAPTER 6

MY LUCK held; Hunter was in the shop, and I explained the situation to him. "... and I need to go home. I hope you're not mad at me for leaving on such short notice. If you want, once I have this sorted out with my father, I can come back and work off my two weeks."

"Don't worry about it, Kipp. I'll be sorry to lose you, but you do what you have to do."

"Thank you."

"Does your guy know?"

"Yes, I just got off the phone with him. Wait, how did you know...?"

"I happened to see him kissing you, and I had a little conversation with him."

"Um... yes?" My face felt hot. "May I ask what about?"

"You're too polite, Kipp. I told him if he hurt you, I'd come after him with the crowbar I use to open the big wooden boxes."

"Oh! Then you don't mind that we're... we're dating?"

"God bless you both! Now tell me: How are you fixed for money?"

"I'm all right. I have most of my last paycheck, and I sold some of my books back to the bookstore."

"What about the others?"

"I'll donate them to Goodwill."

"Why give them away when you can get something for them?" He sounded shocked.

"I can't." I didn't bother shrugging—he couldn't see me. "These are useless; the professors have written new editions of their textbooks."

"Bring the books to me. I'll take care of them for you."

"But, Hunter, they're asking for student ID in the bookstore now."

"Don't you worry, Kipp. I'll sell them online. Are you keeping your checking account open?"

"Yes." My paycheck was automatically deposited into it. "For the time being, anyway." Until I knew exactly what Sir needed of me.

"Then I'll put whatever I get for the books into it. And Kipp, your job will be waiting for you if you want to come back." Hunter had never encouraged physical contact, but I wondered if he would have hugged me if we'd been face to face. "Just drop the books off here, okay?"

"First thing tomorrow morning."

"Why don't you bring them by now?"

"I've got one more final."

"Then bring them by afterward. I'll buy you dinner."

"Oh, you don't have to—"

"No, but I want to. It's been a pleasure having you work for me."

I could feel myself blushing again. "Thank you!"

"And Kipp, make sure you wear something suitable for Gabarelli's."

"Oh!" That was one of the most upscale Italian restaurants in Charlestown. All its dishes were amazing, or so I'd heard—as a college student, I couldn't afford even its appetizers. It was especially known for a pasta puttanesca so mouthwatering chefs from other restaurants had attempted to obtain the recipe through any means, including having their own line chefs infiltrate Chef Pasquale's kitchen. "All right; thank you." I might as well take advantage of my freshly pressed clothes.

"Now, be here as soon as you finish that final."

"Yes, Hunter."

"I've got to go. Someone's just come in."

"Thank you again."

He was silent for a moment. Then he said gruffly, "You're welcome. And good luck on that exam."

IT WAS almost five forty-five when I dropped off the finished test on Dr. Fordham's desk. He peered at me over his glasses again. "I understand you'll be leaving us, Mr. Llewellyn. I must say I'm sorry to hear that. You were one of the few students I've actually enjoyed teaching."

"Um… thank you?"

"Don't let it go to your head." He picked up a red pen and drew the first of the pages I'd turned in toward him. "Results will be up on the department's website by the end of the week. Good evening."

"Have a good summer, Dr. Fordham."

He grunted and began reading my answers, and I returned to the dorm to get changed and gather up the books Hunter was going to try to sell for me.

DINNER was everything Gabarelli's reputation promised. I wished I could have invited Ham to dine there with me, but there were no prices listed in the menu, and I knew what that meant: they would wind up being exorbitant. Hunter didn't let me see the bill—he wouldn't even let me get the tip—and the food was well worth whatever he paid, but dinner could have run to more than I had in my checking account.

"I'll drive you back to your dorm."

"Thank you."

"You're welcome." The drive was accomplished in silence, but when he pulled up in front of my dorm, he said, "Remember, I'll always take you back." He drew me into a hug and kissed my cheek.

"Thank you, Hunter." I worried my lower lip. Did I kiss him in return? Did I shake his hand? "Um…."

"You'd better go. I'm sure you have a lot of packing to do. And as I said, I'll make sure to deposit what I get for your books into your checking account." He raised a hand. "And don't thank me again. This is what friends do for each other."

That decided me. I leaned forward and kissed his cheek. "Thank you, Hunter," I whispered and opened the passenger door of his car. He'd always been so nice to me, right from the start. "Good-bye."

"Good-bye, you sweet boy."

I hurried around the car and jogged up the steps, turning to give him a final wave before letting myself into my dorm.

Andrew Scott was in our room, once again lounging on my bed. He'd obviously gotten lucky; his eyes had a sated look, while the unfastened collar of his shirt revealed a hickey below his Adam's apple. How could someone go out to take a final and come back smelling of sex?

He looked me over. "Wow. You clean up pretty good! Where've you been, Kippers?"

"I had dinner with my boss."

"Oh, yeah? My boss never did that."

"Scott, you don't have a boss."

"Well, I did back home. And besides, it's the principle of the thing."

I shook my head and pulled out my duffel bag. "Mind getting off my bed?" Since the dress code at Armand was so relaxed, all I'd needed were a few pairs of jeans, some sweatshirts, T-shirts, and jogging shoes. I'd pack all my casual clothes and keep out a clean dress shirt and what I was wearing for tomorrow. Sir wouldn't be pleased if I appeared in informal clothes.

Grudgingly, Scott got to his feet, the sated look replaced by something more petulant. "Did that pathetic old queer try to get in your pants?"

"*What?*"

"That fag you're working for. Everyone knows he's gay."

"In the first place, he's not old." Hunter was maybe in his mid-forties. "And in the second—So what?"

"What do you mean, 'so what'? He was probably just waiting to nail you in the stockroom!"

"Is that a euphemism for ass?" I found a couple of plastic grocery bags and stuffed both pairs of my jogging shoes into them before packing them in the duffel.

"Huh?"

"Hunter never made a pass at me." I took a handful of underwear from the top drawer of the dresser I'd used all year. "I think my feelings are hurt."

"Are you serious?"

"Yes. I'm a nice-looking guy, wouldn't you say? Why didn't he come on to me?"

"Are you crazy? Did you want him to… to… to *touch* you?"

"No, but that's only because I'm sort of involved with someone else. Hunter is a nice guy."

"He's a homosexual!" He spoke slowly, in case I couldn't understand the word otherwise.

"Scott, you're an asshole." He shied back. I'd never said "boo" to him before, but it had suddenly occurred to me that I was tired of all his bullshit, and I wouldn't have to put up with him anymore after this evening.

"I'm just trying to be a good friend to you."

"Why? You never bothered before. Or is it that you just discovered who my father actually is?"

"Who… what… uh…." But he turned a dull red, and I wondered who'd spilled the beans and if he wished he'd been nicer to me.

"It doesn't matter to me, anyway," I told him. "Hunter was a good boss, and I'm going to miss working for him."

There was a perfunctory knock on the door and then it was thrust open. Riley Tarleton, a friend of my roommate's, stood there, grinning. "Hey, Scottso, the party's already underway. What's the hold up?"

"Llewellyn's a fag!"

"The correct term is gay," I said cautiously. Was Tarleton going to beat me up over this?

"And you just found that out now? Jesus, Scott, what planet are you living on?"

"What?" Scott looked dumbfounded.

"Yes, what?" I was pretty baffled myself.

"You looked good in jeans, but in that suit...." Riley came in and ruffled my hair. "You were always so busy," he murmured.

"Oh, my God, you're gay too!" Scott's voice sounded like one of the Chipmunks.

"Actually, yes. And your skinny white ass was safe all this time. Makes you wonder where you'd gone wrong, doesn't it?"

I bit back a laugh to hear my words paraphrased.

"Now, are you coming to the party?"

Scott rushed out of the door, and I sighed. "He's going to spread the news to everyone in the dorm, and probably on campus."

"Fuck him."

"No, thanks."

Tarleton laughed. "I'm serious, you know. It was a shame you were always busy. We could have had some good times together." He didn't give me a chance to answer him. "Are you coming to the party?"

"No. I have to catch an early bus tomorrow morning."

He nodded. "It might be a good idea for you to lock your door."

"Scott's got a key."

"I'll get him drunk and keep him off your case."

"If he lets you near him. Thanks, Tarelton."

"Call me Riley. We're family, after all."

I guessed we were, in a manner of speaking. "I'm... I'm sorry we didn't get to know each other better."

"Maybe next semester."

"I won't be coming back."

"Bummer. Give me your e-mail address. We can keep in touch."

"I'd like that." And I was telling the truth. If I hadn't been so intrigued by Ham, I'd have regretted that I'd let what happened with Daniel keep me from exploring a friendship with Riley. We exchanged addresses, and then he hugged me and sauntered out to rejoin the party.

I gazed around the room. Sheets, towels, the mini fridge I'd bought my freshman year.... Even if the bus driver allowed it, there was no point in taking all that home with me. I went looking for Lee Carpenter, my RA. He'd know if it could be stored for an incoming student.

"Thanks, Llewellyn, but actually...."

"What?"

"There's a house in town for kids who've been thrown out by their families. Would you mind... ?"

"That's a great idea. Take whatever you can use: towels, sheets, blankets. Oh, and the surge protector."

"Thanks," he repeated, and he squeezed my shoulder. "I hope everything goes well for you."

"Thank you, Lee."

We shook hands, and I returned to my room. Once I'd finished packing, I decided to take Riley's advice, and I locked the door.

I stripped down to my boxer briefs, hung up my suit in readiness for the morning, and got into bed.

My last night at Charles T. Armand University. It had been a good three years, in spite of the stress of having to come up with scholarships to avoid being asked to leave.

I pulled the covers over my shoulders and closed my eyes.

Of course going to sleep was another matter entirely.

God, those people were loud!

I NEVER overslept, but I did the next morning; as a result, I only just managed to grab a bite for breakfast and make it to the bus depot. The driver didn't give me a hard time, which I appreciated. He stowed my duffel in the storage compartment and told me to find a seat.

The air-conditioning was out, so I opened the window next to my seat. I had my laptop with me, but there was nothing I needed to do; I didn't feel like reading the e-books I'd saved to my hard drive, and I didn't want to waste my battery playing solitaire or Mahjong Titans.

Instead I plugged the ear buds into my Zune and turned it on. Technology went out of date almost as soon as you brought an item home—in fact this was three years old and only had eight gigabytes of storage—but I treasured it because Granddad had given it to me for my graduation, and he'd made sure it had all my favorite music.

Of course that was before he'd learned I planned to major in interior design. I sighed.

This was the first time I'd be returning to Martinsburg in three years. Most of my classmates had lived for going home for the Christmas holidays or summer vacation, but it had never bothered me that I'd remained at Armand U. Even when I'd been shipped off to boarding school when I was eight, I'd never had a problem with being away from the house I'd grown up in. Life at home was cold.

But Sir wanted me there now!

I leaned my elbow out the window and turned my face into the spring breeze, enjoying the feel as it ruffled my hair. I closed my eyes and smiled, thinking about our upcoming reunion. He'd hug me, stroke my hair, and for a change he'd call me Kipp.

CHAPTER 7

MY EUPHORIA lasted the length of the bus ride. The Greyhound pulled into the Martinsburg depot, and I put my Zune away, gathered up my laptop, and bounced down the steps, looking for Pierce, the underchauffeur.

He wasn't there.

All right, he might have hit traffic. I'd just wait, and he'd be here any minute. He was a nice man, and he'd always treated me so much better than Jackson.

I'd never particularly liked Sir's head chauffeur. On the rare occasions when he'd been required to pick me up, he'd kept me waiting, with the result that Sir would be furious with me for being late for whatever event at which I needed to appear.

The bus driver tossed me my duffel, and I caught it, placed it beside me, and waited.

Before very long I was standing there alone. The bus passengers had all disembarked and gone their separate ways.

Pierce still hadn't shown up.

My shoulders slumped. Why had I thought that this time things might be different? I took out my cell phone and called home.

Higgins answered. "Llewellyn Manor."

"It's Kipp. I'm at the bus depot. Can you tell me when Pierce will be here?"

"Both he and Jackson are unavailable. You'll have to make your own way home."

I felt as if I'd been smacked. I doubted that both chauffeurs were busy, but I didn't need Higgins to tell me why neither one would be picking me up. This was Sir's way of punishing me for not arriving yesterday.

"Was there anything else?" Higgins asked.

"No. Thank you." I disconnected the call.

It would be a long walk to the house I'd grown up in, and the shoes I wore weren't the most comfortable, but did I have enough cash on me to take a cab? I pulled out my wallet. Aside from my debit card and a couple of credit cards, there were four twenties, a ten, and three singles in it. Right. The cash I'd gotten for selling back books that had cost almost six hundred dollars.

I was about to close my wallet and place it back in my pocket when I saw the piece of paper with a phone number and the letter H scrawled under it. Not only was the number logged in my cell phone, but it was burned into my memory; I didn't have to keep the paper Ham had written it on. It was a silly, sentimental act to hold onto it, but....

I folded the paper, tucked it behind my ID, and put my wallet away. Then I looked up and down the street.

There was a taxi stand at the end of the block. I slung the strap of my duffel over my shoulder, picked up my laptop case, and walked toward it.

A buzzer sounded as I opened the door, and the dispatcher looked up. "Help you?"

"I need a cab, please."

"Sure thing. Hey, Alec, get your ass out here! You have a fare!"

I heard the sound of a toilet flushing, and then Alec Stuart came out of the bathroom, casually zipping his jeans. He didn't notice me at first.

We'd gone to Martin High together. Maybe he wouldn't recognize me.

"Who is it?"

The dispatcher nodded toward me. Stuart narrowed his eyes and looked me up and down.

For a second it was as if he was stripping off my clothes with his eyes. He'd never looked at me that way in high school, and while I didn't like it, I wasn't going to let him see it bothered me. I made my expression politely inquiring.

He shrugged and nodded toward the door. "Let's go."

I exited before him, and my spine continued to feel like something was crawling over it. "Which cab?"

"The Ford Focus."

The car he pointed to was actually taxicab yellow, with a checkerboard detail. I walked toward it, startled when he bounded in front of me and opened the rear passenger door.

"Th-thank you." I tossed my duffel onto the backseat and climbed in, barely getting my foot inside before he slammed the door shut. "Hey!"

He sauntered around to the driver's door, every inch the cocky jock he'd been in high school. He got in and made a production of adjusting the seat, the rearview mirror, the steering wheel. And all the while, the meter was ticking.

Should I tell him that the addition would be deducted from his tip?

"Okay, where to?"

I told him, and he stared at me through the rearview mirror. "Do you need directions?" He shouldn't—everyone in Martinsburg knew where Llewellyn Manor was—but I couldn't resist the dig.

"No." He put the car in gear and burned rubber peeling away from the curb.

"I'd like to get home in one piece, if you don't mind?"

"Sissy!" he spat under his breath, but I heard him anyway. "You don't recognize me, do you?"

"Should I?" Of course I did, but I wasn't going to let him know. He'd been part of Daniel's immediate clique, and I had no doubt he'd been one of the instigators of that nightmare night. "I mean, I haven't been back to Martinsburg in three years."

"You always were a stuck-up son of a bitch."

"Excuse me?"

"Forget about it."

No, I didn't think I would. Obviously he'd had a problem with me, although I could never tell why. I'd been too reserved to say anything to anyone back in those days, but I'd learned a thing or two in college. Hunter's unquestioning support had bolstered my confidence, as had knowing that Ham looked forward to seeing me in Georg's.

"I didn't expect to see one of Daniel Richardson's friends driving a cab."

"You...." He glared at me through the rearview mirror. "You do recognize me."

All the boys Daniel was friends with were from the same social and financial circles. Why would any of them have to do something as menial as driving a cab?

I had no intention of asking, though. It was none of my business. But I wasn't going to let him know that, so I let my lips curl into a smug grin.

He spat out a curse, turned on the radio, and didn't say another word for the remainder of the drive.

If I'd realized I could shut him up so easily, I'd have said something years ago.

Well, no, I wouldn't have, but it was a nice dream.

The music coming over the radio was crap, which didn't say much for his taste. Who knew there was such a thing as country rap?

The walk would have taken me a couple of hours, whereas the drive was only ten minutes. Still, I wondered if I would have preferred the walk.

Actually, what I would have preferred was to be in Charlestown, getting ready for my date with Ham tonight. So, all right, he was about forty, but that wasn't old. After all, Humphrey Bogart was twenty-five years older than Lauren Bacall when they married.

And what was I doing, thinking of marriage? Even though it had become legal a couple of years ago for same-sex couples to exchange vows in this country, Ham and I hadn't even gone on our first date.

I closed my eyes and began to weave a little fantasy about him anyway. We'd get married, and I'd take care of him.

I frowned and opened my eyes. He wouldn't need me to take care of him—from what he purchased at Georg's, he must have plenty of money.

Still, it was my fantasy; I could do whatever I wanted. I went back to it.

Sir wouldn't be happy about me marrying a guy—man—and I wasn't sure how Geoff would take it, but that didn't matter. I could divorce my family. It wouldn't be much of a hardship.

Well, except for Granddad, but I hoped he wouldn't mind that I was gay....

I frowned again. Why did I keep ruining my daydream with the reality of what my family was? I hadn't heard from Granddad since shortly before I'd left for college. He hadn't been pleased when I'd told him what I planned to major in. Maybe because he thought that meant I was gay? In which case he *would* mind, and....

I went back to the fantasy with a little less enthusiasm.

I didn't have a great deal of money, since Granddad had cut off access to my trust fund, but once I turned twenty-five, no one could stop me from using that money. In the meantime, I didn't have to go back to college. I could work at Georg's. Hunter liked me, and he'd said my job would be there if I wanted it.

Ham and I would live in a cozy little apartment. I'd have someone who loved me, and life would be wonderful....

"That'll be twenty bucks." Stuart roused me from the futility of that last imagining, and I looked around. He had pulled into the circular drive at the front of the house my father and brother lived in.

I took a twenty and the three singles out of my wallet and handed them to him, then got out of the cab, making sure I had my duffel and laptop. No way was I chasing after one of Daniel's "best buds," even if Sir let me borrow the Mercedes M-Class SUV that was his pride and joy.

Higgins came out onto the top step. His face was expressionless, but there was something in his eyes....

"Mr. Llewellyn expected you yesterday."

"I had finals."

"He expected you yesterday."

"Is that why Pierce wasn't at the bus depot to pick me up?" Was that some kind of punishment? I'd suspected as much, but I was startled to realize I'd said that last out loud.

He straightened and fastened his eyes at some spot over my shoulder. "He's waiting for you in his study, Master Kipp."

Higgins should have stopped calling me "Master Kipp" when I'd reached my eighteenth birthday three years ago, but I wasn't going to challenge him on that.

"Yes." I put my shoulders back, even as my stomach began to tie itself into knots. As much as I might hope otherwise, much more than water had gone over the dam for me to expect the fatted calf. Too much more.

Higgins stepped aside to allow me to enter, and I worried my lip to the point where it started to hurt.

But this wasn't doing any good. I went into the house.

"If you'll leave your luggage here? I'll take it to your room shortly."

"Thank you." I took my laptop with me. I wanted to show Sir my grades and what I'd accomplished.

Higgins led the way down the long corridor that ran through this part of the house before curving to the left. Sir's study was the last of the numerous rooms that branched off it.

The double doors were closed. I stood there, my heart pounding. It had been a long time since I'd seen Sir. Why did he want me home? Had he missed me enough to realize he loved me? What could I do for him that Geoff couldn't?

Higgins knocked.

"What is it?" Sir didn't sound happy, but then he rarely did.

Higgins opened the door. "Master Kipp is home, sir."

"Well, get him the hell in here!"

"Yes, sir." He stood aside.

I took a deep breath, held it for a moment, then let it out and walked into the room. "Good afternoon, Sir."

He grunted and scowled at me, then turned his gaze to his butler. "Higgins, get me a drink!"

Higgins hurried to the liquor cabinet, took out a bottle of Ladybank Single Malt, and poured a healthy portion into a glass.

Sir took the glass without bothering to thank him. "Now get out of here!"

Higgins gave a polite bow. Always the perfect butler, his face was blank. He left, closing the door firmly behind him. It wouldn't have caught otherwise, and anyone passing by would have heard the conversation that would be taking place in here.

CHAPTER 8

"DON'T stand there hovering like a—a—" Sir's lips were in a tight line. "Put that goddamned case down and sit!"

"Yes, Father."

"Don't call me that!"

I felt as if he'd struck me. I sank down onto a chair, my laptop on the floor beside me, and sat, stiff-backed. What a fool I was to think that after all these years Sir could have come to care for me!

"I suppose you're wondering why I had you come home." He glowered at me from over the rim of his glass.

"Yes, Sir."

"I have a marriage arranged for you."

"M-marriage? But this is 2017, not 1817."

"How like you to state the obvious," he sneered.

"I can't...." I swallowed, feeling the blood leave my face. This was the worst of all possible times to confess my sexual orientation, but it seemed I had no choice. "Sir, I...." I took a breath and then blurted out, "I'm gay."

"Did you think I was unaware of that?"

"But... how did you know?"

"Seriously? Do you think you have the capability of concealing something so obvious from me?" Both his expression and his tone mocked me.

"But... then... I don't understand. How could you ask me to marry a woman?"

"You're the most stupid boy! I'm not asking you squat. You'll marry who I tell you to marry. And of course it won't be a woman. She'd demand an annulment as soon as she realized you couldn't perform."

"If she signed a prenup?" And what was I thinking, offering a solution to what would be insoluble to me? I shuddered at the thought of being naked in bed with a woman.

"No prenuptial agreement on earth would expunge the scandal you'd bring down on my name!"

"Who...." I swallowed and licked my lips. "In that case, who would you expect me to marry?"

"Hyde Wyndham."

"Who?"

"Are you deaf or just a fool?" Suddenly he was looming over me, his breath in my face, and as much as I wanted to shy away from him, I couldn't because there was nowhere for me to go. "I said Hyde Wyndham! Jesus, boy, don't you read the *Wall Street Journal*?"

I had no desire to become part of his empire—that was what Geoff aspired to. I shook my head, but Sir didn't appear to notice, or else he just didn't care.

He turned on his heel and strode across the room, then paused to glare at me over his shoulder. "And shut your mouth! You're gaping like a beached fish!"

I did as he ordered, then licked my lips again and asked, "But why would Mr. Wyndham want me?"

"The man's as queer as a three-dollar bill." Sir curled his lip. He added grudgingly, "And you're not hard on the eyes. Wyndham came to me and told me he wanted to buy shares of Llewellyn, Inc. When I told him they stayed in the family, that I had no intention of ever putting them up on the open market, he offered a compromise: you'll marry him, and once I'm gone, he'll get your shares."

I finally realized "why," in this case, me and not Geoff. Geoff was straight. As a matter of fact, he was so straight he had a new woman every other week, and of course Sir was proud of that fact.

"It's clear you have no respect for him, Sir. Why would you want to connect our family to him?"

He muttered something I didn't catch and went back to sit behind his desk.

"Excuse me?"

"That's none of your fucking business! You may as well prove useful! Just don't disgust him."

"What? What do you mean?"

"When you're in his bed, be restrained. Lie there and let him... do whatever it is he has to do." He narrowed his eyes and sneered. "Why do you think Daniel dropped you?"

I gasped in shock. How did he know Daniel and I had dated, for however short a period of time?

"Of course I knew!" he snarled, answering my unspoken question. "I know everything that goes on in this house! You were so pathetic, sneaking out to see that boy. Just like your—"

"But you never said anything!"

"Why would I? Daniel taking you as a lover would have given me a hold over Jacob Richardson, and an 'in' to Richardson Industries."

"I don't understand. Mr. Richardson is your friend. Why did you need—" I shut up. I'd seen that look on Sir's face before when he'd been plotting to make another killing, and for a second I thought I was going to throw up.

"I didn't *need* it at that point. I *wanted* it. But you had to ruin that!" He was shouting now. "You were too uninhibited, too unrestrained. Of course Daniel bolted!"

I shook my head. "Daniel is straight. We never would have been lovers."

"Immaterial. Your looks are enough like your mother's. Straight or not, Daniel would have been tempted by you, and when his grandfather learned of it, learned it was a case of like father, like son...." He picked up his glass, seeming to study the amber contents, and smirked, and I swallowed bile. Then his gaze fell on me, and his expression darkened. "If you just hadn't been so goddamned out of control!"

Sir would have used me to blackmail his way into Daniel's grandfather's business?

"Right now I'm stretched a little thin, but with Wyndham's backing, things will turn around in no time." If it was possible, Sir's eyes would have shot sparks. "You won't ruin *this* for me!"

"How long have you two been planning this?"

"A month? Two?" Sir waved away my question as unimportant. "I wasn't going to agree to it—the man's been a thorn in my side since—but when it became obvious how much he wanted the Llewellyn shares...." The twist to his lips wasn't pleasant. "Well, let's just say that I squeezed him until I got the deal I wanted!"

He was *selling* me? I shivered, and then I said to myself, *Enough! Find your goddamned backbone!* I drew in a deep breath and straightened my spine. "I'm sorry, Sir; I can't marry him."

"*What?*" The sound his shot glass made hitting his desk was like a bullet exploding from its chamber, and I jumped in spite of myself.

"I can't—I'm in love with someone else."

"Oh, is that all? Part of the agreement is you remain faithful for a year. After that.... Have an affair, if you like. Have a hundred. He won't care."

I was horrified. "I wouldn't do that to someone I'd pledged to be faithful to!"

"Why not? It's what your mother did!"

"*Excuse me?*"

"I said it's what he intends to do. Pay attention, for God's sake!" A thin trickle of blood began to ooze from his left nostril, and he spat out a curse, reached into a pocket for his handkerchief, and blotted his nose.

The door to the study opened. "Not *now*, Higgins!" Sir looked up, irritated. "Oh, Wyndham." His expression smoothed to a smile he offered those he considered not quite his equals. He put the handkerchief away. "I wasn't expecting you. Come in and meet your fiancé."

Fiancé. I was going to be tied to someone I didn't know. I was so miserable I sat there staring at my fingers, unable to meet the gaze of the man who wanted Llewellyn shares so badly that he was willing to buy me to get them.

"Llewellyn."

I knew that voice. I spun around and nearly fell off my chair. "Ham?" He closed the door behind him and strolled into the study. He was wearing a charcoal gray pinstripe suit, a pale gray shirt, and a charcoal tie, and he looked so good I couldn't take my eyes off him. But.... "What are you doing here?"

"I decided I didn't want to wait to have dinner with you." He had beautiful lips, and the way they curved into an open smile.... My heart turned over and I started to smile at him in return.

"*Ham?*" The disgust in Sir's tone drew my attention from Ham. The quasicongenial look on Sir's face had been replaced with irritation, and his antipathy radiated out to encompass both of us. "Wyndham, what's the meaning of this?"

"Kipp and I have met before."

"You know Wyndham?" Sir stalked to the liquor cabinet and retrieved the bottle of Ladybank. The glare he leveled at me was venomous.

"No!" I protested. I knew... *thought* I knew... someone named Ham.

"You do, Kipp," Ham assured me.

"You... you're Hyde Wyndham?" I stared at him blankly. My pleasure in seeing him was gone.

"Yes."

"Why didn't you tell me?" I shivered. All I could think was that it was another bet. Oh, God, this couldn't be happening!

"Your father—"

"Goddammit!" Sir turned that glare on Hyde Wyndham, who simply raised an eyebrow.

"I was led to believe you were aware," Mr. Wyndham said smoothly.

"Led by whom? I never...."

He ghosted his tongue over his lips, and I couldn't take my eyes off his mouth. Those kisses? That embrace? He'd thought they indicated I had knowledge of Sir's plans?

Cold. I felt so cold. "And you want to marry me, Mr. Wyndham?" He'd been nice to me all along, but lately he'd become more—what had Sir said? Their negotiations had become more *intense* in the past month or so.

"I'm still Ham, Kipp."

No, he wasn't. Ham was someone I'd fallen—I'd come to care about, and I'd let him inside my defenses because I thought he cared about me. I didn't know who Hyde Wyndham was.

Worst of all, he didn't care if I remained faithful to him. In fact, he'd had it put in the contract that after a year I could pretty much fuck whom I wanted.

What a stupid, *stupid* fool I was.

"All right, then, Wyndham. Everything is settled; the boy will be pleased to marry you."

"His name is Kipp!" Mr. Wyndham corrected sharply. He took a step toward me and extended his hand, and I shied back. He frowned. "Kipp?"

"Why do you want to marry me?" Sir had explained the arrangement—if Mr. Wyndham wanted those shares, he had to take me along with them. Was I really hoping that for once I would come first? "No, don't bother answering that." I could see he was at something of a loss at my rapid about-face. God, I was so pathetic. I forced myself up from the chair I'd been virtually frozen in and edged away from both him and my father. "Thank you for asking—" Although, come to think of it, he hadn't asked. Sir had simply told me what I was to do, including lying there and thinking of England. "However, the answer is no."

"You can't say no!" Sir's face turned red, something I'd never seen before, since he'd always been very much in control, even when he'd been slicing his business opponents to virtual ribbons. And as for his eyes....

"You did tell Kipp about this, didn't you?" The ice in Mr. Wyndham's words distracted me, and I turned to him and blinked. He was staring at Sir, his gaze frigid and the expression on his face.... No one had ever regarded Sir in that manner, not to my knowledge.

"The boy was informed when I felt it was necessary for him to be informed. If you've touched him—" He muttered something that sounded like, "*Pervert!*"

"I haven't. Although I have to say it was difficult." His words were warm now, and he smiled at me again. It was the same smile he'd used when we'd met at Georg's. Was he trying to soothe me as if I were a nervous colt?

"In that case, there's nothing to stop this deal from being carried out." Sir glared at me again. "You *will* marry Wyndham!"

"I won't." I cringed at how petulant that sounded, but I wouldn't be tied to someone who didn't love me, who didn't care if I remained faithful to him or not. I turned to leave the room.

"Think carefully, boy! If you step outside this room, you won't set foot in my house ever again!"

"Shouldn't you be a little more conciliatory toward your son if you expect him to do what you want?" Mr. Wyndham stood with his arms folded across his chest. I'd run my fingertips over it once. And God, his shoulders were—No. I wouldn't let myself be distracted by how broad they were, how that action stretched his gray suit jacket snug over them.

"I'll speak to him however I damned well please!" Sir snarled.

"You're an asshole, Llewellyn! Kipp—"

"I'm sorry you went to the bother of driving all this way, Mr. Wyndham." I could barely get the words past lips that felt wooden.

"Where do you think you're going?" Sir demanded.

"Back to Charlestown. Back to college."

"And how will you afford it? If you think I'm going to cover your tuition—"

"You've said this is no longer my home. Why would I expect anything else from you?" I clenched my hands into fists at my side. "I know you never cared about me, but weren't you interested in anything I did?" No, I could see he wasn't. "Neither you nor Granddad have paid my tuition for the past two years."

Reenrolling shouldn't be a problem, but the scholarships I'd applied for would probably be given to someone else, and I'd have no choice but to wait for the winter semester. Fortunately, I could fall back on Georg's, so at least I'd have a job. Getting back in the dorm, though.... Maybe Hunter would let me sleep in the stockroom until I could get myself together?

"Kipp!" Ham—Mr. Wyndham took a step toward me, and I sidestepped him.

"It must have amused you to toy with me, Mr. Wyndham." I thought of his kisses, of how he'd made me feel worth kissing, of that silly fantasy I'd woven of a future with him. Sir was right: I was a fool. But I'd never let Mr. Wyndham know how much of a fool I was. I did my best impersonation of Sir. "I'd ask why, but frankly? I don't care enough."

As I walked out, Sir raised his voice. I'd never heard it so strident. "This is your fault, Wyndham! He's always been an obedient brat! What did you say to him?"

"Llewellyn, get out of my face!"

I didn't want to hear any more. I closed the door, giving it the firm tug that was necessary to be sure the latch caught.

CHAPTER 9

HIGGINS was hovering in the hallway. "Master Kipp—"

"Did you take my duffel to my room? I'm sorry for the inconvenience, but I won't be staying. Please have it brought down." I'd left my laptop in Sir's study. I couldn't go back in there. I ran a hand through my hair, scrambling to come up with a plan.

I'd tell Higgins to call me a cab, and while he was so occupied, I'd slip down to the kitchen and talk to Mrs. Wales. Our cook had always liked me, and perhaps she could go into Sir's study after things quieted down and retrieve it for me. I forced myself not to think of the Zune stored in a side pocket of the case, or all my grades and work that were on the hard drive.

"And call a cab for me."

"I was about to say you have a phone call."

"I'm not taking any calls."

"Your grandfather...."

At times when things became too stressful in this house, I had known I could go to Granddad's home for a week or two or three, until the contretemps was over—I was never missed.

Of course Granddad loved Geoff, but in this case I knew I was loved more, because I looked so much like our mother.

He'd been so angry with me, though, when I'd told him I wanted to study interior design, that I didn't want to follow in his footsteps and take over his factory after he retired; he hadn't spoken to me since I'd gone away to college.

I'd been hurt, but in spite of that, I would never refuse to take his call. I went to the phone on the console table in the library. "Yes, Granddad?"

"It's Beauchamp, Master Kipp." For some reason it didn't bother me that Granddad's butler called me that.

"Well, hello. How's everything?"

"Not good."

"What's wrong?"

"Your grandfather knows you've got your own life, but if you could come to see him...."

"What's wrong?" I repeated.

"His cancer has recurred—"

"*What*? What do you mean *recurred*? When did he get sick?"

"Two years ago. He doesn't have long. Please... he wants to see you."

"Of course. Is he at home or in the hospital?"

"He's at Promise Hospice."

Martinsburg wasn't a large city. There was only one hospice. "I'll be there as soon as I can get a cab."

"He'll... he'll be pleased to see you. He's missed you so much."

I wasn't about to point out the gifts I'd sent that first Christmas that had been returned—although as it turned out, the money wound up coming in handy—and the phone calls that hadn't, until finally I'd given up.

"Tell him I'm on my way." I hung up and then dialed the local cab company; I didn't have time to wait for Higgins to make the call, and besides, God had given me fingers that worked perfectly well. "This is Kipp Llewellyn. I want a car sent to Llewellyn Manor immediately. And I'd prefer any driver but Alec Stuart."

I didn't care if that got him in trouble. Too much had happened, and what I could do without most right then was someone sneering and snarking at me, even if it was only for fifteen minutes.

CHAPTER 10

I DIDN'T need the time it took to drive to Promise Hospice to consider why I'd felt so betrayed by Ham—by Mr. Wyndham. It had seemed as if I were about to get my heart's desire: someone who wanted *me* for myself. That foolish fantasy was torn from me; my only use was as a pawn in Sir's business plans.

"We're here, Mr. Llewellyn." The driver sounded nervous. Because he was afraid I'd refuse to have him drive me again? No one had ever been afraid of me before. I didn't particularly care for the hollow feeling it gave me.

After paying the fare and tipping him, I had forty-five dollars left. I'd have to find an ATM once my visit with Granddad was done. I'd also have to find a place to stay. I didn't bother considering the Saratoga Trunk. It was the most exclusive—for exclusive, read "expensive"—hotel in the area. The Alden Arms was owned by the Aldens, and while it was no longer the five-star hotel it had once been, it was still out of my price range. And it wouldn't be Sir's house, since that was no longer home, and I couldn't rely on being welcome at Silver Birch, Granddad's home, either.

It looked like I'd be spending the night at the local Y. Would they let me check in without luggage? I'd been in such a hurry to get to Promise Hospice, I'd totally forgotten my duffel. I pictured myself storming Llewellyn Manor to get it back, and shook my head. As if that would happen. I did know when Sir would be at his office and when Higgins was likely to be away. I'd call Mrs. Wales, and hopefully, she and Pierce would be able to get my duffel and laptop to me.

However, depending on Granddad's condition, I might wind up needing an apartment. If that was the case, college would be on hold and I'd have to find another job. Maybe Hunter knew someone in the vicinity of Martinsburg who'd be willing to hire me.

I walked into the spacious foyer of Promise Hospice. Late-afternoon sunlight streamed through the windows with their plantation shutters. Potted plants and vases of fresh flowers gave the area a feeling of welcome, and if there was a scent of illness elsewhere in the building, there was none here.

"I'm here to see Bradley Martin," I said to the receptionist at the front desk. "I'm Kipp Llewellyn, his grandson."

"He's in the garden." Her smile was filled with compassion. "Mindy, please take Mr. Llewellyn to the garden."

"Sure." The girl who came to the desk looked vaguely familiar. She was a pretty brunette wearing a beige shirt and slacks, with an amethyst scarf threaded through the belt loops at her waist. "Hi, Kipp. It's nice to see you. Come on, it's right this way."

"Um...." I followed her down the corridor, trying to peer unobtrusively at the name tag clipped to the breast pocket of her shirt. It just read *Mindy*, which I already knew.

"I guess you don't recognize me. I'm Mindy Richardson. You were a few years ahead of me in high school."

"That's right. Daniel's sister." It must have been the family resemblance—the gray eyes and light-brown hair—that made her seem familiar, because I didn't remember her from high school at all. "I guess you'll be graduating next month," I murmured for want of something better to say.

"Actually I graduated in January. I'll be getting married in June."

"Congratulations."

"Didn't you know?"

"No. Sorry. I'm not much in touch with what goes on in town." I'd never been good with the social niceties. It was just as well I'd turned down Mr. Wyndham's proposal. He would have been disappointed with me as a spouse. And I had to change the subject. "You're volunteering here?"

"Yes. Mummy says I should. She said your mother used to be involved in all kinds of volunteer work."

Mummy? That was kind of cute. Not something I'd ever have called my own mother, but somehow it suited Mindy. "Your mother knew mine?"

"Oh, no, but you know how everyone talks in Martinsburg."

"That's the truth." I didn't know how I'd lucked out with the fiasco with Daniel never coming to light.

"Anyway, after your mum passed, Mr. Llewellyn wouldn't let anyone else take her place doing all the things she did."

"Yes." As the wealthiest man in our city, Sir had a say in everything, and I knew that after my mother died, no one woman was permitted to run all the charities she had.

"And I shall!"

"Shall what?"

"Get to be responsible for all the charities!"

"Uh… you can do that?" I wasn't going to ask how she expected to, since she was only eighteen.

She gave a little bounce. "You see, my grandmother was an earl's daughter, so she knew all those things. Mummy learned from her, and she's going to teach me!"

"And Sir is letting you?"

"Oh, that was Geoff's idea. He insisted."

"Geoff?"

"Yes. He likes to say that after we get married, I'll be first lady of Martinsburg."

I started choking.

"You're marrying my brother Geoff?" Why hadn't Sir mentioned this? Why hadn't *Geoff* called to tell me himself, or e-mailed me the news? If Sir hadn't called me home because he had something he wanted of me, would I have ever been informed of my brother's wedding?

"Didn't you know?" she repeated.

"As I said, I've been kind of out of touch." I'd also been raised to keep family secrets in the family, and I wouldn't say anything else to Mindy.

"I know how that can be. We haven't heard much from Daniel in more than two years."

"Oh?"

"Yes. He and Daddy had the world's worst row when he came home from college that first Christmas. Daniel said some horrible things, and Daddy said even worse." Her pretty mouth took a downward turn. "I wanted Daniel to come home for my wedding, but Daddy wouldn't hear of it."

"I'm sorry." I hadn't been in touch with Geoff at all since I'd left for college, so I could hardly look down on Daniel for not staying in contact more with his mother and sister.

"No, it's okay. For our honeymoon, Geoff's planning on a layover in Boston. I'll get to see Daniel then."

"That's right; he always said he intended to graduate from Harvard Law."

"Yes. He starts law school in a year. I—" She opened a French door. "And here's the garden! It's pet-therapy day, and Sunshine is with your grandfather."

Granddad was sitting on an upholstered chair, and in spite of the balmy May weather, he wore a coat and had a throw tucked around his legs. An oxygen tank was positioned behind him, and he had a nasal cannula fitted into his nose. His eyes were closed. At his side was a golden retriever, whose head rested on his lap, and he ran his hand through the silky fur of her neck.

Beauchamp sat on a bench beside him, reading aloud from a paperback.

"Zhenshchina?" He knew that voice, although the deadliness in it now had never been directed at him.

"Yes, I'm here." The warmth radiating from her body was like a benison in this cold place.

"Sorry." He couldn't stop himself from shivering. He'd been stripped and beaten and.... "Didn't want to let them use me to get to you."

Her hands were gentle as she stroked back his hair. "So you allowed them to brutalize you?"

"This is nothing!" he managed to get past split lips. "I've had worse done to me."

"Yes, I know. In that other place." She ran her fingertips over his ribs, and in spite of the gentleness of her touch, he couldn't help hissing in pain. She leaned close to his ear. "I will get you out of here. Trust me!"

"Always do." He'd be inclined to laugh if he didn't know how much it would hurt. Someone was about to learn just how dangerous this woman could be when she was crossed!

Mindy cleared her throat. "You have a visitor, Grandfather."

I jerked around. Why was she... oh, of course—she'd be marrying into the family.

"Yes. Melinda?" Granddad opened his eyes, and they lit with pleasure. "Kipp!"

Oh, God, he looked so worn and old!

"Granddad, I'm glad to see you again!" I crossed the space with rapid steps, dropped to my knees beside him, and put my arms around him. It scared me how thin and fragile he felt.

"I'll go now, sir." Beauchamp rose and placed the paperback upside down on the bench.

Dangerous When Crossed? The woman on the cover was a leggy blonde whose black jumpsuit seemed painted on her lush figure. In one hand she held what appeared to be a scalpel, while in the other was a gun that looked like it could take down an elephant. Behind her was a man, also blond, also in black, with a semiautomatic in each hand.

I swallowed a laugh. Since when had Granddad developed a taste for lurid spy stories?

Beauchamp met my eyes. "Mr. Kipp." We'd never been particularly friendly, but now he seemed pleased to see me. "I beg your pardon for slipping earlier."

"That's all right. Higgins still calls me 'Master Kipp'."

Beauchamp frowned. "In that case, I'm doubly sorry." There had never been any love lost between him and Sir's butler.

Granddad didn't notice. "Thank you, Beauchamp," he said. "For everything. You'll follow my instructions?"

"Of course, sir." Beauchamp touched Granddad's shoulder, stooped to pat the golden, said, "Good-bye, Sunny," and walked out.

"Do you want to keep Sunny with you, Grandfather?"

"Yes, Melinda. Her handler won't be here for another half hour."

"All right. I'll just leave you two to catch up."

"Thanks, Mindy."

"Yes, thank you." Granddad waited until she left, then ran his hand over my hair. "I imagine you're aware Geoff is marrying her."

"Yes, although until she told me just now, I'd had no idea. I haven't spoken to Geoff in a few years."

"So it wasn't just me?"

"Granddad, that isn't fair! You never answered my phone calls—"

"And when I finally decided to, you felt it was only fair play to not answer mine?"

"What? You never called me!"

"I did. It was just after I was diagnosed the first time. I told Marcus I wanted to mend fences with my grandson. He said he'd have to talk to you first. It was a week before he finally got back to me and said you refused to allow him to give me your number."

"Oh, Granddad, since when has Sir allowed anyone to refuse him anything?"

He squeezed the bridge of his nose. "After everything he's done, why did I believe him?" The golden nudged his hand, and he stroked her head. "I'm sorry, Kipp."

"So am I, Granddad. I've missed you so much!" I rested my head against his shoulder. The odor of illness clung to him, and I could have wept. "If I'd known you were ill, I'd have come right home."

He gave a heavy sigh and began to cough, a deep, ratchety sound, and he pulled out a handkerchief. When he took it away from his mouth, it was stained with blood.

I jerked back, horrified, and landed on my butt. "Should I call a nurse?" I felt like an idiot as I righted myself.

"No. She'll just give me a shot of morphine, and I'll get fuzzy. I want to stay alert to talk to my favorite grandson."

"Thank you, Granddad, but if you need something...?" He shook his head, and I settled myself on my knees and studied him. "So tell me what's been going on. Beauchamp said you'd been sick for two years."

"It will be two years this coming August. They took my colon. The prognosis wasn't good—it had already metastasized. They didn't want to tell me, but I made them."

"You always wanted everyone to do things your way." I leaned up and rubbed my cheek against his shoulder, not wanting him to see my tears. "What kind of treatment did you have?"

"I refused chemotherapy. You never knew your grandmother...."

"No." She'd passed away before I was born, but I'd seen pictures of her. Mother had had her coloring—blonde hair and blue eyes, just as I did, although my hair was a good deal lighter.

"... breast cancer," Granddad was saying, "and what the chemo did to her—I was willing to accept radiation therapy. It was just supposed to be palliative, but it actually seemed to send the cancer into remission. Now, however...."

It was back, and from the looks of him, he didn't have much longer.

"If I'd known you were ill, I would have come, no matter what." I wanted to make sure he knew that.

"You always were my good grandson. Geoffrey hasn't come to see me since my cancer recurred. Does Marcus think it's catching?" he muttered under his breath, but I was close enough to hear him.

Oh, Granddad....

"I'm sorry I gave you such a hard time when you told me you planned to become an interior decorator. That was so...." He shook his head.

Had he been about to say it was so gay? Well, that only made sense, since I was gay.

"How did you know I was home?" I asked, deciding it might be better to change the subject.

"It's the talk of Martinsburg, your wedding to Hyde Wyndham."

"I'm not marrying him."

"You aren't? Well, whyever not, boy?"

I rose to my feet and walked away from him, curling my fingers into fists. "Please don't call me that." I didn't flinch, not even when I inadvertently dug the nails into my palms.

"I'm sorry, I know.... Kipp, Wyndham's a good man. And he's ten times richer than your... than Marcus. So what's holding you back?"

"Hyde Wyndham doesn't want me. All he wants is a way to eventually gain shares in Sir's company." I opened my hands and stared at the crescent marks I'd left in the skin. "I met him almost a year and a half ago. He never told me who he was."

"He never struck me as the sort of man who'd marry for anything but love, especially considering—"

"Well, apparently he is. And what do you mean, 'never struck you'?"

"I know him. I'll tell you another time."

I thought he should tell me now, but he had other ideas.

"Now, come back and sit beside me, and tell me what happened."

CHAPTER 11

IT WAS like old times, and I sank down next to him again. "I met him at Georg's—"

"Gay *what?*"

"Georg, Granddad. It's the German pronunciation of George."

"Humph." He beetled his brows at me, and I couldn't help smiling. "So what's this *Georg*? A club?"

"No; it's the shop I worked in."

"Just a second, young man! What do you mean *work?*"

"Granddad, if I wanted to eat and have clothes without holes in them, I needed a job."

"Why?" There was steel in his tone, and I looked into his faded blue eyes, puzzled.

"What do you mean, 'why'? I didn't have access to my trust fund, and Sir stopped paying my tuition."

"He *what?*" He folded his lips into a thin line, and I was about to ask if he was in pain, if I should call for that nurse, when he said, "I'm so very sorry, Kipp. You needed me, and I failed you. Just as I failed—" His voice cracked.

"Granddad?"

"I'll call Carter and tell him... no, he's gone. Who's my CFO now? Orsino? Malvolio? Why do I keep thinking it's something from Shakespeare?"

It scared me so much to see him so vague I didn't even think to ask where Carter had gone to.

Granddad patted my hand. "I'll talk to Beauchamp about it, but you'll have your trust fund available as soon as possible. Now. Tell me about this job."

"Um…. It started as an internship. When I told Hunter—he's the owner—I'd have to drop it because I needed a job to cover expenses, he gave me that job. It wasn't much to begin with, but it was enough to keep me in groceries and supplies—"

"And clothes without holes?"

"Yes, while I applied for scholarships. I have to tell you: Hunter was so nice to me…."

"Nice in what way?" He sounded suspicious.

"He's a good man, Granddad, and I think you'd like him. I mean, he is gay—"

"Kipp!" He was shocked. "I'm ashamed of you! What does that have to do with anything?"

"Well, you know Sir would cross eight lanes of rush-hour traffic blindfolded and on his hands and knees rather than walk on the same side of the street with someone he perceived to be gay. And you and Sir are the same generation." It had never been a secret that Sir was only a couple of years younger than Granddad. "I assumed you'd feel the same way. Especially since you were so angry with my choice of career."

"You know what they say happens when you assume."

I couldn't help smiling. "Yes, Granddad. But was I wrong?"

"I just didn't want everyone to think you might be gay."

All right, here it was. It had been difficult coming out to Sir, but to my grandfather, who I loved and who I had no doubt loved me….

"I am gay, Granddad." Something occurred to me. "And you had to have some idea of that, because why else would you say it was all right for me to marry another man?" I knew that in his younger years he'd had a reputation as being a hard man to work for, but he'd always been good to me, and if I'd been straight, I couldn't see him pushing me into a relationship with another man.

"You're right, Kipp."

"What gave me away?"

"Does it matter?"

"That's more or less what Sir said."

"Unlike Marcus Llewellyn, I want you to be happy."

"And I'd be happy with a man who only wanted me as part of a package deal? Did you know he only expects me to be faithful to him for a year?"

"What?"

"It's in the contract. Sir told me."

"And knowing Marcus Llewellyn, you believed him?"

"But Granddad, he's my father. Why would he lie to me about something like that?" And in spite of how Sir treated me, I kept hoping for the best.

He opened his mouth, but then closed it and shook his head. "He lied to me about you not wanting to talk to me."

It was my turn to open and then close my mouth. I sighed. "You have a point."

"Do you really think that was Hyde Wyndham's idea?"

I shrugged. "Does it matter whose idea it was? He signed the contract. That means he has to have agreed to it."

Granddad ran his palm over my hair again and then tugged my ear. "Oh, my dear grandson. Tell me something. If that clause wasn't in the contract, would you have given some thought to marrying him?"

"Maybe." I looked into his eyes, with their yellow-tinged whites. Had the cancer affected his liver as well? "I don't know. I met him in Charlestown, and I thought he was... perfect. I'd have—" I could hardly tell Granddad I'd been so aroused by this man I would have let him have me the first time I'd seen him. I changed what I'd been about to say. "He could have told me his name at any time, but he never did."

"Kipp—"

I shook my head. "That clause in the contract.... Why marry me?"

"Haven't you looked into a mirror recently?"

"Of course. 'Item, two lips, indifferent red—'"

"I'll thank you not to quote Shakespeare to me, young man! Hyde Wyndham would be getting Beth Martin's son, and that would be worth even more than the shares in Marcus Llewellyn's company."

"You have to say that, Granddad." I kissed his wrinkled cheek. He was so ill. I ducked my head so he wouldn't see the tears that were back in my eyes. "What I meant was, why buy the cow when he could have the milk for free?"

"Don't be crass, young man!"

"I apologize." I should have known better than to mention sex to someone of Granddad's generation. Something else occurred to me. "But why would Sir be willing to sell shares in Llewellyn, Inc.? He doesn't need Mr. Wyndham's backing. I mean, even if things aren't going well with the company, Geoff is marrying Mindy Richardson, and—"

Granddad was shaking his head. "As wealthy as the Richardsons once were, they don't have an iota of Wyndham's money."

"Wait, *once* were? What happened to their money?"

"Bad judgments in his investments, bad decisions in his personal life... Aaron Richardson made them all. His fortune is a fraction of what it was."

"Aaron? Jacob let him do that?"

"You've really been out of touch, haven't you?" Granddad gave a bark of laugher. "Jacob's been gone these past two and a half years."

"Oh." I'd never particularly cared for Jacob Richardson—he'd been a big man who always seemed to be frowning down at me from an enormous height. And in spite of John Donne's words, I had to admit I didn't feel Mr. Richardson's death diminished me. "And what of Sir's fortune?"

"The Families were in dire straits, and so he backed the Aldens and the Stuarts."

"I'll bet it must have killed them to ask for his help." There were four Families in Martinsburg, and I'd grown up knowing that. They'd always treated Sir as the outsider, even though he'd married Mother.

For them to have to go to him.... "But why didn't they ask you for help?"

"They did." His tone was so cold I knew better than to push for more information.

"Alec Stuart is driving a cab," I murmured absently, wondering why his father hadn't given him a job at the Saratoga Trunk. The Trunk had been in the Stuart family for more than a century, coming as part of the first Mrs. Stuart's dowry.

"Yes, I'd heard he had to get a job. How are you aware of that?"

"He drove me home from the bus depot."

"Ah."

"So Sir's broke?" That would explain why I'd had to take a bus home instead of the jet.

"I wouldn't put it that way."

"How would you put it, Granddad?"

"Marcus doesn't have the wealth he once had, but...."

"He needs an infusion of cash?" He shrugged, and I felt my temper begin to fray. "And I'm to be the sacrificial lamb, is that it? No, I'm sorry. I'll never marry for a reason like that." I'd lived the twenty-one years of my life without my father's love; I wouldn't spend the rest of my life tied to another man who didn't love me.

"Frankly, Kipp, it would give me a great deal of comfort to know you're being looked after by someone who cares for you."

I was about to remind him that I was an adult who didn't need anyone looking after me, but his last words distracted me.

"He cares about me?"

"Yes, I do, Kipp."

I whirled around to find Mr. Wyndham standing in the doorway to the garden.

The golden got to her feet and approached him, waving her plume of a tail gracefully. He ruffled her ears, then glanced at me.

"You forgot your laptop. It's in the car, along with your duffel bag. I gathered you wouldn't be returning to that mausoleum."

"You're right." Sir had made it clear I was no longer welcome. "Thank you."

I was relieved beyond belief, mostly because I didn't have to take the laptop from him. My fingers would have touched his. They'd have trembled, but I'd have made no effort to avoid the contact, and he would have seen that in spite of everything, I was still in lo—infatuated with him.

"I'm sorry to hear you're not doing well, Bradley." He spoke to Granddad but kept his gaze on me.

"*Ce qui sera, sera.*" Granddad shrugged. He was right. What must be, will.

"Do you have any objection to me marrying your grandson?"

"Geoffrey? God, yes! For one thing, he's straight. And for the other, he's about to get married!"

"That isn't funny, Granddad!" I snapped, not liking the idea of my brother anywhere near the man standing before us.

"You know I'm talking about Kipp," Mr. Wyndham said smoothly.

"Yes, I do." Granddad grimaced.

"Do you need a nurse, Granddad?"

"No." He gripped my hand and glowered at Mr. Wyndham. "And if Kipp is willing to marry you, then I have no objections."

"Wait!" I panicked. "I never said anything about being willing!"

"You're better off with Hyde than with... Marcus." He turned his attention back to Mr. Wyndham. "However, I expect you to treat him well. I may no longer have the kind of money I once did, but I have enough to hire a hit on you!"

"Granddad!"

"I'm a dying man, so it wouldn't bother me to have you killed if you hurt my grandson."

"Granddad!"

"I love you, Kipp. I didn't do well by you the past few years; I did even worse by your mother, but I'm going to make up for that, for however much time I have left." He glowered once again at Mr.

Wyndham. "And what's this bullshit about letting Kipp take a lover after a year?"

"Just what you said: bullshit. I intend to take those vows seriously, and I expect Kipp to as well. If he marries me, it's going to be for forever."

"Ham—"

"Hyde, Kipp. Call me Hyde."

"Hyde." I could feel myself blushing. "Why didn't you tell me who you were?"

"Too many times people want me for what I can give them: social status, money, investment tips, sex—"

"Sex?" My voice came out in a squeak, and I cleared my throat. "Sex?" I scowled at him. "You thought I was like one of those parasites?"

He opened his mouth, and I wanted to punch him.

"If you say it was because I'm Marcus Llewellyn's son—"

"No, Kipp! At first I thought you must know who I was, but when it became obvious that you didn't.... It was... cute, the way you flirted with me. *You* were cute. You still are."

"And that's supposed to make me feel better? When were you going to tell me who you were? I'll tell you one thing: it wouldn't have been the day we exchanged vows!" Sir would have probably let it go that long, but there was one thing he'd taught me, however inadvertently: always read the fine print, and I would have. "So were you going to tell me on the day that contract was presented to me?"

"I was going to tell you at dinner tonight. Only Llewellyn sent for you. I should have expected something like that from him, but I was so keyed up—all I could think about was asking if you'd be willing to let me slip this on your finger." He took a small, vintage jewelers box from his pocket and opened it.

"Blue diamonds?" They were set in white gold. I stared up at him, trying to keep my jaw from dropping and my eyes from popping out. "You were planning on asking me to marry you?"

"Tonight, yes. I hope you don't think the ring is too flashy. I was looking at platinum bands, but then I saw this, and I know the diamond is your birthstone. I hope you'll give us a chance, Kipp." He closed the box and put it back in his pocket, then came to me and took my hand, bringing it to his lips. "Will you?"

Was I setting myself up for a world of heartache? The honey brown of his eyes was warm, and I seemed to tumble into them.

But I didn't want him to think I could be had with just a few tender words. I tightened my fingers around his and said, "I'll... think about it."

"Kipp!" But Granddad was laughing.

"Well, this is a serious decision to make. We're talking about the rest of our lives, here. And... well.... 'If I am not worth the wooing, then I am surely not worth the winning.'"

"You're very literary today, Kipp. First Shakespeare and now Longfellow." Granddad continued to chuckle.

"Yes, Granddad." I peeked at Hyde though my lashes. "Still, it would be nice to be courted." To know someone wanted me that badly.

"I've never courted anyone."

"What about—" Granddad started to ask something, but Hyde sent a glance in his direction, and he coughed. "Sorry, I forgot what I was going to say."

"Now, as *I* was about to say, it will be my pleasure to court you."

"That sounds reasonable, doesn't it, Kipp?" Granddad sounded so hopeful.

"All right, I've thought about it."

"And...?"

It didn't matter. I wanted him, and it seemed as if he wanted me.

"I'll marry you. But I still get to be courted!"

Hyde pulled me into his arms. "Yes, you do."

CHAPTER 12

THE golden's handler came to get her, and the nurse came to get Granddad. She had a wheelchair with her.

"It's time for your dinner, Mr. Martin." She frowned. "You're breathing heavily. I hope you weren't overexcited."

"I'm fine. The day a visit from my grandson is too much for me is the day you can lay me out in my casket. Kipp, come back and see me tomorrow." He gripped my hand and tugged until I bent close enough for him to whisper in my ear, "I'm glad you didn't keep him waiting for your answer. I haven't long, and I want to walk you down the aisle."

"I couldn't make him wait, Granddad." I'd taken one look at Hyde and had fallen hopelessly in love. And in spite of everything, that hadn't changed. "And there's no one I want more to be there with me." My heart was starting to ache, and I knew in a second I'd be crying all over him, which he wouldn't appreciate, so I turned to the nurse. "Do you need some help?"

"No, I can manage better by myself. We have a system, Mr. Martin and I. But thank you."

I watched as she set the brake on the wheelchair and maneuvered him into it. "I'll see you tomorrow, Granddad."

"Thank you." He looked pleased. "You come too, Wyndham."

"Yes, sir."

"And for God's sake, if you're going to court my grandson, take him out to dinner. He's thin as a rail!"

"Any suggestions?"

"Chantilly Lace." How had he known I'd always wanted to go there? I'd never said anything about it, since Granddad didn't particularly care for French cuisine. "The food is good, and Kipp has never been there. And see you get him home at a reasonable hour."

"Granddad, I won't be going home. I'm no longer welcome there."

"It's nothing less than I should have expected." Granddad's face flushed, and I grew concerned.

"I'm sorry; I shouldn't have told you that." I picked up *Dangerous When Crossed* and gave it to him, hoping it would distract him. "You won't want to leave this behind."

He took it, but it didn't have the desired effect. And although his next words were addressed to me, he glared at Hyde. "Where are you planning to spend the night?"

"Oh, at the Y. I'll get to an ATM tomorrow and—"

"You'll go to Silver Birch tonight, which is what you should have planned from the start."

"But, Granddad…."

He waved away whatever I might have said as inconsequential. "Beauchamp has instructions to see your room is ready for you."

"You'll let me stay there?"

"Kipp…." He covered his face with a hand. "I've been a bad grandfather."

"No, you haven't!"

"I have, but I swear to God I'll make this up to you!"

"Granddad." I went to him and bent down to whisper in his ear, "You're a good grandfather, and you're a better father than Sir ever was." I kissed his cheek. "Now go before this nice nurse gets angry with us and won't let us see you tomorrow."

He reached for my hand and squeezed it, before saying gruffly, "A reasonable hour, Wyndham."

"Of course." Hyde's tone was earnest, but I could see the amusement in his eyes.

And then we were alone in the garden.

"Would you prefer to go somewhere else?" I asked. "We don't have to go to Chantilly Lace." That was the restaurant where the Families went, and because they did so, everyone else in Martinsburg who could afford it wanted to as well. In addition, it had a very stringent dress code.

"I want to take you there."

"All right." The blazer I wore was suitable, as was Hyde's business suit. I leaned forward and dusted off my knees. Fortunately, the pavement I'd knelt on had been clean and dry.

We walked out to the parking lot, and I stole surreptitious glances at him. While I couldn't tell if his trousers were snug over his hips and ass, I'd seen him once in chinos, so I didn't have to imagine what he looked like. I licked my lips and couldn't help grinning to myself.

He took out the key fob and pressed a button on it. There was a chirrup, and the lights of a sleek black Mercedes SUV blinked as the doors unlocked.

"Sir has an M-Class just like this!"

"Who?"

"My father."

He turned to look at me. "You call your father 'Sir'?"

"Yes." We'd never reached the point of talking about anything really personal, so of course he wouldn't know the dynamics of my family.

He shook his head as if baffled, then grinned. "Llewellyn wasn't happy when that chauffeur of his came to tell him a newer model was in the driveway and it belonged to me."

"I can imagine not." And I was willing to bet Jackson hadn't been thrilled either. He was used to having the newest models. "This is a 2017, isn't it?"

"Yes." He opened the front passenger door and leaned forward to point out some of its features, which wasn't strictly necessary. I was familiar with Sir's SUV. But Hyde's nearness caused my mouth to go dry and my dick to twitch.

I always had that reaction to him, but oh, God, I hoped he didn't notice. Sir's words about restraining myself were all too fresh in my mind, and besides, I remembered Daniel's reaction when we'd gone to see the eclipse.

"Are you sure Chantilly Lace is all right?" He nodded toward the seat, and I slid into the SUV.

"Yes, it's fine," I repeated. Geoff had always taken his dates there; Daniel had hinted that we might go there for brunch one Sunday, but now Hyde was taking me there for dinner!

"All right, then, Chantilly Lace it is." He shut the door, and grinning to myself, I fastened my seat belt and stretched out my legs, crossing them at the ankle.

I watched—not from the corner of my eye, but full on—as he buckled up and pressed the start button, and the engine hummed to life.

"Why did you tell me to call you Ham?"

His lips parted in an easy smile. "My friends used to call me that. It's short for Wyndham."

"Isn't there a Wyndham family in Prud'homme?" That was a few towns over, and although I didn't know it well, I was aware that they were the equivalent of the Martins here in Martinsburg.

"Yes. They're my father's people."

"I see." I could also see he was reluctant to talk about that. "Hyde. That's an unusual name." And then I put my foot in it. "Like Dr. Jekyll and—Oh!" My words trailed off, and I could feel a blush rise up to the tips of my ears. "I'm sorry." Things had been easy between us when I'd worked at Georg's, but he wasn't just a customer anymore.

And I was usually better at guarding my tongue.

"It's all right." The expression in his eyes was kind. "It was my mother's idea. She always had a fondness for Robert Lewis Stevenson."

"But Mr. Hyde was evil!"

"Yes, but I was a large baby, and she had a tough time delivering me; by the time I was born, she was so out of it she got the two confused. Which was good. Can you imagine if she'd named me

Jekyll?" He was chuckling as he steered the Mercedes out of the lot and onto the main road, and I couldn't help laughing along with him, although I wasn't exactly sure what we were laughing about. "She didn't tell me until I brought the book home to read for a high school assignment."

"Did it bother you?"

"Actually, no. As I said, my friends all called me Ham, and I liked that, because it meant I was one of the gang. But my family always called me Hyde, and I'd prefer it if you do also."

"All right." I sat there with my hands folded in my lap and pretended to study them. I didn't want him to realize what his words meant to me: I was going to be part of his family too. "Are your parents still alive?"

"My mother is. Dad's been gone more than twenty-five years."

"I'm sorry."

"Thank you. He was a good man, and I miss him."

"He couldn't have been very old. May I ask what happened?"

"Non-Hodgkin's lymphoma is what happened. If his family had helped, he might have lasted longer."

I sat quietly. I knew how miserable family could be.

"They were furious with him for marrying a woman of color, even though if you didn't know, it would have been very hard to tell." He brought the car to a stop at a red light, then turned to look at me. "What about you?"

"What about me?"

"How do you feel about marrying a man of mixed race?"

"Your color has nothing to do with how I feel about you." I studied his honey eyes. "How do you feel about marrying Marcus Llewellyn's son?"

"I won't be taking Marcus Llewellyn to my bed."

"I should hope not." I couldn't help smiling. "The light's changed."

He eased down on the gas pedal and drove down the street. "What about your name? Is Kipp a nickname? A family name?"

My smile faded. "Sir didn't tell you?"

"Oddly enough, he spoke very little of you."

Not oddly, when I was the least loved son.

"My mother wanted me named Kipp. No one knew why." I changed the subject. "Are you familiar with Martinsburg? Do you need directions to Chantilly Lace?"

"Actually I lived in Martinsburg. After my father died, my mother couldn't afford to stay in Prud'homme anymore, and so we moved here."

"You did? Where did you live?"

"The only place Mom could find was on Topeka Road."

That was on the other side of the tracks, one of the roughest—I folded my lips together. How could the wealthiest family in Prud'homme allow one of their own to wind up in the poorest section of Martinsburg?

"She got a job as a cook." Hyde kept his gaze on the road. "I bussed tables at Chantilly Lace after school and on weekends from the time I was sixteen until I left Martinsburg when I was twenty." He turned his head to look at me again. "The same year you were born."

"How did you know what year I was born?"

"It was quite an occasion."

"Yes. Quite an occasion. Mother died and Granddad got stinking drunk." And Sir never once came to the nursery, instead hiring a nurse to bring me home from the hospital and look after me. Before I'd been sent to boarding school, the kids I'd come into contact with had been all too willing to share that with me.

I stared out the window, feeling a burning in my throat.

"I'm sorry," Hyde murmured.

"Don't be. It happened a long time ago." I felt like an idiot for bringing it up. What was wrong with me? "I have to apologize; I've become maudlin. Would you mind if we talked about something else?"

"Not at all. Tell me about Greek life," he suggested.

That was a strange topic. "Well, Granddad was Sigma Chi. Geoff was Beta Theta Pi, as was Sir."

"And you?"

"Oh, no, I never joined."

"Excuse me? They didn't want you?"

"They did." I had that to be proud of. "I was rushed by those fraternities, as well as Alpha Omega Chi. I just couldn't afford the fees." I bit my lip. The last thing I wanted to come across as was poor little me.

But Hyde said, "We have that in common."

I was glad of that, but I regretted he hadn't been able to enjoy an aspect of college life that he obviously would have liked to experience.

"What college did you attend?"

"John the Baptist while we were living here in Martinsburg, and then Columbia when I moved to New York."

"And you studied business?"

"Not to begin with. I wanted to be a veterinarian."

"John the Baptist has an excellent veterinary medicine program." Hadn't he been able to transfer those credits to Columbia University? "So you had two years' worth of credits—"

"Actually, four. I took accelerated courses, and I would have graduated that spring."

"What made you switch your major?"

"I realized I had a greater need for a business degree." The muscle at the hinge of his jaw was jumping, and I decided to drop the subject. Maybe another time he'd tell me about it.

He was quiet for a couple of miles, and to distract myself I began to study him as unobtrusively as I could. Stubble was starting to darken his cheek and jaw, and I wondered what it would feel like under my palm. His nose arched from a dip between his eyes, a sure sign of a Wyndham, now that I knew what I was looking at. His hair was slightly disheveled, and I knew how soft it was from when he'd kissed me and I'd run my fingers through it. My fingers tingled with the urge to touch it again.

He brought the car to a smooth stop and let it idle, once again turning his head to meet my gaze.

I realized I'd been flat-out staring at him, and I blushed.

CHAPTER 13

"WE'RE here." He smiled at me.

Because I was so obviously enthralled by him? "Excuse me?" I blushed even harder and could have cursed my fair complexion.

"Chantilly Lace."

"Oh! Yes, we are!"

Since Chantilly Lace had valet parking, he put the car in park and left the key in the ignition. An attendant came jogging up.

"I'll take good care of your Mercedes, Mr. Wyndham!"

"Thanks, Chuck. Kipp?"

I scrambled out of the SUV and made myself walk sedately around to where he stood.

"You know him?" Was this how it started? Hyde was so gorgeous, and this bozo was so... *friendly*. I wasn't sure if I should worry or not, but I wasn't going to ask Hyde about it.

"Yes."

"Are you going to tell me how?" Shit. I guessed I was going to ask him.

"His family owns Chantilly Lace." A smile was there and then gone so quickly that I wasn't sure if I'd actually seen it. He ushered me into the foyer.

"That doesn't exactly answer my question," I muttered under my breath, and I didn't care if he heard me or not.

The hostess looked up, a polite smile on her face. "Good—Hyde! I didn't know you'd be dining with us tonight!"

"Good evening, Corinne. This was rather spur-of-the-moment. May I introduce my fiancé, Kipp Llewellyn? Kipp, this is Corinne le Blanc." Their eyes met, and they seemed to be sharing a private joke. "She's married to the owner."

"Who is also the chef. Welcome to Chantilly Lace, Mr. Llewellyn."

"Thank you, Mrs. le Blanc." I was used to hearing myself addressed as "Mr. Llewellyn" by some of the faculty of Armand U, but it felt weird being called that by a woman who was old enough to be my—sure, why not?—my mother. After all, Mother had only been nineteen when she'd married Sir.

"Please, call me Corinne."

"In that case, call me Kipp."

"Kipp. I don't believe I've seen you here before."

"No, I've been away at college."

"Ah. I loved my college years. I went to Penn State. As a matter of fact, I met Antoine when my sorority sisters and I happened to drive through Martinsburg." Her expression revealed how pleased she was with that twist of fate.

"Do you have a table for us, Corinne? I know this is short notice, but—"

"Oh, of course we do! Come right this way."

The gentle pressure of Hyde's palm against my lower spine urged me to follow her. She led the way to a table at the center of the room and placed the leather-bound menus on the place settings.

I spotted my brother seated at a long rectangular table some feet away. He was talking to his fiancée. Mindy saw me and gave a little wave, and Geoff turned in his chair. I mouthed "hi" at him.

He glanced from me to Hyde, his expression stony, and then he turned back to Mindy. Was he angry with me about something?

Aside from the occasions when he remembered he had a younger brother, we'd never had much interaction, especially given the eight-year difference in our ages.

Geoff had never seemed to blame me for our mother's death, but Llewellyns were good at concealing their emotions. It was very possible he did, and I'd just never realized. I knew *I* had resented him even as I loved him.

"Jean will be your server." Corinne interrupted my thoughts, and I was grateful for that. "I'll just let Antoine know you're here." She bustled off toward the rear of the restaurant, where I imagined the kitchen was.

"Hyde, why does everyone here seem to know you?"

He pulled out my chair and motioned for me to sit down, then took his seat across from me. "I told you I used to bus tables here. Well, Tony worked on the line. When the original owner decided to retire, Tony got in touch with me to see if I'd be interested in investing in the restaurant. Corinne is his wife, Chuck is his son, and so is John. Tony insisted they take the French version of their names because—"

"I can imagine why." The Families of Martinsburg could be very snobbish. "So now they're Charles and Jean?"

"Exactly."

"Ham!" A chunky man in a chef's hat and houndstooth trousers came rushing up to our table. "It's been too long!"

"Tony!" Hyde rose, and they embraced and pounded each other on the back. He turned to me, and they stood shoulder to shoulder. They were about the same height, although Hyde seemed taller, possibly because his weight wasn't carried all in his gut. "Kipp, this is Tony White—Antoine, the best chef in Martinsburg."

"Are you kidding? I'm the best chef in this entire part of the country! Corinne said you brought your fiancé." He looked me over, and then he grinned, but it didn't reach his eyes. "It's nice to meet you."

"May I say the same, Chef?"

He offered his hand, then leaned down to whisper in my ear, "Hurt my friend, and I'll come after you with my biggest knife."

"Um... all right." I didn't know if he was serious or if he was teasing, but I wasn't going to put it to the test.

And isn't it interesting that while I've worried about Hyde hurting me, his friends might have had the same concerns regarding me?

He clapped me on the shoulder, nearly sending me sprawling off my chair, then turned back to Hyde. "So when's the happy day?"

"We haven't discussed that yet." Hyde hitched up his trouser legs and sat down.

"You'd better have the reception here!"

"Actually, we're thinking of having it at the Saratoga Trunk." *We were?* "Since you and the family are invited, the last thing you'll want to do is spend the entire time in the kitchen when you could be dancing with your lovely wife."

"You're right. And this will give me the perfect opportunity to scope out my competition."

"Their sous-chef is promising. You might want to look into hiring him."

"I just might." He looked down at the menus, frowned, and gathered them up. "I'll make something special, yes?"

"Thanks, Tony."

"I have something in mind for an amuse-bouche. And a champagne to go with it."

"Oh, you'll want to see my ID." I reached for my wallet.

"I will?"

"You're not carding me?"

He swallowed a laugh. "I'll have my sommelier do it."

CHAPTER 14

I SHOWED my ID to the sommelier, who brought out a champagne bucket on a stand and filled two flutes with chilled champagne the color of pale gold.

"Here's to our new life together." Hyde raised his flute and waited as I scrambled to do the same. He tapped his flute against mine, and together we took a sip. It was crisp and dry.

My freshman year in high school, Granddad had taken me aside and taught me the difference between whites, reds, and rosés—"God knows Marcus never will!"—and to distinguish a good champagne from a mediocre one. This one was excellent.

"Tell me about yourself," Hyde murmured after we'd set down our flutes. "We never got to talk about much except furniture and accessories at Georg's."

"There's nothing to tell. Between making sure my GPA was high enough so I'd keep my scholarships and working at Georg's, I didn't have time for much else."

"Not even the occasional date?"

"No. As I said, no time." Or was it more that I hadn't been willing to trust anyone enough to let them past my barriers? I thought briefly of Riley Tarleton.

"That's a shame, Kipp. You're twenty-one years old, you've just finished your junior year at Charles T. Armand; this is the best time of your life."

How did he—For a second I didn't know if I should wriggle like a happy puppy that he'd been so interested in me that he'd looked into my background, or whether I should castigate myself—*stupid,* stupid

Kipp!—for not accepting that it was only good business sense to investigate his prospective spouse.

And then I really wanted to kick myself in the ass. Of course he knew that. *I'd told him.*

I shook out my napkin and placed it on my lap, restlessly pleating it, not sure what else to say.

And *then* I thought, *Screw it!* So I'd had a sucky experience when I was in high school. So my father only cared about me if I could enhance a business deal. That didn't mean the rest of my life had to suck.

And that fucking clause in the contract? He'd agreed with Granddad that it was bullshit. Even so, I'd make him fall so in love with me that he wouldn't even remember it!

I stared pensively at Hyde. There was a lot of porn online. Not that I'd surfed those sites frequently, but I learned best through visual demonstrations, and I'd make sure there was enough time before the wedding for me to pick up whatever manner of tricks were available. By the time of our first anniversary, he'd be happy in my bed.

But meanwhile, he was curious about me!

"Kipp?"

"What did you want to know?" I asked.

"I don't want to pry into your personal life, but I feel I should know if there's anyone who'll announce his objections in the middle of our wedding ceremony."

"Oh, no problem with that."

"Excuse me?"

"They don't do that anymore," I murmured innocently as I raised my glass and took a sip of champagne.

"Kipp!"

I grinned at him over the rim. "No, no boyfriends."

"Not a one? I find that hard to believe. Martins produce incredibly good-looking offspring."

"That's an odd way to phrase it."

"Think about it. Both you and your brother resemble your mother's side of the family rather than Llewellyn's."

"Do you think so? Oh, I've got Mother's coloring, but Granddad has shown me photo albums, and no one seems to have the chin or cheekbones that I've got."

He waved it away. "Recessive genes. You're still incredibly good-looking."

"Well... um...." My cheeks felt hot. I wasn't used to compliments. Oh, sure, Granddad would tell me I was smart or a credit to the Martins, but that was what grandparents did. "Thank you."

"So. No boyfriends ever?"

"No. Well...." I found myself telling him, "I fell in love with a boy in high school, but we weren't really boyfriends. He... it didn't work out."

"And you haven't let anyone get close to you since? I can understand that. What happened?" He didn't say anything about puppy love, which was kind of him. And even if he did know the pathetic story, it was only fair he hear my take on it.

"He took me to the movies, and then suggested we drive up to Lila's Hill in his Jaguar. There was supposed to be a lunar eclipse that night."

"Was there?"

"I don't know. I was too miserable to notice."

"Did he assault you?" His words were clipped, and he looked furious, as if he'd like nothing better than to tear off Daniel's head, reach down his neck, and yank his dick up through his body.

"Oh, no, nothing like that." I felt my cheeks start to burn, but not in pleasure this time. How could I tell this man how stupid I'd been? "That is to say, he told me in the car he was straight."

"Were you out at school?"

"No."

"Then why did he do something so idiotic?"

"I asked him the same thing—well, except for the 'idiotic' part— and it... it was to more or less enhance his reputation as a stud." I found I couldn't say it was to win a bet.

"Well. That's beyond idiotic. It's outright stupid!"

"He was eighteen."

"That's no excuse. How bad were the repercussions?"

"There weren't any."

"What, none?" He narrowed his eyes and stared at me. "I know your father, Kipp. Well, his reputation," he corrected. "He's wildly homophobic. He'd never forgive you for being gay."

"Unless he could use me to seal a business deal," I reminded Hyde. I didn't want him to know how relieved I'd first been when it occurred to me why I liked boys better than girls, and then, after that thing with Daniel, how terrified I'd become when I'd realized that if Sir found out he would send me away to one of those "retreats" to be brainwashed and conditioned until I was no longer Kipp Llewellyn. I'd spent the months until I'd left for college creeping around the house, desperate not to draw his attention. "For whatever reason, he never brought it up. Back then I thought it was because he didn't know, that word hadn't gotten around. You see, I'd sneaked out of the house after it got dark, and no one saw me when I came back in. A number of boys showed up on Lila's Hill: Alec Stuart, Eddie Alden"—and that had hurt, even though we hadn't been friends for ages. "Daniel promised me—"

"Daniel? Daniel Richardson? Aaron's son?"

"Yes. How would you—"

"Those families always stayed together. Twenty years wouldn't have changed anything."

Of course he'd know that, having spent some years in Martinsburg. "He was very popular during high school. I shouldn't have—"

"No. Don't say it." He was quiet for a moment before reaching across the table to lace his fingers through mine. "He was an asshole, and I'm glad for my own sake he didn't realize the diamond he let slip through his fingers."

"That's kind of you to say."

"That doesn't make it any less the truth. And I'm not kind. Anyone who's done business with me will tell you that." He squeezed my fingers. "You know what? There's supposed to be an eclipse of the moon tonight."

"No, there isn't."

"Humor me, Kipp. After dinner, what do you say we take a drive up to Lila's Hill and not watch it?"

"Oh!" My dick got hard, and I laughed. Did my laugh sound as breathless to him as it did to me? "In that case, I say yes!" What a nice man he was! I was going to like being married to him. I might not know him that well, but.... "And... *I* think you're kind."

"Kipp—" His eyes were again warm, but whatever he was going to say was left unsaid as he raised his gaze.

Someone had approached our table, and I turned my head to smile politely up at him, thinking it must be our waiter with the amuse-bouche, but it wasn't.

"Well, well, well, if it isn't Hyde Wyndham. I hardly expected to see you here."

"Hello, Ron," he said lazily. "Why not? Martinsburg is going to be seeing a lot of me. Kipp, this is—"

"I know. Good evening, Mr. Richardson." I recognized Daniel's father from the times Sir had the wealthy Families of Martinsburg to dinner. Those dinners were always very formal, and I'd peeked over the banister to watch Higgins take the furs from the women and the dark overcoats and white silk scarves from the men.

"Robbing the cradle now, are we? How old is he? Sixteen? Seventeen?" He ran his gaze over me and curled his upper lip in a sneer. I would have jerked my hand free, but Hyde tightened his grip on it. "Quite the boy toy."

"Hardly my toy, Ron. Do you mean to tell me you don't recognize Marcus Llewellyn's younger son?"

"Oh, the brat Marcus always had hidden away? We all thought there was something wrong with him, that he was Mongoloid or something of that nature, especially after Marcus sent him away."

"It was to boarding school, and no, I don't have Down syndrome." The spitefulness of his words clawed a hole in my chest. A lot of the rumors had gotten back to me, but I'd never heard that particular one.

He pointedly turned back to Hyde. "Is he any good in bed? He looks like he might be fun to train, but he's so young; shouldn't you worry about your heart? Is he supposed to make you feel like I—like you did when you were twenty?"

"Do you really want to get into a pissing contest with me, Ron? Remember, I know...." Hyde leaned forward and whispered something, and Mr. Richardson got so red in the face I thought the top of his head might explode. Hyde didn't seem perturbed, but his grasp on my hand remained tight. "Kipp's age is none of your business, and neither is what we do in bed. He's my fiancé, and as such, you'll treat him with respect."

It was stupid and clichéd, but my heart swelled with pride.

"And besides, why should you care who I'm with after...?" He let the rest of his sentence hang in the air, unfinished.

"He's too young for you." Mr. Richardson gazed at Hyde. His eyes had become hot and hungry, and my stomach clenched. He wanted Hyde. "You need someone more mature!"

"He's more mature than he should have to be, Aaron." In contrast, Hyde's voice and eyes were cold. "Now, I'd ask you to join us, but this is a special occasion. Kipp's accepted my proposal and we're celebrating. You understand, I'm sure."

"You're going to marry him?" Mr. Richardson turned white, and now I thought he was going to pass out. "Word was—But I never thought—"

"Mr. Richardson?" I jerked my hand free from Hyde's grip and looked around for a waiter, but there was my brother just a few feet away, and this was a family matter. "Geoff!"

He was buttering a slice of bread, and he paused, turned to face me, and raised an eyebrow. I'd always wanted to be able to do that, but while both he and Sir could, the ability escaped me. Every time I tried, I wound up raising both eyebrows.

He seemed annoyed with me—well, I hadn't been exactly discreet in calling his name—and suddenly I wasn't sure if he would do anything, so I tried to gesture discreetly toward his future father-in-law. Geoff got to his feet so abruptly I thought his chair was going to topple over, but he steadied it and hurried to join us.

"I don't think Mr. Richardson is feeling well," I whispered.

"Thank you, Kipp," he said softly. "Aaron, come back to our table." He put his hand on Mr. Richardson's arm. "The rest of our party has arrived, and Mrs. Richardson would like us to order."

"Yes." Color was coming back into Mr. Richardson's cheeks. "It was good seeing you again, Hyde. Maybe you'd like to get together for drinks sometime?"

"I'll see when Kipp has some free time, and we'll let you know."

"That wasn't what—I'll be in touch."

I watched my brother gently urge him toward their table.

Mr. Richardson seated himself beside the woman who I recognized as his wife. Mindy looked more like her mother than her father.

Mrs. Richardson tilted her head toward him, and he said something to her. She glanced over her shoulder and studied first me and then Hyde before turning back and resuming the conversation with the person on her right.

I looked at Hyde too. I had a feeling there was something between him and Aaron Richardson; when Mr. Richardson called about having that drink, I was willing to bet he would find some way to avoid inviting me to go with them. But would Hyde go along with that? Thinking about it gave me nervous knots in my stomach.

However, Hyde's attention was on the waiter, who had arrived and was placing the amuse-bouche on the table. Artfully arranged on a platter were one-inch cucumber rounds filled with something I didn't recognize.

"Dad got in a shipment of the choicest prawns earlier this afternoon," the waiter was telling Hyde, "and he made them into a prawn salad for you."

"Thank you, John. Please tell him this looks delicious."

"He'll be glad to hear that. But he'll want to know that it actually *tastes* delicious."

"All right." Hyde chuckled. He picked up a round and offered it to me.

I put my plate under it, but he shook his head. "Hyde, what...?" And I caught my breath as I realized he wanted to feed me.

I knew I was blushing, but I was smiling too. I leaned toward him and took a bite from his fingers.

"Mmm." I chewed and swallowed, then finished the round with another bite. Hyde licked his fingers, and I bit back a moan.

"Good?" He picked up a round for himself and put it in his mouth, his pleasure in its taste evident. "Mmm. Scrumptious, John, and I'd have expected nothing less. Here, Kipp." He was going to feed me another one.

"This is—" Warmth crept up from my torso to my forehead, and sweat began beading at the base of my skull. "This is—" My palms were itchy, and I suddenly felt nauseous. Before I could even clap a hand over my mouth, I'd thrown up what little there was in my stomach all over myself.

"Kipp!"

I didn't have time to be mortified—I'd never vomited in public— I started to wheeze. And then there was a ringing in my ears, and my vision began to blur around the edges. My tongue felt like it was swelling up.

Help me! But nothing came out of my mouth. I tugged at my tie and tore at the collar of my dress shirt, hoping that would ease the constriction in my throat, but it did no good.

I tried to get to my feet, but my knees gave out from under me, and I pitched forward, clutching at the tablecloth and dragging everything down on top of me as I hit the floor.

Pain shot through my left palm. Oh, God, what had I done to my hand?

"Someone dial 911!" Hyde shouted. He came onto his knees beside me and put his arm around my shoulders, while he gently slapped my cheek with his other hand. "Goddammit—"

As long as I keep my eyes on his, I'll be all right. I wound my fingers into his shirt front and stared up at him.

"Kipp!"

Don't... don't let me die, Hyde!

And then everything went black.

CHAPTER 15

"KIPP? Baby?" A warm hand was stroking over my hair, along my cheek, down my arm.

I managed to get an eye open. "Hyde?" He looked haggard. "What happened? Where are we?" My words came out scratchy.

"You had a reaction to the prawns; you're at Martinsburg Memorial."

I realized the hospital bed was at a forty-five degree angle and I was just wearing my undershirt and boxer briefs. Well, at least I wasn't in one of those gowns that left my ass on view to whoever might care to look. Although... I wouldn't have minded if Hyde was there to view it. I couldn't help a weak smile at that thought. Hyde took umbrage.

"Dammit, Kipp, why didn't you tell me you were allergic to shellfish? I'd never have let you eat them!"

"Didn't know." My mouth tasted awful, and it felt so dry I thought I should be able to spit sand. "Water, please?"

Hyde poured some from a carafe on my bedside table into a plastic cup, put a straw in it, and held the straw to my lips. I'd have told him I could do it myself, but my hands were shaking, and I knew I'd just wind up slopping the water all over me.

He let me take a few sips before he took the cup away. "That's enough for now."

"Thank you."

"This is the first time you had a reaction to shellfish?"

"It's the first time I've had shellfish."

"A reaction like that—it isn't logical. Your body would have needed previous exposure to the antigen. You had to have had it before."

"I don't remember!" And it scared me. I'd never wanted to spend the money on shrimp or crab or scallops in college, but suppose I had? When I was pulling an all-nighter, I'd often eat alone in my dorm room. I could have had a reaction to shrimp toast or crab cakes or even clam chowder and....

I couldn't stop shaking.

"Oh, blue eyes." Hyde put his arms around me, and his body absorbed the shudders of mine. "It's a good thing the fire station is just down the road from Chantilly Lace. The paramedics barely got the lights and siren on before they arrived."

I burrowed against him. "I was so scared."

"You and me both. After we're married, I'll make sure our cook knows never to bring any seafood into the house."

"Not even tilapia?"

"Well...."

"Knock, knock." The door to my room was pushed open, and Geoff poked his head around it. "Is it all right if I come in? You two aren't doing gay stuff, are you?"

"Hardly, Llewellyn." Hyde frowned at him. "And that's not amusing."

"I know. Sorry."

"Geoff! Is something wrong?"

"Yes." He came to stand next to the bed. "My kid brother is in the hospital. How are you feeling?"

"Like crap." I was still shaky, and the pulse in my throat and temples felt like it was trying to hammer its way out of my body. On top of that, there was a bandage on my left palm, and I held up my hand. "What happened?"

"You landed on a piece of broken glass."

I swallowed. "How many stitches?"

"A dozen."

The knowledge of the exact number of stitches made my palm hurt even worse. "Why does my thigh hurt?" I asked Hyde peevishly.

"The paramedics gave you an injection of epinephrine."

"Did they think I was Dracula? It feels like they stuck a stake in it. And it's not funny, Hyde!"

"No, but I'm…." He squeezed the bridge of his nose.

Another twinge caught my attention. "What happened to my arm?"

"Tetanus shot. No one knew the last time you'd had one."

I leaned back on the bed, closed my eyes on the tears that were burning behind the lids, and turned my head away. I'd had one when I'd started college, but no one had cared enough at home to realize that.

All right, enough with the self-pity. That was the way it was with my family. I'd just have to suck it up. I drew a ragged breath and opened my eyes, brushing the tears out of them before I faced Hyde again.

Of course he saw. "What's wrong? Are you in pain? Goddammit, *where's the goddamned call bell?*"

"No, I'm fine."

"Sure you are."

"Well, I'm not in pain," I conceded, hoping he wouldn't realize what a bald-faced lie that was. And then I saw the blood on his shirt. How had I not noticed that? "Hyde! You were hurt!"

"What?" He looked down. "Oh, that. No." His mouth was tight. "You were holding onto my shirt. It's your blood."

"Are you sure you're all right? Let me see."

"Are you going to be this bossy when we're married?"

"Yes. Get used to it."

He huffed, but the tight look around his mouth eased.

I made him unbutton his shirt, but he was wearing an undershirt that was also smeared with blood. I tugged on the material.

"Stop. You'll open your stitches." He pulled up the undershirt.

Oh. His skin, that rich caramel, was unmarked aside from a thin scar on his left side just above his waistband. Dark hair feathered over his chest. His nipples were small and tight and looked like dark chocolate. I swallowed. Would they taste that sweet on my tongue, between my lips?

The thin line of his treasure trail disappeared down behind his fly…. My fingers twitched with the urge to touch him, maybe follow that trail down, but Geoff made a sound deep in his throat, reminding me Hyde and I weren't alone.

"Uh… is it all right if I talk to my brother alone for a minute, Wyndham?"

For a second I thought Hyde was going to get up in Geoff's face, but instead he contented himself with glowering at him. "Sure. I want to go find a doctor anyway. Just don't upset him."

I watched as he crossed the room, muttering under his breath as he tucked in his shirt. That pulled his trousers snug across his seat. I took the opportunity to ogle it: the man had an awesome ass, and it was going to be mine!

His suit jacket dropped down to cover that ass, and the door closed behind it.

"Kipp?"

"He's going to be your brother-in-law, Geoff." I met his eyes. They were blue like mine, but unlike mine, they didn't have a ring of darker blue around the iris. "You might as well start calling him Hyde."

"You're really going to go through with this?"

"Why not?"

"He's not one of us."

"No, he's originally from Prud'homme, and he's a Wyndham."

"Are you being deliberately obtuse?"

"I don't think so."

"He's… he's…."

I waited, but Geoff couldn't seem to get whatever Hyde was past his lips.

"Are you referring to the fact that he and his mother had to live on the other side of town? Or that he's a self-made man?"

"No, I'm not! There's his skin color." He scowled at me when I had nothing to say about that. "It's darker than yours!"

"Did you think I hadn't noticed? And frankly, Geoff, pretty much everyone's is. Including yours."

"What about the matter of his age?" He sounded like he was starting to get desperate.

"Sir was older than Mother when he married her."

"And we all know how well that worked out."

"Excuse me?"

"Never mind. If this is what you want—"

"No."

"All right. I'll handle Father—"

"You can handle Sir?" I hadn't thought anyone could do that.

"Yes, so don't worry about him." Geoff gave an absent nod. "And I'll get rid of Wyndham. You won't have to—"

"What are you talking about? Why are you getting rid of Hyde?"

"So you don't have to marry him."

"I want to marry him!"

"Then why did you say you didn't?"

"I didn't—Geoff, you can't say something about Mother and Sir and then refuse to clarify it. Look. I never got to know Mother. No one ever talked about her to me."

"Granddad—"

"She was his daughter, he loved her, and as far as he was concerned, she was perfect. Geoff... what kind of mother was she?"

"What do you want to know, Kipp? That if she'd lived, would she have loved you?"

"Could I have more water, please?" That was exactly what I wanted to know, but I felt like an idiot asking.

"Grown-ups think because you're little, you don't realize something's wrong." He handed me the cup, then held onto it when he saw how shaky my hands still were and helped me bring the straw to my mouth. "I knew from as far back as I could remember that Mother... oh, she loved me, but she didn't seem to like me very much. I could never figure what I'd done to...." He brushed the hair back off my forehead.

"Geoff?" He'd never been one to touch me.

"Those last months, though, when she was pregnant, she seemed so happy. She hugged me and told me I was going to have a baby brother or sister. So, yes, I think she would have loved you very much." He looked away. "More than she ever loved me."

"But you have Sir's love."

"Have you had enough water?" I nodded, and only after he put the cup back on the table did he turn to meet my eyes. "I'm the firstborn son, Kipp, the crown prince. Father loves me well enough, but that's what means so much to him. One day Llewellyn, Inc. will come to me—"

"I never wanted it, you know. But...."

"But?"

"If you ever need your offices redecorated...." I waggled my eyebrows.

His desolate expression lightened, and he ruffled my hair. "You really scared us, you know." He found a chair, pulled it closer to the bed, and sat down. "The area around your table at Chantilly Lace looked like a warzone."

"Excuse me?"

"Plates and glasses smashed to bits, the centerpiece under the table three tables over, champagne spilled all over the floor. And the blood."

I looked down at my palm. "I scared me too. I thought allergies were hereditary. Neither you nor Sir has any. Do you know about Mother?"

"Ask Granddad. He won't talk to me." He sat back and crossed his legs.

"He said you haven't seen him since his cancer recurred."

"Not… uh… not by choice. Father's been running me ragged, and then there's all the plans for the wedding—*my* wedding."

"You could have called him." He looked… guilty? I sighed. That was my family, living at Dysfunction Junction. "Which reminds me, congratulations on your engagement to Mindy."

"Thanks, Kipp. You'll be there, won't you?"

"At the wedding? Am I invited?"

"Of course you are!"

"All right." I wasn't going to ask him why he hadn't let me know. I was too tired to quarrel with him. "Is Hyde invited as well?"

"He's a very busy man. I'm sure he has other things—" He huffed out a breath. "Don't put on that stubborn expression of yours." I didn't say anything. "Oh, all right, he can be your plus one."

"Thank you. Wait a minute; why are you involved with the wedding?"

"It's my wedding, as I may have mentioned?"

"But that falls to the bride's family."

"If they can pay for it. The Richardsons can't, not a wedding of the magnitude Father wanted. He hadn't been pleased nothing came of your involvement with Daniel—he'd been hoping to get—"

"Good grief!" Did *everyone* know about me and Daniel? "Is that going to haunt me the rest of my life?"

"Face it, kiddo. We're half Martin. Everyone in town wants to know our business."

"I could never understand why Sir didn't hound me over that."

"Oh, he would have, but I happened to find out shortly after it happened. I told him if he didn't leave you alone about it, I'd instigate a hostile takeover of Llewellyn, Inc."

"You'd have done that for me? But, Geoff… he's your father."

"He's yours too, although God knows he's never acted like it."

"I never thought you noticed."

He looked away, but not before I saw the painful shade of red that tinted his cheeks. "Well, don't make a big deal over it. I doubt I'd have been successful, but Father wasn't expecting it, and so he backed down."

"Thank you. I really appreciate that."

"You're welcome. Anyway, that thing with Daniel was before he realized Richardson Industries was tanking."

"I don't understand this at all. Sir said he wanted me to become Daniel's lover, but he's one of the biggest homophobes in Martinsburg. I'd expect him to disinherit me rather than host my wedding!"

"You know how Father can get when he loses his temper."

"Yes, but this was—Geoff, Daniel is straight. How could Sir come up with such a *stupid* plan?" He gave me a peculiar look. "What?"

"Kipp, Daniel is gay."

CHAPTER 16

"WHAT?" Daniel Richardson, the straightest boy in Benjamin Martin High? "Since when?"

"I think he came out his freshman year at Harvard."

"Mindy said something about an argument between Daniel and his father."

"She doesn't know the half of it." Geoff shrugged. "Aaron nearly had an aneurism when Daniel came home for Christmas and the whole sordid mess came out."

"Wait, what happened? What was so sordid? I wasn't home that year, if you'll remember. I missed all of this!" I pictured Daniel hanging out on a street corner peddling his ass, a cigarette dangling from the corner of his mouth, his shirt open to reveal an exotic tattoo on his hairless torso, and his pants so tight a casual observer would be able to tell if he'd been circumcised or not.

"Apparently he wanted to bring his roommate home with him."

"That was all?"

"They were going to share Daniel's room."

"Yes, so?"

"The roommate was a guy."

"Geoff—"

"Kipp." He was becoming impatient. "There was only one bed in Daniel's room."

"They couldn't bring in a futon?"

"You know how big the Richardson house is. There was no need—"

"Y'know something? He could have saved all that aggravation if he'd just kept his mouth shut."

"Would you have done that?"

"Done what?"

"Brought a... a boyfriend home and asked that he stay in your bedroom?"

"Uh...." I boggled simply at the thought of Sir allowing me to invite *any*one to visit.

"You see? You were raised better than that!"

"I hate to disillusion you, brother mine, but it has nothing to do with how I was raised. If I cared about someone enough to bring him home"—and that would have been to Silver Birch, not Llewellyn Manor—"it's for damned sure I'd stay in a hotel with him."

"You'd *what?*"

"Oh, for the love of...!" What century was he living in? "If I'm attracted to someone, why shouldn't I explore that attraction?"

"Have you... uh... done any exploring?"

"No. But that was simply because I hadn't found anyone."

"What about Wynd—Hyde?"

"Are you asking if I've gone to bed with him yet? No, I haven't. But will I? You bet! That's what being gay means." Oddly enough I didn't worry about displaying unrestrained enthusiasm around my brother.

"Don't remind me. When I think—never mind, I *don't* want to think about it."

"Then don't. So what happened? With Daniel and his father," I prompted, when Geoff seemed at a momentary loss.

"Oh. Aaron said no, that no son of his would be gay, they had that huge blowup, Jacob apparently got involved, and you want to know what the kicker is?"

"I have no clue, but you're going to tell me, aren't you?"

"Daniel destroyed his relationship with his father for someone who left him a couple months later, right before Valentine's Day."

"Oh." I couldn't say I was sorry for him after his callous treatment of me—I wasn't that altruistic—but this had a kind of poetic justice. "So has he decided he isn't gay anymore?"

"No, he's still gay. That's why Aaron's refusing to let him come to the wedding."

"But it's your wedding. I mean, if Sir said I couldn't come, wouldn't you still invite me?"

No, the expression on his face told me he wouldn't go against our father's wishes. I felt the pulse in my temple pound even harder.

"I need an aspirin."

"You'll be better off with ibuprofen."

"I don't care what it is." I looked around for the call bell. "I just hope my doctor left an order for it." If he didn't, I knew Hyde would do something about it. Hyde.... "Geoff, how did Hyde get involved in this?"

"He didn't tell you?"

At least he hadn't expected Sir to have told me. I shook my head, then flinched as pain shot through it.

"A few years ago, things began to go downhill among the Families. Do you remember Thomas Chapman?"

"Sir's lawyer? Of course." He'd come to the manor often enough, and the way he'd looked at me had always bothered me.

"He was found dead in his garage of carbon monoxide poisoning about two and a half years ago."

"Oh, my God! I had no idea!"

Geoff shrugged. "I was trying to get Father to replace him."

"Is that what did it?"

"No. It turned out he was being investigated; there were some sick things on his computer. He swore he didn't.... But of course no one believed him, and even Father had to back away. Well, you know if muck starts getting flung around, it doesn't care who it sticks to."

"Wow."

"Around that time, the Stuarts and the Aldens began having financial problems, and they asked Father for a little help."

"Granddad mentioned something about that. Do you know why he wouldn't help them?"

He shrugged.

"So they'd had no choice but to go to Sir."

"Yes."

And of course he would have been only too delighted to offer it, since it would give him a hold on them.

"He was stunned when it looked like it was Llewellyn, Inc.'s turn. Grandfather had become ill, and Carter refused to do anything."

"I'll bet that annoyed Sir!" Granddad's CFO had worked for him for almost thirty years, and he'd never liked Sir.

"That's not the word for it. If Grandfather hadn't recovered, Father would have seen Carter out on his ass. He passed away almost a year ago."

"I'm sorry to hear that." So that was what Granddad meant when he'd said Carter was gone. "He was always nice to me. He was young, wasn't he?"

He gave me an odd look. "He was almost sixty."

"That's not old. What happened?"

"His heart just gave out one day."

"That's too bad." I wondered if the stress of dealing with Sir had anything to do with it, but I wasn't going to bring that up to my brother. "Who's the CFO now?"

"Grandfather brought in an outsider. His name is Yorick...."

I couldn't stifle a burst of laughter. "Alas, poor Yorick!" Granddad was right; the name was from Shakespeare, but he'd gotten the play wrong. It was *Hamlet*, not *Twelfth Night*.

Geoff smiled wryly. "I know. He must have taken a lot of flak over it. He's very competent, however, and Grandfather seems happy with him."

When he could remember the man's name? "That's good. I know he wanted me to take over the factory, but I just don't have the brains for it."

"Don't put yourself down. You've got the brains."

"Well, let's just say I don't have the ambition, not for that. Anyway, you were saying?"

He shook his head but let me return to the original subject. "Neither the Stuarts nor the Aldens could repay what they owed Father, although to their credit, they did try. Aaron Richardson was the only one who seemed to have his head above water, so Father went to him and proposed they combine their finances and ride out this fiasco."

"By you marrying Mindy?"

"Yes. We've had to wait until she turned eighteen. Father wasn't happy about that, but I wasn't going to push Mindy into doing something she'd regret."

"How did she feel about this?" I remembered what I'd said to Granddad about being the sacrificial lamb, and for Pete's sake, she was younger than me!

"She was thrilled." He blushed. "She's always had a crush on me. By the time Father realized Aaron was sucking wind, the invitations had been sent out, Mindy had chosen her dress—" I'd taken an elective in wedding planning; I knew how much those dresses could cost. "Fuck, she'd chosen the menu!"

"You could have called off the wedding."

"No, I couldn't. You see, I love Mindy. One day I looked up and… she just knocked me off my feet. Figuratively, you understand."

"I understand." I bit back a snort of amusement. "So you've sown your last wild oat?"

"Yes, I have."

"Because, y'know, if Mindy loves you that much, and if you screw around, you're going to break her heart."

"I said I have. You haven't been around to see, but… Mindy is what I was waiting for. I never knew, and that's probably why I went from one girl to another."

"That's good. 'Cause, you know, I was starting to wonder if maybe you were gay and were using all those girls as beards."

"Fuck you, little brother." But there was a crooked smile on his face.

"All right. But if finances are tight, why not downsize the wedding?"

"Father won't hear of it. What would all the people who'll be coming from out of town think? And besides, it would break Mindy's heart." Did he realize he'd put Mindy after Sir?

"Geoff, this isn't a good idea. Oh, not if you want to marry her; go to city hall. But to have this much debt hanging over your head...."

"You know Mother's jewels came to me." He uncrossed his legs.

"What? Yes. What about it?" Other than in the painting on the wall in the formal living room at Granddad's house, I'd never seen them, and so it hadn't mattered to me that Geoff had gotten them, especially since I was gay and would never have a wife to give them to.

"I sold them."

The light went on. "Is that why you haven't been to see Granddad?"

"He'd be so angry if he realized everything was gone." His shoulders sagged. "Some of those pieces were Grandmother's. He... uh... he'd feel I should have saved something for you."

"What would I do with them?"

"Wouldn't you want something to remind you of Grandmother?"

"I never knew her either, Geoff. Why would it matter?"

"You're not making me feel better about it, Kipp."

"I don't mean to. Seriously, Geoff. I never saw Mother wearing her jewels."

"Photographs? Her portrait?"

"That doesn't count. I've got no ties to the jewels." I had no ties to Mother. "I'll talk to Granddad about this. He doesn't have long, you know, and it's stupid for the two of you to be at loggerheads when there's no reason for it. I'm going to Promise Hospice tomorrow. Why don't you come with me?"

"I'll think about it."

"Fair enough. So what did you use the money for?"

"I'm giving Mindy the wedding of her dreams."

I thought that was a waste. If I was that short of cash, I'd get married at city hall. But then I'd had the last three years to learn to budget my money. Geoff had never had to do that. He'd had his college education handed to him on a platter—which I wasn't going to bring up—and after he'd graduated with his MBA a couple of years ago, he'd been given a high-paying job at Llewellyn, Inc. Well... the boss's son.

"When is the wedding? Mindy just said it was in June."

"In about four weeks. The fourteenth."

"Flag Day? Any particular reason?"

"It's in the middle of the week."

"I'm not following you."

"We're having the reception at the Saratoga Trunk." He ran a hand through his hair. "It was the only day I could afford."

I felt bad about judging him. "Wouldn't Mr. Stuart give you a break?"

"He would if he could, I'm sure, but he doesn't have any say in it. He's barely holding onto the Trunk."

"Oh. Um... wow. Well, Hyde and I will be there."

"Thank you." He leaned forward in the chair, his hands dangling between his knees. "I can't help Father. I can't help Mindy's father."

"Then don't."

"It's not easy." For the first time I noticed how drawn he was. "It's a good thing you have your trust fund, because I wouldn't be able to help you either, Kipp."

"I haven't been able to access that money. Granddad was angry when I chose interior design as my major, and Sir stopped paying my tuition after my freshman year."

"Oh, shit, I'm so sorry!"

"Don't be. I've been managing on my own."

"Because you'll be marrying the richest man on the Eastern seaboard?"

"No! God, no! I only met Hyde a year and a half ago. Besides, I'd never take money from him! Geoff, how much is left?"

"Less than there had been. Father wanted to lay off half the employees, but it wasn't their fault if he overextended, and I managed to talk him out of that. It's still difficult. That's why Father agreed with Wyndham when Wyndham came to him with his proposition."

I slumped back against the pillows. "And Sir made him pay."

"It's not like Wyndham can't afford it."

"Do you honestly think knowing that will make me go skipping down the aisle with him?"

"You shouldn't let it stop you. I saw the way he was looking at you, kiddo."

Oh, really? That was interesting. "How does he—"

The door opened, and a doctor in green scrubs walked in. "I'm Dr. Alden, Kipp; I'll take care of you while you're at Martinsburg Memorial. I'd like to examine you."

CHAPTER 17

I DIDN'T recognize the man, but I recognized the name. His was one of the four Families of Martinsburg, the wealthy and elite. They'd all gone to school together, much as their sons and grandsons had, and some of those sons had married some of the daughters.

In spite of the fact that he'd married Beth Martin, Sir would never be considered one of them. Even his astronomical wealth, when he'd had it, couldn't buy that for him.

The Families weren't angels; there were Alden, Stuart, and Richardson bastards all over the country, considering they went to Ivy League colleges on the East Coast and Stanford on the West, but one thing the Families never did was toy with each other. Maybe that was why I'd been willing to believe Daniel was interested in me.

That was one thing I'd learned from Sir—not because he followed that edict, but because he didn't. When I was seven, Eddie Alden had been my best friend, until the weekend we'd had a sleepover at Llewellyn Manor. His mom came to pick him up on Sunday afternoon, and Sir cornered her in my playroom. She'd kneed him in the groin, grabbed Eddie by the hand, and dragged him out. The next day at school, Eddie had told me he wasn't allowed to be my friend anymore.

I didn't throw a tantrum—Llewellyns didn't do anything as puerile as that—but for the longest time I refused to talk to Sir. Not that it made a difference. I might as well not even have been there.

"Hello, Rick." Geoff got up and walked to the end of the bed to give him some room. "Of all the hospitals in all the towns in all the world, my brother has to wind up in yours."

"Geoff." Dr. Alden grinned at him and winked. He was of average height and slightly overweight, but charisma seemed to roll off him in waves.

"Rick is going to be my best man, Kipp."

I remembered now. Rick Alden was Geoff's best friend. Apparently Sir hadn't screwed up Geoff's friendship with this Alden.

I stole a glance behind him. Hyde was there, and I could feel my face light up. He studied my expression and then seemed to relax.

"If you'll look this way, Kipp? Yes." Dr. Alden aimed a flashlight at my eyes. "Checking your pupils." I knew that. "They're all right." He took my wrist, counting my pulse. After fifteen seconds, he nodded. "Your pulse is still fast, but not as bad as when you came in."

"Do I have to stay overnight?"

"Yes." But it was Hyde who'd answered. He turned to glare at my brother. "It's a good thing you didn't upset Kipp, or your fiancée would be going to your funeral instead of her wedding. Go home now. Kipp needs to get some sleep."

Geoff glared back at him. "I'll leave, but only if Kipp tells me to go!"

"Guys, if you upset my patient, I'm going to send both of you home!"

It was Dr. Alden's turn to get glared at, but he didn't seem impressed.

"Could I have an ibuprofen?"

"Of course. I imagine you must be feeling a little achy from your muscles tightening up. I'll write an order for it and have your nurse bring it to you. Anything else? No? In that case, and if you have a quiet night, I'll discharge you in the morning. Geoff, I'll see you at the bachelor party. Good evening, Mr. Wyndham."

"Hold on a second, Rick. I'll walk out with you. Kipp, I'd better go before Hyde attempts to beat me into submission with another dirty look. Mindy was worried. She'll want to know how you're doing."

His fiancée, but not our father. I sighed.

"And yes, you're invited to the bachelor party."

"What about Hyde?"

He rolled his eyes and said, "Him too."

"Thank you. And thanks for coming to see me."

"Don't be an idiot. You're my brother; of course I'd come to see how you are."

"Well, I still appreciate it."

He squeezed my big toe under the blanket, and I suddenly remembered him doing that when I was little and had had a nightmare. My brother had been good to me. What had happened to put the distance between us?

"Good night, Wyndham." Geoff caught my frown—maybe things were getting better, but I'd told him Hyde was going to be his brother-in-law, and I wanted him treated as such—and he corrected himself reluctantly. "Hyde. I'll see you tomorrow at Promise, Kipp."

I was relieved to know he'd decided to see Granddad. "I don't know what time I'll be able to get there, so maybe you'd better call me. You have my cell number, don't you?"

"You didn't change it, did you?"

"No." I'd had the same number since I'd gotten the phone for my sixteenth birthday.

"Then I've still got it."

"Good." Only then did I admit to myself that I'd been afraid he'd deleted it from his contacts. "We'll see you there."

"All right."

Hyde turned to look at me. "We will?"

"We will."

"If I didn't...." He shook his head. "Good night, Geoff. Doctor."

Dr. Alden and my brother walked out of the room, and finally it was just me and Hyde.

"I'd better get myself together for bed."

"Do you need some help getting to the bathroom?"

"No." But he still stood ready to catch me if I pitched forward on my face again. I liked that someone cared enough about me to do that.

As with all the private rooms at Martinsburg Memorial, this one had a bathroom attached. Inside were a stack of towels, a yellow basin for bed baths if the patient wasn't capable of using the shower, and a small kit containing a tiny bar of soap, toothbrush and toothpaste, mouthwash, a disposable razor, and a comb.

"You don't have to stay, you know," I called through the door as I relieved myself. "I'll be fine."

"Shut up. I'm staying."

"All right." I couldn't stop grinning, and I hummed a few bars from the song that had been playing in Hunter's stockroom.

Because of the bandage on my left hand, it was awkward washing up, but I managed to wash my right hand and my face. And then I raised my face to brush my teeth and saw what was grinning back at me in the mirror. My reflection jolted me. I was so pale, and the rings under my eyes were so deeply etched that I could have gotten a job as an extra in an end-of-the-world movie.

Hyde must really care about me if he could stand me the way I looked right now.

"Kipp? Are you all right in there?"

"Yes. I'll be right out." I finished brushing my teeth and then rubbed my knuckles over my cheekbones, hoping to put a little color into them. No sense putting this off.

And at least now I didn't look *quite* so much like something from *The Walking Dead*.

CHAPTER 18

"HYDE," I said as I walked out of the bathroom, "would you mind apologizing to your friend for me when you—Oh!"

He wasn't alone. A nurse who looked to be about ten years older than he was chatting with him.

"Good evening!" Her smile faded as she studied my face. "No, it hasn't been a good evening for you. I have the ibuprofen Dr. Alden ordered."

"Thank you." I climbed back into bed, and she checked my wristband before giving me a small paper cup holding two tablets.

"Are you staying, Mr. Wyndham?" she asked.

"Yes."

"But there's no place for you to sleep. I mean...." I wouldn't have minded if he slept with me, but I'd never shared a bed, especially one as narrow as this, and I wasn't sure if either of us would get much sleep.

"Yes, there is! Didn't you notice this chair?" The nurse pointed out an upholstered chair by the window. "Let me show you." It folded out into a single bed. "I'll just get some sheets and a blanket."

They were in a tall, skinny closet in the corner, and she took them out, along with a couple of pillows. She made up the bed, lowered mine as much as it would go, and then dimmed the light.

"Do you need anything else?"

"No, thank you."

"Well, if you do, you have the call bell. Don't hesitate to use it."

"I won't. Thanks."

"Anything for Beth Martin's boy." She nodded and bustled out, closing the door behind her.

"Your mother was much loved by the people of this town."

"I guess." Maybe they did love her, but no one would ever talk to me about her. I turned on my side to face Hyde, being careful of my injured hand. He had taken off his suit jacket and was now slipping off his shoes. "I'm... I'm not really sleepy. I had plenty of sleep earlier."

"You were unconscious earlier, but never mind. Would you like to talk about something?"

"Yes, please, but what?"

"Anything but how you almost scared me out of twenty years of my life, and believe me, I can't spare those years." He grinned at me. "Not if I'm going to keep up with my young spouse."

I made myself comfortable. I didn't want to think of the gap between our ages. "You choose, Hyde. I'm easy."

"Hardly. Who did you want me to apologize to?"

"Your friend who owns Chantilly Lace. From what Geoff said, I made a real mess of his dining room."

"He's dealt with worse."

"I'm still sorry about it."

He sighed. "I'll pass on your apologies."

"Thank you, Hyde." I gave him my best innocent look.

He laughed and shook his head. "All right, then, you wanted to have a conversation with me."

"Yes, please."

He looked thoughtful for a moment, and then resolute. "You didn't ask why I left town twenty years ago."

"And I won't, not unless you want to tell me." I kept my tone neutral. I knew Martinsburg. It was a nice little city for the wealthy families, but there wasn't much in the way of jobs for the younger inhabitants. The only choice for them was to work in Granddad's factory or the others' hotels and companies, and none offered much in the way of advancement.

"I got the shit kicked out of me."

"*What?*"

"I said—"

"But you're not a little man."

"My size didn't help; there were six of them, and I... I was with someone I felt needed to be protected."

"A girl?" That depressed me, which was foolish. Just because he wanted to marry me didn't mean he was gay. He could be bisexual, and that meant I'd have to worry about both men and women catching his eye. I sighed.

"No, actually a boy."

"Oh? Oh!" I couldn't help it. I felt much better. Of course I was sorry he'd been gay-bashed, but... I'd only have to worry about half the population instead of all of it!

"I'd gotten to the point where I was actually imagining a wedding: an arch of ivy and gardenias for us to stand under, a reception at the Saratoga Trunk."

"But that's the most expensive place in town!"

"I know. And I knew it wasn't possible, not here in the States, not then, but we could have moved to Denmark or Norway and had a registered partnership. I'd been saving up for a new pickup truck, but that could go toward a ring and the airline tickets instead, and setting up a new household. I was really fucking stupid, y'know?"

"No!" How could someone like Hyde think of himself as stupid? "You loved him enough to make those wonderful plans!"

"I should have known better. Mom and I didn't have money anymore—almost all of it had gone for my college education, and this wasn't Prud'homme, where my last name meant anything. I was just a poor kid." He touched his cheek. "Who was only part white. I went to the Alden Arms to arrange for a special dinner. I didn't want anything to interfere with the romantic illusion, so I paid for the meal upfront. The manager must have been laughing his ass off as he took my money. I figured out later that he was the one who called my guy's father."

"Could 'your guy' have said something that caused the attack?"

"No, he didn't know. I was going to surprise him. He met me on one of the back roads to Lila's Hill; we were going to take my pickup—it was just a beat-up old heap like any of the poor kids drove, but his father had just given him a Jaguar. Everyone in town knew it. He was already waiting for me. I got out of my truck to open the door for him, and he ran up to me and threw himself into my arms." His gaze seemed to look inward. "And that was when those bastards jumped us."

"What happened to them—the men who attacked you?"

"Nothing."

"Excuse me?"

"They broke my nose and three ribs. One of those ribs punctured a lung. My liver was lacerated and my spleen ruptured—it had to be removed. That's the scar you probably saw on my side. And it was written up as an accident."

I could believe that. The sheriff's department of Martinsburg was bought and paid for by Sir. If he told them to look the other way, they would.

"But why would Sir care who you slep—dated?" I corrected.

"Because of who the boy was."

"Who was he?"

"Aaron Richardson."

"Oh, my God!" Jacob Richardson, Aaron's father, had been Sir's golfing partner. He'd been as homophobic as Sir.

"And make no doubt about it—I slept with Aaron. I don't know which chaffed old Jacob's ass more, that his son was getting fucked, or that I was the one fucking him."

Hearing Hyde Wyndham use a word like "fuck"... I suddenly pictured him over me, pushing my legs back and sliding into me.... I bit back a whimper. The blanket should hide my erection well enough, but I hoped he wouldn't notice.

"I had no idea Aaron Richardson was bisexual." And I *hadn't* been imagining things at Chantilly Lace. He still wanted Hyde.

"He wasn't back then. His father might not have wanted to acknowledge it—hell, he may have been completely unaware—but we knew the guys who hung out at the Garage. Ron liked rough trade."

I wanted to kick "Ron" for making Hyde see himself that way. "The Garage? I've never heard of it."

"You wouldn't have. It was a dive a little outside the city limits. All the kids from the wrong side of the tracks met up and spent time there, but we were a lure for the kids from the rich side of town. After what happened with me and Aaron, Old Man Richardson ordered it torn down as a hazard to the youth of Martinsburg."

"Would you have taken me there? If it hadn't been torn down?"

"Why do good boys want to play with bad boys?"

"I never wanted to play with bad boys."

"And you're a good boy?"

"Of course I am."

"So you'd want to go to a place like that?"

"If I was going with you?" I grinned and reached across the space that separated us.

"Kipp?"

"Shh." I took his hand from where it rested beside his pillow and brought it to my mouth, then probed the space between his fingers with my tongue. His lips parted, and he squeezed my hand.

"Are you sure you're a good boy?"

"Sir would have a fit if I wasn't." I rubbed my thumb over Hyde's knuckles. And thinking of Sir, was I being too... whatever with Hyde? Reluctantly, I released his hand. "Anyway, you were saying?"

His fingers curled into a fist, and I could have kicked myself for pushing the topic.

"Hyde, you don't have to—" But I might as well have kept my mouth shut.

"When I regained consciousness, I was here in Martinsburg Memorial, although not in a room like this one, and Tom Chapman was there as well."

I felt cold. Why was Sir's lawyer involved in this?

As if I'd asked the question aloud, Hyde said, "He told me he was representing Richardson. If I left town, all my medical bills would be paid and I'd be given a check for a hundred thousand dollars."

"What happened?"

"I tore up the check. I told him I couldn't be bought and that Aaron and I loved each other. He laughed at me."

"I never did like him."

"He took great delight in telling me that Aaron loved me so much he was off touring Europe while I was here in the hospital."

I remembered hearing that the Richardsons had relatives in Great Britain. Back when I'd been lingering on Daniel's every word, he'd spoken of the old family estate. Foolish me, I'd hoped that one day he might even take me there.

"It didn't matter. I was certain Aaron would come back to me."

Because if their positions had been reversed, that was what Hyde would have done. I was certain of that. "But he didn't."

"No, he didn't. That was when Chapman told me Aaron was engaged to his cousin, and the wedding would be in a matter of days. I waited. I wasn't going to take that son of a bitch's word for it."

"But he was telling the truth."

"Yes. Four days later he showed me an article from the society column with a picture of Aaron and his bride."

"Could it have been photoshopped?" *Shit!* I wished I'd kept my big mouth shut. I couldn't think of anything more devastating than to learn I'd been kept from the one I loved by a ruse. "Don't pay any attention to me. That was more than twenty years ago, and I'll bet Chapman's office didn't even allow programs like that on their computers." Time for a distraction, but the best I could come up with was, "Was the woman who was at his table earlier Mrs. Richardson?"

"You didn't recognize her?"

"She wasn't in Martinsburg often, and when she was, well, we didn't go to the same church." I felt silly telling him that—Sir never believed in going to church, and so Granddad was the one who took me to Saints Peter and Paul Episcopal—but I hoped Hyde wouldn't realize I hadn't answered his question.

"She was a pretty girl. I wanted to hold it against her that she took Aaron away from me, but...." He shook his head. "At any rate, the article said the engagement had been longstanding but kept private due to the ages of the young people."

"Did you believe it?"

He shrugged. "It didn't matter. After that, Aaron was separated from me by more than the width of the Atlantic. I'd never interfere with something as sacred as wedding vows. I still won't."

"I'm so sorry, Hyde."

"Don't be. Aaron looked utterly miserable in that picture, and while I knew I shouldn't have, I felt a sense of satisfaction that he was as unhappy as I was. And this time when Chapman offered me the check, I kept it, and as soon as I could, I left town. But I promised myself that I was going to come back, and when I did, I'd see the Richardsons, the Stuarts, and the Aldens all in hell."

Was that the reason behind his changing his major from veterinary medicine to business?

"I understand the Richardsons, but the others—" I drew in a sharp breath. Of course, they'd all stick together to protect one of their own. "But you can't fight them! Aside from Sir and Granddad, they're the most powerful men in this part of the country!"

"Once, maybe, but not anymore." He turned his head to meet my eyes, and this time it was he who reached across the space that separated us and took my hand. "Don't worry about me."

I remembered Granddad telling me about the bad choices Aaron Richardson had made. Could Hyde have had something to do with that? Well, if he did, it was nothing more than Mr. Richardson deserved. But....

"Do you... do you still love him?"

"Good God, no! If I did, I wouldn't be marrying you!"

"Thank you for telling me about this." We were both silent for a while, and then I couldn't help myself; I had to know. "Hyde, do you... what do you feel for me?"

He let go of my hand, turned onto his back, and stacked his hands under his head. "Do you remember the second time we saw each other?"

"Of course." How could I forget? "I had a sneezing fit, and you let me borrow your handkerchief."

"And if I recall correctly, you never did return it."

"No. Every time after, I'd apologize and tell you I didn't have it with me, even when I did. I wanted to have something to remember you by."

"Do you know, that's the most romantic thing anyone has ever done for me?"

My cheeks felt hot, and I was glad the light was so dim. I didn't want him to see how I was blushing.

"Anyway, I thought you were adorable. I asked Hunt about you. He's a good friend to you, you know. He refused to tell me anything beyond the fact that you were majoring in interior design and that your family disapproved. He wouldn't say anything else for the longest time. I could have forced him to talk. I hold the papers on Georg's."

"But you didn't."

"No, I wouldn't do something like that to him for being a good friend."

"I knew it! You can't fool me! You're one of the good guys!"

He turned his head and raised an eyebrow. Why was it everyone could do that except me?

"Now, go on. What did you do?"

"Finally, I told him I could hire a private detective—"

"You would have?" My voice came out breathless, and how gauche was that?

"And you find that… what?"

Maybe if there was something in my life I didn't want known I'd have had a different reaction, but right then I thought that was intriguing! Romantic! *Hot*!

Of course I wasn't going to admit to that.

"So did Hunter cave at that point?"

"No. He said, 'But you won't.' And of course I didn't."

"See? One of the good guys. But... how did you find out about me, then?"

"I can't tell you all my little secrets, Kipp."

"Tease." I yawned. It hadn't slipped my notice that he hadn't told me how he felt about me. Oh, he thought I was cute, but that wasn't the same as love.

All right, so maybe he didn't love me, but he wanted to marry me. He'd also said he believed in keeping his wedding vows. My heart would be safe with him.

I yawned again.

"You'd better try to get some sleep. How are you feeling?"

"Much better, actually, but I think you're right. I can barely keep my eyes open. G'night, Hyde."

There was rustling as he pushed aside his blanket, and then he stood beside my bed. He leaned down and brushed his lips over mine.

"Good night, Kipp."

Before I could tell him I wanted another, please, he was back in his own bed.

In spite of my words, I didn't fall asleep right away—that kiss had roused me in more ways than one. I lay there listening to his breathing deepen and even out.

"I'm glad you stayed," I whispered, when I was sure he was asleep. I pulled the blanket up around my shoulders and closed my eyes.

Just as I was falling asleep, I heard him murmur, "I wouldn't be anywhere else."

CHAPTER 19

THE next morning, I stared at my clothes in dismay. "I can't wear these!" Not only were they covered in champagne, regurgitated prawns and cucumber—the mere thought made my stomach want to empty all over again—and blood, but they were in pieces, since they'd been cut off me in the emergency room. Although it was odd they'd left my underwear alone.

"No, you can't. Eat your breakfast. I'll find something for you."

"Hyde—" But he was out the door.

I sighed and peeked wistfully under the covers of the dishes on the tray someone—I'd seen her leaving the room, and from the clothes she wore I doubted she was on the hospital staff—had brought in for Hyde. I hadn't had that kind of breakfast in a long time. Eggs over easy, bacon, sausage, and ham, and whole wheat toast. Maybe the toast was supposed to make up for all that cholesterol on his plate, but the amount of butter slathered on it sort of defeated the purpose.

Oh, well. The nurse who had come in to check my vitals at o-dark-thirty had promised me breakfast, and yes, it was breakfast, but stewed prunes?

And I didn't even get coffee.

No one was around. I could filch a strip of bacon and then rearrange the others so it wouldn't look like one was missing.

I'd feel too guilty, though, so instead I dipped the plastic spoon into the bowl of Frosted Flakes and morosely began to eat.

But I wasn't eating those prunes!

A few minutes later, Hyde strolled back in with my duffel. "Shower and get changed as soon as you're done eating. Then I'll drive you to your grandfather's house."

"Dr. Alden has to discharge me first."

"All right." Hyde looked at his watch. "He should be here shortly. And then I'll drive you to your grandfather's house."

"Why?"

"You need a place to stay, and we both know that won't be at Llewellyn Manor."

"Where are you staying?" I asked as innocently as I could.

"I have a suite of rooms at the Saratoga Trunk."

Recalling how Hyde had told me the manager of the Alden Arms had betrayed him and his lover, I didn't ask why not that hotel. As a matter of fact, if it had been me, I'd simply have remarked that if my money hadn't been good enough for that place once, I'd be damned if I let them have a penny of it now.

"Good choice," I said, taking another spoon of my Frosted Flakes. They were getting soggy, but there was enough sweetness to the cereal that I didn't really care. "The Alden Arms has been going downhill for the last four years."

"Has it, now?"

"Oh, yes. The junior prom was a disaster. The bathrooms backed up, security overlooked the bottles of alcohol that were sneaked in, one girl wound up having to get married and two others transferred to another high school out of state. The principal of Martin High forbid all future classes from having their proms there."

"What a shame." But something about Hyde's tone told me he really thought otherwise. That didn't surprise me, considering the hardship he'd gone through due to the manager of the Alden Arms, but I wasn't going to hold that against my fiancé.

"Yes, isn't it?" I asked innocently and took another spoon of cereal. My fiancé. I loved the sound of that.

"I enjoyed my prom."

"Oh, I did too. A senior offered to be my date; Phyll—" I looked up to see him scowling.

"A senior boy? But I thought you weren't out at school."

"No." I couldn't help laughing. "A girl. She was so nice to me. I couldn't understand why...."

"Why wouldn't she be nice to you?"

"No, I meant I couldn't understand why she'd want to go to the junior prom. But she danced every dance with me, and afterward we went to the Main Street Soda Shoppe and had a burger and fries and a shake." My enthusiasm dimmed as I recalled going there the following year with Daniel and what a disaster that had turned out to be. Determinedly, I pushed that memory out of my mind.

"Did you kiss her?"

"Of course!" I laughed again, his expression effectively clearing my mind. "On the cheek, Hyde."

He tugged a lock of my hair. "Tease."

"Anyway, getting back on topic: Why don't I go with you?"

"You are going—Wait, to my hotel?"

"Sure. I've never been to the Saratoga Trunk. We might even...." I peeked at him through my lashes.

"No. Not until our wedding night."

"I didn't take you for a traditionalist."

"Well, I am. Kipp, I really think it would be a good idea for us to wait."

"For what?"

His expression became exasperated, and I realized he was talking about our wedding night.

"Oh! Hyde, do you think I'll try to wheedle you into bed?"

"Won't you?"

"No." He didn't know me very well. "Well, you told me no."

"Are you always going to obey me so readily?"

I opened my eyes wide—I didn't even bother trying to raise an eyebrow—but I didn't say I was really obeying Sir. The last thing I wanted was to have Hyde react to me the way Daniel had.

Earlier that morning, I'd noticed Hyde's trousers tented from his morning wood. That sight had made me hard—well, harder—and my fingers had itched to close around his dick. Just wondering what it would feel like was driving me crazy, and I had to battle the urge to go to him, curl a leg around his waist, and rub myself shamelessly against him.

But once we were married.... He'd said he believed in those vows. He'd have to stay with me no matter how uncontrolled I became. Wouldn't he?

"So does that mean we can't even make out?"

"Kipp."

I hopped off the bed. "I'll take that shower. Eat your breakfast before it gets any colder."

CHAPTER 20

I CAME out of the bathroom, and Hyde looked up from a newspaper someone must have brought him.

"Geoff called. He takes lunch at one, so he'll meet us at Promise Hospice then."

"All right. Have you heard from Dr. Alden?"

"No." He tossed aside the paper and stood, his eyes growing hot.

"Uh…." I was wearing black 501 Levi's and a black T-shirt that said *What I really need are minions*. It had been a toss-up between that or the one with *Looking for love (will settle for green jelly beans)* across the front, but I was actually embarrassed to have Hyde see me in that one.

"Those pants are hugging your body the way I'd like to," he said.

"Should I change?"

"Not for me." He looked me up and down, grinned, and licked his lips. I could feel my cheeks heat.

It was my turn to lick my lips, so I did. I walked up to him, folded my arms behind my back, and tilted my head back. I smiled a little and closed my eyes.

His lips were warm when they touched mine.

"Ohhhh!" I slid my arms around his neck, but as much as I wanted to hold on for dear life, I forced myself to keep my grip loose.

He took advantage of my parted lips to slide his tongue into my mouth. He tasted of coffee.

"Ah-heh-hem. Pardon me, but I'm here to collect the breakfast trays."

My eyes flew open and I tried to step back, certain Hyde would be dismayed to be caught making out like a horny teenager, but he wouldn't let me go. I buried my head against his chest but stole a look to see what was going to happen.

He raised his head and looked toward whoever had entered the room. "Go away."

"Uh...."

"Go. Away." He turned his head back to me, tipped my chin up, and gazed into my eyes. "Now, where were we?"

IT WAS almost four hours later before Dr. Alden came in to write up my discharge. "Sorry to keep you waiting."

"We found something to occupy us." Hyde smiled, but it wasn't the wholehearted expression I'd seen on his face at other times.

I knew I'd come on too strong! I'd kept a rein on my actions as much as I could, but when you're kissing the man you love more than anything in the world.... Sir's words echoed in my brain, but it wasn't easy to be restrained, and finally I'd had to let him go and put some distance between us.

Meanwhile, Dr. Alden had glanced at the television. "*Maury*? Really?" He shook his head and looked puzzled when I choked on a laugh.

"What took you so long?" Hyde asked. His tone was deceptively mild, but as much as he'd enjoyed making out with me, I knew he was becoming impatient. He would have called his own physician, but the doctor lived out of town, and it would take him as long to get here as it probably would for Dr. Alden to show up.

"There's an outbreak of measles going around."

"There's a vaccine for that."

"Yes, and every once in a while parents go batshit and refuse to get their kids inoculated. Which results in me running late for my rounds. Okay, now I'm going to give you a prescription for an EpiPen. Fill it in the pharmacy here and make sure you always carry it with you. Although it would be better if you just avoid shellfish."

"Thank you, Dr. Alden. I will. Any other instructions?"

"Drink plenty of fluids. Oh, and your lips look a little puffy. Hmm. I wonder if I should give you another shot of epinephrine."

"No! I mean, I feel fine." I sent Hyde a frantic glance. I didn't want another shot, especially since the only thing wrong with my lips was that they'd been thoroughly kissed.

Dr. Alden must have seen, because he peered at Hyde. "Y'know, if I didn't know Kipp had had an allergic reaction, I'd be willing to swear it was contagious."

"Excuse me?"

"Puffy lips." He swallowed a grin, took my vitals, and then nodded. "Everything seems okay." He took the clipboard that hung from the end of my bed and scribbled something on it. "All right, you can go. Unless you have any questions for me?"

"No." I hopped off the bed and dug a pair of running shoes out of my duffel.

"Oh, I understand congratulations are in order. Geoff told me you're getting married too."

"Thanks. It's going to be a small wedding." I was about to explain that no one other than Granddad and probably Geoff and Mindy would be there, but Hyde overrode me.

"Actually, it's going to be quite a large affair."

"It is?" I stared at him, one shoe on my foot, the other in my hand.

"Yes. We hope this epidemic will be under control by the end of the week. We'd like to see you there." The way he said that made it seem more like a command than an invitation.

"That's kind of you. Who else will be invited, if you don't mind my asking?"

Yes, I wanted to know too.

"Everyone who's anyone in Martinsburg, as well as a good many of my friends and associates."

"I should tell you that I've distanced myself from my father's affairs, Mr. Wyndham."

Hyde just raised his eyebrow. "I hardly think it matters, but I am aware of that."

Dr. Alden was quiet for a moment. "In that case, yes, I'll be there."

"Bring your fiancée as well."

"She has a gown she just bought. She'll be pleased to have someplace to wear it. Just let me know when it will be."

"This Sunday."

"*What?*" I stared at Hyde, aghast. "We can't get married that soon!"

"Why not?"

"Well… well…." I wouldn't have time to surf the Net! "What about all the paperwork that has to be filled out and submitted?"

"It's already done."

"It is? How?"

"Let's just say I have a contact in city hall," he murmured nonchalantly.

"Can you do that?" What was I saying? He had. "Never mind. Don't we have to have blood tests?" I knew they probably weren't necessary, especially since there was no way Hyde could get me pregnant, but I needed to buy myself a little time.

"Not in this state."

"Well, what about the three-day waiting period? And I know the courthouse says to give yourself a month before the wedding date to have the… the legal aspect taken care of." He raised his eyebrow again, and I hurried to explain. "They'll want to see our ID and… and proof that neither of us was ever married."

"Who told you that?"

"I…." I could feel a blush ride up my cheeks. "I checked it out online."

"Did you?" That pleased him, and he ran his fingertips over my cheek. "Well, I have—"

"Don't tell me. Contacts." I threw my hands up in the air. "Fine. Why'd you even ask me?"

"It's customary to propose to the person one intends to marry."

I bumped my shoulder against his. "You know that's not what I meant!"

"However, it's what I meant. Now, if you haven't any more questions—"

"Uh...." But he kept on talking, so it didn't look as if I had much choice. I ducked my head and grinned. Not that I minded.

"—I think we'd better go. You'll need to get settled at Silver Birch before we have lunch with your grandfather." He turned to Dr. Alden. "Thank you for your care of Kipp."

"That's my job." He smiled, suddenly more at ease, but I could still see how tired he was. Had he gotten any sleep last night?

"I'll make sure you get an e-mail with all the pertinent information."

"Thanks." He looked at his watch. "I'm sorry, I have to go. Good-bye for now."

"Good-bye."

"Bye, Dr. Alden."

He waved and left the room.

"Hyde, what's all this about a large wedding?"

"Unfortunately, there isn't enough time for mailed invitations to arrive at their destinations. Of course they'll be at everyone's place setting. As sort of another memento."

"Sh—" I bit my lip. "We don't have Dr. Alden's e-mail address."

"Don't worry about it. Armitage is handling everything."

I remembered him telling me on Monday—oh, my God, it was only two days ago!—that Armitage was his personal assistant.

"You look nervous."

I wanted to tell him I wasn't nervous... well, not very much... but he continued speaking before I could say a word.

"Don't be. I don't want anyone to think that I'm anything less than proud to be marrying you."

My cheeks felt on fire. "Am I blushing again?"

"Yes, you are, and you look adorable."

"Thank you." I wanted to throw myself into his arms, and then I thought, *Why not?* We'd be getting married in four days' time, and I'd have a paper that said I could have my way with him whenever I wanted; it would be legal.

So I went up to him, slid my arms around his waist, and kissed him.

"Kipp." He whispered my name against my lips.

"Hyde," I whispered back.

He gave me one last, lingering kiss, and then set me away from him. "Is everything all right?"

"Yes. Why wouldn't it be?"

"I don't know, I get the feeling—" He shook his head. "Forget about it. Now, you're not taking these with you, are you?" Hyde held up the clothes that had been sliced and diced.

"No." I started to go through the pockets, but Hyde held up my wallet and cell phone and a handkerchief.

"I don't think I know of anyone who travels with less than you."

"I don't need a lot." I put the wallet into a front pocket, clipped my cell phone onto my waistband, and reached for the handkerchief. It was one of mine, with my initials in a corner.

"Not even a set of keys?" He tucked my handkerchief into his own pocket.

"I turned in my dorm keys, and there was no reason for me to take my house keys when I left for Armand U." I tried to raise an eyebrow, but as usual wound up raising both of them, and I gave up in defeat and held out a hand. "My handkerchief?"

"It's only fair, don't you think, since you have one of mine?" He settled his hand on my neck, warm and secure, and gave it a little shake. "Let's go."

CHAPTER 21

WE STOPPED at the pharmacy first, and once I had the EpiPen in the mini drawstring backpack the pharmacist was so kind as to provide and slung it over my shoulder, we were ready to leave.

Even though I'd been in the hospital for less than twenty-four hours, I was glad to walk through the doors and out into the May sunshine. Hyde insisted on carrying my duffel, and he tossed it onto the backseat.

We got in the SUV, and I put the backpack on the floor by my feet. After buckling up, I sat fiddling with the radio—if he was taking me for better or worse, he'd have to take me for changing the radio station as well. There was a slight grin on his face as he eased out of the parking lot and onto the road that would take us to Silver Birch.

He was quiet for some time, and finally I said, "So, we're really getting married on Sunday?"

"Yes. You don't have to do a thing. Armitage is taking care of it all. She's very competent."

"All right. But what 'all' is she taking care of?"

"Arrangements at the Saratoga Trunk. We'll exchange our vows under an arch on the south lawn there. Our reception will follow in the Rampart Room, starting with a cocktail hour offering hot and cold hors d'oeuvres, a four-course dinner giving our guests their choice of a meat, fish, or vegetarian dish, and finally, after we cut the cake, the Viennese hour. That will feature a chocolate fountain and a coffee bar." He waited for me to comment and shifted in his seat when I didn't. "Kipp?"

"Yes?"

"Did you want to say anything?"

"About?"

"All these plans that have been made for your wedding, but without your input?"

"Why?"

"*Why*? This needed to be done very…. Oh, you mean why would you want to say anything?"

"Yes."

"Kipp, are you going to give me a single-word response in answer to every question I ask?"

"No." I swallowed a smile. "Seriously, Hyde, why would it matter to me? I never expected to get married. And I can see this means so much to you." I recalled what he had said in the dim light of my hospital room last night, and if he wanted to give me the wedding he couldn't give Aaron Richardson, then I had no objection at all.

"Most brides prefer to plan their weddings."

"Yes, but I'm not a bride, am I? And watch how you answer that, Wyndham!"

He laughed. "I knew I'd love being married to you."

But did he love me? "We're not married yet." I knew I'd better change the subject, or I'd wind up saying something that would leave him appalled. "But in answer to your question: I took a course in event planning. Although I'm sure you found out about that."

"Actually, Hunt happened to mention it, so…. Yes."

"I thought so. Well, it was fun, but it's a lot of work. Why would I want to spend the next four days running around like a chicken with its head cut off, when I can sit back and let someone else—Armitage, you said?—do that."

"You're a wonder, do you know that?"

"I try." I reached across and ran my fingernail along the seam of his trousers. "These aren't the trousers you wore yesterday," I murmured for want of something better to say.

"No. Armitage dropped off a fresh suit when she brought my breakfast."

"*That* was Armitage?" If the woman stood five feet tall in her pantyhosed-feet that was a lot, and she looked like she couldn't weigh more than a hundred pounds dripping wet.

"Yes." There was a smile in his voice. He pulled into the circular drive of Silver Birch. "Don't let her appearance fool you. If I tell her I don't want to see someone, they'll never get past her. And conversely, if I tell her I want to see someone…."

I grabbed up the mini backpack that contained everything I should no longer leave home without and hopped out of the SUV. If we had a quarrel, would she keep me away from him? And… conversely—I couldn't help grinning—if he wanted me in his office, would he send her to get me?

It was very schoolboy-and-the-schoolmaster-ish, or maybe employer-and-the-recalcitrant-employee, but it was also kind of *hot*.

"Why are you grinning like that?" Hyde asked.

I'd opened the rear passenger door and reached for my duffel, but Hyde was there on the other side before me.

"Your hand."

"I can still carry it with my right."

He raised his eyebrow, and I laughed and shrugged.

"All right, it's all yours."

"Kipp?"

I left him to take the duffel and my laptop, and climbed the shallow steps to the front door. "Because it's a beautiful day and I'm happy," I explained over my shoulder.

It had been a long three years since I'd been here last, and I gazed over the façade with pleasure. In spite of its age, it was in an excellent state of preservation. Martins took care of what was theirs.

Originally it had been just a fairly large farmhouse, but Great-great-granddad had torn it down, replacing it with a three-story edifice that sprawled over half an acre and was more than eighty thousand square feet. It had housed his enormous family as well as an army of servants, although most of the rooms were closed now.

Years ago, before I was born, something had caused a rift on that side of the family. My mother had two sisters and a brother, but my aunts had gone with their husbands and my uncle was in the army somewhere; I'd never met them.

Granddad had talked of donating Silver Birch to the town as a museum, and I'd be sad to see it leave the family. Still, it was his home, his choice, and if his offspring didn't care....

Were they even aware of how ill he was? Should I ask Beauchamp for their phone numbers—he'd definitely have them—and call them?

Hyde joined me at the door and slipped an arm around my waist. "Are you?"

"Am I what?" I pressed a finger to the bell. What had we been talking about?

"Happy?"

I glanced up and smiled into his eyes, but before I could assure him I was *very* happy, something inside the house caught my attention.

Beauchamp was the original dignified butler, even more so than Higgins. He walked at a dignified pace, he spoke in a dignified manner, and if he didn't like you, even the curl of his lip was dignified. That was why it startled me to hear the sound of footsteps hurrying toward the door.

Beauchamp pulled it open and looked relieved when he saw it was me. "Oh, Master Kipp, thank God!"

"What's wrong?" My stomach felt like it was about to climb out through my throat. "Granddad?"

"No, no, I spoke with him last evening, and he was quite all right. Well, as all right as he can be these days. I became concerned when you didn't come home last night. I know you're an adult, but you were never inconsiderate. Higgins had no idea where you were, and—"

"You called Sir's house?" Oh, shit.

"Yes. As I said, I was quite concerned." He frowned at me, and then raised his gaze to Hyde. His expression became cold. "I was about to contact the hospital."

"I'm sorry; I didn't even think to call."

"You'd have been too late, Beauchamp. We left the hospital approximately forty minutes ago."

"Excuse me, sir? Master... I beg your pardon. Mr. Kipp?"

"I had an allergic reaction to some prawns and had to spend the night. I'm fine now, though." I held up the backpack, although I was sure he'd have no idea about its contents.

"P-prawns? No one except... that's...."

"Are you all right, Beauchamp?"

"Oh, I beg your pardon. I shouldn't keep you standing here. Please, come inside. Mr. Wyndham, is this Mr. Kipp's duffel?"

"Yes."

"If you'll let me have it, sir?"

"That's all right. I'll take it up to his room. Kipp, lead the way, please."

I paused by the curving staircase. "Beauchamp, I'm sorry you worried, but I appreciate that you did."

"I'm glad you're all right." There was relief in his tone, and then he became the stoic Beauchamp once again. "Will you be staying for luncheon? Shall I prepare something for you?"

"No, thank you. We'll be going to see Granddad, and we'll have lunch with him. Would you like to come with us?"

"I'm afraid I won't be able to join you today. I need to get the house in order. With the wedding only a few days away, I need to open the entire north wing."

"Excuse me?"

"A Ms. Armitage contacted me. I have to prepare for the relatives who'll be descending upon us en masse."

"Relatives?" I turned to stare at Hyde. "I don't understand. The north wing has eighteen bedrooms."

"Armitage has been busy." He grinned. "Now, let's get your clothes unpacked."

CHAPTER 22

MY BEDROOM was on the second floor of the west wing, in a corner at the back of the house.

I threw open the door, and a single glance told me Beauchamp had been here. The curtains had been drawn back, allowing the sunlight to spill through the windows and dapple the ivy-bordered, puff-top bedspread. The furniture had been polished to a high sheen, and the scent of lemons and oranges filled the room. On a dresser was a vase filled with blossoms from the mock orange trees that Granddad had told me Grandmother loved.

"This has been my room since I was about five." I looked out the window at the forest of birches the house had been named for. It was such a beautiful sight. They marched row upon row for half a mile or more.

"What, always like this?"

"Hmm? Oh, yes. This was Granddad's room when he was a boy, and when I was old enough to understand, I was so proud that he'd let me have it that I wouldn't let anyone change a thing."

"It's very adult for a five-year-old. Where did you stay before then?"

I shook my head. "That was when Granddad insisted I stay with him for a time." He'd been to the manor for Geoff's birthday and had seen Sir cut me to ribbons with his words after I'd spilled my chocolate milk all over the white outfit I'd had to wear. I'd known better than to cry, but being backhanded across the face would have hurt less. "It would have been nice if this could have been my home, but after a couple of weeks, Sir made me go back to Llewellyn Manor."

"Why, Kipp?" He placed my laptop beside the nightstand. "I don't want to upset you, but it's obvious that Marcus—that you're not his favorite."

"Sir might not care about me, but he cares about what the Families think." I went to the pocket doors that opened into the walk-in closet, slid them back, and went in. A luggage rack was folded in a corner, and I brought it out and set it up, then went back into the closet. An armful of hangers should be enough.

Hyde had swung the duffel onto the luggage rack and unzipped it. "I'm so sorry."

"Promise me something, Hyde?"

"Anything."

"If we have children... if we adopt, we'll treat them better than Sir's treated me?"

"Oh, baby." He came to me and took me in his arms. "You'll be the best dad!"

"No, you too, Hyde. If you can't promise me—"

"I promise. I had a good example, until I was fifteen and my father died. He was a good man."

"All right."

He ran his fingers from my cheek, under my jaw to my chin, and used a slight pressure to tip my head back. "Kipp." He kissed me, and I sighed into his mouth and held on.

But just for a minute; I didn't want to come across as a clingy fiancé. I stepped back and looked into his honey eyes. "I'd better put my clothes away or we'll be late. Granddad doesn't like it when I'm late." He didn't get verbally abusive, as Sir would on occasion, but he'd look disappointed, and that was even worse.

I took the jeans and Dockers out of the duffel, slipped them onto the open bar hangers, and went back into the closet. When I came out with a couple of shirt hangers, Hyde was putting the last of my T-shirts into a dresser drawer.

I hung up my dress shirt and tucked away my Nikes in the shoe bench. Somewhere between Chantilly Lace and my room in the hospital, my dress loafers had gone missing. Oh, well. The soles had been getting worn anyway.

The duffel was empty now, and I grinned at Hyde.

"You weren't perving on my underwear when you put them away, were you?"

"I'll have you know I do not 'perv', young man." And then he started laughing. "But I am looking forward to seeing you in those black boxer briefs with the hearts all over them. Were they a Valentine's Day gift? Should I be jealous?"

"Ass." I bumped my shoulder against his. "Target had them on clearance after Valentine's Day."

"Ah. A thrifty spouse. Could you be any more perfect?"

"Hyde, I'm not—"

"Shh. You are." He brushed a kiss across my lips, and then swatted my butt. "I believe you said your grandfather didn't like to be kept waiting?"

"I just have to put the duffel away, and I'll be good to go." I grabbed it up and stuffed it in a corner of the closet, then sent a rueful glance toward the bed—even if we had the time, I wouldn't do that under Granddad's roof. And besides, I didn't want Hyde to think I couldn't control myself. I wanted the first time we made love to be a long, luxurious experience.

I linked my arm though his. "I'm starved. I hope the food is decent at Hospice."

"It is."

"Excuse me?"

But he just laughed, and handed me the mini backpack that contained the EpiPen. "You don't want to forget this."

"No, I guess not." I slung it over my shoulder, and we went downstairs.

BEAUCHAMP was coming out of the study as we reached the first floor. He had a stack of paper in his hand.

"Mr. Wyndham, these e-mails are for you."

"Thank you." He flipped through the pages with obvious satisfaction.

"Beauchamp, do you know if my aunts and uncle have been informed about Granddad?"

He nodded and looked sad. Well, in that case, there was no need for me to contact them.

"We're leaving now."

"Very good, Mr. Kipp. Will you be back for dinner? I'll make a rack of lamb." He knew that was my favorite, and no one made it like him.

"Hyde?"

"Yes, I think so," he said absently. He was reading one of the e-mails.

"We usually dine at eight. Will that be all right?" I didn't know if he had anything planned and would need to eat either earlier or later.

"That's fine, Kipp. Beauchamp, do you have copies of these?"

"Of course, sir."

"All right, I'll take these with me. Armitage is going to need to see them and plan who sits where."

"Very good, sir. One moment, Mr. Kipp. I think you might feel more comfortable going out in... er... public with this." He handed me one of Granddad's sports coats, and I realized I was still wearing the *What I need are minions* T-shirt.

"Thank you, Beauchamp." The coat was a little tight across the shoulders and short in the sleeves, but at least Granddad had good taste. It didn't look like a grandfather's coat.

"You're welcome." Beauchamp smiled and opened the door. "Oh, and please tell Mr. Martin that I'll be in to see him tomorrow."

THE e-mails were on the console. While Hyde was concentrating on the traffic—for the middle of the week there were a lot of cars on the road—I picked them up and looked through them.

"Hyde?"

"Hmm?"

"Elliot Wyndham?" If I remembered correctly, he was Hyde's grandfather.

"What about him?"

"This e-mail says he won't be attending."

"No." He sighed. "I imagine my Aunt Imogene tried to twist his arm, but he always was a stubborn old man, even if my cousin Doug says he's mellowing out in his golden years."

"How do you feel about his not coming?"

"To tell you the truth, I'm glad. This is going to be an important day for both of us, and I don't want his bigotry to spill over onto it. If he showed up, he'd say something hateful to my mother, and then he'd start in on you."

"Me? But he doesn't know me."

"No, but you're a man, and you'll be marrying me."

"I… I see. No, wait a minute. I *don't* see."

He reached across the console and carefully caught my hand. "I waited a long time to find someone like you."

"I'm glad you did, but I still don't understand."

"It makes no difference to you that my mother is a woman of color, that I'm considered the same."

"No, you're not. You're not a woman." As I'd hoped, that got a laugh from him.

He brought my hand to his mouth and then let it go, and I went back to scanning the pages.

"Hyde. These people all say they're coming to our wedding!"

"Yes?"

I couldn't believe the names I was reading. Oscar-winning actors, best-selling authors, creators of long-running Broadway musicals, musicians who were in the Top Forty, businessmen, congressmen, and senators. Names I'd seen in *People* or read about in *Newsweek*, or heard Sir mention.

"Why are they all coming to our wedding?"

"They're friends of mine. Why wouldn't they?"

"But—"

"Oh, don't worry. There will be plenty of seating for your family and friends and the good people of Martinsburg. After we see your grandfather, I'll have to stop at the Saratoga Trunk. Armitage has a command center set up there, and I want to make sure she's on top of this."

"Hyde, they're dropping everything to come here on Sunday!"

"Don't worry about it, Kipp," he repeated. Apparently he felt the need to reassure me. He reached across and patted my knee. "All you have to it show up and look handsome."

"All right." But how could I tell him the only person I cared about coming to our wedding was him? *Dummy! You open your mouth and you tell him!* "Hyde...."

"Yes?"

I sighed. "We're here."

CHAPTER 23

THE receptionist from yesterday smiled at us as we crossed the lobby. "Mr. Wyndham. Mr. Martin is waiting for you in the dining room. Your brother is with him, Mr. Llewellyn."

"Thank you, Madeleine," Hyde said. "I know the way."

I assumed Hyde knew her name from the tag on her blouse, but how could he know where the dining room was? Promise Hospice hadn't been built until about seven years ago. There had been a big to-do over it, with Granddad for the project, and the Families, and most especially Sir, against it. Somehow, Granddad had been able to swing the city council; because things had gotten so bad at the manor, I'd spent six months living at Silver Birch.

They'd been the best six months of my life.

The dining room was a large, airy space with murals of seascapes and landscapes on the walls. There were about a dozen round tables, but only a fraction of them were occupied.

Granddad's table was next to a window that looked out onto the garden. From where he sat, he had a view of the paved walkway that wound its way through masses of flowers. Benches were placed at strategic spots so the occupants of Promise Hospice could rest when they needed to and still enjoy the landscaping. Whoever had been hired to plot out that space had done an amazing job.

"Maybe I'll look into classes in landscape and garden design," I murmured to Hyde.

"If that's what you'd like." As we crossed the floor to join my grandfather and my brother, I could feel the warmth of his palm on my lower back.

Granddad was sitting with his spine taut, a portable oxygen tank in its harness hanging from the back of his chair. Geoff was seated opposite him, and even from where I stood, I could see how uncomfortable Geoff looked.

Had he confessed about selling Mother's jewelry?

"Hi, Granddad. How are you feeling today?" I leaned down and kissed his cheek. I'd never have attempted something like that with Sir, but Granddad had always encouraged it.

"Angry."

Shit. How did I address that? "I'm sorry to hear that." Perhaps if I changed the subject? "Geoff. I hope we didn't keep you waiting. Hyde was helping me get settled in my room." I felt a blush heat my cheeks as I realized that could be taken another way. Fortunately, neither Granddad nor Geoff appeared to pick up on it.

Instead, Geoff said, "I told Grandfather about Mother's jewelry."

"I had a feeling. You didn't have to, Geoff. Sir gave her jewels to you."

"Well, he should have set some aside for you," Granddad snarled. "She was your mother too. You should have a ring or that opal pendant to remember her."

"It's all right." I patted his hand. I didn't want to tell him they wouldn't have helped—nothing would. "If opals aren't your birthstone, they're unlucky for you. I really don't mind, you know."

"Kipp," Hyde murmured as he pulled out a chair on Granddad's right and motioned for me to sit down. I hung the backpack from the back of my chair—I understood why people would *forget* to take it with them—and gave him a broad smile. The last thing I wanted was for him to feel sorry for me.

Granddad looked me up and down. "How are *you* feeling?"

"I'm fine, thank you. Why?"

"*Why?* Your brother tells me you spent the night in the hospital, and apparently I'm the last to know...."

"I'm sorry. I didn't want to worry you." I glowered at Geoff. There hadn't been any need for him to tell our grandfather, especially since I *was* fine now.

"Next time something like that happens, I expect to be notified immediately. Is that clear, Wyndham?"

I started to object, but no one was paying attention to me.

Hyde smiled at him and rested a hand on Granddad's shoulder. "Of course, Bradley. I apologize. I should have thought of that—"

"You damned well should have!" Granddad complained.

"—but I was a little distracted by what was happening to Kipp." He took the seat on Granddad's left.

"What did happen? All Geoffrey would tell me was that Kipp grew unwell at dinner and had to be taken to the emergency room. If Chantilly Lace is serving substandard food—"

"No, Granddad! I just had an allergic reaction to the prawns. It wasn't anyone's—"

"Shellfish?" He turned so white I thought he was going to collapse off his chair.

"Granddad, what's wrong?" I jumped to my feet and reached for him. "Nurse? Nurse!"

Hyde was on his other side, holding him steady.

Geoff's chair tipped back as he scrambled out of it and rushed to Granddad's side. "What can I do to help?"

"Give me a little room, please." A nurse wearing scrubs with kittens and puppies all over them came to us.

"No, no, I'm fine!" Granddad tried to wave us away.

"You don't look it."

"Don't baby me. I said I'm fine, and I'm... fine." He batted at the nurse with ineffectual hands, but she ignored him and checked his pulse and heart, then took his blood pressure.

"It's a little high, Mr. Martin. I'll need to inform your doctor."

"Go ahead and tell him, then. I'm trying to have lunch with my grandsons. Oh, and see trays are brought out for them," he ordered. He might be on borrowed time, but he was still large and in charge. "Tattletale," he growled.

"You've got that straight, Mr. Martin." She chuckled and turned her sunny expression to include me and Hyde. "We're having orange glazed chicken, rice pilaf, and broccoli."

"Sounds good," Hyde said.

"I'll bet yours won't be cut into bite-size pieces," Granddad groused. "I'd give a month of my life for a thick, juicy T-bone. Medium rare." He sighed and licked his lips. "With roasted tarragon asparagus and artichokes." His gaze became wistful.

I'd made that for him two weeks before we'd had that row. Beauchamp had taken his vacation, and I'd been staying with Granddad. Apparently Grandmother had not only enjoyed cooking, but she'd been an excellent cook. The recipe was one of many that I'd found in her recipe box.

Geoff returned to his seat, looking green. I went to him and leaned down. "What's wrong?"

"Is this how it was for you?"

"How what was?"

"Being shut out?"

I straightened. "I'm sorry. I didn't mean to—"

"*Stop fucking apologizing!*" He flinched at the sound of his own voice and pinched the bridge of his nose. "I never realized what it must have been like for you at home. It never occurred to me... but now I can see how often you were ignored, how Father would...."

"It doesn't matter."

"It does. I'm so—Go sit down. We'll talk another time." He took his napkin, snapped it out, and placed it over his lap.

I returned to my chair just as a couple of aides brought out our trays and set them before us, along with cartons of apple juice and lemonade.

Granddad shook himself out of his reverie and pushed his tray to the side. "You say you had a reaction to the shellfish?"

"Yes. That's why I've got this." I gestured to the backpack. "It's got my EpiPen. I was talking about this last night with Geoff, and while I know he and Sir aren't allergic, he couldn't tell me about Mother."

"Your mother didn't have any allergies."

Well, that was great. "It's supposed to be hereditary. The one thing I get to pass on and it can kill my kids. I guess it's a good thing I won't be having any."

"Oh, I don't know, Kipp," Hyde mused, his expression pensive. "I think a baby with your blue eyes would be an adorable addition to our household."

"Yes?" I tried to be casual about my response, but the thought of raising a child or two or three with him had my heart pounding. And then I looked into his honey-brown eyes and couldn't catch my breath. "A baby with your eyes would be pretty adorable too." A little girl.

I fixed my gaze on my chicken, trying to concentrate on cutting it, but the bandage on my left palm was making it awkward.

"Let me do that for you." And Hyde came around to me.

"Thank you."

His cheek was just inches away. I inhaled his aftershave. If I leaned forward, I could—

Granddad made a sound deep in his throat, reminding me we weren't alone. "And what's this about?" He gestured toward my injured palm.

"It's nothing. I landed on some glass and cut myself."

He turned his head and glared at Geoff. "Why didn't you tell me *that*?"

"What would you have done, Grandfather?" Geoff asked tiredly.

"I'd have... why, I'd have—"

"You'd have fretted about it," I said simply, "and it wasn't necessary." I stole a surreptitious glance at the elegant line of Hyde's back as he returned to his seat.

"I do not fret, young man."

"Of course not, Granddad. Now eat your lunch, please."

He frowned but drew his tray back toward him and did as I'd instructed.

I looked around him to Hyde. "So you're suggesting we adopt?" We'd touched on that briefly earlier.

"Surrogacy."

"Oh!" Hyde's baby. I'd hold her and sing to her about the brown-eyed handsome man who was her daddy. For a second it was so real I could feel her in my arms, smell the scent of her baby powder, but then

I was forced back to the here and now as reality came crashing down. "What about the allergy?" I asked morosely.

"We're not having shellfish for you, so it won't be a problem for her. And when she's older, we can have her tested to be on the safe side."

"*Her?*" Had he shared my vision? Or.... I shifted in my seat. "Do you know something that I don't?" I didn't want to ask in front of Granddad or Geoff if Hyde had gotten a woman pregnant, perhaps in response to the hurt Aaron Richardson had caused when they'd been younger.

No. I couldn't see Hyde retaliating in that manner to anything.

He smiled at me. "I don't have any children, if that's what you're wondering about."

"All right." I blew out a sigh of relief. "So this is just a hypothetical girl child?"

"Yes."

"Elliot Wyndham had two girls," Granddad observed.

"Oh, was one of those the Aunt Imogene you spoke of, Hyde?"

"Yes. My father was the only son, and I was his only son. I do have a couple of uncles on my mother's side who have daughters."

"So we can get the girl from you and the boy from me." I was pleased to have it settled so neatly.

Geoff stared from me to Hyde and back, and I could tell something was bothering him.

"Geoff? Haven't you and Mindy talked about having children?"

"Uh... yes. She's looking forward to it."

Granddad's smile was tinged with sadness. "I'd love to still be around to see your child, Kipp."

"And Geoff's too, right, Granddad?"

Hyde stared at him thoughtfully. "How much do you want that, Bradley? I have connections.... It wouldn't be easy, though, and it could just as likely decrease the time you have left."

"I don't think so, Wyndham; I've made my peace with God. But I appreciate the offer. And yes, Kipp. I'd love to see your brother's children also."

Geoff looked relieved, but he didn't know Granddad as well as I did. Granddad was just saying that to placate me.

"Now, let's talk about your wedding," he suggested. "Are you going to make it a double wedding with Geoff and Mindy?"

"That's not fair to her!" Geoff objected.

"No, and there's no need take the spotlight from Mindy on her special day." Hyde raised his napkin to his mouth, and then he murmured, "We already have the date picked out."

I stared at him, wide-eyed, and then grinned when he winked at me. *Yes, we did!*

Granddad glowered at Geoff. "I was going to divide your grandmother's jewelry between the two of you, but I think, considering your actions, that it's only *fair*," he said, emphasizing the word, "that Kipp get those jewels."

"I have no objection, sir," Geoff said quietly, and I cringed to hear him address our grandfather by that word.

"Seriously, Granddad, what would I use them for?"

"Seriously, Kipp? They can be reset for you. Or your husband."

That startled me. I hadn't even given that a thought. I leaned my elbow on the table and propped my chin on my hand. "Hmm." Granddad had let me see Grandmother's jewelry a few times. "There's a necklace, you know the one, Granddad, with the brown diamond pendant? It's large enough that if it was cut down, it would make a ring"—an eternity ring, even if I was the only one to know it—"as well as a tie clip and cufflinks! Shirt studs too!"

I stole a glance at Hyde. A warm red colored his cheeks.

He was blushing!

If Granddad gave it to me now, I could have it ready to give to Hyde for our child's birth. And....

"Hyde, if we get started on picking out a surrogate right away, we might at least have ultrasound pictures to show Granddad."

"I think we should get married first."

"I have to agree with that," Granddad said. "And we're back to when your wedding will be."

"We'll be married on Sunday, at the Saratoga Trunk." Hyde tore off a piece of his roll.

"You know, I really don't need anything fancy," I said as I speared a forkful of the glazed chicken.

"I think you do."

"You do."

"You have to!"

Hyde, Granddad, and Geoff all spoke at the same time.

I chose to address my brother. "Why do I have to?"

Hyde answered instead. "Because you deserve it. You've been treated like Cinderella all your life."

"Oh, and now I get to go to the ball?" I sniped.

"Yes. Now, as I said, the ball—" He touched his napkin to his lips, hiding his grin, but I could still hear it in his voice. "That is, the wedding is this Sunday. The ceremony will be intimate, just us and the minister."

"I insist on being there," Granddad said.

"Me too. You'll need witnesses. And a best man." Geoff's lips were tight. "Me."

"Thank you, Geoff. I appreciate that." I'd never thought of my brother standing up for me when I got married. Well, I'd never thought of getting married at all.

Granddad looked from Geoff to me and then said, "I want to walk down the aisle with you."

"All right." I was glad he would be there with me on an important day like that.

"What time will it be on Sunday?"

"That's Hyde's worry. Oh, but the reception's going to be amazing! You won't believe who's coming, Granddad!" I thought of all the e-mails from Hollywood and New York and Washington, DC. "Plus everybody here in Martinsburg will be there!"

"Including the Richardsons?" Granddad raised an eyebrow. Dammit, how come everyone but me could—I huffed out an annoyed breath.

Hyde was rolling that piece of his roll into a ball. "They've been invited, yes."

I had to bite my tongue to keep from asking why. Mindy would be there with Geoff, but why would the rest of her family—the rest being mostly Mr. Richardson—have to come? And then it occurred to me: he was Sir's friend. Of course Sir would invite him.

"Well, the Rampart Room will fit everyone. Kipp, are you done?"

I stared down at my plate, surprised to see it wiped clean. And I didn't even care for broccoli. "Yes."

"In that case, Bradley, would you mind if I stole your grandson away? He needs to get measured for his tux."

"I thought you needed to touch base with Armitage," I reminded him.

"You need your tux more. And besides, that's what cell phones are for."

I felt like a leaf on the tide, but it was nice being the focus of his attention, and I wasn't going to object.

"I'll come to see you again tomorrow, Granddad. Oh, and Beauchamp said he'll see you tomorrow too. He's getting Silver Birch ready for all our guests. Geoff, why don't you and Mindy join us for dinner tonight? I can call Beauchamp and tell him there will be two more."

For some reason, he looked a little dazed. "Thank you. I'll need to make sure Mindy is free, but yes, I'd like that very much."

"All right, don't let it go too long. Beauchamp might need to go shopping." I looped the backpack over my shoulder and squeezed Granddad's shoulder. "Take care of yourself and listen to your nurses. Bye."

As we walked away, I could hear Granddad say, "Now, Geoffrey, I want an explanation."

I would have gone back to explain to Granddad that I really had no problem with Geoff selling our mother's jewelry, but Hyde cupped my elbow and urged me out.

"We've got a busy day ahead of us!"

CHAPTER 24

I LEFT the backpack in Hyde's SUV, and we entered Putting on the Ritz, the shop where he wanted me to get my tux.

"It would be a better idea to rent it," I said.

"No fiancé of mine will wear an off-the-rack tux."

"That's pompous!"

Hyde raised an eyebrow at me.

"And supercilious!" I tried once more to raise an eyebrow, but when he bit back a grin, I knew I'd only succeeded in looking like a startled rabbit. I'd been told more than once that was the result.

"Mr. Wyndham? It *is* you! I'm so glad to see you again!"

"Hello, Archie. How've you been?"

"Good. I'm doing good! If you check with Armitage, you'll see I only have about a year's worth of payments left!"

"Excellent." Hyde twined his fingers with mine. "This is Archie's second location. His flagship facility is in DC."

"My brother runs that one. And we're thinking of opening another one in Manhattan."

"Make an appointment with Armitage, and we'll crunch some numbers."

"Thanks. So, I hear you're getting married."

"Yes. This is my fiancé, Kipp Llewellyn. Kipp, Archie is the best tailor in the state."

"I'm pleased to meet you, Mr. Llewellyn."

"Same—"

Before I could finish my sentence, Hyde spoke. "He needs a tux."

"You've come to the right place."

"Th—" I tried to complete another sentence, with the same amount of success.

"Archie: price is not an object."

"You'll get the best. Now, let's get down to work. Color, material...." He and Hyde put their heads together.

Well, considering how much I'd added to the conversation, I might as well have not even been there.

I began to stroll around the shop, examining the mannequins.

"No, no, no!" Archie suddenly yelled. "You insult me by even suggesting I might have polyester in my establishment!"

"As long as we have that straight."

"This is nice." I held out the sleeve of the tux that had caught my eye.

Archie frowned. Hyde looked thoughtful. I waited to hear them tell me I had no taste at all.

"Your young man has a good eye. I think he'll look excellent in this. Ian, get this model in a... thirty-six slim. I want you to try it on, Mr. Llewellyn. If you're happy with it, I'll take your measurements."

Ian came back with the tux, took my arm, and ushered me into the fitting room. Once there, he stripped me out of my clothes, giving a snort of laughter when he saw my T-shirt.

"Here." He handed me first a shirt, then the trousers, and finally the jacket. "We'll skip the cummerbund for now." Then he turned me around to face the mirror.

"Oh." I stared at my reflection. "Oh!"

"Is that a good 'Oh' or a bad 'Oh'?"

"I'll let you know in a minute." I walked out into the showroom. Archie was studying color swatches, but Hyde was on the phone, probably talking to Armitage. "Um...." That drew their attention to me. For a second I felt like a deer in the headlights, but then I took a couple of steps forward, spun on my toe and took a couple of steps back, then faced them again and held out my arms. "I know by rights the groom isn't supposed to see his... um... groom in the... uh... tux before the wedding, but...?"

"I'll call you back." Hyde disconnected the call and stared at me for a full minute. I was starting to get nervous when, "Archie?"

"Yes, Mr. Wyndham?"

"This is the tux!"

MY CELL phone rang while I was standing with my arms outstretched as Archie measured from my shoulder to my wrist. We'd already selected the color—black, and the material—wool.

"Get that please, Hyde?"

"Kipp Llewellyn's phone."

I couldn't hear the other end of the conversation, but Hyde's made me curious.

"Tomorrow evening? No, I'm afraid we have something planned. Actually, we'll be flying to Las Vegas. Kipp told me he's never played the slot machines, so I thought I'd broaden his horizons."

Hyde was going to broaden my horizons! My mind went straight to the bedroom, and I had to think of winters at the university so I wouldn't get an erection.

He noticed me watching him, and he smiled. Damn. Too late. "Sorry," I whispered to Archie.

"He does that to people." Archie grinned at me and jotted down some numbers.

Meanwhile, Hyde was saying, "Well, that's hardly your concern, since he's twenty-one." He shot his cuff and glanced at his watch, the epitome of indifference. "And that's not your concern either." He listened for a moment, studying his fingernails and frowning. "You did say he was no longer welcome in your home, so where he sleeps and who he sleeps with...." This time as he listened he walked around me, studying my body, and I shivered at the almost palpable caress. Then he broke the spell, saying briskly, "Well, I had promised Kipp, but if it means so much to you... I'll ask him and get back to you. Good-bye."

"What was that about?" I asked uneasily.

"Marcus is having a dinner party for us."

"Tomorrow?"

"Yes."

"Do we have to go?" I rarely dined with Sir, but on those occasions when I did, my stomach would tie itself in knots and I'd have to excuse myself from the table before I lost my dinner in front of everyone.

"I told him I'd ask you. If you don't want to...."

"No, it's all right." I wasn't going to be a baby about it.

"Are you finished, Archie?"

"Yes, sir, Mr. Wyndham. I can have this ready by—"

"The wedding is Sunday, so it will be ready by Saturday, yes?"

"You bet!"

I was startled. "I'm sorry; doesn't it take three to four weeks to get a suit made to measure?"

"Oh, that's express. Usually it's six to eight weeks. But I'll have all my boys working on it. Anything for you, Mr. Wyndham!"

"Thanks, Archie."

"Hyde!" I whispered. "He can't drop everything to work on my tux!"

"Of course he can. He's getting paid for it."

"But... but... you can't go throwing money around like that!"

"Sure I can."

"But think of all the kids in Africa!"

"Do they want tuxes too?"

I gave a snort of laughter and shook my head. "Call back and let Sir know we'll be there."

"I rather thought you'd want to make him twist a bit."

"If he was preparing dinner, I would. But Mrs. Wales was always nice to me, and I don't want her stressed any more than necessary."

"You're...." He ran his fingertips over my shoulder, then down my arm to my hand, which he brought to his mouth. Then he turned away to call Sir on his phone.

My phone rang again. "Valley Forge. This is George Washington."

"What? Kipp, is that you?"

"Uh... sorry, Geoff." I could almost see him shaking his head at my silliness. "What's up?"

"I'm calling about this evening. Mindy's free, and she'd love for us to have dinner together."

"Great. Dinner is at eight. We'll see you then."

"Kipp...."

"Yes?"

"You're out shopping with... with Hyde, right?"

"Yes. We just ordered my tux."

"Will it be ready in time?"

"According to Archie it will."

"Archie? You're getting your tux at Putting on the Ritz?"

"Yes." He was quiet for a minute. "Geoff?"

"Do me a favor. Get yourself a suit and some appropriate shirts. Father is having a dinner party for you and your fiancé, and if you show up in one of those T-shirts he'll have a coronary."

"I know about dinner. And thanks for having such faith in my sartorial selections."

"Right. I'll see you later."

I hung up and then called Beauchamp. "It's Kipp," I said. "Geoff and Mindy will be joining us for dinner. Do you have enough or would you like us to pick up more groceries?"

"I have everything. Thank you for letting me know. Miss Mindy enjoys my lemon lush. I believe I'll make it for dessert."

"All right; there should be plenty of time to freeze it. Are you sure there's nothing we can get for you?"

"I'm sure."

"We'll see you later, then."

We hung up, and I turned to Hyde. "Geoff and Mindy are coming over this evening. He mentioned the dinner party Sir's having and suggests I get some new clothes. Apparently he doesn't approve of what I'm wearing."

"I can't imagine why. Archie, do you have anything suitable? Unfortunately we don't have time for something made to measure."

"You bet, Mr. Wyndham. I got just the thing. Ian! Go find the suit Alec Stuart ordered but never came back for." He studied my frame. "You're pretty much the same size." We were? He'd always seemed much larger to me. "We'll just need to take it in a bit around the hips, waist, and seat. And I have a nice selection of shirts. Pick out whatever you want." He exchanged glances with Hyde. "It's included in the cost of the suit." And he bustled off.

I had a shirt, but it was three years old, and it would be nice to get a new one.

"Oh, and Archie, he'll need shoes as well!" Hyde called after the tailor.

"Those are next door!"

"As soon as we're done here, we'll get the shoes for you. You can't go around all the time in running shoes."

"No, but Hyde, this is going to cost a fortune." I could see the dollar signs racking up. "Listen. You want to buy me the tux, and that's fine." I wasn't a fool, no matter what Sir might think, and there was no way I could throw that kind of money around. Well, I just didn't have it. But, "I've got enough in my checking account to pay for the suit."

"And shoes?"

I nodded.

I was afraid he was going to give me a hard time, but he just smiled. "All right."

"Thank you. That reminds me. May I invite Hunter to the wedding?"

"Yes, you may, and anyone else you'd like to celebrate the occasion with us."

"Excellent."

Ian came out with the suit. "Sorry for the delay," he said. "It took me a while to find it. It was stored in a plastic bag behind everything."

"That's all—" My mouth went dry as he held it up. Oh, shit. I should have realized when Archie said "Alec Stuart" it was going to be an expensive suit, but I'd been blinded by the cost of my tuxedo and hadn't thought. Did I even have enough to pay for this? "Uh… Ian? Is it all right if I pay part of this with my debit card and then charge the rest of it?"

"Whatever works for you, Mr. Llewellyn. Now, why don't you come back to the fitting room with me?"

I trailed along after him, juggling figures in my head, and not seeing any way I could afford this. But how could I ask Hyde to buy me these clothes as well?

Maybe Granddad wouldn't mind lending me some money?

But it just so happened the suit wasn't as expensive as I'd thought. Yes, it would cost a pretty good chunk of change, but Archie had propped his hands on his hips and said, "Ian, you know we always discount special order suits if the original purchaser doesn't return for them."

"Uh… oh, yes! Sorry, boss. I… uh… got distracted."

"Well, don't get distracted again!"

So as it turned out, I had more than enough to cover it in my checking account. Which was a good thing, because I looked *great* in that suit!

One look into Hyde's eyes told me so.

CHAPTER 25

"SO, WHERE to now?" I asked as we left the shoe store next to Putting on the Ritz and walked toward the car. I was now the owner of not only a sleek pair of Concerto patent leathers for my wedding, but a pair of Boss dress shoes suitable for tonight's dinner party and tomorrow night's engagement party at Llewellyn Manor. I'd lucked out: the Boss shoes, which usually ran almost three hundred dollars, had been reduced.

I swung the bags from my right hand, while Hyde carried the garment bag containing my suit and shirts.

"I really do have to touch base with Armitage. Would you mind coming to the Trunk with me?"

"I wouldn't mind going anywhere with you." I wanted to wind my fingers in his, and would have in spite of the bandage on my left hand, but public displays of affection were severely frowned upon by Sir, and I wasn't sure how Hyde would feel about them.

"You're not too tired? Last night had to be an ordeal for you. It was for me," he said softly, and I could hardly catch my breath. That was so sweet of him to say!

I couldn't help smiling at him. "Well, it's not something I'd care to repeat. But no, I'm fine."

"Okay." He stored the garment bag in the back of his Mercedes along with my shoes, and then opened the passenger door of the SUV, turned my face to him, and brushed his lips over mine. I stared into his eyes, and he smiled. "I hope you don't mind."

"N-no. I don't mind at all." I'd have thrown myself into his arms and peppered his face with kisses, but Sir's words and the memory of

Daniel's reaction convinced me to keep my emotions in check. Once we were married, though....

"I'm glad. I...." His smile became rueful, and he shook his head. "Get in."

I scrambled into the front seat and buckled up, then waited until he was behind the wheel and driving toward the Trunk before taking a breath, crossing my fingers, and asking, "Do I get to see your suite?"

"Certainly." Before I could contemplate the possibility that maybe we could spend some time kissing—that last brush of his mouth over mine was too brief to count as a proper kiss, and I wanted to nibble and lick his full lower lip, preferably while we were on a bed, until I drove both of us out of our minds—he continued, "On Sunday, as I'd told you."

"Spoilsport," I muttered under my breath.

He grinned. "You're pretty irresistible, you know."

"You could've fooled me."

He reached across and ruffled my hair. "Once I complete my business with Armitage, I'll make sure we have some time alone."

"You're a tease."

"But you love me anyway."

"Well, of course!" But I said it in such a way that he'd know *I* was teasing. He probably didn't realize I'd never have agreed to marry him—no matter what Sir said, no matter what Granddad said—if I hadn't cared about him.

"Kipp." He suddenly sounded very serious. "This is your wedding too."

"Yes?"

"The catering manager will be available to show you the Rampart Room and the facilities that are part of it."

"And?"

"I want you to feel free to make any changes you want. Flowers, food, decorations, the bands."

"Bands, plural?"

"Of course. Webster, the catering manager, suggested having music both generations could enjoy, and it sounded like a good idea."

"It does."

"Now, you see? You're just going with the flow."

"All right, Hyde. If there's anything I don't like, I'll kick it to the curb."

"I'm serious, Kipp. I want you to be happy with this." He pulled into the parking lot and turned off the ignition.

"I told you before that I'm happy."

"Yes, but you've been pressured into this wedding."

"Excuse me? Hyde, in case you don't remember, I walked out of Sir's study yesterday." Had it only been the day before?

"But then your grandfather pushed for you to marry me—"

Oh, for Pete's sake! "If I didn't want to marry you, I wouldn't. Don't you know that by now?" I unfastened my seat belt and got out of the car.

Hyde came around to meet me. "Kipp—"

"Or... or are you sorry you asked me?" It didn't matter that we were having an exceptionally warm May, that the temperature was about eighty degrees. I began shivering so hard Hyde couldn't miss seeing it.

"Oh, baby, no." He pulled me into his arms. "I want you so much."

Okay, want and love were two different things, but I'd known from the beginning I was just part of a business deal. But... I'd also known him for a year and a half, and I trusted him not to hurt me. I tucked my head under his chin and held on.

"Oh, my God! Why don't you two get a room?"

Hyde stiffened and let me go. "What are you doing here, Alden?"

"I have some unfinished business with Cameron Stuart."

"Is he here?"

"Oh, yes, although since you bought out the note he signed for Llewellyn and he has to dance to your tune, he spends most of his time in the bar."

I turned to stare at Hyde. "You own the Saratoga Trunk?"

"Didn't he tell you?"

I scowled at Robert Alden. I'd never liked him.

"I just own some shares." Hyde studied Mr. Alden.

"*Controlling* shares. That was part of the agreement with your father," Mr. Alden spat at me. "Marcus needed cash, and in exchange for that note, Wyndham gave it to him."

"I hold your note as well, Alden," Hyde said mildly.

Mr. Alden suddenly looked sick. "I have to go."

"We'll see you tomorrow evening."

"Eh?"

"I'm sure Llewellyn invited you to his son's engagement party."

"He did."

"Then we'll see you tomorrow."

"Yes, tomorrow." He turned to walk away.

"I thought you had to see Mr. Stuart." I didn't have to raise my voice; he was close enough to hear me.

He froze before glancing at his watch. "There's no point. He'll be tanked out of his mind at this hour." He hurried away.

"He didn't sound too overjoyed about coming to our engagement party."

"He didn't, did he? Kipp... is this going to change anything between us?"

"Which? The fact that you pretty much own the Trunk and didn't mention it, or that you don't think I'm happy at the thought of marrying you?"

"Either? Both?"

"Should they?"

"No." He sounded cautious, though. "I want to marry you. I just want you to have a good time at our wedding."

"Then I will. But I do have a question for you. Why wouldn't you give my brother a break?"

"Excuse me?"

"Geoff had to switch the day of his wedding because having it on a Sunday was more than he could afford."

"I have nothing to do with the day-to-day running of this hotel, Kipp. Are you going to ask me to do something about this situation?"

"I don't get involved with the way my fiancé runs his businesses." I felt bad for Geoff and Mindy, but it was their choice. And the last thing I wanted was for Hyde to think I was marrying him for what he could do for me. Unless it was in bed. I grinned up at him. "Shall we go in now?"

He put his arm around my shoulders, and we walked from the parking lot to the front of the property.

CHAPTER 26

THE Saratoga Trunk was a three-story Victorian with quite a history. It had been built in 1882, damaged by fire and rebuilt twenty-five years later, and used as an infirmary during the outbreak of the Spanish influenza in 1918. It had been remodeled around the same time Promise Hospice had been built, and it was the only building in the area to vie with Silver Birch for the amount of square-footage. It looked gorgeous.

An expansive, well-tended lawn ran from the veranda to a private road that curved around to the parking lot in the rear. The veranda—of course Mr. Stuart wouldn't have anything as pedestrian as a porch for the hundred and thirty-five-year-old building—wrapped around three sides of the Trunk. Adirondack chairs were scattered along the length of it, and large windows let in the afternoon sun.

We climbed the steps and crossed to the double doors that led into the main lobby of the hotel. The ceiling here was about thirty feet high, and I stared up at the mural of an English countryside that covered it.

"Impressive, isn't it?"

"Yes! My senior prom was held here, and I'm sorry now that I missed it."

"Why did you?"

"Family matters," I said, waving it aside with an airy hand. I didn't want to tell him that it had been just a few days after that incident with Daniel, and unlike the *A* Hester Prynne had to wear, I felt as if there was a big *F* for fool etched on my forehead.

We crossed to the reception desk. The young woman behind it looked up and then jumped to her feet.

"Mr. Wyndham! Ms. Armitage is in the grand conference room. Everything has been set up there."

"Thank you, Phyllida. This is my fiancé, Kipp Llewellyn."

"Hello, Mr. Llewellyn." Phyllida Carter was the daughter of Alexander Carter, the man who'd been Granddad's CFO. She had been a year ahead of me at Benjamin Martin High, and while I'd built and staged sets for the drama club, she'd been onstage rehearsing her heart out.

"I thought I was Kipp to you, Phyll."

"I wasn't sure...." In spite of her standing in the school, she'd always been nice to me, to the point of asking to accompany me to my junior prom. "Kipp." She beamed.

"Phyllida—Phyll? Are you the young lady who went with Kipp to his prom?"

"Yes, I am. I hope you don't mind."

"How could I, when it was before I knew him? But I want to thank you for giving him fond memories of it."

She blushed. "We had fun. Now, what can I do for you?"

"Would you mind letting Mr. Webster know we're here?"

"Not at all!" She sat down, reached for her phone, and punched in a couple of numbers. "I have Mr. Wyndham and Mr. Llewellyn here to see Mr. Webster," she murmured. "He is? Yes, ma'am. I'll let them know." She hung up. "Mr. Webster is on an international call, but his secretary will let him know you're here."

"Thank you. As I mentioned, he's the catering manager," Hyde told me. "He'll give you a tour of the facilities while I see what Armitage has for me."

"All right, but you know I'm good with whatever you've chosen."

"Oh, Kipp, you don't want to do that!" Phyll had a hand over her mouth to stifle her giggles.

Before I could ask what she was talking about, Hyde's cell phone rang. He took it out and checked the screen. "I have to take this, Kipp. Excuse me, please."

"Sure."

"Thanks for getting back to me, General." He walked away, and I wondered briefly if the general was going to be at our wedding too. Hyde seemed to know a good many important people.

I turned back to my former schoolmate and stared into her blue eyes. "Now, what shouldn't I do?"

She opened her eyes very wide, trying to disguise her amusement, but not doing a very good job of it. "Let him know you think the sun rises and sets on him."

"*Shh!*" I felt myself blushing.

Her eyes widened even more. "I was only teasing, but you *do* think the sun rises and sets on him! Does he know?"

I shook my head. He might not want that from me. Not that I didn't think he liked me well enough, but the last thing he needed was a fiancé who was all clingy and.... "Would you mind keeping that between the two of us?"

"Of course not. I shouldn't have said anything. It's—" The phone on her desk rang. "Excuse me, please?" She didn't ask me to step away, so I eavesdropped as she took the reservation for one of Hyde's Hollywood friends. Her voice was smoothly professional, but her eyes were enormous. When she hung up, she said in a hushed tone, "Do you *know* who that was?" She didn't wait for me to take a guess, just went ahead and told me.

"Hyde knows some interesting people, doesn't he?" I grinned.

"I'll say! I almost expected him to make me sign a confidentiality statement. If the paparazzi ever learned who'll be coming…!"

I'd never thought of having that problem. Certainly I was the son of a very wealthy man, but I lived in a small city and I'd never done anything to draw attention to myself. I thought for a moment of that debacle with Daniel, and I shivered, imagining it splashed all over the scandal sheets.

"Kipp? Are you okay?"

"Uh… yes. It didn't occur to me that I could be hounded by the paparazzi." Would Hyde feel the need to see I had a bodyguard? Oh, God, I didn't even want to think about that! I decided to change the subject. "I was sorry to hear about your father." Damn. That was more abrupt than I'd intended, but before I could apologize....

"Thank you. It was a heart attack, you know."

"Yes, my brother told me. Did he have a history of heart trouble?"

"If he did, he kept it hidden from Mom."

"I'm so sorry," I repeated.

"Your grandfather made sure Mom and the younger ones were taken care of, and there was Dad's life insurance policy. But...." She shrugged. "Mom couldn't deal with being on her own, so I... came back from New York."

I'd met her mother once when the drama club was putting on *Pygmalion*. She was nice but what Granddad would call high-strung: she fussed over the least little thing, like when one of the props for the play went missing. Phyll and her leading man had worked around it, and I was positive the audience had no idea they'd improvised, but Mrs. Carter had reacted as if it was the end of the world.

Losing her husband was, of course, much more serious than a missing handkerchief in a high school production, but to ask her daughter to give up the one thing she wanted more than anything in the world....

Phyll's dream had been to make it on Broadway, and she was so good it wouldn't have surprised me, especially since she'd been voted "girl most likely to bring home a Tony." We'd talked once while she was being fitted for a costume and I was putting together something that would look like a mountain of mattresses, and we'd agreed: neither of us had wanted to work in the factory.

"I was lucky to get a job here at the Trunk," she said now, her expression wistful.

"How do you like it?"

"You know, it's interesting, especially with all the reservations coming in for your wedding. We're almost completely booked up!"

"You'll be referring them to the Alden Arms once you are?"

"Oh, yes. Mr. Stuart gets on pretty well with Mr. Alden. Well, the Families." Obviously they were capable actors if she didn't realize what little regard they actually had for each other. She finished entering something on her computer and then smiled at me, but I could tell that as interesting as this job might be, she missed the theater.

"Ever think of putting on a show in the barn? You could have all the big critics from Broadway down, you know."

She looked puzzled for a moment, then picked up on my reference to the movies from the thirties and forties and laughed. "I'm an actress, not a producer or director. But if *we* could put one together...." She waited expectantly.

"Oh, I don't know what Hyde's plans are."

"Why don't you think about it? It would be a million laughs."

Now she was referencing those movies.

I couldn't say yes or no, but I didn't want Phyll to think I was turning her down flat, either. I really didn't have any idea what Hyde might want to do once we were married, but....

A hand on my shoulder made me jump. Hyde must have concluded his phone call and rejoined us, but he'd been so silent I hadn't realized he was there. He raised an eyebrow, and I sighed.

"What's wrong, baby?"

Okay, I was being silly. What did the eyebrow thing matter when I had an awesome man who cared enough about me to want to marry me?

"Phyllida is an amazing actress. Martinsburg doesn't have its own theater—"

"Shall I change that?"

I bumped my shoulder against his. "—but the high school auditorium is larger than most Broadway theaters. If she found a vehicle, do you think you could get some of your friends down to attend?"

"Kipp, I wasn't serious!" She looked scared.

"Why not? If you can't go to Broadway, we'll bring Broadway to you. Right?" I smiled up at Hyde.

"Whatever you'd like." He took out a business card and scrawled something on the back. "This is Armitage's number."

"She's his assistant!" I said sotto voce.

"She'll handle everything."

"Th-thank you!" Phyll said faintly. "I don't know what else to say."

"You don't have to say anything else," he told her.

"By the way, are you busy on Sunday, Phyll?"

"No, that's my day off." She stared up at Hyde as if he was the burning bush on the mountain.

Well, he pretty much was. At least he was the burning bush on my mountain.

"Then I'd like you to come to our wedding."

That seemed to jolt her out of her reverie. "That's sweet of you but I... I couldn't afford it, Kipp."

I leaned on the counter and spoke confidentially. "I couldn't afford to come to my wedding either, Phyll, but Hyde's paying for everything. And if you're worrying about a gift, don't. He's one of the richest men in the country: he doesn't need anything."

"Wrong," he said. He smiled at me and took my hand. "But as it turns out, I'm getting exactly what I need."

I smiled back again, feeling heat rise in my cheeks.

"Mr. Wyndham, do you have a brother?" Phyll asked.

"I'm afraid not."

"Of course not. You're so lucky, Kipp!" She made a moue, but then giggled happily. "Well, thank you both very much. I'd like to come."

"Oh, and bring a guest." I didn't have many friends here in Martinsburg, and it would be nice to show Hyde I wasn't a total loser.

"Kipp, are you sure—"

"You bet."

"I still feel I should bring a gift."

"In that case, make a donation to Promise Hospice in our names."

"That's a great idea!"

"Yes, it is." Hyde brushed his fingertips over my cheek, then frowned and glanced at his watch. "Where's Webster?"

"He should be here shortly, Mr. Wyndham."

"Kipp, I have to see Armitage, but I'll try to join you before you're done."

"Go ahead." I stroked his sleeve. "I'm a big boy."

"Are you?" His gaze dipped down below my waist—the first time he'd done something so blatant—and then came back to mine, and I shivered. He wound his hand around my neck, drew me to him, and skimmed his lips over mine, nipping the upper one, then tugging on the lower one until they parted and I could hardly catch my breath. He let me go and ran his thumb over my eyebrow. "Don't let this stress you out."

"Yes, Hyde." I watched him walk off. Would I ever grow tired of admiring his butt? I didn't think so. And on Sunday, I'd get to see and touch it in all its naked glory.

"You're so lucky!" Phyll murmured. "Was that kiss as sweet as it looked?"

"Do you remember that song about kisses being sweeter than wine? This was even sweeter."

"I'm happy for you, Kipp. Daddy would have been too. He used to mention how difficult things were for you at Llewellyn Manor, how much happier you were with your grandfather."

Fortunately, her phone rang just then. I knew what Martinsburg was like, and I wasn't about to discuss my home life. The last thing I wanted was to be thought of as the town's poor little rich boy.

Phyll hung up and frowned. "I'm sorry, Kipp, Mr. Webster is still tied up."

"That's all right. Catching up with you isn't a hardship."

"Why, Kipp Llewellyn! Are you flirting with me?"

"Phyll! You know I'm engaged!"

"I know. I was just teasing."

I worried my lower lip. "Phyll, did I strike you as being gay when we were in high school?"

"Truthfully?"

Oh, boy, here it comes.

"You're going to think I'm the world's most conceited person, but... Do you remember when we did *Streetcar*?"

"Did you doubt it?" That was her senior class's swan song, and they'd outdone themselves. "Everyone was surprised you took the role of Stella rather than Blanche."

She blushed. "Do you want to know why? Daniel Richardson was playing Stanley."

Of course. "But you weren't one of his girls."

"No. Well, he was a junior."

"Did that ever matter?"

"I guess not. To tell you the truth, I was a little insulted he never even once made a play for me. I mean, what was wrong with me?"

"Nothing, Phyll. And I can understand your wanting to grab the opportunity to kiss him." Even if it was just in a play. It was more than I'd ever had.

"Yes. But that scene at the bottom of the stairs when he was kissing me—Stella? I happened to open my eyes, and I saw you in the wings, watching us. There was such a look of longing on your face...."

"Oh, God!" I buried my face in my hands.

"No." She touched my shoulder. "Kipp, I thought that was directed at me. I thought you wanted to be the one kissing me."

My head jerked up. "Excuse me? Is that why you treated me so... so kindly the rest of the year? Why you went to the prom with me?"

"You were a junior, and...." Her blush darkened and she nodded. "I told you it was conceited."

"No, that's really sweet." Wrong, but sweet.

"But anyway, to answer your question, no, it never occurred to me, even when you just kissed me on the cheek. As a matter of fact, you could have knocked over pretty much everyone in Martinsburg with a feather when news got out that you were marrying Hyde Wyndham—Kipp, what's bothering you?"

Not quite everyone—Daniel and his friends had to know what my orientation was.

I couldn't tell her that. From what she said, it sounded like she still thought Daniel walked on water, and I wasn't going to burst her bubble. I scrambled for an excuse. "I suddenly realized—I need to find something to give him. For our engagement."

"You've got some time until Mr. Webster gets done. Why not check out Clio's Trunk?"

"Excuse me?"

"That's the Trunk's exclusive boutique. It's got everything: clothes, accessories, last-minute gifts." She winked. "It's right at the end of this corridor. See?" She pointed to my left. "Go check it out. I'll call Clio's when Mr. Webster gets done."

"Thank you!"

"You're welcome, Kipp."

CHAPTER 27

I HURRIED to the boutique. I didn't want to take a chance Hyde might turn up.

Clio's Trunk was interesting. I skipped the clothes and accessories that Phyllida had mentioned and homed in on a case of jewelry. I didn't care for the signet rings—too bulky, and besides, I had no doubt the markup was extravagant.

And then I saw the ID bracelet. It was pretty perfect—sterling silver and fourteen karat gold, with a hidden clasp, but it cost three hundred forty-five dollars, and that was without the engraving. A few years ago that wouldn't have mattered in the least to me, but after buying my suit I'd more or less drained my checking account. I still had the paycheck that was due me, and a credit card that had a decent limit. I chewed on my lower lip. Granddad had said he'd release my trust fund, but with so much going on, would he even remember? It would be better if I depended on myself. I could probably pay it off in about six months.

"May I help you, sir?"

I nearly jumped. I hadn't realized the man behind the counter had approached me. "Thanks. This ID bracelet I'm looking at—would you be able to—"

"I don't think so."

"—engrave—Excuse me?"

"The items in this boutique are very expensive." His eyes seemed riveted to my torso. I looked down to see that Granddad's sports coat hung open and the *Minions* T-shirt was very visible. I buttoned the coat, concealing the words—something I probably should have done earlier, but it was a warm day, dammit!—and he curled his lip. "I don't think you could afford them."

My jaw dropped and I stood there staring at him. Granted I wasn't well thought of at home, but I'd always been treated well in Martinsburg.

The phone behind the counter rang, and he fixed a gimlet eye on me. "Stand right there and don't touch anything!" He reached over the counter, keeping that eye on me. "Clio's Trunk, this is Sanderson. Oh, hello, Ms. Carter. Can I get back to you? I was just about to call Security. There's a person—I beg your pardon? Who?" He turned a pasty white. "Are you sure? Yes. I'll… I'll let him know." He hung up and turned slowly toward me. "Mr. Llewellyn. I'm sorry, I didn't recognize you. Especially dressed like that," he muttered under his breath.

"What's wrong with how I'm dressed?"

"Nothing! Heh, heh, heh. Not a thing! Er… Ms. Carter wanted me to let you know that Mr. Webster would join you in about ten minutes. That should give us plenty of time to find the ideal ID bracelet. Now, you were interested in one of these?"

"Yes, this one."

"That really isn't top-of-the-line. Perhaps this one? It's titanium, onyx, and diamond."

It also had a top-of-the-line price tag, and as much as I wanted to buy the best for Hyde, I couldn't afford it. And what kind of gift would it be if he wound up paying for it?

"No, I'd really prefer the one I pointed out. I'd like it engraved in script on the back as well as the front."

"Well… if you're very sure?"

"I am. I want my fiancé's name on the front. On the back I want 'Always remember I love you.' And sign it 'Kipp'."

"Very well. Let me just write it up."

"There's just one thing more: I want to give this to him tonight. Can you have it ready for me by the time I leave the Saratoga Trunk?"

He looked like he was sucking on a lemon. "Of course. However, I'll need about an hour."

"Thank you. Shall I pay for it now?"

"If you wouldn't mind?"

"Not at all." I took out my wallet.

He took my credit card and began to process the transaction. "And if you'll print out what you want engraved?"

Once that was done, I signed the receipt and put my copy in my wallet, along with my credit card.

I glanced at my watch. "I'm sorry, I need to hurry. I'll see you later."

"Mr. Llewellyn. I want to apologize for my attitude earlier. I thought...."

I really didn't want to know what he thought. "Apology accepted."

"Thank you. I'll get right on this."

"Thanks." I could see us doing round after round of thank-yous, and I hurried out of Clio's Trunk.

Phyll glanced up from her computer as I approached the reception desk, and a smile lit her face.

"Did you find something, Kipp?"

"Yes. Mr. Sanderson is going to engrave it, and I'll pick it up before Hyde and I leave."

"I'm glad. Was Sanderson giving you a hard time?"

"Frankly, I thought he was going to boot me out of the boutique. It was a good thing you called when you did."

"He tends to take his position as assistant manager very seriously."

"Did he honestly think I was going to shoplift something?"

"Wellll...."

"Seriously, Phyllida? I'm a Llewellyn!"

"But you're not exactly dressed like one."

I'd gotten used to dressing more casually at college, and I wasn't going to dispute that with her. "Well, it was either this one or the one that said *Looking for love (will settle for green jelly beans).*"

She began giggling. It was infectious, and after a few seconds I joined her. Oh, not giggling, but more a manly chuckle.

Her phone rang. "I wonder who it's going to be this time!"

"I'll let you get back to work, but I'll see you on Sunday, yes?"

"Yes. Oh, and Kipp? Congratulations!"

"Thanks, Phyll."

A tall, angular man dressed in an Armani suit came striding across the lobby. "Mr. Llewellyn. I'm Clarence Webster. It's a pleasure to meet you!"

"How do you do, Mr. Webster? I know you must be very busy this time of year, and I appreciate you taking the time to talk with me."

"Not at all, not at all! Whatever we can do to accommodate Hyde Wyndham. As I'm sure you know, your fiancé has selected the Rampart Room for your reception. If you'll come with me, I'd be delighted to show it to you."

I turned to Phyllida. "It was nice seeing you again, Phyll."

"Same here, Mr. Llewellyn."

I tried to raise an eyebrow, but as usual both of them wound up trying to hide beneath the hair that spilled over my forehead. She cut a glance toward the catering manager, and I nodded. She'd probably get into trouble if it seemed she was being familiar—not with me, but with Hyde Wyndham's fiancé.

Mr. Webster linked his arm through mine and almost dragged me around the corner and down the broad hallway.

"I've heard the Rampart Room can seat a thousand people."

"Indeed, yes! Of course you'll only be having five hundred."

Only five hundred? I swallowed a laugh. My graduating class had *only* numbered a hundred and fifty.

"I'm sure that's simply because of the short notice," Mr. Webster was saying. "And here we are!" He flung open a pair of huge doors and gestured for me to enter.

The room was nothing short of breathtaking. Crystal chandeliers were hung in a spiral that started at the center of the ceiling and expanded outward. One entire wall was windows draped with white silk.

"As you can see, we're getting everything ready for Sunday."

"Yes," I said faintly.

Men and women in aprons and gloves were setting up fifty tables—white linen tablecloths, crystal goblets, fine china dishes, sterling silver flatware. The tables were around the perimeter of the room, leaving the center cleared for dancing.

"You'll have centerpieces of roses, carnations, and baby's breath, with some ferns to add a touch of green. There's also to be an ice carving. Mr. Wyndham has chosen a pair of hearts with your names and Sunday's date inscribed in it. However, if you prefer, we can have a castle instead."

"Yes," I repeated. "I mean no. I mean...." I was starting to wonder how Mindy dealt with all these details. Sure, I'd taken that course, but to make those decisions for my own wedding.... I was relieved Hyde had spared me this. "The hearts will be fine."

"And of course you'll have a chocolate fountain with a variety of fruits to dip—kiwi, mango, pears, mandarin oranges—along with a coffee bar that will offer espresso, cappuccino, latte, and macchiato."

"Is that all?" Hyde had mentioned both the fountain and the coffee bar, but I hadn't given either much thought. For a second the image of coffee mounded high with whipped cream and chocolate cascading down in a waterfall took my breath away. Sunday was going to be awesome in more ways than one.

"Oh, my, my, no! There will also be—Oh, you're teasing. Heh, heh, heh." Were all the employees of the Trunk taught to laugh like that?

"Sorry."

"Not at all, not at all. Now on your special day the waitstaff will be dressed in tuxedo trousers and white dress shirts."

I wasn't going to say "yes" again. Instead, I asked, "What about music?"

"Live, of course. A violin, cello, and viola trio will be off to the side; they'll play a mixture of classical and easy listening music while everyone is dining. Afterward, Mr. Wyndham has arranged for two bands to alternate sets."

"He mentioned two bands, although I didn't realize it was his idea."

"Ah… yes." Mr. Webster didn't seem to know how to respond to that. Then he shrugged and said, "Actually, the idea was mine. He chose the bands. JC and the Factory Boys are for the younger guests. They cover current songs. Have you heard of them?"

"No, I can't say that I have."

"They're quite good. I understand they have a contract in the offing. They're also local—Mr. Wyndham has tried to hire within the community."

I knew I was beaming, but the idea that Hyde would care for my city…. "And the second band?"

"That would be Harry Dorsey and His Martinaires. They play pop standards for the over-fifty crowd. Is that all right? If you'd prefer other entertainment… it's rather short notice, but I have no doubt we can—"

"No, I'm sure both bands will be fine."

"Excellent! Now, if you'll come this way, I'll show you the south lawn where Mr. Wyndham has requested the ceremony itself take place."

The south lawn was immense, at least the size of two football fields. It was enclosed by a wall of neatly trimmed hedges that rose more than ten feet in height. The arch Hyde had said he'd imagined for his wedding to Aaron Richardson was the only thing that interrupted the empty space.

"There are no flowers." The trellis was bare, just a white, wooden structure.

"It's too soon. On Sunday, a few hours before the ceremony, our people will transform that plain arch into a wonder to behold. You're going to love it!"

"It doesn't matter what I think of it. Hyde wants ivy and gardenias."

"And that's precisely what will be wound through it!"

"All right."

"And there will be a white carpet laid down for you to walk to your groom. It will start here, wind around in a semicircle, and then lead you across to him." He took my arm again and actually walked me around the path I would be taking.

The grass was thick and lush, and that gave me something to be concerned about. "My grandfather wants to walk with me, Mr. Webster. Can the lawn and carpet accommodate a wheelchair?"

"Hmm." He tugged on his lower lip. "I believe for something like that, a wooden walkway would be called for. Yes, of course we can make it work! If this is satisfactory?"

"Thank you, yes."

"Excellent. In that case...." He led me back into the Rampart Room.

I gazed around. "There's an awful lot of white going on."

"Well, Mr. Wyndham thought it would be suitable."

"*Excuse me?*" Was Hyde intending to announce to the entire city that I was a virgin?

"Since it's a first marriage for both of you."

"Oh." Well, having embarrassed myself.... "May I see the menu?"

"If you'll come this way?" He ushered me to the kitchen and flipped a light switch. The room—another huge, *huge* space, this one lined with stainless-steel appliances and butcher-block counters—was empty. He offered me a handwritten menu. "Of course this is the chef's copy. We'll have the final choices printed up especially for your wedding and placed in a leather folder. These folders will have your names and the date stamped on them in twenty-four karat gold—quite an elegant touch; your fiancé must care for you a great deal. And of course they'll be a lovely souvenir your guests can take home with them."

Souvenirs? Hyde had said something about the invitations being used as souvenirs. In spite of that course in event planning, I'd never even thought.... No wonder it was costing Geoff a fortune.

I glanced over the menu and abruptly shivered. "We're having bacon-wrapped jalapeno prawns?" Just reading it made my throat feel like it was starting to close up.

"Yes. That's one of Chef Edouard's most acclaimed appetizers."

"I don't want to deny this to my guests, but is it possible to see that I'm not served any shellfish?"

"That won't be a problem at all. Chef will come up with something to tempt the most finicky palate."

"It's not a question of finicky. I'm allergic. I can't eat any shellfish."

"Oh, my! Not even the broiled lobster?"

"I'm afraid not." I pictured Hyde dipping a chunk of lobster into butter, painting my lips with it, and then sliding it into my mouth. I could almost taste the butter on my tongue, and I sighed. "I can't take the chance. Even if I had my EpiPen with me, it would put a damper on the festivities, don't you agree?"

"Yes, indeed! However, not to worry, we shall do everything in our power to accommodate you!"

"Thank you. Everything on the menu looks delicious." A choice of French onion soup or tomato bisque, house salad or Caesar, a sorbet to refresh the palate, and then to the serious part of the meal: filet mignon with a mushroom-wine sauce and broiled lobster tail stuffed with jumbo lump crab and Boursin cheese blend, blackberry chipotle glazed salmon, quail with bourbon-pepper jelly glaze, or wild mushroom, asparagus, and onion polenta for the vegetarians.

"Chef will be pleased you approve. Now, of course we don't have the cake ready, but let me show you a sketch of what the baker has promised us. As you can see, it's eight tiers and almost six and a half feet tall."

"It's beautiful." I didn't have to ask for ivy and gardenias this time. The cake was awash in them.

"And the flowers are made of wafers and spun sugar."

"This is very impressive."

"I'm so pleased you think so!" He positively beamed.

"May I see the wine list?"

"Indeed, yes!" He handed me a very elaborate card covered with elegant swirls and curlicues. I studied it intently. One thing I'd learned at Armand U was that fancy could hide a multitude of sins.

And sure enough…. "Who selected these wines?"

"Why, Mr. Stuart himself."

"Did my fiancé approve this list? Did Ms. Armitage?"

"They were very busy. Mr. Stuart saw no need to disturb them."

"I've heard many things about Mr. Stuart, but none that indicated he was a connoisseur of wines."

"I… I…."

"Is he trying to foist second-rate vintages on us?"

"I've seen the invoices for these wines. They're very expensive!"

"That doesn't change the fact that they're second-rate. Do you have a pen?"

"Yes, sir, of course." He removed one from his pocket and handed it to me. His hand was shaking.

"Thank you." This was the second time someone had had that reaction to me. I didn't like it any better than the first time.

One by one, I drew a line through the wines—through the champagne Hyde and I would have drunk to toast each other, through cabernets, chardonnays, and pinots, through dessert wines and liqueurs. And then I began writing. "These will replace Mr. Stuart's choices."

"Mr. Llewellyn, the cost will be greater than what Mr. Stuart charged!"

I stared at him without responding.

"I…." He tugged at his collar. "I don't know if we can obtain all these on such short notice."

I took out my cell phone and dialed the number for Promise Hospice. "I'd like to speak with Bradley Martin please. This is his grandson."

In a matter of moments Granddad was on the line. "Kipp, is something wrong?" He didn't even think it might be Geoff.

"Actually, yes, Granddad. The wine that was chosen for my wedding is dreck."

"Who chose it?"

"It seems that was Mr. Stuart."

"I'll have to have a little chat with him. Apparently he thinks that because I'm not well, I can no longer make sure my grandson isn't taken advantage of. Do you have a list to replace this dreck?"

"Yes."

"Bring it to Beauchamp."

"It's a lot of wine, Granddad."

"I have a lot of wine in my wine cellar, and I'm not going to be around to drink it. It may as well be put to good use."

"Thank you."

"Let's get on to more pleasant things. Did you order your tux?"

"Yes, and it's gorgeous!"

"You're pleased with it?"

"More than I can say." The important thing was that Hyde was pleased with it too.

"And will it be ready on time?"

"Archie says so."

"Good man. Oh, Hyde called to tell me of the dinner party your father is hosting for you."

"Yes, I know."

"I've informed Marcus that I'll be joining you."

I knew that too. Hyde had told me. "Do you feel well enough?"

"Yes," he snapped.

"Don't bite my head off, Granddad!" I laughed. "I'll see you tomorrow, then. And thank you again. Bye."

"Good-bye, Kipp."

I put my phone away. "I believe we're done here, Mr. Webster."

"Yes." He had a handkerchief out and was mopping his forehead. "I apologize for this misunderstanding."

"I'm sure it wasn't your fault. However, my grandfather will be taking this up with Mr. Stuart. Now, can you point me in the direction of my fiancé?"

"He's in the grand conference room. Let me escort you."

"Thanks, but that isn't necessary."

"Oh. All right, then. Just go back the way we came and turn left at the end of the corridor. That will lead you to the lobby. From there it's three doors down on the left."

"Thank you."

He smiled nervously and mopped his forehead once again.

CHAPTER 28

MY HEART was still pounding from that confrontation. I'd never done anything like that before, but the thought of Mr. Stuart trying to make Hyde look like a fool.... Because I had no doubt that he'd snicker and sneer behind Hyde's back and tell everyone those wines were his choice.

I stopped at Clio's Trunk. Mr. Sanderson gave me a weak smile. "Mr. Llewellyn, it's all ready, and if I may say so, I think you'll be very pleased with it!"

I examined it carefully, making sure the spelling was correct. "This is perfect. Thank you very much." I handed it back to him. He polished it with a royal blue cloth, placed it in a slender box, and returned it to me.

I slid the box into the breast pocket of Granddad's jacket.

"Thank you again. Have a good day."

"Oh... er... you too, Mr. Llewellyn."

I walked past the reception desk. Phyllida must have left for the day; a man in his middle twenties had replaced her.

"Good evening, sir," he said politely.

I nodded at him and continued down the corridor.

And then I realized what he'd said. *Evening?* I checked my watch and forgot all about my pounding heart. It was a quarter to six; I needed to get home and get ready for dinner!

The door to the grand conference room wasn't quite closed. I pushed it open in time to hear Aaron Richardson say, "He's just a child! You need someone who shares the same memories." His arms were around Hyde's neck. "You've missed me, I know you have! Kiss me, darling! Kiss me!"

Well. This was an interesting situation. I stood there for a moment, uncertain as to what to do. Was Richardson right? Had Hyde missed him?

But it suddenly occurred to me that it didn't matter for two reasons. One: Hyde had asked me to marry him, and two: he'd never go after a married man. He'd told me that himself.

I decided my fiancé needed rescuing. "Gentlemen. Am I interrupting?"

"Yes!" Richardson said. He leaned against Hyde, his mouth swollen and triumph in his voice. "You're not wanted here! Go away, little boy!"

Hyde removed Richardson's arms from around his neck. In spite of the caramel tones of his skin, he was actually looking pale. "Kipp."

"Hello, darling," I husked, deepening my voice and doing my best impersonation of Julie Andrews in *Victor/Victoria*. I pulled Hyde's head down, wiped my palm over his mouth, and then kissed him.

His lips clung to mine almost desperately. "Kipp."

I drew back and ran my fingertips along the curve of his cheek before turning to meet Richardson's eyes. "I'll let my fiancé tell me if he no longer wants me, Mr. Richardson. Meanwhile, I think you're the one who's not wanted."

"Hyde! Are you going to let this… this… *child* talk to me like that?"

"Yes, I believe I am. You'd better go."

"Bastard!" But it was me he spat the word at. He stormed out, slamming the door behind him.

I opened my eyes very wide. "He hurt my feelings!"

"Kipp, that wasn't what it must have looked like."

"No? It looked like you were being assaulted." At some point he'd removed his suit jacket. His shirt was out of his trousers and his hair was disheveled.

"It won't happen again, I promise."

"I believe you."

"I don't know why you would. If I caught you kissing another man—"

"What would you do? Beat me?"

"I'd never hurt a hair on your head, Kipp. But I'd ruin him." His eyes were cold, and I knew beyond a shadow of a doubt he would do exactly what he said.

"Well, I have no intention of kissing anyone but you, so there's no one you'll have to ruin." I leaned against him, partly to relish his warmth, but mostly to erase the feel of Richardson's body from his memory and replace it with mine. "So what happened?"

"I thought you trusted me."

"Of course I do. That doesn't mean I'm not curious."

He laughed a little. "I sent Armitage home for the day and continued wrapping up some... loose ends."

"What loose ends?" I asked idly. I was more interested in undoing a couple of his shirt buttons, slipping my fingers in the space, and exploring his chest. My fingertips were teased by the feel of the hair I'd discovered. Why wasn't it Sunday yet?

"Nothing for you to worry about. The door opened, and I thought it was you. I smiled, and I guess Ron took it the wrong way, because the next thing I knew he was trying to see if I still had my tonsils."

"Didn't he know from when you were engaged?"

"We didn't talk about things like that."

"No? Hyde, do you still have your tonsils?"

"I think I'll let you find that out for yourself."

"Yes? Now?" I couldn't catch my breath. I was certain he could feel my dick against his hip. This would be the ideal time for him to.... I closed my eyes and imagined him slipping his hands past the waistband of my pants and into my boxer briefs, imagined the heat of his broad palms against naked skin, closing over my buttocks and squeezing them....

"You'll be the death of me!"

"We wouldn't want that," I breathed in his ear. I was so close to losing control, and I wanted Hyde to lose control along with me.

He gave a full-body shudder. "I'm... I'm done here. Let me just gather.... I'll drive you home and come back here to shower and change."

I kissed the hinge of his jaw. "You know, you could shower and get changed now. It would save you from having to drive back and forth. And once I'm home, it won't take me long to get myself together."

"You're really determined to see my suite, aren't you?"

No, I was determined to see his naked body. If I needed to use the bathroom while he was showering...? I peeked at him through my lashes.

"Okay, but you'd better behave."

"Don't I always?"

"Too damn much."

"Excuse me?"

"Nothing."

"Um... just out of curiosity.... What would you do if I...?"

"I don't think you want to know."

I felt cold. Would he call off the wedding?

"Kipp?"

"Ye—" My voice cracked. God, my mouth had gotten so dry. I swallowed and tried again. "Yes?"

He cupped my face in both hands and then pulled me gently into his embrace, wrapped his arms around me and rested his cheek against my hair.

We stood like that for a long minute, and I savored the sensation. I'd have savored it even more if I'd been able to feel the length of his body, but I forced myself to keep a chaste distance this time.

Finally, he stepped back and smiled into my eyes. "It is getting late. Let's go up to my suite. You can watch the six o'clock news while I shower."

"I don't watch the news. I don't want to encourage them."

"MTV, then."

"I don't watch that either."

"Why not?"

I hunched a shoulder. MTV didn't really air music videos anymore. If I wanted to watch them, I'd go to iTunes on my laptop. But if Hyde remembered MTV from when it did, I wasn't going to say anything about it.

He chuckled. "In that case, you can select the suit you'd like me to wear. No peeking, though."

I sighed and let him urge me toward the door.

CHAPTER 29

As soon as we entered Hyde's suite, he strode down the long corridor that led to the bedroom, while I hurried after him. He tossed his jacket onto a chair, removed his shoes and socks, and then stripped off his shirt and trousers. "I'm sorry; I don't want to make you late."

He reached for the hem of his undershirt and yanked it up over his head, and my heart began beating in a slow, heavy rhythm. I ran my tongue over my lips and pretended to be busy with something else. I kept glancing over my shoulder as I walked toward the closet, though, and I nearly smashed my nose on the door. It would have been worth it to get a glimpse of him naked, but to my disappointment, he left on his aquamarine boxers. Where had he found that color? It went so well with the caramel skin tones of his back and legs.

And, oh, God, his butt! I started to drool.

It occurred to me that he'd have to walk out of the bathroom in nothing more than a towel. Gravity doing its thing, the towel might even....

Hyde crossed to the closet and gave me an absentminded smile. "Excuse me, please."

I was in his way. I stepped aside, and he opened a drawer in the organizer and took out a pair of black boxers.

"Well, damn," I muttered.

"Did you say something, Kipp?"

"Um... are those silk?"

"Yes."

I wanted to ask if I could touch, but I could hear Sir whispering in my ear, *You're not married yet, and if you disgust him, you'll never be married!*

The opportunity passed me by as he strode to the other side of the room. I sighed again. "I was wondering, Hyde. Do you want me to send this suit out to the cleaners?"

"No, the Saratoga Trunk has an excellent dry cleaner on-site. There's a bag for it behind the closet door. If you'll put the suit in the bag and leave it on the stand, the valet service will pick it up and return it for tomorrow." He unfastened his wristwatch and placed it on the nightstand. "I'll hurry." And he went into the bathroom and closed the door.

"Hmm." I walked over to the nightstand and picked up his watch. It was a Cartier. I turned it over, and on the back it was engraved, *I'll always love you. D.* Well, at least it wasn't *A.* But I couldn't help wondering who *D* was.

I set the watch down and went back to the closet. Hanging inside the door, as Hyde had said, was a plastic bag. I took it out, and then emptied the pockets of his suit, smiling when I came across my handkerchief. It would be his choice what to take with him, so I placed the handkerchief, along with his wallet, cell phone, and keys on the nightstand beside his watch. Once the suit was in the bag and the bag on the stand, I went back to the closet, moving the various suits on their hangers from one side to the other as I studied them.

Oh, this one was *very* nice! I walked across to the bathroom and tapped on the door. "Hyde?" I could hear the sound of the shower, and I knocked harder and raised my voice. "Hyde, would the Paul Smith London be all right?" It was a black suit with flat-front trousers and a zip fly.

"I told you the choice was yours," he shouted back.

"All right." I stood there for a moment, picturing him standing under the spray. Four more nights counting tonight, and then I'd be able to join him in the shower. I pictured myself caressing his chest, his nipples becoming erect under my fingertips, and then running my palms down past his waist, finally gripping his dick.

And what would he be doing? Telling me to turn around and brace my hands against the tiles? Stroking along my spine to the cleft of my buttocks? Maybe even dipping into the crevice, finding my hole? Or would he drop to his knees, spread my buttocks, and drive his tongue into me?

I shivered and swallowed, then reached into my jeans to squeeze my dick before I came in my pants.

I took out the suit and laid it across the king-size bed, found a shirt I thought would go well with it, socks, and a tie. Shoes too. I found a pair I liked and placed them at the side of the bed.

There was nothing else for me to do now except wait for Hyde to come out of the bathroom and get dressed.

I didn't bother turning on the television. As I'd told him, I didn't watch the news or MTV, and I had no desire to watch any of the sitcoms or reality shows that were mostly reruns anyway.

Instead, I wandered through the bedroom, running my fingertips over the modern, whitewashed pine furniture. It wasn't to my taste, but it suited this suite. Floor-to-ceiling window treatments that matched the gray and black bedspread were tied back, allowing the late-afternoon sunlight to pour into the room, giving it a warmth I was sure it would lack otherwise.

The suite was arranged in an almost zigzag configuration. I strolled back along the hallway. A half bath was to the right of the front door. Another hallway led to an exceptionally large space. On one side was the living room, and a quick glance at it surprised me.

The walls were painted burnt umber—again, not my taste, but it made quite a statement. It was furnished with an oversized couch and a couple of armchairs, all shades of gray. The abstracts staggered on one of the walls were original—obviously, none of that hotel art for the Trunk—while a fifty-five-inch flat screen took up a good deal of space on the other. An outside wall had doors rather than a window, and they opened onto a balcony. The view was pretty.

In an alcove was the work station, complete with Wi-Fi, a multi-line phone, and a fax; I didn't know if all the suites offered that or if management set it up specifically for Hyde.

Finally, directly opposite the living room, was the dining area, useful for those times when Hyde had his people working late? The table was round and glass with a stainless steel base, and I recognized its elegant lines as something by an exclusive designer who worked out of Rome. Four chairs of the same spare design circled the table.

I wished I could have said the décor of this suite left a lot to be desired, but I'd have been lying. Mr. Stuart's decorator had done a very good job.

I wandered back into the bedroom. There were no buildings nearby, so no one would get an eyeful of Hyde's luscious body, but I pulled the drapes closed anyway.

I was just turning on the recessed lighting when Hyde came out of the bathroom, his hair slightly damp. And okay, he didn't have that towel wrapped around his hips as I'd fantasized, but the black boxers he wore were quite satisfactory. They hugged his package and were snug over his ass, and all I wanted was to touch.

He fastened his watch to his wrist, frowning when he saw the time. "I'm sorry, I didn't realize…."

"It's all right. I'll call Beauchamp and tell him we're running a little late."

"I won't take long, Kipp." He slid his arms into the sleeves of his shirt, and the frown line between his eyes deepened as he fastened the buttons.

"Don't rush." I took out my cell phone. "Hyde? Who gave you that watch?"

"My mother. It belonged to my father." He sat on the bed and pulled on his socks.

"It's very nice." I was glad I hadn't chosen a watch for him.

"Thank you." He drew his trousers on over his long legs.

I leaned against the doorframe, dialed Silver Birch, and watched as he continued to dress.

Four more days, and then he'd be doing that in reverse, I'd get to take advantage of him, and no matter how out of control I was, he wouldn't be able to turn me loose.

CHAPTER 30

BEAUCHAMP opened the door, both his eyebrows raised. "You don't have very much time, Mr. Kipp."

"I know, I'm sorry." I thrust Granddad's suit jacket and the mini backpack at him, took the garment bag containing my suit and the bag with my shoes from Hyde, and headed for the stairs. "I'll hurry."

"Mr. Wyndham, may I pour you a drink?"

"A diamond fizz, thanks. Kipp, there are some details I need to go over for Sunday." He'd brought along his PC tablet.

"All right, Hyde."

"The study is just that way, sir." Beauchamp pointed him in the right direction. "I'll fix your drink and bring it right to you."

"Thanks very much." Hyde disappeared through the door.

"Beauchamp!"

"Yes, Mr. Kipp?"

"What's a diamond fizz?"

"Oh, it's a gin fizz with sparkling wine instead of carbonated soda."

I nodded and jogged up the stairs. I'd have to learn how to make it.

I'D JUST threaded my tie through my collar and realized there was going to be a problem when there was a knock on my door.

"Beauchamp, can you give me a hand with—" I opened the door. "Hyde!"

He ran his gaze from the black socks on my feet to my tousled hair and gave a low wolf whistle.

"Oh, um...." I could feel my cheeks heat up, and I raised a self-conscious hand to smooth my hair, barely managing to repress a wince as I used my bandaged hand. "Thank you. I thought you were going to be busy downstairs."

"It could wait. I wanted to thank you for this." He held out his left wrist. Fastened snugly around it was the ID bracelet I'd bought him earlier. How could I have forgotten it was in Granddad's suit pocket? Beauchamp must have given it to Hyde. Although why he hadn't brought it up to me....

"Do you like it?"

"Very much so. I like even more what's engraved on the back."

My cheeks had begun to cool, but at those words, they felt as if they were on fire. "You weren't supposed to see that."

"No?"

"No. Not until we'd had a fight."

"I don't understand, Kipp."

"I was going to put the bracelet on you myself, and I was going to tell you to never take it off."

"Okay. No, not okay. You've completely lost me. Why didn't you want me to see what was on the back?"

I sighed. "See, we'd have this horrible quarrel, and I'd tell you it was time for you to take off the bracelet. You'd think it was because we were through, but then I'd turn it over and you'd read what was engraved on it."

"So it was to prove to me that no matter what happened, you'd...."

"Yes." I bit my lip. Was this going to strike him as unrestrained?

"Do you really think we'll have a horrible quarrel?"

"Don't all married couples quarrel?"

"Never having been married, I couldn't say. But... 'horrible', Kipp?"

"I'm sorry. That was stupid."

"Actually, I think it's one of the sweetest things anyone has ever wanted to do for me." He leaned toward me, and I tipped my head back. For a moment I stared into his eyes, and then I let mine close.

Nothing happened, and I opened them. "Hyde?"

"You look tired, Kipp. I'm sorry. This afternoon was too much for you. I should have brought you directly home so you could have rested."

"I'm not a baby, you know. But I can always sleep in tomorrow if I have to." I was a little tired, though. Who'd have thought an allergic reaction could take so much out of a person?

"Nevertheless, I should have—"

"Hyde." I rested my forearms on his shoulder and smiled into his eyes. I wanted to feel his body against mine; I wanted that so badly, but I forced myself to keep some distance between us. "I'm fine."

"And you're really pleased with the arrangements?" He smoothed his fingers through my hair.

"Yes, I'm really pleased." God that felt good! For a second I thought I was going to melt into a puddle at his feet! "Well, except for the wines Mr. Stuart selected. It's a good thing I got to take a look at the wine list. He was trying to put one over on you."

"Oh?" The word was ice cold, although his eyes burned with anger.

I decided the hell with it and tentatively raised a hand—not the one with the bandage, because that would be rough against his skin—to stroke his cheek, ready to back off at the least sign that I was overstepping the bounds by touching him. Instead, he brought his hand to mine to keep it there and turned his head.

"It's... it's all right." Was my voice shaky because of how warm his lips were against my palm? "I'm replacing the wines he selected with bottles from Granddad's cellar."

"You don't have to do that."

"Actually, I'm not. Granddad is. You haven't paid Mr. Stuart the entire amount for the wedding, have you?" He shook his head, the motion causing his lips to graze over my palm repeatedly. I could hardly speak for how aroused I was. "Just... just deduct the cost of the wine," I murmured huskily.

"You're a wonder, do you know that?" He squeezed my hand before releasing it.

"But... I'm just me."

"Yes, you are." He tipped up my chin, and I closed my eyes and savored the soft pressure of his lips across mine.

"Hyde." In spite of myself, I leaned into the kiss.

He pressed one last kiss to my mouth, and then raised his head. "Now, what do you need a hand with?"

"Hmm?" I still had my eyes closed. Abruptly, I roused to the here and now. Damn! I straightened and held out an end of my tie. "I'm having trouble tying this." The bandage on my left palm made it a little awkward.

He took both ends and fashioned it into a Windsor knot.

"Thank you."

"You're welcome. Where are your cufflinks?"

"On my dresser."

He went to it and opened the box that contained the links and the tie clip. "They're very old-fashioned."

"They're Granddad's." I'd always liked them, liked the small sapphires that formed an elegant spiral; I'd been pleased and surprised and very touched when Beauchamp said Granddad had called and suggested I borrow them.

"In that case, I apologize. But they're still old-fashioned. Wear these instead." He took a jeweler's box from his pocket. Inside were cufflinks and a matching tie bar. They were platinum, and I took out a cufflink. *KL* and *HW* were entwined around each other.

"Ah!"

"Do you like them?"

"Oh, yes!" I handed him the cufflink and held out a wrist. He was smiling a little as he fastened the cuffs, and once he was done, once the tie bar was also in place, I stood in front of the mirror above my dresser and admired how they looked.

"They're not as romantic as the gift you gave me...."

"They're absolutely perfect, Hyde!" And I thought, *The hell with what Sir said*, and I kissed him.

AT 7:30 P.M. the doorbell rang, and since Beauchamp was busy in the kitchen, I hurried to answer it.

"Mindy, welcome." I kissed her cheek when she offered it to me. "You look lovely." She was wearing a lavender sheath that nipped in her waist and flowed over her hips. Geoff couldn't seem to take his eyes off her. I'd never seen such a fatuous look on his face.

"Thank you." She blushed. "You look very nice too."

Geoff spared me a glance and nodded as he shook my hand. "Father would approve." I was wearing the midnight-blue suit with a white shirt. "I even think he'd appreciate your choice of tie."

I'd completely forgotten ties, but Ian hadn't. He'd pulled out a dozen, in solids, stripes and prints. I'd been trying to choose between a green and gold paisley, a black with tiny red roses, and a blue that he said matched my eyes, when Hyde joined us, looked them over with unconcern, and said, "We'll take them all."

So now the tie I wore was a navy-blue one with diagonal burgundy stripes banded by slim gray stripes.

"How are you feeling, Kipp?" she asked.

"Fine… oh, you mean because of the reaction I had last night? I am fine, thank you."

"You gave us all a scare!"

Surely not everyone, and although I didn't say it, Hyde must have thought so as well.

"Well, he gave *me* a scare." Hyde came up beside me and slid an arm around my waist, his hand comfortable on my hip.

I leaned into him, losing myself in his honey-brown gaze. "Mindy, do you know my fiancé?"

"I'm sorry, no. We haven't met."

"In that case, Melinda Richardson, Hyde Wyndham."

"It's a pleasure to meet you, Mindy."

"Mr. Wyndham."

"Call me Hyde. We're going to be in-laws, after all." He smiled at her, and although she smiled back at him, I thought it was a little hesitant.

Apparently Geoff did as well, because he went to her. "I'm starved."

"Beauchamp has the hors d'oeuvres set out on the side porch," I told him.

Mindy's eyes lit up. "That's a wonderful idea! It's such a beautiful, balmy May evening."

"It is, isn't it? I think we've lucked out this spring." Geoff offered her his arm.

"I just hope our wedding day will be as lovely." The expression on her face as she looked at him…. Geoff had said she'd had a crush on him forever, but this was the way a woman looked at the man she loved. She linked her arm with his and threaded their fingers together. He led her through the house to the side porch.

"Me too," I said. "Um… I mean, my wedding. Of course, I hope you have good weather too…."

Hyde chucked. "Come on, blue eyes. There's an hors d'oeuvre with your name on it." He leaned closer to me and murmured, "I spoke with Beauchamp earlier. No shellfish, Kipp."

"Thank you." I'd known that from looking at the offerings, but I appreciated his care of me. He was going to be the best partner, and I was going to love being married to him.

"Wine?"

"Yes, please, Hyde." I accepted a glass of the chilled Riesling Beauchamp had left.

"You can have a glass too, if you like, Mindy," Geoff told her.

"No, thank you. Daddy wouldn't like it. I'll have a Coke, please."

Beauchamp, being the quintessential butler, had put a can of Coke next to the Riesling in the ice bucket.

Geoff popped off the top and poured it for her with a flourish and a polished twist of his wrist, and she jumped up and kissed him.

How would Hyde react if I jumped up and kissed him like that in front of family and friends?

Well, I could do it on Sunday after we exchanged vows.

I took a prosciutto crostini with lemony fennel slaw, and picked off the slaw. Beauchamp had never cared for me being around him in the kitchen, but when shooing me out was unsuccessful, he'd given in and taught me how to slice the baguettes and brush them with olive oil. He'd place them in the oven to brown, because he didn't trust me to not burn my fingers. I'd always loved the toasted rounds.

Then I took another one and fed it to Hyde. He encircled my wrist with his fingers and held me there as he took neat bites of the hors d'oeuvre.

Mindy enjoyed the caramelized onion tarts with apples, and as a matter of fact, she appeared to be fascinated by them. She kept her eyes on them, constantly making "yummy" sounds, and sending only occasional glances at me or Hyde.

Geoff kept going back for the spiced beef empanadas with lime sour cream, and in between bites he brought me up to date with what was going on with Llewellyn, Inc. Mindy hung on his every word, and Hyde seemed interested. I pretended to be, but mostly I watched Hyde eat the various finger foods and unconsciously lick his fingers.

At eight, Beauchamp came out onto the porch. "Dinner is served, Mr. Kipp."

Geoff seemed taken aback. Because Beauchamp addressed me rather than him? Or because he'd addressed me as "Mr."?

"Thank you, Beauchamp." I offered Mindy my arm.

Hyde grinned at my brother, probably enjoying Geoff's surprise at the realization that I was host this evening, and offered Geoff his arm.

Geoff gave a snort of laughter. "Thanks, I think I can manage on my own."

And we all went in to dinner.

CHAPTER 31

SINCE it was just the four of us, we ate in the informal dining room. I sat at the head of the table with Mindy on my right and Geoff on my left. Hyde sat at the bottom, but in reality he wasn't more than six feet away from me.

"Do you need help cutting your lamb chops, Kipp?"

"I can do it for him, Wynd—" Geoff flinched as I kicked his ankle under the table, and he changed what he'd been about to say. "Hyde."

"Thank you both, but I think I can manage." Truthfully, it was even more awkward than trying to tie my tie, but I wasn't having my fiancé and my brother getting into a pissing contest over who would cut my meat for me.

"If you need any help?"

"Yes, Hyde. I'll ask you to do it for me."

Geoff grumbled under his breath.

"Well, really, Geoff, doesn't it make sense? I'm not your little brother anymore."

"You'll always be my little brother." He reached over and gripped the back of my neck gently.

"Thank you." I smiled at him and Mindy, but mostly at Hyde. "Bon appétit, everyone."

After her reticence on the porch, Mindy became very talkative. However, all she wanted to talk about was her wedding and the changes she planned to make to their suite in Llewellyn Manor—

"You'll be living there?" That came as a surprise to me. Didn't every bride want a home of her own?

"Yes. Father Marcus thinks it will be more convenient if he needs to talk to Geoff...."

I lost the rest of what she was saying. All I could think was that it was a good thing Sir's first name wasn't William. Father William. I tried to swallow my laughter and nearly inhaled my wine.

Geoff took that opportunity to nudge my ankle.

"Sorry," I whispered. "I apologize, Mindy. That was inappropriate of me. You were saying?"

She looked a little confused, but continued. "We'll have the entire third floor. And as a wedding gift, Grandpapa is giving me a blank check to redecorate."

"That's Mrs. Richardson's father, Kipp," Geoff told me. "I don't know if you're aware that Jacob Richardson passed away a few years ago."

"Granddad mentioned it yesterday." Good grief, was it really only the day before? I couldn't believe how much had happened in such a short space of time.

"Oh, uh...." He looked uncomfortable. Well, he *could* have called to keep me informed.

"That was a horrible Christmas. It was right after Daddy had that quarrel with Daniel." Mindy looked so sad. "They'd locked themselves in Daddy's study, you see, and all we could hear were raised voices. Finally, Daniel came out looking sick. He kissed Mummy, hugged me, and said good-bye. I... I didn't think he meant *good-bye* good-bye, but he hasn't been home since then."

I sat staring at her. How could she so casually reveal what went on in her family? Sir would have seen me locked in my room for a month if I'd done anything like that.

Geoff touched the back of my hand.

"What?"

He leaned closer to me and whispered, "We're her family now."

"Yes, of course." I could feel a blush rising in my cheeks. I should have realized that, especially since she'd called Granddad "grandfather". I reached for my glass and took a sip of wine.

"As for Grandfather Jacob," Mindy was saying, "he yelled something about it all being Daddy's fault and that he should have shipped him off to England sooner than he had. After that, he stormed out of the house. 'Stormed.' That sounds positively Victorian, doesn't it? But that was just what he did. Of course Daddy wanted to make it up with him, but Grandfather Jacob must have had a heart attack on the drive home. He crashed into a tree." She sighed.

"Fortunately, that tree was all he hit," Geoff muttered.

"I'm sorry for your loss, Mindy," Hyde said. But of course he must have known about that, and he couldn't say he was sorry to hear of the old bastard's passing, because after what Jacob Richardson had done to him, he wouldn't be sorry.

"I'm sorry also, Mindy. As I said, I only heard yesterday." In an effort to cheer her, I asked, "Will your other grandfather be here for your wedding?"

"Oh yes. He couldn't be there when Mummy and Daddy got married, but he's always said he'd be at my wedding come hell or high water." She giggled. "He'll be flying over about a week before the wedding."

"That's nice."

"I can't wait until he gets here. I want to show him what I plan to do with our suite. It's going to look wonderful." She paused to sip her soda before asking, "And where are you going to live, Kipp?"

I met Hyde's eyes across the table. "Wherever Hyde wants to live."

"Kipp, I don't...." Geoff looked torn.

"Don't what?"

"I...." He shook his head and reached for his wine glass.

I laid my fingers on his wrist. He'd be doing the driving, and I didn't want him to get into an accident. "I'll be all right. Don't worry."

"You're my baby brother. Of course I'm going to worry."

"Why now, Geoff?"

"I've always worried about you. I just… I couldn't show it."

"Dysfunction Junction," I muttered under my breath and shook my head. Hyde narrowed his eyes as he watched me, and I forced a smile. This conversation was pointless. "Mindy, would you care for more roasted potatoes?"

"Thank you. Beauchamp is an excellent cook."

"Yes, he is."

"Are you going to continue college?" she asked.

"I only have a year left to go on my degree, so I'd like to."

"And as long as I have a computer and a phone, I can conduct business anywhere." Hyde picked up the bottle of Cabernet Sauvignon and raised an eyebrow.

"Yes, please." I started to stand, to go to him, but he held up a hand to stop me, then came and filled my glass.

"So if you want to go back to Armand U, we can find a place to live in Charlestown for your senior year."

"Thank you." He did have such lovely honey-brown eyes.

"You're welcome." He tugged a lock of my hair, then bent forward and stroked a kiss over my mouth. He winked at me and strolled back to his seat.

I could have wriggled like a happy puppy. I touched my tongue to my upper lip, and Geoff nudged my ankle again. Only then did I remember I had guests.

"Sorry. What about you, Mindy? Mindy?"

Her mouth had dropped open, and she stared from Hyde back to me. She put her fork down and swallowed. "Excuse me? I'm sorry. It's just that I've never seen two men kiss."

"What, never?" Hyde wasn't pleased.

Neither was Geoff. "I think we should change the subject!"

I wasn't going to let this go. "Hyde and I are going to be married, just as you and my brother are. No one objects if you kiss, but my fiancé can't kiss me?"

"Yes, I know." Mindy looked like she was ready to cry. "I just didn't think... I'm sorry."

"No, I'm sorry." I patted her hand. I'd made a guest uncomfortable; Granddad would be unhappy with me. And Sir would have hammered home that this was what happened when one didn't control oneself.

The wedding was on Sunday, but Hyde could call it off if he realized how abandoned I could be. I had to.... Hyde was trying to catch my eye. I sent a smile his way, avoiding his gaze.

"Geoff's right," I said. "We should change the subject. What college will you be going to, Mindy?"

"Oh, I'm not going to college." There were no words to describe how relieved she looked to be talking about anything other than men kissing. "I'll be staying home and keeping house for Geoff and our children. We want to start a family immediately. That's partly because I want my children to know their great-grandfathers. Life is so fragile. I hope Grandfather Martin will still be here."

"And you'll be the first lady of Martinsburg, so there will be a lot of things to do for the city," Geoff murmured as he stretched a hand across the table to take her hand.

Sir would have disapproved of that action, and Geoff should have known that. From the time I was permitted to use a knife at the dinner table, it had been pounded into me that we always kept a hand on our lap unless we were using both fork and knife. Geoff wasn't setting up his fiancée to face our father's displeasure, was he?

"Well, I hope it works out for you," I said. She was a sweet girl, in spite of having Aaron Richardson for a father and Daniel Richardson for a brother.

"Oh, it will!" She was so sure. I was only three years older than her, but I felt ancient. "You must be thrilled about tomorrow evening's dinner party. Father Marcus gave one for us about a year ago so we could officially announce our engagement, and we had the most delicious food! He had it catered by Chantilly Lace. Mrs. Wales is a gem, and I'm so pleased she'll stay with us, but a party that size would have been too much for her."

I wondered how many people Sir was inviting for my engagement. I had the feeling it wouldn't be a quarter as large as Geoff's.

"Geoff, Mindy tells me you'll be stopping in Boston on your honeymoon." I hoped he'd take that as the olive branch I intended.

"We are. We're going to see Mindy's brother."

"Will you spend your entire honeymoon there?" I still couldn't believe Daniel was gay.

"No, just a couple of days. Then we'll be flying down to New York. I've booked a room at the Algonquin Hotel."

"It's so exciting!" Mindy was positively bubbling now. "We're going to see the Round Table and everything! And Geoff got us tickets for *Wicked, The Lion King,* and *Mary Poppins*! And we're going to ride around Central Park in one of those horse-drawn carriages! And we'll go to the Statue of Liberty and the Museum of Natural History."

"It sounds like you'll have a lot of fun." And it did, but it also sounded more like a school excursion. My boarding school had arranged for us to spend four days in Manhattan. I was glad I'd been able to go on that trip, because at the end of that term, Sir had decided I should go to Martinsburg High and had pulled me out.

And then I realized, of course! Mindy was underage. Geoff wouldn't be able to take her to any of the popular clubs in Manhattan.

Well, at least Hyde wouldn't have that problem with me, no matter where we went.

"Where do you want to go on our honeymoon, Kipp?" Hyde was watching me steadily.

My jaw dropped, and I finally met his eyes. "I never thought...."

Geoff started laughing. "You are entitled to a honeymoon, kiddo."

"Well, yes, but this has happened so fast!" I was dazzled. "Hawaii? Perhaps Australia to go snorkeling in the Great Barrier Reef?" I grinned at Hyde. "Or Las Vegas?" Actually, any place that had a bed would be fine, but I could hardly say that in front of my brother and his fiancée. "Can we discuss it later?"

"Of course. It won't take long to make the arrangements."

"You'll leave it all to Armitage?"

"Of course," he repeated.

I couldn't stop grinning. Geoff looked at me, surprise on his face.

"I don't think I've ever seen you this happy, Kipp."

"That's because I've never been this happy." I met Hyde's eyes across the table. He raised his glass of wine to me, and I pursed my lips and blew him a kiss.

GEOFF and Mindy lingered, until finally Hyde said, "Llewellyn, I'm sure you want to kiss your fiancée good night. Please go so I can do the same with mine."

Mindy giggled. I'd thought she was having a hard time accepting that Hyde and I were a couple who did couple things—well, who *would* do couple things once we were married. It was probably one thing for her to know a portion of the population was gay, but to actually sit across from them at the dinner table....

But by the time Beauchamp brought out the lemon lush, she seemed more comfortable with us.

Geoff, on the other hand, looked like he was having a hard time keeping the lamb he'd eaten down.

He forced a smile. "Sounds like a good idea, Wyndham." He glowered at me. "And if he can call me by my last name, I sure as hell can call him by his!"

I held up my hands. I wasn't going to get into another argument tonight.

"All right, then. We'll see you tomorrow evening."

There was a chorus of "Good nights," and then Hyde closed the door behind them.

"Alone at last." And he reached for me.

"Beg pardon, sir."

I couldn't help laughing. Beauchamp stood there.

"Yes, Beauchamp?"

"I'm about to retire for the evening. Mr. Martin always preferred that I lock up when Master Kipp was here." But I saw the look in his eyes before he turned his gaze over Hyde's shoulder.

I felt the laughter fade. Even Granddad didn't trust me to control myself.

"You may as well go, Hyde. I'll—"

"Very well, Beauchamp. Go lock up the rest of the house."

"I already have, sir."

"I see." Hyde's eyes no longer looked like warm honey. In fact, it suddenly felt as if the temperature in the room had dropped twenty degrees. "In that case, Go. And Do It. Again."

"Very good, sir." Beauchamp had the strangest look on his face. He coughed lightly, turned, and left us.

"Now, where were we?" Hyde's voice sent shivers down my spine, but I couldn't afford to lose control.

"You were about to leave." Beauchamp had saved me from making the biggest mistake of my life. Too bad he hadn't been around when I'd let Daniel talk me into going to the movies with him. As much as I wanted to kiss Hyde and keep kissing him until neither of us could see straight, I kept it to a peck and stepped back.

"Not quite yet." He pulled me into his arms.

All right. One kiss. One kiss wouldn't send me out of control.

Only it did. One kiss led to another, and another, and another until I was rubbing myself against him shamelessly and uttering whimpers and moans I'd never have expected could come from my mouth.

Finally, humming with pleasure, he said, "I'd better go now." He unwound my arms from around his neck.

"Must you?" I opened my eyes and had to blink a number of times to bring them into focus. "Please stay." I slid my arms around his waist.

He laughed. "I like you like this. But if we don't want to shock Beauchamp any more than we already have—"

"His quarters are at the other end of the house, and you know my room is in the west wing. Please, Hyde?" Daringly I let my hand wander below his waist, over the curve of his ass. The muscles were firm, and I wanted to feel them naked under my palms as he pushed into me. "Please?"

He removed my hands from his body and kissed me, a chaste kiss he could have given anyone: his mother, a child—but not his fiancé.

I'd done it. I'd disgusted him. I held myself stiffly, waiting for him to tell me what a disappointment I was to him.

"I'll see you tomorrow." He dropped a kiss on the tip of my nose—was my nose more appealing than my lips?—turned and opened the door, and left.

Wait, what happened to "baby"? To "blue eyes"? Shit. He couldn't even fumble behind him for the doorknob because he couldn't take his eyes off me?

I watched as he got in his SUV, gave a nonchalant wave, and drove away, and then I shut and locked the front door. So what if Beauchamp was going to double-check it?

I went up to my room, stripped, showered, and changed into my pajamas.

CHAPTER 32

WE WERE naked on my queen-size bed, and I was on top, my knees framing his hips. I buried my fingers in his thick, soft hair and covered his lips and cheeks and jaw with hungry, uninhibited kisses.

"I love you," he murmured against my throat, and I groaned.

No one had ever....

His dick was hard and slick against mine, and his long fingers imprisoned them. I drove into his grasp, desperate for the orgasm that was a glimmering promise almost within my reach.

"That's it," he whispered, his voice hoarse and unrecognizable.

I'd brought him to this state! I'd wielded this power.

And when he took it from me—when he fondled my ass with his other hand, tracing the crevice between my buttocks, finding my opening and teasing it—I surrendered it willingly.

I spread my legs wider and humped against him, frantic now to come.

"Almost there, babe. Are you—"

"Yes, I'm—"

Unrestrained! *I could hear Sir shouting at me, and the thought of him coming across me and my lover in such an intimate moment had me scrambling off the warm body beneath me.*

Unrestrained! *Who would want someone like that?*

I curled into a ball, weeping. No one. Of course, no one.

But Hyde had said he loved me. I wiped the tears from my eyes and crawled toward the body on my bed. Wouldn't he—

He raised his head, and I looked into gray eyes, not brown.

Oh, my God, I'd been having sex with Daniel? *Nausea roiled in my stomach. I clapped a hand over my mouth, rolled away from him, and—*

Toppled off the bed.

I shot to my feet and then fell over as my pajama pants tangled around my legs. Pajamas? But I'd been....

I yanked them up as I whipped my head around, searching the shadowy corners. I even looked in the closet and under my bed, but except for me, my room was empty.

A dream? It had been a... a fucking *dream*? I should have known. Hyde had never said he loved me.

I sat down on the edge of the bed and cradled my head in my hands. That was the last time I'd have a glass of dessert wine with the second slice of lemon lush so late at night. I'd had such indigestion that I'd had to go in search of a bottle of antacids. As luck would have it, I'd found them in one of the downstairs bathrooms, and on my way back to my bedroom, I'd stubbed my toe so badly that I thought I'd broken it. The upshot of that was I'd gone back downstairs to the kitchen for some ice and had spent an hour icing my toe.

And then as tired as I was, I couldn't fall asleep. I'd tossed and turned until it was almost dawn. My brother didn't approve—was I doing the right thing? My father thought I didn't have an ounce of control—was that going to scare Hyde away?

And when I'd finally fallen asleep, it was to have that dream.

My head was pounding, and I peered through my fingers at the clock radio on the nightstand. It was 8:08 a.m. My room wasn't very light, but it was on the west side of the house, and even at the height of summer it wouldn't be much lighter than this at this time.

My cell phone rang, and I jumped and slid off the bed again. God*damn* it!

I grabbed the phone and touched the screen to answer it. "Hello." My voice sounded like I'd swallowed broken glass.

"Kipp? It's Hyde. Are you all right? You sound—"

"I'm fine. You woke me up."

"Oh? Dreaming about me, blue eyes?" Dammit, he was in a chipper mood.

"What did you want?"

"Not a morning person, baby?"

Why was he calling me pet names when I'd cheated on him? Wait, did a dream count? Oh, God, I was losing my mind!

"Sorry. I had a bad dream."

"I'm sorry to hear that. If you have bad dreams after we're married, I'll wake you with kisses."

He could have done that last night, if he'd stayed with me! I only just managed to bite back the words.

"Kipp?"

"Sorry, Hyde. I've got a bit of a headache." And then I regretted saying that. He was going to think I was hungover from the wine I'd drunk the night before.

"I'm sorry to hear that too. I was going to pick you up for breakfast."

"*No*! I mean, thank you, but I wouldn't be good company. And I don't have a hangover!"

"All right." He sounded amused.

"I... I hurt my hand when I fell out of bed." If I told him about my indigestion, he was going to think I was always getting sick, and he wouldn't want to have anything to do with me.

"Wait, you fell out of bed? That must have been a really bad dream! Did you pull the stitches?"

I looked at the bandage on my palm, which was staining red. "No."

"All right. I'd like to pick you up for lunch, but—"

"I... Look, Hyde, I'm not at my best right now. I'm... I'm going to go back to bed." I waited, hoping to hear him say, "Well, then, I'll come and join you," but he didn't.

What he did say was, "In that case I'll see you this evening."

Not before then? *Well, fine.* I'd just show him I didn't need him. For *anything.* "All right," I said coolly. And then I said, "Um... I'll see you at the manor, then?"

"Of course not. I'll pick you up at Silver Birch at a quarter to seven."

"Why so early?"

"Your grandfather is coming with us."

Right. Hyde had called him while I was choosing shirts, and Granddad said he wanted to be there.

"I know he told me he's feeling well enough, but is he?"

"According to his oncologist, he'll be fine as long as he takes it easy."

"Hyde. Thank you."

"Don't be silly. Do you need a doctor to see to those stitches? Or is that allergy kicking in again?"

"No. I'm... I'll be all right. I just need a little more sleep."

"Okay. Listen, Kipp. I...."

I held my breath, waiting to hear what he was going to say.

"I'll see you later." And he hung up.

I did something I had never done in my life. I hurled my cell phone across the room, breaking not only it but the window it hit as well.

I FOUND Beauchamp in the kitchen. "A window in my room is broken. Would you mind calling for a glazier?"

"I'll see to it, Mr. Kipp."

"And I'll need to borrow the Porsche." I'd drive to the mall and get a new cell phone.

"Very good."

"And would you bring Granddad's black suit to Hospice? And whatever else he's going to need: socks, shoes, shirt, tie? And remind him Hyde and I will pick him up at seven."

He nodded. To my surprise, he took my hand and turned it over. "Tsk. You'll need a fresh bandage for this."

"It's fine."

"It's bleeding."

"I said it's all right. I'll change the bandage later."

"Very well. Would you care for some breakfast?"

Not really, but I'd better eat something. "I'll make myself some toast."

He poured a cup of coffee and put it on the table. He stood there, holding out his hand.

"What?" I was being surly, but Jesus, wasn't I entitled to be out of sorts once in a while?

"Some ibuprofen, Mr. Kipp."

"I don't have a hangover!"

"No, but you look like you've gone a few rounds with whatever is disturbing you, and you didn't come out the winner."

I'd known Beauchamp all my life; he was only a couple of years younger than Granddad. How could I tell him to fuck off? I swiped the caplets from his palm, tossed them into my mouth, and washed them down with the coffee. "Happy?"

He bit back a smile. "You're very like Miss Beth."

"My mother?"

"Yes. Many were the mornings after when I'd give her a Tylenol."

"Mother had mornings after? Who'd she have the evenings before with?" I was willing to bet it hadn't been Sir.

"I'm sure I don't know." For a second he had been almost warm, but now he was back to his usual stiff self. "I'm the butler, not *her* father."

"Right." I finished the coffee and got up. "I'll skip breakfast. Don't forget Granddad's stuff when you go."

"Master Kipp...."

We were back to that, were we? I didn't need him to call me that to remind me I was acting childish. I'd broken my cell phone as well as a window, I'd pulled the stitches in my hand, and on top of that, my wedding was a few days away and my groom seemed fine spending the time away from me.

I walked out of the kitchen.

CHAPTER 33

IT HADN'T been a good day, and there was still the dinner party at the manor this evening. No matter what, I had to face it.

The only good thing was that even though my phone was wrecked, the SIM card wasn't; I was able to transfer my contacts to my new phone. And I was able to keep my number.

After the new phone was activated, I discovered that someone—not Hyde, so I didn't pay it much attention—had been trying to reach me all afternoon. Hyde had called once more during the morning and three times in the afternoon.

Dammit. Then again, why had he called four times? Did he.... I thought back to last night when I'd groped him. Did he not like me touching him like that?

I puzzled over that while I stood in line at Sbarro in the food court at the mall, ordering a slice of pizza and a medium Coke when the girl behind the counter got to me and asked what I wanted. After I paid for it, I found an empty table, and while I nibbled on my pizza, I programmed my ringtones, not that there were that many people I actually cared to give specific tones to: Hyde, Granddad, Geoff, Hunter.

When my phone rang shortly after I returned home to Silver Birch, it was the generic ringtone. I glanced at the screen. The area code wasn't local, but even though I didn't recognize the number, I picked up anyway. Hyde could be using someone else's phone.

Well, he could be.

"Hello?"

"It's Armitage, Mr. Llewellyn."

Oh. All right. "Good afternoon, Ms. Armitage. How may I help you?"

"I've been trying to reach you all afternoon."

"On Hyde's phone?"

"Oh, no, I've been using mine."

Was this it? Was Hyde breaking our engagement, and having his personal assistant do it? Well, it was better than being texted or faxed by him. I stiffened my spine and waited for the ax to fall.

"When I couldn't contact you, I called Silver Birch. Mr. Wyndham was becoming a little concerned when he couldn't reach you on your cell phone."

"Really?"

"Oh, yes."

"My... uh... my phone stopped working and I had to get a new one."

"Ah. Mr. Wyndham will be relieved it was nothing more than that."

"Really?"

"Yes." There was a smile in her voice. She wouldn't smile if she was going to give me bad news, would she? "I must say, he's very fond of you, Mr. Llewellyn."

"Really?" She was going to think I was an idiot, repeating myself like this, but.... Had I been overreacting? Usually I had a better grip on my emotions, but between an unexpected engagement and a wedding planned in less than a week's time, finding out I was deathly allergic to shellfish, a night spent in the hospital and another spent suffering from acid reflux topped off by that stupid dream....

I wanted to smack myself. Of course I was overreacting. I was letting Sir get in my head. What was wrong with me? Shouldn't I know better after all this time?

All those miserable things—not the engagement or wedding, but the stress of the past few days and my nerves getting the better of me— they had to mean that by the time Sunday came around, nothing worse could happen and my wedding day would go off without a hitch. *Didn't it?* I gave it more careful thought.

Yes, it did.

Meanwhile, Ms. Armitage was saying, "I've never seen him act this way with anyone he's dated before. And of course yours is his first engagement."

"Um...." Ms. Armitage was Hyde's employee, not his friend. If he hadn't told her about Aaron Richardson, then I wasn't going to say anything either.

"Although perhaps I should say yours is the first engagement that will come to its natural conclusion."

So she was aware. I felt obliged to say, "Well, he did care about his first fiancé."

"Who didn't care enough about him to stand by him."

"It didn't matter. Once Hyde's fiancé became engaged to someone else—"

"He was engaged to Mr. Wyndham first."

"So you're saying.... What are you saying?"

"Mr. Richardson didn't love him enough. Mr. Wyndham deserves better than that. And if I may be frank? I think he's found that 'better' in you."

"Really?" Suddenly I felt much better. After all, *I* was the one he was marrying.

"Really. At any rate, I just wanted to inform you that Mr. Wyndham has been called away."

"On business?"

She made a noncommittal sound.

"Sir—my father isn't going to be pleased that Hyde will miss the party."

"Oh, Mr. Wyndham won't miss it. He will be a little late, however. He wanted me to contact you so you wouldn't be waiting for him to come for you and your grandfather. Shall I arrange for transportation for you?"

"No, that won't be necessary." I had to sit down, I was so relieved. "I'll take one of Granddad's cars." I was more comfortable driving the Porsche, although Granddad preferred the Mercedes. Beauchamp drove it now, so it would be in running condition. Once Granddad had gone into Hospice, Beauchamp told me, there hadn't been a need for him to keep a chauffeur, full- or part-time. I missed Ferguson. Between him and Pierce, they'd done a good job teaching me to drive.

"Very good," Ms. Armitage said. "I didn't have the opportunity to congratulate you on your coming nuptials. Congratulations."

"Thank you."

"I... I'd just like to say I've never seen Mr. Wyndham this happy."

"Really?" Oh, God, I was repeating myself again.

"Yes. He's a very reserved man. I know this because I've worked with him from the beginning," she hurried to explain. "Now, to hear him whistling and laughing out loud.... Well, I'm sure you and he will be very happy."

"Uh... today?"

"Excuse me?"

"Did he seem happy today?"

"Oh, very much so." I could hear the smile in her voice again.

All right, maybe he might not love me, but I made him happy, even if I couldn't keep from fondling his ass.

"Oh, and as soon as you decide on your honeymoon destination, let me know; I'll make all the arrangements."

"Do you know if Hyde has any favorite places?" It shouldn't be all about me. He was the groom as well.

"He's traveled all over the world on business."

"But is there any one place that he keeps going back to?"

"Well, he did enjoy the time he spent in Fiji."

"All right. Thank you." I couldn't tell her to go ahead and make the arrangements without talking to Hyde first. And then I thought, *why not*? "Ms. Armitage, Fiji it is. Please arrange everything?"

"Yes, I will. There's this lovely little island that has a single cottage on it—"

"Has Hyde been there with anyone?" I was startled by the flash of jealousy that seared through me.

"Oh, no, he has no idea... I'll tell you a little secret, Mr. Llewellyn. I don't travel, but I love to make plans. That island...." Her sigh was dreamy.

"Is there anyone you'd like to go there with?"

"Yes, but I'm afraid he doesn't see me as anything more than Mr. Wyndham's competent Armitage." She paused for a moment, and then said, "Please excuse me. I'm a foolish woman."

"I strongly doubt that." As a matter of fact, she sounded like a really nice lady. I'd have to talk to Hyde about this. Maybe he'd know who she was referring to and would give the guy a boot in the ass. Meanwhile, I didn't want Ms. Armitage to know what I was thinking. "Well, I'm sure you're very busy. Thank you again for taking the time to call me."

"You're welcome." She was once again Hyde's competent Armitage.

"By the way, you're coming to the wedding, aren't you?"

"Yes, I am."

"Great. I look forward to seeing you then. Good-bye."

"Good-bye, Mr. Llewellyn."

I disconnected the call and then dialed Promise Hospice. "This is Kipp Llewellyn. May I have Bradley Martin's room?"

"One moment, please."

I tapped my foot restlessly and began counting the rings. I'd gotten to eight before someone finally picked up.

"Martin's Funeral Home."

"Wha—*Granddad*? Is that any way to answer the phone?" I really couldn't talk, considering how *I* answered it at times, but that wasn't funny! "And where were you?"

"I was in the bathroom. Kipp? Is something wrong?"

"No. Hyde's away, so—"

"Away where?"

"I don't know. His assistant didn't say. Anyway, I'll pick you up this evening, and I just wanted to make sure you're feeling well enough to do this. Are you? If you'd rather not go...."

"Of course I'll go! I wouldn't miss my favorite grandson's engagement party!" That was the only thing that had gotten me through the times Sir remembered he had a younger son—that there was someone who cared about me.

"All right. Beauchamp is bringing your black suit—"

"He's already brought it here."

"Where has the day gone?" I couldn't help smiling. "I'll pick you up at a quarter after seven. Granddad, I love you."

"Kipp, what's wrong?"

"Not a thing! Can't I tell my favorite grandfather that I love him? I have to go now. I'll see you later. Bye." I hung up and checked the clock. I had a few hours before I needed to start getting ready for my engagement party. Maybe I'd go ahead and finally have that nap.

CHAPTER 34

BEAUCHAMP tapped on my door, waking me from a fortunately dreamless sleep.

"I'm sorry to disturb you, Mr. Kipp, but you'll need to get ready." He hung up the midnight-blue suit I would be wearing.

"Did I spill anything on it?"

"No. I just gave it a good brushing, as I did your grandfather's suit before I brought it to him. Now, I've shined your shoes," he said as he set them neatly beneath my suit, "and ironed the shirt you chose to wear with this as well."

"Thank you." I swung my legs over the side of the bed and sat up. "Beauchamp, about this morning.... I apologize for being in such a bad mood."

"Mr. Kipp, you've never seen your grandfather when he was in a bad mood."

No, I hadn't, but I'd seen Sir.

"What you had was nothing more than a minor... a *very* minor... outburst."

Great. I couldn't even pitch a fit properly. I sighed. "Well, thank you."

"Not at all." He nodded and left me to get myself together.

I went into the bathroom down the hall, stripped off my clothes, and turned on the water. While I waited for it to heat up, I made sure my pockets were empty before I dropped jeans, shirt, and underwear down the laundry chute.

My palm was feeling better, but I didn't want to take a chance with it, so I put a latex glove on my left hand and wound a rubber band around my wrist so water wouldn't get inside.

As I showered, I wondered if Hyde had thought of me while he'd been showering yesterday. I tipped my head back and closed my eyes, letting the water pour down through my hair, and I thought of making love with Hyde in the shower. He was taller than me by about four or five inches, but if he bent his knees, or if I leaned forward and canted my hips, his dick would fit perfectly between my ass cheeks. *Mmm, yes.* I raised my hands to lather my scalp. Would he urge me to lean against the tiled walls and take me like that? Would he curl his fingers around my dick and leisurely jerk me off, or would he drop to his knees and go down on me?

The fantasy was as nice as yesterday's, but the actuality was better—being alone in my own bathroom, I could take full advantage of the images behind my eyelids.

I grinned and ran a soapy hand along my dick while I cradled my balls with the other, carefully because of the damned bandage and latex glove. I wanted to make it last, but picturing Hyde on my bed with me, *on* me, our fingers entwined, set me off like a firecracker, and I gasped and climaxed.

My legs were a little shaky, but I didn't mind. Still grinning, I rinsed off, turned off the water, and took a towel from the heated bar.

After I wiped the moisture from my hair and body, I leaned toward the mirror so I could see my reflection. Since I'd had the fan going, the mirror hadn't fogged up.

My facial hair was slightly darker than the hair on my head. I didn't have to shave often—it would take almost a week for me to cultivate enough to achieve the scruffy look, and would Hyde like that?—but as I ran my palm over my cheeks and jaw, I thought I wouldn't skip it today.

I stripped off the glove, put on a fresh bandage, and shaved, then splashed on some aftershave and applied deodorant.

Back in my bedroom, I plugged a set of miniature speakers into my little Zune player and turned it on.

A glance at the bedside clock told me I needed to get moving, and as I dressed, I began humming along about my brown-eyed handsome man.

THE cufflinks Hyde had given me were in my cuffs, and I was just inserting the tie bar when there was a tap on my bedroom door. Last night, when someone knocked on my door, it had been Hyde. Had he returned sooner than he'd anticipated?

I rushed to the door and yanked it open, but it was only Beauchamp. He raised both eyebrows at my appearance. I didn't even care that at least I wasn't the only one who couldn't raise a single eyebrow.

"This came for you, Mr. Kipp." He held out a florist's box. Through the clear plastic I could see a red rosebud nestled on a bed of white tissue paper.

"Is there a card?"

He handed me a small envelope. I opened it and took out the card.

I saw this and thought of you. It's appropriate, don't you think?—Hyde

Red, for true love? I tucked the card into my dresser mirror where I could look at it, then reached for the box and took out the rosebud, cradling it my hands. The scent was heady; I could get intoxicated from it.

What a relief that I'd gotten those pre-wedding jitters out of my system. The next time I saw Hyde, the hell with whatever Sir said, I was going to kiss him like he'd never been kissed!

"Would you like some help with that, Mr. Kipp?"

"Yes, please." I gave him the rosebud, slipped my arms into the sleeves of my suit jacket, and shrugged it over my shoulders.

He pinned the beautiful flower to my lapel. "You look—" For a second I thought he was going to hug me, but he didn't. What he did do was smooth his hands over the shoulders of my jacket, down the sleeves to the hem, and give them a tug. "Mr. Martin instructed me to give you this."

He held out his hand. In his palm was a man's platinum wedding band.

"He knew you wouldn't be likely to have time to shop for a ring for Mr. Wyndham."

"More likely he knew I'd never be able to afford something of this quality." I didn't need to look inside the band to know it was 950 platinum. "It's not his."

"No. He found it in Miss Beth's little keepsake box."

"But it's a man's ring."

"Yes." His voice cracked, and when I looked into his eyes, they were sheened with tears.

"Thank you, Beauchamp." I took the ring and put it in the inner pocket of my suit jacket. I'd thank Granddad when I saw him.

"Congratulations, Kipp. I...." His upper lip quivered for a moment. "I hope you'll both be very happy."

"Th-thank you." That was the first time he'd ever addressed me simply by my first name.

"I've brought the Mercedes around to the front for you," he continued briskly. "Now, I suggest you hurry. Your grandfather doesn't care to be kept waiting."

"No." I checked the mirror one last time to be certain my hair wasn't every which way, made sure I had my wallet, cell phone, and handkerchief—Hyde's handkerchief—then turned off the Zune and drew in a deep breath. "Thank you, Beauchamp."

"One second. Do you have your EpiPen?"

"No. I won't need it. It's dinner at the manor, and I'm sure Geoff told Mrs. Wales I can't eat shellfish." He murmured something I didn't catch. "Excuse me?"

"Nothing, Mr. Kipp. Have an enjoyable evening," he called as I trotted down the stairs.

I brought the rosebud to my nose and inhaled. Yes, I was certain that I would.

CHAPTER 35

WE WERE running late, but fortunately, Sir had Jackson and Pierce to do the valet parking. I left the keys in the ignition and ran around to the passenger side. Pierce had already opened Granddad's door.

"I'll help him, but would you mind holding this?" I handed Pierce the portable oxygen tank in its harness. "All right, here we go. Easy, Granddad."

"I can manage fine."

"Of course you can. Thanks," I said as Pierce slid the strap of the harness over my shoulder. "Ready, Granddad?"

"Yes." He was a little out of breath as he took my arm and we climbed the stairs to the front door of Llewellyn Manor.

Higgins had the door open. "Good evening, Mr. Martin, Master Kipp."

I was twenty-one years old. Was he going to call me "Master Kipp" until I was old and gray?

"Your father has been expecting you for the past half hour."

"He can blame a sick old man," Granddad said, frowning at him. "It took me some time to get dressed, and then I insisted that my grandson drive under the speed limit. I don't want to meet my Maker any sooner than I have to."

"As you say, sir." Higgins had always been cautious around Granddad. "Hors d'oeuvres are being served in the small dining room. The bar is also set up there. May I get you something to drink?"

"No, thank you," I said. "We'll help ourselves. Ready, Granddad?" I leaned down—when had I become the taller of us two?—

and whispered, "Do you need to sit down for a second?" His breathing was erratic, and his fingers were digging into my upper arm; it was all I could do not to flinch.

He exhaled audibly. "Let's go."

"Back to Hospice?"

"To the small dining room."

I blew out a quiet breath of my own so he wouldn't know how terrified I'd been that this was too much for him. "All right." I kept my pace slow. "Thank you for the ring, Granddad."

"No need to thank me. It's not as if it was an heirloom, which a good many of your mother's pieces were!"

"Please let it go. Be angry with Sir if you have to. Geoff did what he felt he needed to do."

He snorted, and I knew he was going to keep picking at it, so I began chatting about yesterday's shopping trip and the visit to the Saratoga Trunk, not really paying attention to what I was saying.

Whose ring was in my jacket pocket? Why had it been in my mother's keepsake box? Would it fit Hyde?

"And this suit you're wearing had been ordered by young Alec Stuart and never paid for?"

"Excuse me? Oh, yes."

"Hmm. I'd heard the Stuarts were having financial difficulties. I wonder if it's karma."

"I'm not following you, Granddad."

"This isn't the place to talk about it."

"Perhaps that's why Mr. Stuart tried to foist off second-rate wine on us."

"Perhaps, although I'd be more inclined to view it as a way for Cameron to get a bit of his own back, thinking he'd made a fool of Hyde. And I wouldn't be surprised if he planned to pass that information on to the Families."

At our wedding? So everyone would laugh at Hyde? I'd suspected as much, but to hear Granddad more or less confirm it…. I was furious.

And Granddad could see it. Was he going to tell me to control my temper?

"I think you should ask Hyde to let you deal with the bill for the Trunk."

"You're a devil, Granddad."

"I am, aren't I?" His eyes glittered wickedly. He patted my hand. "I'm a little hungry." We were at the small dining room.

"Small dining room" was a misnomer. There were twenty-five people already there, and it could easily hold twice as many.

"Bradley!"

"Martin!"

"Darling!"

"It's so good to see you!"

We were engulfed by the men and women Granddad had known forever, as well as their adult children, and I could feel his hand tremble on my arm.

"If you'll give Granddad some room? Let me get him settled, and you can chat with him one or two at a time."

They stared at me in consternation. I could tell what they were thinking. *How dare this boy instruct us in how to greet our friend?* More than ever I wished I could raise an eyebrow. I sighed. I'd have to settle for tipping my head back and peering down my nose at them.

"There's a chair—"

"Bradley, I'm pleased that you could join us!" My stomach flipped. Where had Sir come from? He hadn't been here just a moment ago. "You're looking well."

That was an outright lie. Granddad was gaunt, and even though his suit had been taken in, it still appeared to swim on him.

"I expected you sooner." Sir looked me up and down, and I felt as if I was a dust bunny the maid had missed in her cleaning.

"I'm sorry, Sir. I—"

"He was accommodating an old man," Granddad said. "Talk to Higgins. I don't have the energy to repeat myself. Kipp has always been a good grandson."

"If you say so."

"And speaking of grandsons, where is Geoffrey? And his lovely little fiancée?"

"Something came up and they couldn't make it." Sir's lips were a thin white line. He turned back to me. "Where's Wyndham, boy?"

"Hardly a boy, Marcus. He'll be a married man on Sunday."

"*If* Wyndham shows up. Don't tell me you've managed to misplace him already?"

"No, Sir. He'll be here. He's just running a little late."

"Humph. When I was engaged to your mother I made it a point to always be at her side."

Granddad gave him a sour look. "Kipp, will you help me to that chair you pointed out earlier?"

"Of course. If you'll excuse us, Sir? It looks like there's a nice selection of hors d'oeuvres, Granddad. I'll pick some out for you, and get you a glass of wine." I'd checked with his doctor while the aide had been helping him dress, and it wasn't a question of what he couldn't have but more whatever he felt like eating.

"Of course he was always at your mother's side. Like a goddamned leech," Granddad snarled under his breath. "What? Oh, yes, choose whatever looks good. And then go and tell Stuart I'll talk to him."

CHAPTER 36

GRANDDAD had a plate of hors d'oeuvres and a glass of white wine, and Mr. Stuart was off in a corner licking his wounds. I'd kept my expression bland, but it had been a pleasure hearing Granddad tear into him with cool precision.

A couple approached, and he gave a tight grin. "Robert, Helena. How nice of you to join us."

"We wouldn't dream of missing it," Mr. Alden said, although the look in his eyes denied that.

"Kipp, Helena is Robert's wife." She couldn't have been more than ten years older than me.

"You're the—I mean, you cute thing, you!" She fluttered her lashes.

"Mrs. Alden." They must have gotten married after I'd left for college. Mr. Alden had divorced his oldest son's mother about twenty-five years ago, and then he'd divorced Eddie's mother shortly before we'd started high school.

Martinsburg was a small city, and everyone knew everything about everybody.

Mr. Alden raked his gaze over me, his expression cold. "I imagine congratulations are in order."

"We're quite pleased to have a Wyndham joining our family," Granddad said.

"Of course it helps that he has so much money." The latest Mrs. Alden toyed with the garnets that dangled from her ears. What happened to the Alden rubies?

"He could be flat broke and I'd still marry him."

"That's easy to say when he isn't broke."

"Are you calling my grandson a gold digger, young lady?"

"That's not what she meant at all, Bradley." Mr. Alden closed his
fingers around her arm, and she didn't flinch, but the lines between her
eyes became very pronounced. "Is it, darling?"

"Of course that isn't what I meant. I'm so sorry if it sounded
otherwise."

"Kipp."

"Yes, Granddad?"

"Why don't you get yourself something to nibble on?"

"Yes, Granddad." I wouldn't ask if he'd be all right, not in front
of Mr. Alden and his witch of a wife. At any rate, I had no doubt he
could deal with them.

I went to the buffet and was trying to decide which hors d'oeuvres
called to me when an older man came up beside me.

"These mozzarella and tomato things looks interesting."

"They are." Cherry tomatoes and tiny mozzarella balls were
fastened together by toothpicks, separated by a basil leaf and brushed
with basil oil. "Mrs. Wales makes the best appetizers." I smiled at him
and offered my hand. "I'm Kipp Llewellyn. Thank you for being here."

"Thank you for having me. I'm Douglas Livingston."

"Are you an acquaintance of Sir's?"

"Who?"

"My father."

"Ah. No, actually, I'm here for Hyde."

"I'm so glad someone he knows is here. Everyone else is from
Martinsburg. How do you know Hyde, if you don't mind my asking?"

"We... grew up together, you might say."

"Really? You're one of the guys from the Garage?"

"He told you about that?"

"A little."

He grinned and shook his head. "I'm five years older than Hyde,
so when he was raising hell at the Garage, I was getting my MBA.

Actually, I knew him before he left Prud'homme. So," he said, changing the subject abruptly, "you're going to marry him."

"Yes." I couldn't help giving a small bounce. "Sorry. On Sunday."

"You seem a little excited."

"Just a little? He's so…. But if you know him, you know what a great person he is."

He raised an eyebrow, and I scowled.

"What is it?" His voice was suddenly like ice. "Are you having second thoughts?"

"About what? Marrying Hyde? It would take an act of God to stop me!"

"Well, something's bothering you."

"You'll laugh."

"I won't. I promise."

"All right, but remember, Mr. Livingston, you promised." I raised both eyebrows.

"Yes?" I'd obviously confused him.

"I can't raise just a single eyebrow."

"Excuse me?" He raised one again.

"There, you see? Everyone can do that except me!"

He burst into laughter, and Sir's guests turned to look. "I'm sorry. I know I promised." His laugh was so infectious that I grinned back at him.

"That's all right." I finished the last tomato on my skewer. "If you'll excuse me, I want to see if my grandfather needs anything." The Aldens had left him, and for the moment Granddad was alone.

"I heard he's been ill. I'm sorry to hear that."

"Thank you. He went into remission once, and I'm hoping he will again, in spite of what his oncologist says."

"You're a caring grandson. I hope we'll be able to chat more." He seemed sincere.

"I'd like that." I beamed at him and returned to Granddad. "Can I get you anything, Granddad?"

"Another of those peanut chicken skewers. No one makes them like Mrs. Wales." He caught my sleeve. "Who was that you were talking to?"

"He said he's a friend of Hyde's. His name is Douglas Livingston."

"Hmm. What else did he tell you?"

"He's from Prud'homme."

"Hmm."

"Granddad?"

"If I remember correctly, Elliot Wyndham's oldest daughter married a man named Livingston."

"Yes, so…?" It suddenly fell into place. "He's Hyde's cousin?"

"I wouldn't be in the least surprised."

"How come everyone knows these things except me?"

"Well, if you'd read the *Tri-Community News*—"

"Sir always called the *Tri-Comm* a scandal rag and wouldn't permit it in the house. Is…." I worried my inner cheek. "Do you think Mr. Livingston is here to make sure Hyde isn't making a mistake?"

"Wyndham isn't making a mistake, and he wouldn't appreciate anyone, even a relative, insinuating that he is."

"That's a relief."

He patted my hand absently. "Have you heard from your fiancé?"

"No."

"Hmm."

"Granddad? Are you all right?"

"I'm fine. Go get me another of those skewers before they all disappear."

I did as he asked, and when he waved me away, I looked around for Mr. Livingston. It would be interesting to learn more about Hyde from someone who'd grown up with him, but I didn't see him.

Oh, well. I went to see what else I could find to munch on.

CHAPTER 37

HIGGINS rang a little bell, getting everyone's attention. "Dinner is served in the grand dining room," he announced.

"If you'll excuse me?" I'd been talking to Mrs. Richardson. She was a nice lady, and if I were straight, her English accent would have had me melting in a puddle at her feet.

Another reason why I liked her was because she'd married the man Hyde had thought he wanted, leaving Hyde for me.

"Of course. Go fetch your grandfather. I'm looking forward to chatting with you more about redecorating my bedroom."

"Thank you. I think it will be fun." And she'd assured me that Mr. Richardson wouldn't care what we wound up doing with the room. I had a sneaking suspicion that he might not share that room with her, and that that was why it wouldn't matter to him how it looked. I made my way back through the crowd pouring out of the small dining room. "Granddad, how are you doing?"

"I…" He looked pale, and his breathing seemed labored. "I think I'll have to forgo dinner. Kipp, would you mind if we left?"

"Not at all." Dammit, he had overdone it! "Let me tell Sir, and then I'll have Pierce bring around the Mercedes."

"I've ruined your party. I'm sorry—"

"Don't apologize. It's no fun without Hyde here, anyway." Although I'd been having a surprisingly good time, as long as Sir wasn't glowering at me. "Will you be all right for a couple of minutes?"

"Yes."

I ran through the house to the kitchen, where the servants were sitting around the table having their own dinner. While Mrs. Wales had done all the cooking, Sir had hired waiters to serve the guests, and Higgins was busy seeing they did it properly.

"Hi, Mrs. Wales." I kissed her cheek.

"My, my, you have grown, Mr. Kipp." It had been three years since we'd seen each other, and I'd had that growth spurt my freshman year at Armand U.

"And I'm getting married soon too. You'll come, won't you?"

Jackson snorted and walked out.

"You don't need to come," I called after him, and then I turned to the underchauffeur. "You're invited too, Pierce."

"Thank you, Mr. Kipp." He smiled at me. "We... uh... Mrs. Wales and I were afraid we might not get to see you again."

"I'd have made sure we were able to visit once more before I left town. Maybe when you took Mrs. Wales grocery-shopping."

His smile broadened. When I was little, I'd wheedle my way into going with them, and Mrs. Wales always saw to it that I had a treat, whether it was a piece of candy or a cookie.

"I never did like Jackson. And you did not hear me say that." He winked. "Was there something you needed?"

"Yes. I'm sorry to disturb your dinner, but would you bring Granddad's Mercedes around to the front?" He'd know it was the silver E-sedan. "Thanks very much."

He grinned and gripped my hand. "Congratulations."

"Thank you." I shook his hand, and then shook Mrs. Wales's as well. "I'd love to catch up, but Granddad isn't feeling well, and I want to get him back to Hospice."

"Your father isn't going to be pleased."

I was very aware of that, but *ce qui sera, sera.*. "Bye for now!" I sang out as I hurried out of the kitchen and to the grand dining room.

A quick glance around told me Sir wasn't there.

"Excuse me, has anyone seen Sir?"

"Who?" Mrs. Alden curled her lip at me. God, I wished Mr. Alden hadn't brought her with him. Actually, if it came to that, I wished they'd both stayed home. Still, an invitation from Sir was more like a command, and no one said no to him.

"His father," Mr. Livingston said, raising his eyebrow. He grinned and winked at me, and I grinned back at him.

Mrs. Alden pointedly turned to say something to Mrs. Richardson. I was tempted to roll my eyes. According to some of the gossip I'd overheard tonight, the latest Mrs. Alden, back before she'd become Mrs. Alden, had had friends in the area, and while she'd been visiting, she'd made a play for Sir. She was a blue-eyed blonde, though, and apparently that was no longer Sir's type. Once she realized Sir wasn't interested, she'd gone after Mr. Alden.

I shuddered to think how close she'd come to being my stepmother, and while I felt a little sorry for Eddie, I was relieved it was him rather than me.

Mrs. Richardson ignored her. "Come join me, Kipp." She nodded toward the empty seat between her and Mrs. Alden, her smile warm. "Marcus said you're to sit here, and I must say I'm very pleased about that."

"Thank you, Mrs. Richardson. That's kind of you to say, but Granddad isn't feeling well and we'll need to leave. I'm sorry."

"That's too bad. Bradley is a nice man, and it's a shame he's so ill."

I nodded. "Have you seen—"

"Oh, he took Robert, Cameron, and Aaron to his study to discuss some business matter. Nothing we need to be concerned about." Mrs. Alden sent a smirk from me to Mrs. Richardson. "Marcus told us to start without them. This pineapple-ginger shrimp cocktail is delicious."

"Thank—" I paused. Before each guest was a shrimp cocktail. Strips of bell pepper and pineapple spears made for a very attractive offering. Before each guest, including the seat beside Mrs. Richardson which was supposed to be mine. My throat felt as if it was closing up just from looking at it, and the cut on my palm began to itch. Hadn't Geoff told Sir I couldn't eat shellfish? There had to have been some kind of miscommunication. "Uh… thank you."

I walked out of the dining room and down the hallway.

The door to Sir's study hadn't been quite closed, which meant Sir hadn't been the last man into the room. I'd learned forever ago that it needed to be shut with a firm hand or this would happen.

Once I informed Sir that Granddad and I would be leaving, I'd make sure the door was securely closed behind me so he could continue his business meeting undisturbed.

I was about to tap on it and enter when I heard his voice, the irritation in it evident. "... told you that repeatedly. It all goes back to Jacob, and the bastard was smart enough to have a heart attack before the shit hit the fan. You can be sure otherwise I'd have seen he'd faced the music with the rest of us!"

"You can't talk about my father like that, Marcus!"

"Grow up, Aaron. This is your fault, you.... If you hadn't been so willing to bend over for that—" I recognized Mr. Alden's voice, and the distaste in it was obvious. "It would be nice if you'd at least gotten it out of your system, but I'm aware of that piece you're keeping in Philadelphia."

"What I do in my own time is no one's business but mine! I could understand my father having a problem with Hyde, but why did you two get involved?"

"The Families stick together. If Wyndham went after you, how safe would our children be?"

"If you hadn't noticed, Robert, Wyndham's a faggot." In spite of myself, I flinched at Sir's use of such a crude term, although I supposed he could have used an even more derogatory term relating to Hyde's color.

"Well, then, our sons. And tell me, Llewellyn, how does it feel now the shoe's on the other foot and your son is involved with Wyndham?"

"Hyde loved me! He still does!" Richardson spat. "I don't care if he's marrying your son, Marcus. You made sure that provision was in the contract, didn't you?"

"Yes, but—"

"There, you see? What does Hyde need with a child? I'm going to get him back, if not now, then within the year!" Richardson must have been close to the door, because I could hear him mutter, "Especially since my father won't be around to stop me this time!"

I clenched my hands into fists. His father wasn't around, but *I* was.

"How would your wife feel about that?" Mr. Alden's tone indicated how delighted he was to bring up Mrs. Richardson.

"You're a fine one to talk. You're on your third wife, who's the biggest slut in town, and by the way, how many mistresses is it you've had now?"

"Shut your foul mouth, Richardson." Mr. Alden snapped. "We're all your seniors, and you'd better remember that."

"Oh? And I'm supposed to show respect to the men who ruined my life?"

"Hardly ruined it. You have a wife and two children. Would you have had that if we hadn't stepped in?"

"I'd have had love!"

"Oh, please. That's a fairy tale for children."

"Gentlemen, gentlemen." If Sir intended that tone to calm them, it didn't have the desired effect; in fact, it was like pouring oil on fire.

"And how much would Wyndham love you if he knew you hadn't lifted a finger to help him?" Mr. Alden snapped.

"There was nothing I could do! There were so many, *too* many!"

"There were six, and if you'd stayed to help, he wouldn't have wound up in the hospital."

"*There was nothing I could do!*"

You keep telling yourself that, you miserable excuse for a man! I thought savagely. I remembered the scar on Hyde's side where his spleen had been removed. I'd never let Richardson near Hyde again!

"I'm assuming you didn't bring us in here to discuss Aaron's weakness, Llewellyn." Mr. Stuart spoke for the first time.

Sir stated flatly, "Wyndham's not getting my business."

"Well, of course not. The bastard will just get half." Mr. Alden sounded snidely pleased about that. "As well as getting your son."

"He won't get a fraction of a percentage of it! The contract is worded that he must marry my son."

"But he is."

"The boy he's engaged to is no relation to me!"

I felt the blood drain from my face. I wasn't Sir's son? How could I not be?

I was afraid I wouldn't be able to hear the rest of what Sir was saying, not only due to the uproar his words caused, but because of the roaring in my ears, but somehow I managed.

"*What*? Llewellyn, what are you saying? That boy's lived under your roof all his life!"

"What difference does that make? My servants have lived under this roof for years, but that doesn't make them related to me."

"But...." Confusion was evident in Mr. Stuart's tone.

"You're not deaf all of a sudden, are you, Stuart?" Too often I'd heard that smug, self-satisfied tone of voice, and I shivered. "And it's exactly as I say: the boy is not my son. That bitch I married got herself pregnant by another man."

That caused even more of an uproar.

"Don't you *dare* malign Beth!" The savagery in Mr. Alden's voice shocked me.

"Oh, please, Robert. Did you think I wasn't aware you were in love with my wife since she graduated high school? How do you think her father would react if he ever learned you'd have coerced her into marriage?"

"The way you did? At least I loved Beth and would have made her happy, whereas you just wanted her because she didn't want you. That she was young and blonde and lovely made her the perfect trophy to have on your arm!"

"My deceased wife is not what I called you in here to discuss."

"What, then?" Mr. Alden asked sullenly.

"Your nose is starting to bleed, Marcus," Mr. Stuart murmured.

"What? Dammit!"

"How frequently has that been happening?"

"None of your goddamned business!" His voice became muffled as he probably blotted at his nose. "Now, as I was saying, the contract has been worded to the effect that in order to gain half of Llewellyn, Inc., Wyndham must marry my son. As soon as he and the boy exchange vows, that agreement will be worthless."

"But... but...."

"Close your mouth, Aaron. You're as bad as the boy with your imitation of a beached fish!"

"Wyndham's going to learn of this!"

"Of course he is, but not until after I'm gone, which won't be for a very long time. But at that time, he'll get a copy of the boy's revised birth certificate, along with the results of the DNA test, which will show beyond a shadow of a doubt that the boy is none of mine."

Sir had proof I wasn't his son? Then why had he kept me all these years?

"Meanwhile, with Wyndham's backing, my investors have been more than willing to extend my line of credit. I'll be laughing up my sleeve, knowing I've had the pleasure of one-upping the arrogant son of a bitch! And best of all, the boy will be off my hands."

Hyde was marrying me in order to get half the shares of Llewellyn, Inc. Oh, I was sure he cared for me well enough, but I doubted he'd have wanted to marry Kipp Llewellyn if those shares hadn't been part of the deal.

I could hardly breathe, and I began shivering uncontrollably as my world crashed down around me. I couldn't marry him now. He'd hate me....

"Marcus, are you sure this is a smart idea?" Mr. Alden asked urgently.

"That's the only kind of idea I have."

"Honestly? I fail to understand why you felt the need to share this information with us." Mr. Stuart's words were musing. "Wouldn't it have been safer to keep this to yourself?"

Yes, he's right. Why would Sir do this?

"It will be nice to have my genius admired while I'm still alive to enjoy it." That made no sense at all! "In addition, I want the three of you to keep an eye on Wyndham and the boy whenever they're in town. I can't be everywhere, after all."

"Marcus, are you all right?" Mr. Stuart sounded concerned, genuinely concerned, not as if he was pretending so he could get on Sir's good side.

"Of course I am!"

"Your eyes look.... Never mind. I still think this doesn't make sense."

So I wasn't the only one to think so!

"Need I remind the three of you that I wouldn't be in this predicament if you'd handled your own affairs better?" Sir was losing his patience.

"It came out of left field, Llewellyn!" Mr. Alden growled. "After all this time—How could we know the way we'd dealt with Wyndham twenty years ago would come back to bite us in the ass?"

"Yes. How were we to know he'd take the money Jacob gave him and turn it into a fortune?" Mr. Stuart mused.

"I could have told you Hyde was a genius when it came to making money. Even when he was studying to be a vet." There was pride in Aaron Richardson's voice, but if he was so proud of Hyde, why had he allowed his father to ship him off to marry his cousin?

"He was a *busboy*!"

"He was also Elliot Wyndham's grandson!" Richardson reminded them.

"Who he disowned!" Mr. Alden pointed out smugly.

"This is getting us nowhere." Now Mr. Stuart was losing his patience.

"It isn't, is it?" Sir sounded as if he was enjoying hearing Richardson and Alden tearing each other apart. "Just keep in mind, the three of you, that I know where all the proverbial bodies are buried. You'll keep your mouths shut! If I learn word has gotten out...." He let the threat linger for a moment. "Now, let's go in to dinner. I think you might find it amusing."

"Marcus, my wife can't know about that apartment!"

"Oh, for—is that all you're worried about, Aaron?"

"You don't understand! If my father-in-law learns—"

I backed away from the door. It didn't matter what Richardson's father-in-law learned. If Sir found out I'd eavesdropped on this conversation, I'd be lucky to escape the aftermath with my skin intact.

I had no time to get myself under control, but on the other hand, I couldn't let Granddad see me like this. I ducked into the half bath just off the library and leaned my head against the cool porcelain of the sink, fighting nausea.

I'd have to tell Hyde I couldn't marry him.

Oh, God, I'd have to tell him *why*!

No. I wasn't giving up. I wasn't going to let Sir get in my head as he had earlier.

Granddad…. Granddad would know the truth.

I drew in a deep breath, and once my stomach had settled down and I'd stopped shaking, I walked to the small dining room.

I thought back to earlier in the evening when Beauchamp had wished me an enjoyable evening and I'd thought it would be. Could I have been more wrong?

CHAPTER 38

THE sun hadn't quite set, but even so the lights at the front of the house were on, illuminating the drive.

Pierce had the Mercedes at the front door, and he helped me get Granddad settled in the backseat. I put the oxygen tank and its harness on the seat beside him.

Just as I shut the door, another car pulled up, and Geoff and Mindy got out.

"Kipp! Where are you going?"

"What the fuck do you care?"

"Don't swear in front of Mindy!"

I'd never in my life raised a hand to anyone, but I was so hurt, and so furious... I punched my brother in the face and knocked his feet out from under him.

"Geoff!" Mindy ran to him. She was wearing a violet chiffon cocktail dress tonight, and it floated around her knees as she knelt by him. "What's wrong with you, Kipp?" she spat at me.

"I'll tell you what's wrong with me! I've got a son of a bitch for a brother!"

"What are you talking about?" He started to get up, and I put up my fists to let him know I'd knock him down again. "Kipp?"

"Jesus, Geoff, I'd expect something like this from Sir"—well, no, I wouldn't, but it wouldn't have surprised me—"but you're my brother, goddammit. I thought you cared about me!"

"Expected what?" He stared up at me, holding his hand to his nose. But color rose in his cheeks.

"Here, baby. Take my handkerchief." Mindy glared at me. "You're nothing but a meanie, Kipp Llewellyn!"

I began to laugh uncontrollably. Was that even my name?

"What's going on, Kipp?"

"You set me up. Hyde isn't going to want to marry me now. Why should he? You wrote up a contract that said in exchange for cash and incidentally marrying Sir's son, Hyde got half the shares of Llewellyn, Inc. But I'm fucking *not Sir's son!*"

"What are you talking about? Of course you are! All I put in the contract was that after a year if you wanted to walk away, you could, with no repercussions! Wyndham got a prorated amount of his money back, and you got control of your trust fund."

"Oh, yeah? And what about the clause about it being okay for either of us to break our marriage vows?"

"I put that in there to—"

"Tempt him? Sure, why not?" I asked bitterly. "What man would want to stay faithful to Marcus Llewellyn's son?"

His cheeks turned even redder. "I was just trying to protect you. Wyndham's a player; he's left a string of boys in his wake, and he broke—" He glanced at Mindy, and I was positive he was going to say Hyde broke her father's heart, but I knew it was the other way around. "He'd have broken your heart."

"Maybe he *might* have, but you know something, brother mine? You've *definitely* broken it." I started to walk away.

"Kipp, you have to understand!"

"No, I don't." I turned back. "Why are you even here?"

"What do you mean? Where else would I be for your engagement party?"

"Sir said something had come up and you weren't coming."

"Father called to tell me the time had been changed to nine to accommodate Wyndham's tardiness."

I glanced pointedly at my watch. It was a quarter past eight.

"Mindy was hungry."

"Did you tell Sir I'd had a reaction to shellfish?"

"Of course I did."

"Take a look at what he's serving." Maybe I shouldn't have punched Geoff for the shellfish thing, but he'd still put together that damned contract.

"Kipp!"

I walked to the car and got in.

"Kipp, what was that all about?" Granddad rasped. "Why did you knock down your brother?"

I buckled up and put the car in gear, but I kept my foot on the brake. I met his eyes in the rearview mirror. He wasn't looking good, but he'd look even worse if I told him about the contract, about the shrimp cocktail, about not being Sir's son. God, he could have a heart attack and die right here.

"I'll tell you at Hospice, all right?"

"Kipp...."

"At Hospice."

"All right."

THE drive to Promise Hospice passed without any conversation. I turned on the radio, and as if to mock my pain, Buddy Holly was singing his version of "Brown-Eyed Handsome Man."

Goddammit! I changed the radio station, but every goddamned station had that song on it. What the fuck?

By the time I realized it must be a CD, the next song had come on: "Because I Love You." I stabbed at the eject button, and the disc slid out. A glance told me it was something called *Reminiscing*.

Beauchamp used this car; the CD must be his. Was he a Buddy Holly fan?

I didn't know. I didn't really care.

I had to blink hard to keep tears from falling.

CHAPTER 39

I FOUND a parking spot close to the front door of Promise Hospice. "I'm going to get you a wheelchair. Will you be all right for a little bit?"

"Yes." But, oh, God, his voice was so faint!

"Do you want an aide?"

"No."

I ran into the building, called out, "Wheelchair?" and when the receptionist pointed, I followed her gesture toward a corridor that ran in the opposite direction to the garden. I found a wheelchair in an alcove and hurried back out.

"I'm sorry I took you away from your engagement party," Granddad said as I helped him into the wheelchair.

I wasn't. I forced a smile at the evening receptionist and wheeled him to his room. "Do you want me to ring for an aide?"

"No. I think we need to talk, and a third person will just be in the way."

"All right." I removed my suit jacket, folded it over the back of the easy chair that had been brought from Silver Birch, and then helped him get out of his suit and into his pajamas.

This was the first time I'd seen his colostomy bag, and I swallowed and shivered.

"Do you need an aide to empty your bag?"

"No, it's fine. Stop asking if I need an aide and tell me what's wrong."

"Let's get you in bed first." Once he was in it, I used the controls to raise the bed to a sitting position. "Comfortable?"

"Yes."

"All right, then." I disconnected the oxygen hose from the portable tank and hooked it up to the port on the wall.

"You didn't have dinner."

"It doesn't matter. I couldn't have eaten it anyway. Sir was having shrimp cocktail as the first course."

"That—that—"

I pulled over the easy chair and sank down into it. I'd often asked him why Sir seemed to hate me so much, and Granddad had always put me off, telling me I'd just caught Sir in a bad mood. The problem was he always seemed to be in a bad mood when I was around.

I ran a hand through my hair. "I'm not Sir's son, am I?"

"What? What makes you ask something like that?"

"I overheard Sir talking to the heads of the other three Families. He said Hyde wouldn't get my share of Llewellyn, Inc. because I'm not his son. Is that true?"

He was quiet for so long that I didn't think he was going to answer me. Finally, looking utterly defeated, he said, "I'm so sorry, Kipp."

Oh, God*damn* it. "I'd better give you the ring back." I wouldn't be marrying Hyde.

"What ring?"

"The one you found in Mother's keepsake box. The one you had Beauchamp give me."

"Oh, that. Keep it." He looked so uncomfortable that I panicked.

"Are you going to tell me I'm not your grandson either?"

"No, you're Beth's son," he assured me.

"Then who's my father?" It started to make sense—the shellfish allergy that no one else in the family had, my blue, blue eyes and very blond hair, my chin and cheeks, and even the stupid fact that I couldn't raise an eyebrow.

"Shortly after you were born, your—Marcus came to me. He said you weren't his son. I lost my temper. I was just sobering up—I mean—"

"I know about you getting drunk, Granddad."

"He told you that? That son of a bitch!"

"I don't understand how you never saw what he was like."

He looked away. "I avoided him as much as I could. Especially once Beth was gone."

"So Sir came to tell you I wasn't his, and...?"

"I wanted to knock him down, but...."

I had to sit on my hands; otherwise I'd have been tempted to shake him in my impatience.

"I told myself I had to be understanding. I thought Llewellyn was out of his mind with grief; he'd just lost the wife he'd moved heaven and earth to marry, due to what was probably a stupid human error."

"What error?" I hadn't heard this story before.

"Your mother was alone in her room and began hemorrhaging. The call bell should have been clipped to the sheet by her head, but it was out of reach, and she was just too weak to reach it. By the time anyone realized something was wrong, it was too late."

"But his reaction wasn't because Mother died, was it?"

He sighed. "No. I've spoken to you about your mother before, and you know she was the youngest in the family. We all adored her: her mother and I, her sisters and brother, Beauchamp, his son—"

"Wait. Beauchamp has a son?"

"*Had.* Yes."

"Beauchamp was married?" I could hardly wrap my mind around that.

"Yes. Beth probably should have been a spoiled brat the way everyone doted on her, but Beauchamp's son kept her steady. They were the same age, and they were very close. None of us thought anything of it until they graduated from high school. Then they came to us and told us they wanted to get married. Your grandmother wasn't pleased."

"How did Beauchamp take that?"

"He was even less pleased. He was a staunch believer in upstairs/downstairs, and the idea that his son had the temerity to break with that tradition—"

"Granddad, this is the twenty-first century, not the nineteenth."

"We're talking thirty years ago."

"All right, the twentieth century." I was starting to lose my patience again.

"A Beauchamp came over the mountains with old Benjamin Martin."

"Yes, but still—" I shook my head. "Well, obviously it didn't mean anything, since she married Sir."

"That was what we hoped, but they kept insisting. Finally we persuaded them to wait until Beth had at least a year of college. Kipling—"

"Who?"

"Beauchamp's son. He knew there was nothing here for him. Well, I'd hardly let him keep his job at the factory, and none of the other Families would hire him. He had to drive over to Prud'homme to find work."

"Oh, Granddad."

"I've disappointed you, haven't I? You have to understand that Beth was my pride and joy. I wanted only the best for her."

"And you thought the best was Marcus Llewellyn?"

He sighed. "Llewellyn came to Martinsburg to look into some property on the outskirts of town, and it was apparent that he was smitten from the moment he saw Beth."

"Granddad... Sir doesn't do smitten."

"No, but we didn't know that at the time. Your grandmother and I thought Beth would be better off with an older, more stable man. In addition, he had all that money, more than all the Families put together. While Kipling—the boy had nothing."

"Did you know Mr. Alden wanted her?"

"What? *No*! My God, he was a married man! Not to mention, a good deal older!"

But Sir was older still. "So you made her marry Sir?"

"No, of course not! She agreed to it. *Alden*?" He looked baffled.

"She was nineteen." I shook my head. "She'd have been better off running away with Kipling."

"We didn't give them the opportunity. We were afraid they might do that, and we kept a strict eye on them both. Finally I convinced Beth to go out to dinner with Marcus. I promised her if he couldn't win her over, I'd back off. Of course your grandmother was furious, but it was the only way I could see to work this out."

"Did you even intend to honor your promise?"

"Kipp! How can you say that?"

I could see I'd hurt him, but the idea of the daughter he claimed meant so much to him being pushed into marrying Sir.... "What happened?"

"They didn't come home until the early morning hours. Beth was pale, but she smiled and said she'd changed her mind and would marry your—Marcus as soon as the wedding could be planned. Nine months almost to the day, your brother was born."

"How did Beauchamp's son feel about this?"

"No one knew. The day after Beth came home from that date with Llewellyn, Kipling left. We learned eventually that he'd enlisted in the army."

"I still don't understand why Sir would say I'm not his son."

Granddad rubbed a palm over his face. "Kipling came home on leave in July of 1995; we didn't know it at the time, but he was about to be deployed to Bosnia." He gazed off into space as if he were remembering that day. "He met with Beth at Chantilly Lace for lunch."

I didn't ask how he'd learned of that. This was Martinsburg. It had probably spread through the city like wildfire as soon as the first person saw them together.

"Llewellyn happened to be out of town at the time on business. He never would have permitted it."

"That doesn't surprise me."

"No. No one saw them after that lunch. They were just... gone."

"Excuse me?" He couldn't mean they'd died! And then I wanted to smack myself in the head. I hadn't been born yet; of course she hadn't died.

"They left town, no one knew where. Marcus was almost insane with worry."

I blinked. Sir never worried about anything, much less insanely, but could my own experiences with him be coloring how I saw this?

"As soon as Marcus returned and learned what happened, he left Geoff at Silver Birch. He was going to search the places Beth usually frequented. Your grandmother had been gone a couple of years at that point, and so it was just me, and thank God I had Beauchamp. It had been a long time since I'd had to take care of a seven-year-old. Just before the end of July, Beth came back. She picked up Geoff and went home to Llewellyn Manor."

I was starting to get the feeling that Llewellyn Manor had been even less Mother's home than it was mine. "Did she tell you where she'd been?"

"No. She just told me that she'd never considered Llewellyn her husband, that he could have a million legal documents saying otherwise, but it wouldn't matter. Shortly afterward, Llewellyn returned."

"Do you think Mother contacted him?"

"It's possible, but it was more likely Higgins. At any rate, Llewellyn told everyone he'd overreacted, that they'd had a foolish quarrel and they'd spent the last few weeks in Manhattan. He'd taken her shopping, and they'd seen the latest shows on Broadway. He also said she'd overdone it physically, and she needed to recuperate, so they were cutting back on their entertaining, starting with the Labor Day party he usually gave."

"Did you see her?"

"No. Oh, I called on the phone and spoke to her, but she reiterated what Llewellyn had said: that she'd overdone it and was very tired. A few months later Llewellyn announced the 'happy results of their second honeymoon': they were expecting again."

I remembered my brother telling me how happy she'd been. "Why is there such a gap between Geoff and me?"

"Beth had a couple of miscarriages and a stillbirth."

"Then Sir should have been pleased she was going to have another baby."

"You'd think so, wouldn't you? If I hadn't known him better, I'd have sworn he was bipolar. One day he was overjoyed, and the next.... But finally it was time for you to be born. It was a difficult birth."

"Granddad, I'm aware of this."

"He told you that too? Why aren't I surprised?" He shook his head, looking more tired, and reached for my hand. "Afterward, I went to her room to see her. Beth was holding you. She looked pale. 'His name is Kipp, Dad,' she told me. I knew Llewellyn would have a stroke if his son was named after the butler's son, but she spelled out your name. 'Anyway, do you think Marcus has any idea what Beauchamp's son's name is? He doesn't know Mrs. Wales's daughter just had a little girl named Marjory or that Pierce's son is dating a girl from Prud'homme.'"

"I knew Marjory, Granddad. We used to play together sometimes."

"Did Marcus ever find out?"

"Of course not. I'd hide in the pantry whenever Higgins came into the kitchen."

His grip on my hand tightened.

"So Mother was certain Sir didn't know Kipling's name?"

"At that point, I don't think she cared. She said, 'Marcus has no say in what I name this baby.' And she made me promise to name you Kipp. I've often wondered if she knew she wouldn't leave the hospital alive."

"Do you think Sir had something to do with that call bell being out of reach?"

"No, no, not at all, Kipp! How could you even—I'm sorry, I'm—"
He couldn't seem to catch his breath.

"Granddad?"

"This... this must be taking more...."

"Let me call the nurse."

"Yes, I think you'd better."

I pressed the call bell, but I wasn't going to wait; I ran out into the hall and down to the nurses' station.

She was already up and coming around the counter. "What is it?"

"My grandfather's having trouble breathing!"

"I'll take care of him. But I'll need you to stay out of the room."

I touched her arm. "I know this is a hospice, but please don't let him die."

"Our aim is to keep him comfortable." She patted my hand and left me outside the room.

CHAPTER 40

I PACED the length of the corridor, turned, and paced back. I peeked into Granddad's room in time to see the nurse remove the blood pressure cuff.

"Lean forward, Mr. Martin, I want to listen to your lungs."

"Excuse me," I whispered. "I'm just stepping out to the lobby. I have to make a phone call."

"Are... are you calling Hyde?" Granddad asked. "Tell him to... to get his... his ass down here."

"Actually, I'm going to call Beauchamp."

"Good... good boy. And... and then call... call Hyde."

"Yes, Granddad." I'd have to, if only to tell him we weren't engaged anymore.

The nurse shooed me out. "Now, a deep breath, Mr. Martin, and blow it out...."

I made my way to the lobby and then out into the May night. There was no moon. I remembered Hyde teasing me about going up to Lila's Hill and not watching the eclipse.

Why had I expected to have something as good as Hyde in my life?

I took my cell phone from my pocket and dialed the number for Silver Birch. It rang twice.

"Martin residence."

"Beauchamp, it's Kipp."

"Is everything all right? I wasn't expecting you for another few hours."

"I had to bring Granddad back to Hospice. He's not feeling well, and the nurse is checking him over right now."

"Thank you for calling. Have you spoken to Mr. Wyndham? He called shortly after you left, but when I told him that, he said he'd see you at Llewellyn Manor."

"No. I must have missed him." I'd spend the rest of my life missing him. "Anyway, I just wanted to let you know where I was. I don't know what time I'll get in—"

"I'll wait up."

"Oh, no, it could be really late...."

"I'll be waiting."

"All right. I'll talk to you later."

We hung up, and I dialed Hyde's number, and then hung up after the first ring. Too much was going on with Granddad, and I really needed to be available. That was what I told myself, at any rate.

I went back into Hospice and resumed pacing the length of Granddad's corridor.

I lost track of the number of times I'd done that, but I was at the far end once more when my cell phone rang. I knew who it was from the ringtone. All right, no time like the present; I had to tell my fiancé he was no longer my fiancé.

I swallowed, drew in a breath, and touched the screen. "H-Hyde."

"Kipp, are you all right?" The concern in his words tore me apart.

"Yes. I'm glad you called."

"You tried to reach me earlier. I had the phone on vibrate, otherwise I'd have picked up."

Say it. "The...." *Say it!* "The wedding is off."

"What? What are you telling me?"

"I've...." I had to shove the words out past a throat that felt as closed as when I'd had that allergic reaction. "I've changed my mind. I—we're not getting married."

"I see. And this is because you no longer want to get married, or you no longer want to marry me?"

"B-both."

"Never mind about that. Where are you? *How* are you?"

"I told you I'm... I'm all right." Why was he asking me that? Shouldn't he be angry, shouting at me for calling off the wedding at such short notice? Armitage would have to contact all those people; it would be so embarrassing.... And expensive. I thought of the leather folders with our names and the date stamped into them in twenty-four carat gold. "I'm at Promise Hospice. Granddad wasn't feeling well—"

"How is he?"

"Not... I don't know. Hyde...."

"I'm just leaving Llewellyn Manor."

"When did you get there?" Dammit, that sounded as if I'd missed him. I shouldn't have asked that. I swallowed and forced the words out. "We left before dinner."

"Thank God! I was ready to tear your brother a new one for not telling Llewellyn about your reaction to shellfish—"

"But he said he did!"

"Yes, he blurted that out, and then I tore into Llewellyn."

"Oh, my." Sir wouldn't have liked that, especially if it was in front of guests.

"Look, I'll be at Hospice as soon as I can."

"Wait!"

"Yes?"

"You don't have to come here. Don't you understand? I broke up with you. We're through!"

"Yes, I understood. I'll be there as soon as I can," he repeated.

"Hyde...."

"Yes?"

"Drive carefully. I don't want you to die getting here."

"I won't, blue eyes. Hang in there." He hung up, and I put my phone away.

I was happy for about two seconds, and then I wanted to kick myself in the ass. How stupid was this? Now I'd have to break up with him all over again.

If it wouldn't have come across as a foolish repeat of my actions earlier today, I'd have thrown my cell phone at the nearest wall.

But... for this short amount of time, he was still mine.

I resumed my pacing and was at the far end of the hall once again when the nurse came out of Granddad's room and looked around. I was already sprinting back to her by the time she spotted me.

"Is he all right?"

She shook her head. "I'm going to call his doctor; I'm concerned about his breathing, and I don't like the way the contents of his colostomy bag look. I don't want to distress you, but I don't know if he'll make it through the night."

"Oh, God. May I—"

"Yes. Go sit with him. Let him know he's not alone."

My hands were shaking as I walked into the room. "How are you feeling, Granddad?" I asked as I pulled the easy chair close to the bed again and took his hand.

"I don't think I should have had that last peanut chicken skewer."

"Oh, Granddad." I laughed because I knew he wanted me to, and I brought his hand to my cheek.

"I'm sorry, Kipp."

"I don't know what you're sorry about, but stop. There's nothing—"

"There is. You were right about the allergy being hereditary. You got it from your father, from Kipling Beauchamp."

I felt cold. So that was why Granddad had nearly passed out and Beauchamp had looked so disturbed when they'd learned about my reaction to the shellfish.

"What happened to him?" Didn't he want me either?

"As I said, he was sent to Bosnia. He was killed by friendly fire. Beauchamp got the notification just after the New Year. I dreaded having to tell Beth, but she seemed to know, although she wouldn't tell me how she knew. I've always suspected your uncle contacted her."

"My uncle?"

"Bradley. He was called Four by everyone because he was the fourth Bradley Martin."

I couldn't help laughing. "It had to be a lot less confusing."

"Yes, although I would have preferred his friends used his name. It's a very good name."

"It is, Granddad. But how would Uncle Brad have found out about my... my father?"

"He was already in the army when Kipling joined, and I believe they kept in touch. Bradley is a colonel, Kipp. I'm so proud. He's been deployed all over the world, and so of course he hasn't had many opportunities to come home to Martinsburg. Perhaps he'll come home now."

"Is there any way I can get in touch with him?"

"Beauchamp most likely knows. Talk to him."

"I will." How sad that it was my grandfather's butler who had any idea where my uncle was. "Do you... do you think Beauchamp has photos of my father that he'll let me see?" Granddad *had* said Beauchamp had been very much against his son marrying.... A thought occurred to me. "Oh, my God, Granddad, he's my grandfather too!"

"Yes, I guess he is. How do you feel about that?"

"I don't know. He was always kind of standoffish, and—do you think he knows?"

"I imagine so. He apologized twice while he was hanging up my suit, although he wouldn't say what he was apologizing for. He also said he'd leave Silver Birch, if I requested that of him."

"It's not his fault!" I didn't say how unpromising that sounded. Didn't... Grandfather Beauchamp... want to be my grandfather?

"No, but you know Beauchamp."

"He called me Kipp tonight. He's never done that before." I ran a hand through my hair, no doubt leaving it disheveled. "Will he talk to me about my father?" And suddenly a measure of relief swamped over me. I'd no longer have to force myself to try to love the man who *wasn't* my father.

"He loved Kipling very much, and I have no doubt he'll tell you everything you want to know."

"Granddad... I'll have to leave Martinsburg."

"Well, certainly. You'll be going with your husband."

"No. You know I can't marry Hyde."

"Do you think he won't want you?"

"It doesn't matter. I won't let him be talked about because of me."

"Where will you go?"

I looked down at my hands. My fingers were twisting together so tightly I thought for a second I would break them. I'd been hoping he would order me not to be such an idiot, that Hyde and I could weather anything together. Obviously Granddad didn't think....

The sound of footsteps racing down the hallway distracted me, and I turned, hoping it was his doctor, and then terrified that it might be him, because of the hurry.

But it was a man dressed in a military uniform. He looked vaguely familiar, but I knew I'd never seen him before. "I don't think you're in the right room."

All the color drained from his face. "Kipp?"

"Do I know you?"

"He's your nephew, not your friend, Four."

Then Hyde came in, and I forgot everything.

"Hyde!" I bounded out of the chair, crossed the floor, and threw myself into his arms before I even realized what I was going to do.

"It makes me very happy to be welcomed this way." He ran his fingers over my hair, smoothing it down. "I'm sorry I wasn't here, blue eyes."

I brought his head down to mine. "Granddad's not doing well," I whispered. "They don't think he'll make it through the night."

He looked at Granddad, and then tightened his hold on me. "I want you to meet someone." He turned toward the door just as the most beautiful woman I'd ever seen walked in.

She had skin the color of café au lait, but her eyes were green. She wore a black lace cocktail dress with three-quarter sleeves and strappy sandals with six-inch heels, making her almost as tall as Hyde. Under her arm she carried a matching clutch bag.

"Mom, this is Kipp."

"So you're my son's fiancé." She smiled at me, and it was Hyde's smile. "I've been looking forward to meeting you."

"Uh... thank you. It's nice meeting you too." I glanced frantically at Hyde. Without a doubt, his mother would be coming to the wedding. Why hadn't I expected her to come to the engagement party as well?

Oh, of course, there wasn't an engagement because *there wasn't going to be a wedding.*

He leaned down and pressed his cheek against mine. "You might as well accept it, my sweet, blue-eyed boy," he said softly in my ear. "You're marrying me."

"But—"

"Now." He gave me a squeeze, and then let me go. "I need to step out for a moment. Mom won't bite. I've already told her she's going to love you."

Oh, God, I wished he hadn't!

"Hyde, we're not—"

"Will you be okay?"

"Yes. Of course." I just wished the floor would open up and swallow me. Why had he brought his mother here? She was going to hate me for making a laughing stock of her son. "But Hyde, we're not—"

"Shh." He tipped up my chin and pressed his lips lightly to mine.

"Hyde," I whispered into his mouth.

"We are, and it will be fine." He ran the backs of his fingers over my cheek. One more kiss, and then he turned and walked out, pulling his cell phone from his pocket as he went.

I was supposed to break up with him! This wasn't—

"What an interesting evening this has proven to be!"

"Excuse me?"

"Of course I'm sorry about.... But I must say it's been a very long time since I've seen my son react so intensely to anything. For the past twenty years he's been quite restrained. He's never been so enthralled by anyone."

I realized abruptly that she'd been watching me, and I shifted uncomfortably.

"I find that hard to believe. I mean, he's gorgeous."

"Oh, he's had any number of people who were attracted by any number of things about him: his looks, his money, his possessions. But he hasn't been drawn to any of them."

He'd been in love with Aaron Richardson, though.

"You, on the other hand?"

"I know," I agreed miserably. "He just has to hold out his hand and I'll fall into it like a ripe plum."

"You care about him, don't you?"

"Do you even have to ask? Isn't it written all over me?"

"I can understand why Hyde's in love with you."

"I can't. And anyway, he's not. He's marrying me to get shares in... that is, he would if... I mean...." I groaned. This was getting so confusing.

"I hardly think he'd marry for such a reason."

"Then why marry me? He won't get anything out of it!" Especially now.

"My grandson doesn't believe what his mirror tells him," Granddad said.

"Weren't you supposed to be talking to Uncle Four?" I used the nickname deliberately, but he just chucked and then wheezed a bit before turning back to my uncle.

"You know, I saw you once when you were a little boy." She smiled, as if this was a fond memory. Was that what a mother did?

"But Hyde told me he left the year I was born. And aren't you concerned about the difference in our ages?"

"Are you?"

"No, it never mattered."

"Then it doesn't matter to me either."

I shook my head, even more confused. "How could you have seen me?"

"I stayed in Martinsburg for a few years afterward; Hyde didn't need his mother underfoot while he was getting himself settled." She brushed aside the hair that had fallen into my eyes. "You couldn't have been more than three at the time. It was the most beautiful autumn day. Your nurse brought you to the park, and you were pulling along a little red wagon you'd filled with acorns. I heard her tell you the squirrels would be jealous of all the acorns you had, and you laughed and clapped your hands. Those acorns made such a racket, but anyone could see how proud of yourself you were."

"I remember that wagon." It had been ages since I'd thought of it. I'd outgrown it and one day it had been put out with the trash.

She touched my hair again, and I felt my eyes start to burn.

Shit, had a frog taken up lodging in my throat? I swallowed around it, not that it seemed to do much good. Finally I managed to get out, "Uh... Do you live with Hyde?"

"Oh, no. I have my own place, so you won't have to worry about sharing your home with your mother-in-law."

"Mrs. Wyndham—"

"Do you think you might call me Mom?"

"Hyde and I aren't getting married!"

"Are you sure?" She chuckled. "In that case, call me Delphie."

"I—"

"Kipp, come and meet your uncle." Thank God! Granddad to the rescue, interrupting this conversation!

"Please excuse me?"

"Certainly. I'll just make myself comfortable in this chair and do a little reading." She sat down and took her smartphone and a pair of glasses from her bag. Would Hyde eventually need reading glasses? They'd make him look so distinguished. "But later, perhaps, you'll allow me to join you and my son for a cup of coffee?"

"Excuse me? Oh, I don't... the hour, the caffeine...." I gave her a weak smile and went to Granddad's bedside.

CHAPTER 41

"HOW are you feeling, Granddad?" He'd sounded stronger. Maybe the nurse was wrong; maybe he'd be all right.

"A little better. I'm sorry I gave you a scare. Brad, this is your nephew, Kipp, spelled K-I-double-P."

"How do you do, K-I-double-P?" His smile was warm. "You look a good deal like my sister and.... You look like both of them." He extended his hand.

"How do you do?" I took it, and before I realized it, he'd pulled me into a hug. "Um...."

"I'm glad to know my sister found a small measure of happiness."

Not sure how to respond to that, I gave *him* a weak smile and backed away. "I see you're in the army." Oh, that was clever. *What gave it away, Kipp? The uniform?*

"Yes. Your father and I were in the same company. He was a good man. You'd have liked him."

My father.... "Granddad said he was killed by friendly fire."

Uncle Brad shrugged. "That was what the word was." He changed the subject. "As I said, you look a lot like Beth, but I can see Kipling in you as well."

"Uh...." Again I was at a loss as to how to respond, and I decided the best thing to do was to change the subject myself. "Why are you here?" I groaned and covered my face with my palm. "I'm sorry; that didn't come out right. How is it that you're here?"

"Your fiancé pulled some strings and got me leave in order to be here for my nephew's wedding."

"We're not getting married!"

He raised an eyebrow—well, dammit!—and the corner of his mouth kicked up in a grin, but he didn't respond to that. "It proved to be fortuitous, since I'll also be able to spend some time with my father, who neglected to tell me just how ill he was."

"Don't talk about me as if I'm not here!" Granddad snapped.

"Well, someone seems a bit better." I rested my hand on his, and he covered it with his free hand.

"Kipp."

My uncle said, "You're probably wondering why you've never met me or your aunts."

"I am?" Frankly, I'd never given them much thought. "Well, I imagine you all had your own lives to live." That was how it was with Sir. I knew there was at least one surviving uncle on his side, but neither he nor Sir's parents had ever made an effort to visit us. I couldn't honestly say it mattered.

"We were so angry with Mother and Father for pushing Beth into Llewellyn's arms."

"Was that what broke the family apart?"

"She couldn't have married Kipling!" Granddad burst out. "Granted he was a good-enough boy, but what would the Families have thought?"

"Oh, Dad, we were the leading family in Martinsburg. What the hell did it matter if the Stuarts or Aldens or Richardsons got their panties in a bunch because Beth chose to follow her heart?"

"You don't understand, Bradley—"

"Yes, I do. You put that above Beth's happiness, and the results—"

"Excuse me for interrupting, but that's old news." And I really didn't want to hear about how they all had abandoned my mother to a man like Marcus Llewellyn. A thought occurred to me. "Granddad, I'll have to change my name!"

"Of course you'll be changing it, Kipp." Hyde was back, and I smiled at him.

No, what was I doing? I couldn't—

And then I saw the man behind him, and I thought I was going to throw up. "You went to get a priest?"

"I don't need last rites just yet, Wyndham!" Granddad sounded ticked off.

"I'm aware of that... Granddad." Hyde winked at him. "He's for me and Kipp." He turned to me. "This is Father Ed. He's chaplain here at Promise Hospice. I thought it would be a good idea for us to get married here in your grandfather's room."

I opened my mouth to shout "Yes!", but then reality slammed down on me. "Didn't you hear what I said earlier? I can't marry you!"

"Why not?"

"Yes, why not?" Mr. Livingston asked.

"Mr. Livingston? What are you doing here?" He must have walked in behind Hyde and Father Ed.

"Call me Doug. You're going to be part of the family."

"Thank you." I could feel myself blushing. "Wait! No, I'm not! Hyde!"

"You are."

"Argh!" He was making me crazy!

"I'm here now because Hyde called me," Doug said. "After the dinner party broke up—you did miss some fireworks, let me tell you!"

"Doug!" Was there a warning in Hyde's tone?

Doug just grinned at him. "I went back to the Saratoga Trunk. Did you know it has a very nice cigar bar, La Isla Bonita?"

"No, I had no idea," I said faintly.

"Well, at any rate, he called, and as soon as he told me he was going to need a best man tonight, I came running."

That distracted me. "I don't have a best man!" This time I covered my face with both hands. "What am I saying? I don't *need* a best man. I'm not marrying anyone! Why won't you listen to me?"

"Because you're talking nonsense. It's obvious you care a great deal about my son. I think you want to marry him more than anything." Delphie had obviously been listening the entire time. "Oh, Hyde, I do like him."

"I knew you would, Mom."

"Weren't you supposed to be reading something on your phone?" I demanded irritably.

She gave me a bland smile.

"You haven't explained why you won't marry me." Hyde's lips curved into such a tender expression that I could barely catch my breath.

"I'm not Marcus Llewellyn's son!"

"And?"

What did he mean, *and*? "You won't get the shares in Llewellyn, Inc."

"And you think that's the only reason why I'd want to marry you?"

"Well, no. Yes! Why would you want me otherwise?"

Granddad started laughing. "'Item, two lips, indifferent red....'"

"Dad, are you all right?" Uncle Brad obviously thought Granddad was losing it, but I remembered quoting that line from *Twelfth Night* to him.

"I'm better than I have been all evening. Kipp, marry the man."

"But Sir will laugh at him, Granddad! He already is! Hyde, he thinks he's put something over on you!"

"And he's discovered he hasn't. When I learned of the nasty, mean-spirited trick he tried to pull on you tonight, I had no trouble informing him that line of credit he's been drawing on is no longer available to him."

Granddad continued to chuckle. "Didn't I tell you about karma, Kipp?"

"Yes, but I thought that was in regard to the Families." For what they'd done to Hyde.

"That's all immaterial at this point. Are you going to marry me, Kipp?"

"I... I.... You won't get the shares of Llewellyn, Inc."

"I hardly need them."

No, I supposed not. I tried one last time. "Everyone in Martinsburg is going to find out what I am."

"And what are you?"

"I'm a...." I couldn't say the word. "I'm not Marcus Llewellyn's son, and you'll be mocked for marrying a... me."

"Is that the only reason why you're saying no?"

"Yes."

"All right."

I felt defeated.

"Your reason is duly noted. And discarded."

He wasn't going to let me go. I stared into his eyes. "Are you really sure this is what you want?"

"Oh, Kipp." He touched my cheek, my ear, my throat, and I shivered from the erotic feel of it. "More than I've wanted anything."

Even Aaron Richardson? But I couldn't ask him that. Suppose he said no?

"Then I guess we're getting married tonight."

"Come stand by my bed," Granddad ordered. "I gave your mother away, but I'm not about to do that for you—"

"Uh... not the bride, Granddad," I felt I had to point out.

"Don't interrupt. And for obvious reasons, I can't stand up with you. However, I *will* be here for you."

"You always have been."

"Not as much as I should have." He reached for my hand and squeezed it gently.

"And if you've no objections, I'll be your best man, Kipp," my uncle said.

"I... thank you."

Father Ed cleared his throat. "You realize this ceremony is just a... um... ceremony?"

"Yes. Kipp and I will go down to city hall tomorrow and file the paperwork." Hyde gazed into my eyes. "Don't say no to me," he pleaded.

I couldn't. I took his hand. "And on Sunday, God willing, we'll have another ceremony, the one you always wanted."

He brought my hand to his mouth. He did like doing that!

"Do we have the rings?" Father Ed asked.

"I have Kipp's, Father." Hyde took the case from his pocket.

"How long have you been carrying that around?" I thought he'd have to use the wrapper from a straw on Granddad's bedside table; I hadn't expected Hyde to have it handy.

"Since the second time I saw you at Georg's."

I didn't believe him, but it was a sweet lie. "Well, I've got a ring for you! Just wait a second!" I reached for my suit jacket and took the platinum band from the inner pocket. I just hoped it would fit. "All right." I clutched Hyde's sleeve. "Are you certain you want to do this, even though you won't be getting the shares to Llewellyn, Inc.?"

"Blue eyes, I told you: I don't need those shares."

"But you wanted them."

"No, all I wanted was you. I knew Llewellyn would be a—would throw all kinds of roadblocks in our path if he didn't think otherwise."

"I hope you know what you're getting into, because I don't have the strength to say no to you again."

"I knew you were smart." He took my hand from his sleeve and rubbed his thumb over my knuckles. "I haven't told you that I love you."

"That's all right. I'll love you enough for both of us."

He tightened his grip on my fingers, and then turned to Father Ed. "If you'll begin, Father?"

"Just a second." I put on my suit jacket, tugged the hem to make sure it fell into place, and fastened the middle button. "All right, I'm ready."

"Wait! Wait!" Delphie was on her feet, looking through her bag.

"Mom?"

"Okay." She waved a handkerchief, her smile already watery. "Go ahead, Father."

The priest nodded. "Dearly beloved, we are gathered here together to join this man and this man...."

CHAPTER 42

GRANDDAD'S oncologist, Dr. Brooks, walked in just as I slid the platinum ring onto Hyde's finger and said, "This is my solemn vow." The ring was a little snug over his knuckle, and we'd probably need to get it resized in the morning, after we visited city hall, but it was on his finger, and he was mine.

"Mazel tov, gentlemen," Dr. Brooks said. "Now, please leave while I examine my patient."

We all walked out, leaving him alone with Granddad.

"Thank you, Father," Hyde said to the priest.

"You're welcome. I'll—"

Hyde took his hand and pressed something into it. The priest looked down at his palm, surprised, and then he flushed.

"Oh, really, this isn't necessary...."

"Please, Father. As a token."

"No, really, this is too much."

"You can donate it to your favorite charity if you choose." Hyde closed the priest's hand around the bills and folded his own hand over it.

"In that case, thank you. I'll return to my quarters now. I hope I won't be needed here again tonight."

I hoped so too.

"Well, this was certainly a wonderful surprise," Delphie said, carefully blotting her eyes. "I came for an engagement party and stayed for a wedding. Hyde, I think I'll go back to the hotel. It's been a long day. Kipp, I hope you won't mind if we have that coffee another day?"

"No, M-mom." I'd never called anyone that before, and I couldn't help grinning happily.

"I always wanted another son."

I knew I was blushing.

She pressed her hand to my cheek. It was softer than any hand I could remember touching me. She hugged me and kissed my cheek, and then turned to Hyde and did the same.

"Thanks for flying in early, Mom. Doug, would you mind giving her a lift back to the Trunk?"

"No problem. Delphie's right. This has been more excitement than I'm used to. Good night, cuz." He shook Hyde's hand, took mine as if to shake it, but then placed a hand on my shoulder and leaned down. "Make each other happy, Kipp," he whispered.

"Um... yes." I shook his hand and patted his arm awkwardly, then stood there watching as the two of them walked down the corridor. "They could have stayed at Silver Birch, Hyde. We have plenty of room."

"Not for long. I called your aunts and their families, and they'll be coming in tomorrow."

"To see Granddad?" They only waited until he was at death's door to put in an appearance? "That's nice of them." I hoped he didn't notice the sarcasm in my tone.

"Well, they will stay for the wedding."

"Is it really necessary? I mean, we're married now."

"Aren't you going to give me the wedding of my dreams?"

"Yes, Hyde. I'll give you whatever you desire." Whatever was in my power to give him, including more relatives, if that was what he wanted.

"Remember that." The expression in his eyes was hot, and my mouth went dry. Could we start our honeymoon now?

I leaned against him and rubbed my cheek against his shoulder.

"So... uh... how long have you known my nephew, Hyde?" Uncle Brad looked from me to Hyde.

That tender expression was on his face again. "Eighteen months and four days."

He'd been keeping track! I bumped my shoulder against his and grinned at him through my lashes.

"Hmm. I'd—" But we never knew what Uncle Brad was about to say.

Dr. Brooks came out of the room, shaking his head. "That man…."

"How…. Is he…?"

"It was indigestion."

"Oh, thank God." I sagged against Hyde. "I guess he really shouldn't have had that last peanut chicken skewer."

"Y'know, I told that stubborn old goat he could eat whatever he wanted, but this…." Dr. Brooks was shaking his head again. "And he informed me he had no intention of dying just yet; he'll be beside you on Sunday."

"Will he be well enough?"

"I think so. However, he'll need a wheelchair."

"That's not a problem, since we'd pretty much planned for that. We'll just have the florist decorate it." Hyde pulled out his cell phone and pressed a number. After a few seconds, he said, "Armitage? Congratulate me. I'm a married man!"

And he was married to me. I sighed happily.

"I'd also suggest you hire a nurse for the day," Dr. Brooks told me, calling my attention back to him.

"Yes, of course."

"Armitage can handle that as well," Hyde interjected before he went back to talking to his assistant. The man could multitask.

"Are you sure he'll be all right, Dr. Brooks?"

"Frankly, Mr. Llewellyn, I'm surprised he's lasted this long. And he'd shoot me if he knew I'd told you that. But on the other hand, let me say this: you've given him something to live for."

"All right. Thank—" My cell phone rang, and I knew from the tone—"He Ain't Heavy, He's My Brother"—it was Geoff calling. "Excuse me, please."

"That's all right; I have to update your grandfather's chart anyway. Good night, and congratulations again."

"Thank you." I took my phone from my pocket and touched the screen. "Hi, Geoff. Dr. Brooks has just seen Granddad, and he's doing all right. Hyde—"

"What? Oh... that's... I'm... Kipp, Father's had a stroke."

"Excuse me?"

"I said—"

"When did this happen?"

"I'm not sure; an hour ago? Two? I've lost track of time. I'm at the hospital, in the ER. I know... look, Kipp, I'm aware how things stand between you and Father now. I couldn't believe it, but...."

"But it's the truth. Granddad confirmed it. Geoff, if... if you'd rather I didn't come to your wedding—if you don't want me in your life.... I understand. I won't like it, but I'll abide by your wishes."

"No, no matter who your father is, you're still my brother, and I want you there. It's important to me, especially since it isn't likely that Father...." There was a hitch in his voice.

Oh, Geoff. "It's that bad?"

"It's... Apparently he's been having transient ischemic attacks for more than a year. Kipp, would you come here?"

"Where, to the hospital?"

"Yeah. I... please?"

"Sure. Give me a few minutes to say good night to Granddad, and then I'll drive right on over."

"Drive where, Kipp?" Hyde must have finished his conversation with Armitage; he was listening in, but he wouldn't have been able to hear Geoff's side of the conversation.

"Hold on a second, Geoff." I covered the mouthpiece of the phone. "To Martinsburg Memorial. Sir's had a stroke."

"I'll drive you."

"I've got the Mercedes."

"It can stay in the parking lot."

"But that's not allowed."

"They won't tow it."

No, they probably wouldn't, if only because everyone in town knew it was Granddad's car.

"Excuse me, but I'll take care of the Mercedes," my uncle said. "Just give me the keys."

I fished them from my pocket and dropped them in his palm.

"Thanks. I'm going to stay here a while longer; I haven't seen Dad in about fifteen years and I'd like to catch up." I must have looked horrified. "Oh, I called him on birthdays and Christmas."

I'd thought the Llewellyns lived at Dysfunction Junction, but it seemed the Martins did as well. Or was it all families, at one time or another?

"Do me a favor, all right? Don't wear him out."

He looked surprised but then smiled at me. "Kipling and Beth's son," he said softly. "You and I need to catch up too."

"I guess we do."

"Kipp? Let your brother know you're on your way."

"Yes, all right. Geoff? Sorry. I'm leaving now. I'll be there as soon as I can."

"Thanks, Kipp. It…. They're about to transfer him to a room. It doesn't look good."

Shit, there too? "Is anyone with you?"

"Mindy is. She's been… I don't know what I would have done without her. She made Higgins give her father's ID and insurance cards, and she drove. I never thought…."

"I guess she'll make a good first lady of Martinsburg. Now, hang in there. I'll see you in a few." I disconnected the call. "Just let me tell Granddad." I went back into his room. His eyes were closed, and I didn't want to wake him, but I touched his hand.

"Eh?"

"It's Kipp."

"I'm not asleep."

"Of course not. I have to leave. Sir's had a stroke, and Geoff asked me to come to the hospital."

"Are you driving?"

"No. I'll leave the Mercedes for Uncle Brad. He's staying with you for a while longer. Hyde will drive me."

"All right. Come see me tomorrow, after you're done at city hall."

"I will." I bent down and kissed his forehead. "Good night, Granddad. Sleep well." *And don't you die on me!*

He put his arms around me, and he murmured against my cheek, "My boy." For a second his voice was gruff. "Good night, Kipp. I'll see you tomorrow."

I walked out of his room. "Thanks, Uncle Brad. You can go in now."

"Uh.... Kipp, do you mind if I spend the night at Silver Birch?"

"Of course not. It's your home. Do you have a cell phone?"

"No."

"All right. I'll have to let Beauchamp know I won't be home tonight but you will." I'd also have to tell him we were related. "Hyde, just let me make this phone call."

"Of course."

I strode down the hall, and as soon as I was out of earshot, I called Silver Birch.

"Martin residence."

"B—" How could I call him Beauchamp when he was my grandfather? "It's Kipp. Uncle Brad will be staying at Silver Birch tonight."

"It will be good to see him again. I'll prepare his room. When may I expect you?"

"I'm not sure. Uncle Brad will be here at Hospice for a while longer, and I—"

"Do you have your key?"

"No."

"I'll keep the back door unlocked for you."

"Just for him. I'm staying with Hyde. We were married earlier in Granddad's room."

"I... I see. Congratulations, Mr. Kipp."

"Um... we're going to have another ceremony on Sunday. Granddad will walk down the aisle with me. Well, roll down the aisle. He'll be in a wheelchair. I was... I was wondering if you would also."

"Me?"

"Yes, please."

"To help with your grandfather; of course I will."

"Not exactly. I'd like you there as part of the family."

"That's very kind of you, but that's hardly conventional. I mean, what would the Families say?"

"I don't care what the Families say." Sometimes I really hated them. I drew in a deep breath. *All right, here goes nothing.* "I... I think you should stop calling me Mr. Kipp."

He was silent for a moment, then asked cautiously, "What did you want me to call you?"

"Just Kipp, Grandfather?"

"Oh, my God. You know?"

"I found out tonight that your son was my father. I overheard Sir talking about it. Is it all right if I call you Grandfather?"

"I... I...."

"Please?"

"I'd be honored."

"No, I will. I have to go now. Geoff called to tell me Sir—his father has had a stroke and has been hospitalized."

I thought he muttered something about it just being a matter of time, but then he said, "Thank you again for calling. And if I may, I hope you enjoy your first night as a married man."

"Thank you, Grandfather. Good night."

"Good... good night, my boy."

Granddad had called me the same thing. I hung up and fumbled for my handkerchief. After I blew my nose and dried my eyes, I went back to where Hyde and my uncle were waiting.

"Kipp, we'd… is everything okay?"

"Yes."

"Are you sure?"

"Yes." I rested my right palm against his cheek. He turned his head and pressed a kiss into it.

"Okay, we'd better get going."

"Yes, Hyde. Uncle Brad, Grandfather said he'd leave the back door of Silver Birch open for you."

"Who? Oh, Beauchamp." He didn't look disturbed by the fact that I had another grandfather now.

"How long can you stay in Martinsburg?"

"I've been given leave for a week."

"Will you be here tomorrow?"

"Absolutely."

"We'll see you then. Good night."

"Good night, Kipp. Hyde, thanks for getting me here in time for my nephew's wedding."

"You're welcome, Four."

Uncle Brad punched his shoulder lightly, and then turned and marched into Granddad's room, every inch the soldier.

"Y'know something, Hyde?"

"What?" He draped his arm around my shoulders, and we walked down the corridor toward the lobby.

"My father was in the army. So is my uncle. How come it never occurred to me to enlist?"

"That's simple. The army couldn't have you. You were destined to be mine."

I liked that thought.

CHAPTER 43

"Do you have any more surprises for me?" I asked my... I sighed happily... my *husband* as he drove toward Martinsburg Memorial.

"Surprises?"

"You knew I wasn't Sir's son even before I told you."

"It wasn't a smart move on Llewellyn's part to think I wouldn't do my research."

"He doesn't have a very high opinion of anyone's intelligence except his own."

"Stupid to underestimate your opponent."

"Well, to underestimate you. I guess he was so used to everyone believing he was my father that he didn't expect anyone to question him. Did he... was he behind the deaths of my parents?"

"Does it matter?"

"I think it does."

"Then I'll find out for you."

"Thank you. So." What else? "Armitage said you were away all afternoon. And that reminds me: we're going to Fiji for our honeymoon."

"We are?" The corner of his mouth curled up in a pleased grin.

"Yes, we are."

"I like Fiji."

"I'm aware. So what were you doing today?"

"Oh, I picked up my mother from the airport. I pulled in some favors to get your uncle leave so he could be here for the wedding. I called Doug and told him I wanted him at the engagement party."

"And in addition he was your best man. You've had a very busy day."

"I guess you could say that. And how did you spend your day, blue eyes?"

"I simply replaced my cell phone and got married." I waited until he finished chuckling before I continued. "And in between I took a nap. So... uh... where are we spending our wedding night? You're not going to make me wait until Sunday, are you?"

"No, I'm afraid I don't have that much fortitude."

"Has it been difficult for you, Hyde?"

"Eminently so."

"Good."

"Scamp. Where would you prefer we made love for the first time? In your bed at Silver Birch?"

"Would you mind if we spent our first night in your suite at the Trunk?" It would feel... strange... making love with my husband while my uncle and my newly discovered grandfather were at the other end of the house, aware of what we were doing. Hyde wouldn't know why I'd made this request, but nonetheless I felt myself blushing.

"If that's what you want." He pulled into the parking lot of Martinsburg Memorial, found a spot, and turned off the ignition.

"Great." I reached across the console and rested my hand high on his thigh.

"Kipp. There's something else." He took my hand off his thigh and got out of the car.

For a second my stomach tried to climb out through my throat. Had I done something he didn't like?

When Hyde realized I was still sitting there, he leaned into the car. "Kipp?"

"I'm... I'm sorry."

"For what?"

"I... I don't know. I've made you angry?"

"I'm not angry. Get out of the car, blue eyes."

I got out and stared at him across the roof of his SUV. The night air was cool, but that wasn't why I was shivering.

He swore and came around to me. "I'm going to take Llewellyn, Inc. apart one location at a time." His voice was tight.

"What?"

"That bastard has made you afraid to love—" He clenched his fingers, as if he wanted to touch me but worried he might scare me, which was ridiculous.

"I'm not afraid to love. I… I don't want to disgust you by being uncontrolled."

"Kipp, you can be as uncontrolled as you like."

"I can?"

"As long as it's with me, yes."

"Oh, in that case…." I stepped close to him until our shoes were touching. "I can do this?" I put his arms around my waist.

"Yes."

"And this?" I slid my arms around his neck.

"Yes."

"And this also?" I stroked the hollow at the base of his skull, and then urged his mouth down to mine and licked along the seam of his lips.

"And I hope you'll do this as well." He took my mouth in a heated kiss, and I grew dizzy from lack of oxygen. Finally he drew back and gave a soft laugh. "My blue-eyed tiger. I think I'd better stock up on Vitamin E."

"You don't need it." I rubbed my cheek against his jaw. His arousal was very evident against my abdomen. "I could stay like this all night."

"I've got a very comfortable bed waiting for us."

"Do you?" I sighed voluptuously. And then reality dawned. "Geoff is waiting for me."

"Okay. But visiting hours are usually very limited." He nuzzled the hair away from my earlobe and nibbled on it.

"You didn't let that stop you the other night, when I was in the hospital."

"Well, I care more about you than I do about any Llewellyns. That reminds me…."

"Yes?" How wonderful it was to just stand here in his arms.

"Your name."

"I'll have to ask Beauchamp if he has any objections to me changing it to Beauchamp." I leaned back and looked into his eyes. "I hadn't told you that. His son was my father. Will... will you mind being married to a butler's grandson?"

"Not as long as he's you. But I was wondering if you'd be willing to share my name."

"You mean Beauchamp-Wyndham? It's a mouthful, don't you think? But I like it."

"I do too. In fact, I think it suits you much better than Llewellyn-Wyndham would." He took my hand from around his neck and brought it to his mouth. "Most people would be having an identity crisis, you know."

"Why?"

"Changing your name after twenty-one years."

"I don't mind. Sir... Marcus always made me feel as if I wasn't worthy of it. And if it turned out that we didn't know who my father was, just that he wasn't Marcus, I'd change my name to Martin."

"That would make your grandfather very proud."

I smiled into those eyes of his. How had I gotten so lucky as to fall in love with this man?

"We'd better go see your brother." He brought me back for one last kiss, and then set me away from him.

My brother.... "Please, Hyde, don't take apart Llewellyn, Inc. Odds are Sir...." How long was it going to take before I stopped calling him that? "Marcus isn't going to make it, and while Geoff could find another job, it wouldn't be here in Martinsburg."

"You don't want to hurt Geoff."

"No."

"All right, then. Let's find out where Llewellyn is." He wound his fingers through mine, and we began walking toward the main entrance of Martinsburg Memorial.

And I completely forgot there was something else he'd wanted to talk about.

CHAPTER 44

MARCUS was in ICU, and I didn't know if they'd allow me to see him, but apparently word hadn't spread yet that I wasn't his son. The nurse behind the desk gave a tired smile and nodded toward a room at the far end of the unit. "Keep the visit short, please."

"Yes." I reached for Hyde's hand, and she didn't object to him accompanying me.

When I entered the room, I was stunned by Marcus's appearance. The entire right side of his face dragged down and his left eye, barely open, looked vague.

And my brother... his face was drawn and his complexion was muddy. "Geoff."

"Oh, God, Kipp, I'm so glad you're here!" He was on his feet and hugging me before I realized he'd moved. Hot tears fell on my neck.

"I'm so sorry." I'd never seen my brother so shaken, and I didn't know what else to say.

He let me go and fished a handkerchief from his pocket. "Sorry. This has been.... Let's step outside." He didn't speak until he closed the door. "Hearing is one of the last things to go, and he may look like he's out of it, but I wouldn't be surprised if he... oh, hello, Hyde."

"Geoff."

"Tell me what happened." I rested my hand on his arm, hoping it would give him some comfort.

"Father was in the dining room demanding to know where you were. I told him you'd left with Grandfather. He wasn't happy to see me, especially when I called him on having shrimp cocktail served. I couldn't believe he'd do something like that. I'd *told* him.... Anyway,

Hyde walked in, and when *he* saw the shrimp cocktail he hit the ceiling."

"Yes, I did," Hyde murmured. "How he could do something like that, knowing it could kill you...."

I left Geoff and went to Hyde. "We talked about him not believing anyone had a modicum of intelligence." I kept my voice low. "Marcus could put out all the shellfish he wanted; I wasn't going to eat it."

Geoff had continued speaking, too lost in his thoughts to pay attention to our quiet words. "... I thought for a minute he was going to knock me down, but when he realized I had informed Father about your reaction to shellfish.... He told Father he was withdrawing his financial support. And then he walked out."

"Well, there was no reason for me to stay." Hyde twined our fingers together. "*You* weren't there."

"Father had Higgins tell the guests the party was over and they were to leave. He went into his study, and I followed him. He had a glass of Ladybank in one hand—you know he won't drink anything else—and a handkerchief in the other. I asked him if it was true you weren't his son. That was when Father began ranting: about Mother, about you, about Wyndham, and how Father was going to come out on top this time. I told him I wasn't going to let him do that, sacrifice you so he could make a few millions." He glanced at Hyde and then at me. "I'm sorry Kipp. I know you want to marry him, but this wouldn't be a good marriage for you, not when Wyndham wouldn't be getting what he thought he would."

I opened my mouth to tell him I was already married to Hyde, but Hyde squeezed my shoulder. "Hush," he whispered.

"Father started cursing at me. How dare I ruin his plans by putting you above our family? I was a Llewellyn, and you were nothing but a... a.... And then he collapsed. Mindy called 911."

"Oh, Geoff." I appreciated him not telling me what his father considered me.

"I didn't even realize she was there, that she'd heard the whole diatribe. I was positive that she'd leave once she made that phone call, but she stayed at my side the entire time. And she made Higgins give her Father's ID and insurance cards."

"Yes, you'd mentioned that."

"I did?" He shook his head and scrubbed his face. "Once the ambulance got Father here, the doctors in the ER ran some preliminary tests, but according to Dr. Van Winkle—"

"Who?"

"He's Father's doctor. He said Father's cholesterol has been sky high and his blood pressure out of control for the past two years. What's surprising is that he didn't have a stroke before now."

"But you said he'd been having those TIAs."

He shrugged.

"Why did he let it go so long?"

"You know how he can be. If he refuses to acknowledge something, then it just isn't relevant."

That was true. How often had he overlooked my presence in his home?

"What's the prognosis?" Hyde asked.

"As I told Kipp, it doesn't look good. They can't determine just yet what his mental status is. If he winds up like a vegetable...."

Marcus had always prided himself on his acuity and intelligence, and if he lost that, would he want to continue living? I imagined being trapped in an unresponsive body, unable to communicate at all, and I shuddered and pressed a fist into my gut.

Hyde noticed, but misread my action. "Kipp, you must be starved. Do you want me to get something for you?"

That reminded me that other than some hors d'oeuvres, I hadn't eaten anything since the slice of pizza at lunch.

"Thanks, Hyde. I don't think the cafeteria will be open at this hour, but whatever you can get will be fine."

"You'll be here for a while, yes? If the hospital doesn't have anything, I'll—"

"Don't tell me you'll send Armitage out for something!"

"I wouldn't do that to her. I'll just drive over to Burger King. Did you want anything, Geoff?"

"Hmm? No, thanks."

"Oh, get me a caramel frappé too?"

"For you, blue eyes? Anything." He caught my left hand, careful of my bandaged palm, and kissed the ring he'd placed on my finger less than an hour and a half before.

I was smiling as I watched him stride away. That was, until Geoff grabbed my hand.

"What the fuck?"

"Ow!"

"Sorry." He eased his grip on my hand. "But what is this?"

"I didn't have the chance to tell you. Hyde and I are married."

"Why?"

"Well, when two people are in love—"

"He doesn't love you, Kipp." He had the courtesy to look abashed when I flinched. "I'm sorry, I shouldn't have been so blunt, but you know the only reason he wanted to marry you was to get your shares of Llewellyn, Inc."

"Which he won't, since I'm not Marcus's son." And yes, he hadn't said he loved me, but he was going to. I had a lot of time—the rest of our lives—to make sure of that.

"When he finds out—"

"He knows, Geoff. How could you think I'd marry him without telling him something so important?"

"I'm... I'm sorry, Kipp. He actually married you?"

"Yes, in Granddad's room at Hospice. We weren't sure if he'd make it until Sunday, so...."

"How is he?"

"Actually, he's better. His doctor said it was just a touch of indigestion."

"I'm sorry I couldn't be there. I was supposed to be your best man."

"That's okay, Uncle Brad was there. But you can still stand up with me on Sunday if... if you want?"

"You're going through with it?"

"Sure. I mean, why not? We've reserved the Rampart Room, and all those people are coming. This is something Hyde really wants, and...."

"What Hyde wants, you'll give him?"

"If it's in my power." I knew it sounded silly, but he'd had one fiancé who'd allowed himself to be coerced into abandoning him, and I intended to make sure he knew I'd be at his side no matter what. "Besides, I've got the most amazing tux, and I'd like to wear it for the reason Hyde bought it for me."

"We'll be there, Mindy and I." He touched my arm. "I don't know how long we'll be able to stay, but...."

"Thank you, Geoff. And speaking of Mindy, where is she? Do you need a ride back to Llewellyn Manor?"

"No, thanks. She's in the ladies room."

"All this time?"

"Kipp, have you ever dated a girl?"

"No."

"Okay, so you won't know that this isn't an inordinate amount of time." In spite of the situation, he grinned.

"If you say so."

His grin faded. "I tried to make her go home but she wouldn't listen to me."

"And why should she? She's going to be your partner, Geoff."

"But I'm supposed to take care of her."

"You're supposed to take care of each other."

"But she's so young!"

"There's only ten years between you."

"Whereas there are twice as many years between you and Hyde."

"Wait a minute. What does that have to do with anything?"

"I don't know." He scrubbed his face again. "I'm sorry. I'm going to sit with Father."

"I'll go with you."

"Why? He's not your father."

"No, but you're my brother."

"Kipp…."

"Geoff." I'd never seen anyone who looked more in need of a hug.

So I hugged him.

CHAPTER 45

FRIDAY was busy, between making sure our marriage was legalized, having Hyde's ring resized, introducing my husband to family I had never met, and seeing Granddad, who looked better.

Saturday was spent having the final fitting of my tux and marveling with Granddad over the list of celebrities who'd be coming to my wedding.

"Um… Hyde? Why is Daniel Richardson's name on this?"

"He treated you like something no one would want, and I intend to show him how wrong he was. I want him to see what he let slip through his fingers."

Granddad looked up, his grin hard. "A man after my own heart."

"Well, he probably won't come." Why would anyone be a glutton for that kind of punishment?

"Oh, he'll be there." And if Granddad's grin had been hard, Hyde's was like titanium steel.

"His father isn't going to be happy."

"Ask me if I care."

Whoa. I'd have to make a point never to get on Hyde's wrong side! "When… uh… when were you going to tell me?"

"I started to the other night outside the hospital, but then you distracted me. And frankly, I couldn't care less about the Richardsons, father or son." He glanced at Granddad. "If you don't mind, Bradley, Kipp needs to rest. He's still suffering from the aftereffects of his allergic reaction."

"I am?" I whispered.

"Yes, you are."

Granddad's smile was warm. "Go ahead. I'll see you tomorrow at the Trunk."

And of course, Hyde saw to it that I got plenty of rest. After he loved me to within an inch of my life.

I GNAWED on a fingernail and stared at the crowd on the south lawn. I knew there were supposed to be five hundred people at our reception, but this looked like more than a thousand! What had happened to the intimate ceremony Hyde had wanted? In addition, the path Granddad and I were about to walk down seemed to be unending; it meandered across the entire length and breadth of the lawn. By the time we finally got into position for the final walk that would end with me beside Hyde, I was sweating and my bowtie had wilted.

The trio started to play Mouret's "Rondeau" complete with horns. Um... all right, but wasn't that supposed to be a string trio?

Everyone turned to look at us.

My heart was pounding so hard I truly thought it was about to do an imitation of a chestburster, and then Granddad murmured, "It's time, Kipp," and he gripped my hand.

I gave him a weak smile and nodded, keeping my eyes on the carpet; we began that long walk.

"Kipp."

"Yes, Granddad?"

He was looking straight ahead, and when I raised my eyes to follow his gaze, it was to see Hyde standing beside Father Timothy, the pastor of Saints Peter and Paul. Hyde's smile was proud. That smile is for you! *I told myself, and I was so relieved I felt as if I could walk on air. I was getting married. Not in a hospice room with the threat of death hovering over my grandfather; not at city hall with other couples waiting to exchange their vows; but here, under a May sky that was unbelievably blue, and beneath the arch where Hyde was waiting for me.*

The tux he wore was amazing, and he looked so scrumptious I was tempted to drag him behind the hedges and have my wicked way with him.

He must have realized where my thoughts were going, because he dipped his eyelid in a slow wink, and I could feel a blush rising as I grew hard.

I released Granddad's hand and stepped forward to take my place beside the man I loved more than.... Another line from Shakespeare came to mind, and I couldn't help smiling. Yes, I loved him more than I'd ever love a wife.

Father Timothy began to speak, and I turned my attention to him. "Dearly beloved: We have come together in the presence of God to witness and bless the joining together of these two men in Holy Matrimony."

We prayed, we sang, we prayed some more, and finally Father Timothy smiled at us.

"I'm sure this is what you've been waiting for, even though you've gone through something similar twice before. Hyde, if you'll repeat after me—"

"No! No, no, no!" someone shouted, and as if we were synchronized, Hyde and I both turned to see who was interrupting our wedding. "What happened to objecting?" Aaron Richardson struggled past guests, stepping on toes, almost knocking people off their chairs, and nearly tripping and falling on his face as he made his way toward the aisle. "There was supposed to be objecting!"

"What the fuck?" Doug muttered.

"Daddy!" Mindy cried.

"Aaron, don't!" Mrs. Richardson hurried after him, her expression stoic, but I could see the humiliation in her eyes.

Behind her was... Daniel? How had I not even noticed him?

"I object to this marriage!" Richardson bellowed.

"Dad, what are you talking about?" Daniel demanded. But his father ignored him, glowering at me instead.

"I know the truth about you, and if you don't leave at once, I'll tell Hyde!"

"What truth?"

"About who your father is! Or should I say isn't?"

"Y'know, I resent that. Why does everyone think I'd do something so despicable as to keep that from my husband?"

"He's not your husband! I stopped the wedding in time. Even though you didn't ask if anyone objected!" He glared at Father Timothy.

"We don't do that anymore, Mr. Richardson." Father Timothy sounded mildly surprised. With that line no longer included in the service, a lot of the drama of a wedding was removed.

"Well, do it now so I can object!"

Doug was right. What the fuck?

"Dad, how can you object to this?" Daniel's face was flushed. He was as handsome as ever, but his looks did nothing for me. "What does it matter to you?"

"Hyde Wyndham was mine years ago, and he's going to be mine again!"

"You... you're gay? Jesus, Dad, you threw me out of the house because of Auggie, and all this time you've been gay?"

Richardson was practically frothing at the mouth, and in spite of the fact that his son was standing beside him, he ignored Daniel completely. "You can't marry him, Hyde! You love me!"

"Aaron, you're married. And so am I."

"No, you're not! The priest hasn't pronounced you anything yet! And I can get a divorce. I will get a divorce!"

"Aaron, I told you eleven years ago I had no intention of being your dirty little secret. There could never be anything between us."

Wait, what? "Hyde? Why didn't you tell me?" I'd thought they hadn't had any contact since Richardson had been sent to Great Britain.

"I didn't think it was necessary. I turned him down, and I saw no reason to embarrass him by bringing up old news."

"I... I see."

"Kipp?"

"So you could have had him then if you'd wanted him."

"Yes, but I told you I wouldn't go after a married man."

No, he wouldn't.

It was rather fitting. All of Martinsburg and half the known world now understood that Hyde wanted me enough to marry me. And they might not be aware at this point that I wasn't Marcus's son, but Hyde had been, and he'd still married me. I caught his hand and squeezed it. *"I wish you'd told me, though. I'm not fond of surprises."*

"I'll remember that."

"It was a mistake for me to come here. I'm sorry." Daniel looked ill. *"I'd hoped we could be friends—"*

"Why would you want to be friends with me? After what happened three years ago?"

"You don't realize what you are, do you? Everyone liked you...."

"Who, me?"

"Yes, you." He sounded annoyed. *"If you'd gone to the prom, you'd probably have been voted Prom King."*

"Me?"

"After that night—oh, God, I realized what I'd done! I tried to talk to you, to apologize, but you looked right through me. No one had ever done that to me."

"I had no idea." I would have run a hand through my hair, but Hyde was still holding on to it. He tightened his grip and smiled into my eyes.

"No, I guess you didn't." Daniel seemed puzzled by that. *"I'd better go. I hope you'll be happy, Kipp."*

"Thank you, Daniel."

I watched as he spoke to his mother and kissed his sister's cheek, which was why I was startled when Richardson grabbed my arm.

"You! Bastard boy! Take your hand off—Oww!"

Hyde had punched him. *"Keep your foul mouth shut, Ron."*

"You... you hit me!"

"Damn straight I hit you, and I'll hit you again if you ever call Kipp anything other than his name! You walked away from me twenty years ago, Ron—"

"Don't call me that! I hate it!"

"—in spite of the fact that we were engaged. I wouldn't marry you now even if you did divorce your wife. Who doesn't deserve what you've done to her." Hyde shook his head and pulled me against his side. *"I'm sorry, Kipp. I had no idea he'd do anything this stupid."*

"Well, it's a good thing we were married twice already." The sense of satisfaction I felt was truly unchristian, but Richardson was not only twenty years too late in deciding he wanted Hyde, he was forty-eight hours too late as well.

"What? What? You can't be married! I stopped it!"

"I'm so sorry." Mrs. Richardson stared after her son's retreating back, and she looked tired and sad and defeated.

"It's not your fault." Hyde reached for something in his pocket but came up empty-handed. *"Dammit. I left my phone in my suite."*

"I have mine, Mr. Wyndham." Ms. Armitage held up her clutch purse and gave a little wave.

"Thank you. Call Webster, please?"

"Yes, sir." She pressed a number. *"Mr. Webster? This is Ms. Armitage, Mr. Wyndham's personal assistant. Send security to the south lawn, please. No, just a minor interruption. Thanks."* She shut her phone and put it away.

"Thank you."

"You're welcome, boss."

"Mindy?" He glanced at Geoff's fiancée and then nodded toward her mother.

Mindy's face was white, but she forced a smile and went to her. *"Mummy, why don't you let me take you inside? It's cooler, and I'll get you a cup of tea."* She slid an arm around her mother's waist.

"I can't stay for the wedding," Mrs. Richardson said. *"Kipp, I'm so sorry—"*

"No need to be." But had she even heard me?

"After the fool Aaron's made not only of himself but of me.... I can't even remain in Martinsburg any longer."

"No one's asking you to, you stupid bitch!" Richardson snarled. In spite of the accident of my birth, he was the real bastard. *"Do you think I don't know you never wanted to marry me? Oh, yes, I knew all about that boy from your village. Your parents wanted you to marry me as much as mine wanted me to marry you."*

Mindy stared at her father as if she'd never seen him before, and then turned back to her mother. *"You can stay with me and Geoff, Mummy."* Mindy glanced over her shoulder, searching for Geoff.

"Kipp...."

"Go, Geoff." I remembered our conversation in the ICU. *"It's all right."* It was more important that he be there for her than for me.

He went to his fiancée's side. *"Mindy's right, Mom. You can stay with us."*

"I knew he never loved me, but I thought he cared about me.... And what he did to our son...."

Her voice became fainter and then faded completely as they entered the Rampart Room.

"I'm not letting you get away again, Hyde," Richardson was insisting, completely disregarding the wreck he'd made of his family. *"Father's not here to stop me this time! We'll be happy together!"*

"Aaron, what don't you understand about 'already married'?"

"But you can't be!"

"Jesus!" Hyde growled.

Fortunately, three men who wore the black-and-maroon security uniforms of the Saratoga Trunk approached just then.

"Please escort Mr. Richardson to his car. And if he gives you a hard time, call the Martinsburg PD and have him arrested on charges of... well, I'm sure they'll think of something."

"Being a public nuisance?" I asked softly. I didn't like the look in Richardson's eyes.

"No!" Richardson jerked free and tried to race back to Hyde.

Bullshit! He'd have to go through me to get to my husband. I was ready to slug him, but the security men grabbed his arms and jerked him to a halt.

"*You're going in the wrong direction, Mr. Richardson. Let us show you the right way.*"

"*No!*"

This time, as much as he struggled, the security men kept their grip on him.

Hyde stood there staring after him. Well, this wasn't good.

"*Hyde.*" *I pressed my palm to his cheek.*

"*I'm sorry, baby. I'm so sorry. I never thought he'd do something so insane.*"

We watched as Richardson was hustled through an opening in the hedges rather than through the Rampart Room.

"*Shall we continue, gentlemen?*" *Father Timothy asked.*

"*I don't know if Kipp wants to marry me again.*"

I did! "*I do!*" *For some reason, I couldn't move, couldn't get to him.* "*I do....*"

CHAPTER 46

"KIPP? Blue eyes, wake up!" Hyde held me so tightly against him, I couldn't move.

"Huh? What?"

"You were dreaming."

"I was?" I blinked and rubbed my eyes. Light was filtering through the curtains. Oh, of course I was dreaming. There was no way I'd be voted Prom King. Also, I had no idea if Mrs. Richardson had loved anyone from her village. And who the hell was "Auggie?" Geoff had never mentioned Daniel's boyfriend by name. God, the subconscious was weird.

"What was it about?"

"Our wedding. There were like a kazillion people there, and Mr. Richardson tried to object to keep us from saying 'I do.'"

"Well, he can do whatever he likes, but that isn't going to happen."

"No, it isn't." I wanted to lean against him and tip my head back for his kiss, but I needed to brush my teeth. "You've been up?"

"I ordered breakfast." He kissed me anyway, and then let me go. "Come on, sleepyhead. It's going to be a busy day!"

I rolled out of bed and pulled on the sleep pants that had somehow wound up across the room.

"Give me five, and I'll be right with you!"

BREAKFAST had been fabulous and we spent most of the morning... thumbing through the brochures Ms. Armitage had seen were brought to our suite. There were a lot of things to do, not only on Fiji, but in the surrounding area.

Just after one there was a knock on our door.

"That's probably your brother and my cousin," Hyde said as he checked his watch and grabbed up his robe. "I'll get it. *You* put something on!"

Well, we hadn't spent *that* much time looking at those brochures.

I put on sweats and a T-shirt that read *He's my first, my last, my forever*, and followed the sound of conversation. Hyde was in the foyer, along with Doug and Uncle Brad.

From the expression on Hyde's face, he approved of my T, but he said, "We have to start getting ready."

"Where's Geoff?"

"He had an emergency call from the hospital." Uncle Brad looked a little frazzled. "Trust Marcus Llewellyn to cause a problem at the most inconvenient time."

I had to agree with him. "Will Geoff be back in time for the ceremony?"

"He said he'd try, but I'm here if he can't make it."

"Thanks, Uncle Brad."

"Hyde, where do I...?"

"The room just down the hall has been reserved for the two of you to get ready. Kipp, your tux and accessories are there, and Brad, your dress uniform should have arrived as well. Doug?"

"I've got my tux right here." He held up a garment bag.

"Okay. The master is straight ahead. You can have first crack at the shower. Kipp, we don't want to be late...."

"Do I get a last kiss before the ceremony?" I asked, doing my best to look innocent.

"Of course."

"No, I don't think so!" Uncle Brad objected. "Look at his neck! What are you, Dracula or something, Hyde?"

I couldn't help blushing. Of course I'd marked Hyde as well, but he'd left some fairly noticeable marks on my neck. I'd seen them when I was brushing my teeth; well, they'd been hard to miss.

Hyde just laughed, tipped my chin up, and gave me a quick kiss. "That will have to do for now, blue eyes."

"All right, but I'm keeping a tally, and I expect you to pay in full."

"I look forward to it. Now go. We don't want to run late."

THE room for me and Uncle Brad was small by the Trunk standards, but we managed not to get into each other's way as we showered, shaved, and began pulling on clothes.

For my first wedding in Granddad's room at Hospice, I'd worn my midnight-blue suit. The next day when we'd had the ceremony at city hall to make it legal, I'd worn Dockers and a dress shirt and the black boxer briefs with red hearts.

Hyde liked those briefs. He liked them even better off my body.

AFTER the official ceremony at city hall was over, we'd dropped off Hyde's ring to be resized, paid a visit to Granddad, and then returned to his—our—suite at the Saratoga Trunk.

He removed each article of clothing that I wore, toying with my nipples until they were pebble hard, tracing the faint line of hair down past my navel, running his fingertips over the length of my dick.

"You're a little overdressed, handsome," I told him.

A warm blush was visible in spite of the caramel of his skin. "I'm not—"

"You are. You're my brown-eyed handsome man, so get used to it." I tossed aside the bedspread and sheet and made myself comfortable. I'd worried that thoughts of the fiasco with Daniel would plague my wedding night, but Hyde had made it so good for me that I hadn't thought of anyone but him. In the morning, I wasn't even slightly sore, and I couldn't wait for him to claim my body again.

AND now today....

In about half an hour Hyde and I would be standing before Father Timothy, who actually *was* the pastor of Saints Peter and Paul, exchanging vows for the third and final time.

Although maybe we'd renew them for our golden anniversary.

I peered into the mirror. Fortunately my eyes were clear and unshadowed; they didn't show a trace of the dream I'd had.

I smoothed a hand over my hair and tugged the hem of my tux jacket.

"Do you need any help with your tie?" Uncle Brad asked as we finished dressing.

I smiled at my uncle. "No, I've got it, thanks," I told him. My palm wasn't completely healed, but it was well enough that I didn't need the bandage.

"You've got a beautiful day for this."

"Yes, we do." The weather was gorgeous and everyone I'd met had been so nice to me. I ran my thumb over my naked ring finger. The only thing that made me unhappy was the fact that I'd had to remove my ring. I said as much to my uncle.

"Well, consider this: once Hyde puts it on your finger this time, you won't ever have to take it off. Hyde's never going to lose you."

"Rather I'm never going to lose him. He's really mine now." I couldn't help grinning. I loved being married to Hyde. "I'm just sorry Geoff won't be able to stay for the whole thing."

"How's your—his—father?" Uncle Brad asked.

"Geoff didn't say?"

"No. He just... what do you youngsters say? Booked. And I'm sorry, I know this isn't a situation to be taken lightly, but I never liked Marcus Llewellyn."

I shrugged. "He's lost the use of his entire right side, and he can't speak—everything comes out garbled—but he's aware of what's going on. Geoff told me he could see it in his eyes. It's killing him."

"Who? Marcus?"

"No, Geoff. In spite of what his father is, he loves him."

"You talk so easily about 'his' father. For twenty-one years you thought Marcus was your father too."

"Yes, I did. Thank God he isn't."

"I suppose I shouldn't be shocked by your attitude."

"I hope not, Uncle Brad. You were willing to walk away from Silver Birch because of what Grandmother, Granddad, and Marcus did to my mother." A tap on the door interrupted the uncomfortable conversation. "Yes?"

The door opened and Doug poked his head in. "Are you ready? It's time."

I smoothed my hair a final time, gave another tug to the hemline of my jacket, and swallowed. Funny, I'd said "I do" to Hyde twice already, but this felt as if it were the first time.

I drew in a breath, held it, and blew it out, then nodded decisively. "I'm ready."

"In that case, let's get going. Hyde's already gone down." Doug grinned at me, and Uncle Brad put his hand on my lower back to usher me out of the room.

It didn't feel the same as when Hyde did that.

Mr. Webster, the catering manager, was holding the elevator for us. "There's been a slight change in plans, Mr. Llew—Beauchamp-Wyndham."

"Oh? The wine arrived, didn't it?"

We got into the elevator, and he pressed "lobby".

"Yes, indeed. It's just that... er... a number of your guests have expressed a desire to witness the wedding."

"Have you talked to my husband about this?" God, I *loved* being able to say that!

"Yes, of course."

"And?"

"He said I should bring it up with you."

Great. Hyde had made all the decisions, and *now* he was turning it over to me?

The elevator came to a smooth halt and the doors slid open. "How many of them?"

"Er... everyone from Martinsburg."

That would be about a hundred and seventy-five people. "Do you have enough chairs to seat them on the lawn? And is there enough time to set up the chairs?"

"The chairs aren't a problem. We already have thirty-six prepared. However—"

"Just a second. *Thirty-six?*" How did an intimate wedding with just me and Hyde, Granddad and Geoff, grow to thirty-six? Uneasily, I recalled my dream and the unexpected mob.

"Mr. Martin sent me a memo. Aside from your brother, who'll be your best man, he said twenty-one will be at the ceremony." Mr. Webster could see I was about to question the remaining guests, and he hurried to explain, "The rest are at Mr. Wyndham's request."

"All right, fine. So what about getting the additional chairs in place?"

"I'm afraid that would cause a bit of a delay."

Why hadn't Hyde thought of this? And then I realized: the reception could have as many people as the Rampart Room held, but he wanted an intimate ceremony. Although thirty-six.... I was going to have a little talk with both my husband and my grandfather once the service was over.

"All right, that solves the problem, then. My grandfathers, my brother's fiancée and her family, my uncle—have my aunts arrived from Silver Birch?" I didn't really know them, but if people I didn't particularly like were going to hear me and Hyde exchange vows, then family I didn't really know were just as welcome.

"Yes, and they've been seated with their families."

"All right. Mr. Wyndham's mother and cousin and whoever else he wants—"

"That would be his aunts and their families, his uncles, and Ms. Armitage."

I nodded. I liked her. "All right, Phyllida Carter and her date, Hunter, Mrs. Wales, and Pierce. Oh, and Mrs. Miller, Granddad's nurse. These are the only attendees. The other guests shouldn't be here this early anyway. How did that happen?"

"I'm sure I can't say. What am I to do with them?"

"Start the cocktail hour early."

He turned pale. "Chef Edouard is still preparing—"

"Mr. Webster, get the bar open. If Chef doesn't have anything ready, serve them cheese and crackers. And if the string trio is here, have them start playing."

"Oh, my. Oh, my." For a second it seemed as if he was going to cry. "I'm so sorry, Mr. Beauchamp-Wyndham, but they'll be playing for you."

Shit. "All right, see if anyone has something suitable on their iPods."

"Excuse me, please. I'll just…. Chef is going to be so distressed!"

"Tell him there will be a bonus for everyone."

"Thank you! That will be sure to help!" Mr. Webster rushed off.

I ran my hand through my hair, and Doug made a choking sound and covered his mouth.

"What?" This was my wedding day, dammit. Well, one of them. Wasn't standing beside Hyde and saying "I do" all I was supposed to do?

"You're mussing yourself." He smoothed my hair.

"Oh. Thank you."

"I have to say it's a pleasure watching you work."

I gave him a distracted look. "Excuse me?"

"I was wondering if you'd throw your weight around and tell the manager to remind Chef Edouard who his employer was."

"That would be rude. And besides, he might spit in my food."

Both he and Uncle Brad began to laugh. "Come on. Hyde is going to think we got lost."

CHAPTER 47

WE STOOD just outside the double doors, my grandfathers and I, and I swallowed hard. Geoff had made it back just in time, and since he was my best man, Uncle Brad had gone to take a seat on the left side of the aisle behind his sisters and their families, while Doug went to stand beside Hyde.

Hyde's mother looked breathtaking in a one-shoulder draped chiffon gown in peach. Mindy wore a strapless knee-length in her signature shade, this time lilac, and Mrs. Richardson carried off a halter tea-length dress in teal with panache.

I was touched that they would make such an effort for me, especially on such short notice.

Doug, his jaw almost on his shoes, was staring at someone, and I was amused when I realized his reaction was to Ms. Armitage's appearance in a ruby V-neck, floor-length taffeta dress.

Well, well.

The trio began to play Pachelbel's "Canon in D Major" and everyone rose and turned to look at us. I knew there were thirty-six people seated beneath the open tent, but it felt like a million eyes were staring at us. The path Granddad and I were originally supposed to take had been altered so that we walked to the rear and then down the center aisle.

There was no problem with Granddad's wheelchair, and Beauchamp... Grandfather, was kind enough to push the chair while I walked alongside, holding Granddad's arm.

"I wish you every happiness, Kipp."

"Thanks, Granddad." Suddenly I was almost giddy with excitement, and he must have seen that in my face as I gazed down at him.

"My boy." He attempted to smile, but his upper lip quivered. He took a handkerchief from his pocket and blew his nose. He didn't sound like a Canadian goose either.

"Are you sure you're up for this?" The ceremony was going to be at least an hour long and most likely longer, since Communion would be offered.

"I'll be fine." He put his handkerchief away and gripped my hand.

"Indeed... Kipp," Grandfather Beauchamp assured me. "I'll keep an eye on him, and if it looks like he's starting to grow weak, Mrs. Miller is here to see to him."

"I'm right here, you know," Granddad groused, more himself now.

"We know, and we want to keep you here." I squeezed his hand gently, and when I looked up, it was to find Hyde watching me.

I knew there were other people there: but as in my dream, everyone faded to nothingness. I released Granddad's hand and stepped forward to take my place beside Hyde.

Father Timothy waited for everyone to be seated, and then opened his book and began the service. I let his words drift over me, recalling the breakfast Hyde and I had shared. He'd ordered caviar but even though it wasn't shellfish, he wouldn't let me have any, no matter how I wheedled. But he'd fed me the lush strawberries he dipped in whipped cream.

I ran my tongue over my lips, remembering the sweetness he'd kissed from them.

And then Father Timothy was saying, "Hyde, if you'll repeat after me....?"

There was no line about objecting, but when I heard rustling behind me, I glared over my shoulder at Mr. Richardson. He turned red, his shoulders slumped, and he looked away.

"Kipp?" Hyde recalled my attention.

"Sorry," I whispered and held out my hand for him to slide the ring onto my finger.

"All right, Kipp," Father Timothy said.

I turned to Geoff, and he handed me Hyde's ring. Then I took a breath and began the vows I'd said twice before. "I, Kipp, take thee, Hyde, to be my wedded husband, to have and to hold from this day forward, for better or worse, for richer or poorer, in sickness and in health, to love and to cherish, until we are parted by death." With the ring back on his finger, I gazed into his honey-brown eyes and said again, "This is my solemn vow."

Hyde took my hand and pressed his lips to the ring on my finger. I cradled his face with both palms and drew him to me for a kiss.

"Kipp," he murmured.

I wrapped my arms around him and held him tight, and whispered softly into his pleated shirtfront, "My heart, my soul, my life." I sighed happily, and then I stepped back and smiled into those eyes of his.

The sound of applause reminded us we weren't alone. Hyde twined his fingers with mine and we turned to face our family and friends—and the two Richardson men—and greeted them for the first time—today—as husband and husband.

WITH the ceremony concluded, we entered the Rampart Room to be met with a rain of confetti.

Thank God I didn't have to worry about everyone wondering what the hell had happened on the south lawn—aside from me marrying Hyde for a third time, nothing had.

We danced our first dance, kissed when spoons tapped glasses, stopped by each table to chat with our guests, and dined on the meal Chef Edouard had outdone himself to prepare for us. The lobster tail looked delicious, but the memory of my reaction to prawns was too current for it to tempt me.

The Venetian Hour was about to start when Mrs. Miller, Granddad's nurse, approached us. "Mr. Martin is—"

I didn't give her a chance to finish. I rose and hurried to his side.

"Granddad, do you want to leave now?" I wasn't going to ask how he was; I could see how tired he looked.

"Yes, Kipp. I know you'll be leaving on your honeymoon tomorrow. Enjoy yourself, and come see me when you get back."

"I will, I promise." I'd offered to postpone it, but he'd insisted we go. "I'll make sure Grandfather Beauchamp brings a piece of cake for you." Granddad loved cake, and this one with cannoli cream filling and whipped cream frosting would be a treat for him tomorrow. "Take care of yourself, and we'll see you in three weeks."

I watched as Mrs. Miller wheeled him out. Hyde put his arm around me. "I've given Ms. Armitage strict instructions to call us if... well, if she feels there's a need."

"Thank you, Hyde." What a wonderful man he was!

"Let's sit down. Doug wants to say something."

Doug, as Hyde's best man, would be giving a speech. He tapped the microphone and grinned at everyone. "Ladies and gentlemen, if you'll give me your attention? I have just a few short remarks...." He pulled out what looked like a huge stack of index cards and got the first of many laughs. "As some of you know, Hyde and I are cousins, and we go back a lot of years." He spoke of events from their boyhood, and later, when he'd been in his late twenties and they'd reconnected.

Did anyone notice the gap in between, when Hyde's grandfather had banished him and his mother from Prud'homme, and when he'd fallen in love with Aaron Richardson?

Probably not. It wasn't something they needed to know.

Doug finished to applause, and Hyde hugged him and I shook his hand, and we gave him the cigar case and flask combo Hyde had had engraved for him with our names and the date.

I didn't expect a speech. Uncle Brad didn't know me that well, and Geoff had too much going on.

"I'm sorry, Kipp, I have to get back to the hospital," he'd said shortly after Granddad left.

"Thank you for being here. And thank you for helping to keep Mr. Richardson away from Hyde."

"Thank *you*, little brother." He pulled me into a hug. "If he doesn't behave, feel free to sic security on him."

"I don't want to cause problems for you."

"You won't." He squeezed my shoulder.

"All right. I'll send cake home for all of you with Mrs. Wales. Call if you need me—"

"But you won't, will you, Geoff?" Hyde asked.

"I won't, Hyde." Geoff's smile was crooked. "I want to thank you too."

"What for?" Hyde looked bored.

"For getting that line of credit extended again."

He shrugged. "It wouldn't look good if my husband's brother wound up bankrupt."

"No, I can imagine how much that would bother you." Geoff held out his hand. "I appreciate it."

"Didn't you have to be somewhere?" But Hyde shook his hand.

"I'll see you in three weeks. Enjoy Fiji."

CHAPTER 48

THE sound of a spoon tapping a glass once again made me laugh, and I turned to Hyde, offering him my lips.

I was stunned when I realized Hunter, my boss at Georg, had risen and picked up the microphone. He was going to make a speech! "Hyde," I whispered, "I don't have a gift to give him!"

"Sure you do."

"No, I don't!" I'd given Geoff his gift, a midnight pocket watch and chain, and Uncle Brad a Coleman multi tool torch-style lighter.

"Oh, ye of little faith. You can give him this." And he handed me a silver-plated USB drive key chain.

"You knew he was going to give a speech?" I bumped his shoulder with mine. "Thank you. I'd have looked like such a cheapskate!"

"You know I'd never let that happen." He brushed a soft, brief kiss over my cheek.

"No one tapped on a glass, Ham." Hunter winked at me, and I turned to stare at Hyde, wide-eyed.

"Yes, Hunter was one of the guys from the Garage. So was Tony."

I wondered how many of his friends he'd helped. What a good man he was!

"Ladies and gentlemen, it's my turn to make a speech," Hunter said. "Most of you don't know Kipp Llewellyn."

Hyde growled deep in his throat.

"Humor me, Ham. I've known him since he was a pup. Actually, I've known Kipp for three years, and in dog years that's close enough," and he went on to talk about how I'd come to him as part of Armand U's internship program, how he'd hired me when I needed a job, and how I'd met Hyde in his shop eighteen months ago. "It gave me great pleasure to see them falling in love."

It was kind of Hunter to say that, and it was so romantic. Of course our guests wouldn't want to hear it was only physical on Hyde's part. But that was okay. I'd love him enough for the both of us.

"I knew they were perfect for each other then, and they're even more perfect for each other now. Ladies and gentlemen, I give you Kipp and Hyde."

I could feel myself blushing, not only from Hunter's words but from the thunderous applause. Hyde slid an arm around my waist and urged me to my feet. We raised our glasses of champagne to our guests and, as if we'd practiced, spoke in unison. "Thank you all, very much."

WE FED each other pieces of our wedding cake, which looked even more amazing than the picture Mr. Webster had shown me only a few days before.

I danced with our female guests, who all envied me my new husband, while Hyde chatted with their husbands or significant others.

We'd long since shed our tux jackets, our bowties hung loose and the top buttons of our shirts were undone, and now the reception was winding down.

"So what did that director want?" I asked as I watched the man lean down to speak to his wife. He was noted for science-fiction movies that didn't have an ounce of gore but that still scared his audience under their seats, and I expected Hyde to tell me he'd asked to be bankrolled for his next opus.

"Actually, he wanted to know if you'd be available to design a child's bedroom for him."

"*Me*? But I don't even have my degree!"

"No, but Hunt suggested you'd be a good bet. Dance with me!" Hyde pulled me into his arms and we began to waltz across the floor.

"He did?"

"Mmm hmm. After we get back from Fiji, I thought we'd fly up to his place on Martha's Vineyard and you could take a look at the room."

"I'd… like that. Thank you." I'd have to thank Hunter too. I rested my cheek against Hyde's shoulder and hummed along to the song the Martinaires were playing, something soft and lush from *West Side Story*.

Someone began tapping on a water goblet with their spoon, and I raised my head and glanced around.

"It's the senator," I said, laughing into Hyde's eyes. "He isn't going to stop until you kiss me, you know."

"And these are the people we elect to run our country." He went ahead and kissed me, though.

I had something to say to him, and I didn't know how he was going to accept it. If he didn't care…. I tucked my head under his chin. "I really do love you, you know; very much. It nearly killed me when I thought I wouldn't be able to marry you."

He tightened his embrace for a moment, and then he cupped my chin and tipped it up so I was looking at him. "I have something for you. I was saving this for later, but when you say something like that…."

"I don't need anything." Not when I had him.

He twined his fingers in mine and led me back toward our table, where he removed a clear plastic bag from the pocket of his jacket. A lime-green ribbon was tied in a bow at the top. Inside were—

"Jelly beans?"

"Green jelly beans. You were willing to settle for them."

"Oh. You saw that T-shirt."

"I did, and I've got something better for you."

I couldn't help laughing. "What's better than green jelly beans?"

"Love?"

"Hyde, what…?"

"I love you, Kipp."

"Do you really?"

"Yes, I do." He tucked the bag of jelly beans into my jacket pocket. "Happy wedding day."

"Happy wedding day, my brown-eyed handsome man." And this time it was I who took his hand and entwined my fingers with his.

FIJI was beautiful, and that little island is simply amazing. The cottage came with a well-stocked fridge, and every other evening we'd take the cabin cruiser we'd been supplied to the main island and have dinner in the capital of Suva.

During the day we fished, we swam, we parasailed, we made love. And at night we made love again.

"Did you have a good time?" Hyde asked as we boarded our flight to Auckland, the first leg on our journey home.

"It was wonderful. Thank you for giving me the best honeymoon."

"It was the best for me too. And you liked the island?"

"You know I did."

"I'm glad. You know that meeting I told you I had to take?"

"Yes." I'd been surprised he'd agreed to it, but if he felt it was necessary, I wasn't about to object. I'd spent the day wandering through the Fiji Museum in the Suva Botanical Gardens on my own, which was enjoyable. That night, though…. Ah, that night. My dick twitched, remembering it.

"Here, Kipp." He was holding out some papers.

"What's this?"

"It's the deed to the island."

"Hyde?"

"It's ours."

EPILOGUE

WE WERE naked on our king-size bed, and I was on top, my knees framing his hips. I'd dreamed of this before, but it had never been so good.

I buried my fingers in his thick, soft hair, and I covered his lips and cheeks and jaw with hungry, uninhibited kisses.

His dick was hard and slick against mine, and his long fingers imprisoned them. I drove into his grasp, desperate for the orgasm that was a glimmering promise almost within my reach.

"That's it!" he whispered, and his voice, normally smooth and contained, was rough and uncontrolled.

I'd brought him to this state! I'd wielded this power.

And when he took it from me—when he fondled my ass with his other hand, tracing the crevice between my buttocks, finding my opening and teasing it—I surrendered it willingly.

I spread my legs wider and humped against him, frantic now to come.

"Almost there, blue eyes. Are you—"

"Yes, I'm—" I groaned and shivered, and came apart in his arms.

And he was there with me, his powerful climax splattering semen up onto my torso.

Finally, after long moments during which he ran his palms from my shoulder blades to the curve of my ass, gave a squeeze, and then reversed the motion, I raised my head and looked down into his beautiful eyes. He made me so happy.

"I'll get a washcloth and clean us up."

"Or we could...." He ran a finger through the semen on his torso and brought it to my mouth. I licked it off, and then did the same to him.

As it turned out, we didn't need that washcloth.

"I dreamed about us doing this," I murmured as we tugged a sheet up over us.

"And?"

I snuggled close to him. "The reality is so much better."

"It is, isn't it?" He held me tight.

What was even better was that when I woke in the morning, he would be there beside me.

BEAUCHAMP'S LEMON LUSH

Mix together until crumbly:

2 sticks margarine

2 cups flour

Add 1 cup chopped walnuts.

Pat into 9x13 pan and bake at 400° 18 to 20 minutes and cool.

1st layer: cream together:

- 8 oz. cream cheese
- 1 cup confectioners' sugar
- 1 cup Cool Whip

Spread on cooled crust

2nd layer: Mix 2 packages lemon instant pudding and 3 cups milk

Spread on 1st layer

3rd layer: spread with layer of Cool Whip.

Freeze well

TINNEAN has been writing since the third grade, where she was inspired to try her hand at epic poetry. Fortunately, that epic poem didn't survive the passage of time; however, her love of writing not only survived but thrived, and in high school she became a member of the magazine staff, where she contributed a number of stories.

It was with the advent of the family's second computer—the first intimidated everyone—that her writing took off, enhanced in part by fanfiction, but mostly by the wonder that is copy and paste. While involved in fandom, she was nominated for both Rerun and Light My Fire Awards. Now she concentrates on her original characters.

A New Yorker at heart, she resides in southwest Florida with her husband and two computers.

Ernest Hemingway's words reflect Tinnean's devotion to her craft: "Once writing has become your major vice and greatest pleasure, only death can stop it."

She can be contacted at tinneantoo@gmail.com, and can be found on LiveJournal at http://tinnean.livejournal.com/ and on Facebook at http://www.facebook.com/Tinnean. If you'd like to sample her earlier works, they can be found at

http://www.angelfire.com/fl5/tinnssinns/Welcome1.html.

Also from TINNEAN

Spy Vs. Spook from TINNEAN

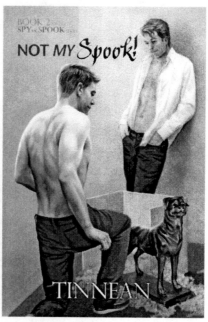

http://www.dreamspinnerpress.com

Also from TINNEAN

http://www.dreamspinnerpress.com

Also from TINNEAN

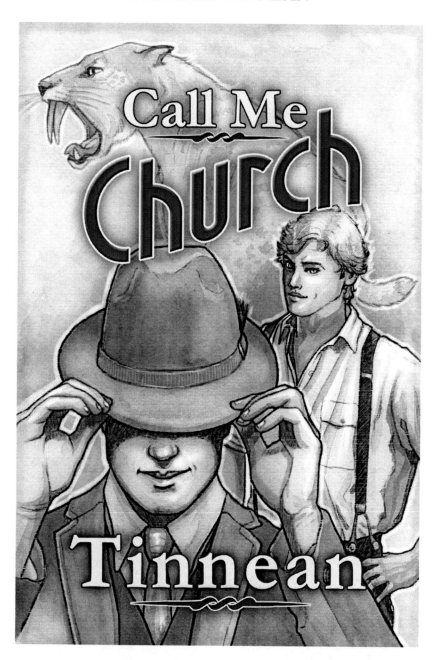

Also from TINNEAN

http://www.dreamspinnerpress.com

CPSIA information can be obtained at www.ICGtesting.com
Printed in the USA
BVOW04s1815231214

380654BV00013B/428/P